The Gypsy Tearoom

Also by Nicky Pellegrino
Delicious

The Gypsy Tearoom

Nicky Pellegrino

First published in Great Britain in 2007 by Orion Books,
an imprint of The Orion Publishing Group Ltd
Orion House, 5 Upper Saint Martin's Lane
London, WC2H 9EA

1 3 5 7 9 10 8 6 4 2

A CIP catalogue record for this book is
available from the British Library.

ISBN-13: 978 0 7528 6130 2 (hardback)
978 0 7528 7362 6 (trade paperback)

Typeset by Deltatype Ltd, Birkenhead, Merseyside
Printed in Great Britain by Mackays of Chatham plc,
Chatham, Kent

The Orion Publishing Group's policy is to use papers
that are natural, renewable and recyclable products and
made from wood grown in sustainable forests. The logging
and manufacturing processes are expected to conform to
the environmental regulations of the country of origin.

www.orionbooks.co.uk

For John Richard Carne Bidwill, of course.

Prologue

The pomegranate tree stood alone in the centre of the courtyard. How much longer it would stand there no one knew. Long ago its twisted limbs had stopped reaching for the sky and now only tender care kept it alive.

Last year, in October, the old tree began to lean like the Tower of Pisa. It was Carlotta, the gardener's daughter, who noticed first.

'It's as though the fruit is too heavy for it to carry a moment longer,' she said sadly to her father, Umberto. 'It wants to lay down its tired branches and rest them on the ground.'

Umberto stopped sweeping up autumn leaves and leaned on his broom. He looked at the pomegranate tree and saw Carlotta was right. The fruit still hung like lanterns amid the sinewy branches, but the tree was pitching forward to the ground.

'It will have to come down,' he said shortly.

'No, Papà!'

'Carlotta, if I don't chop it down, it will fall by itself,' Umberto argued reasonably.

'But, Papà, it's so very old. You've always told me it's been here far longer than either of us has been alive. You have to try to save it.'

Umberto looked at his daughter, at her sharp, pale face beneath the wide-brimmed straw hat she always wore, and her thin arms pressed to her flat chest in entreaty. And then he looked back at the pomegranate tree.

'It's no good, Carlotta, it's coming down. We have plenty more pomegranate trees down there.' He gestured towards the terraces below the courtyard. 'And look, most of the fruit on this tree is bad, anyway.'

'Yes, but when you find one that isn't bad, it tastes so much sweeter than any of the fruit from those younger trees down below.'

She took hold of the broom and pulled it away from her father. 'I'll finish sweeping up these leaves if you'll try to save the old pomegranate tree.'

Half listening to the sound of Carlotta's broom scratching over the flagstones, Umberto stood and stared at the tree. His mouth hung half open, as it always did when he was thinking hard, so all the world could see there was not a tooth left in his head. Next to his bed, he had a set of dentures in a jar, but he had never taken to wearing them, and besides, he and Carlotta so rarely saw anyone these days it hardly seemed worth making the effort.

No one ever visited the pink house beside the courtyard. It was empty and its dark-green wooden shutters were closed tight, as they had been for years. Umberto received a small wage each month for the work he and Carlotta did in the grounds, and they lived quietly in their cottage just beyond the high walls. They were charged only with keeping the gardens neat and tidy, and no one came to check the work had been done. If he chopped down the pomegranate tree, only Carlotta would notice or care.

'It wouldn't take much to get it down,' he called out to her. 'I could probably push it over if I tried.'

'It's roots may be deeper than you think,' she called back.

'We could plant another tree in its place – a sapling. It would grow before you knew it.'

'It wouldn't be the same.'

'Carlotta.' He was exasperated now. 'A gardener can't afford to fall in love with the plants in his garden. He must harden his heart and tear out those that are old or dying or simply no longer look their best. And he must plant afresh.'

Carlotta stopped brushing, but she didn't speak. He looked over and saw she was staring at the tree.

'I can't imagine waking up tomorrow morning and seeing that it isn't there,' she said softly. 'It's been there every morning, every day of my life.'

Umberto threw his hands in the air. 'So how do you suggest I save it?' he asked angrily. 'It's half dead already so how am I meant to keep it alive?'

'It isn't half dead.' Carlotta's voice was measured and patient. 'It's leaves are green and it still bears fruit. But it's old and tired. All it needs is some help to hold its branches up from the ground.'

2

'All it needs, all it needs,' Umberto muttered, pulling the battered old hat from his head and wiping the sweat from his brow with it. It was warm and all this thinking was hard work. 'You're asking too much of me,' he exploded. 'I don't know how I'm supposed to keep the damn thing from falling over.'

He heard a hiss of impatience as Carlotta threw the broom at him. Two minutes later he saw her disappearing down the stone steps that led to the lower terraces, an axe in her hand. She was puffing when she came back and red in the face, and in her hands there was no longer an axe but a thick, long branch with a fork in it that was wide enough to cradle the biggest of the pomegranate tree's trailing limbs.

'It's a crutch,' Carlotta explained. 'If we wedge it beneath that branch firmly enough, it will support the tree and it won't lean over any further than it has already.'

There was some heaving and pushing, but Carlotta was determined and the tree seemed to know it. Finally, it allowed the crutch to be jammed beneath its deformed limb and let it take its weight.

Umberto stood back and surveyed their work. He nodded his head in quiet approval. 'You're a clever girl, Carlotta. I always said so.'

She smiled at him in reply. 'I'd better go and get that axe,' she said, and he heard the happiness in her voice if not in her words. 'I left it down below.'

'No, leave it,' he told her. 'I'll get it later. And I'll cut another crutch while I'm down there . . . just in case.'

She smiled at him again. 'The tree will be here tomorrow when I wake. And the morning after and the one after that.'

'It will die eventually, though, everything does,' Umberto said bluntly. 'And there is no one here to appreciate it while it does live.'

'Oh, you never know.' Carlotta glanced at the pink house with its shutters closed against the light. 'Perhaps someone will come along one summer and open up the house and sit beneath the pomegranate tree to watch the sunset. Until then it's here for just you and me.'

Umberto clicked his tongue against his gums. 'No one will come, Carlotta. They've forgotten this place even exists. It will be empty for ever.'

Raffaella couldn't sleep. She lay on her back in the lumpy old bed she shared with her younger sister and stared into the darkness. The last thing she wanted was shadows beneath her eyes. But her mind was busy with thoughts of the excitement to come and her body was filled with a restless energy. She couldn't lie still any longer.

The sheets rustled as she slipped out from between them, but her sister didn't stir. In the darkness, Raffaella felt her way to the end of the bed, and her fingers found the cedar chest that stood there. Quietly, she lifted the lid and slipped her hands inside.

The embroidered tablecloth lay on top. It was white with sliver thread, and there were eight napkins to match. Beneath them was the bedlinen her grandmother had given her when she was ten and the towels she had been presented with a year or so later. And at the very bottom, neatly pressed and swathed in tissue paper, were the flimsy bits of underwear and pretty nightgowns her mother had helped her embroider.

This was Raffaella's bottom drawer. She'd been adding to it since she was a young girl, and everything inside had remained untouched, aside from the odd airing, waiting for the day when she was married.

Tomorrow the cedar chest would be loaded on to a cart with the rest of the things that made up her dowry and taken up the hill to a new home. And one day later, when all the celebrations were over, she would follow it. She would hang the towels on a rail, put the sheets on the double bed and dress in the finest of the nightgowns. And that night her sister, Teresa, would sleep alone for the first time, while Raffaella climbed into bed with her new husband.

Curled up against the cedar chest, Raffaella rested her head on the stack of linen and imagined what her life would be like. Free to kiss her Marcello's lips as much as she wanted, to lie encircled in his arms and talk late into the night. Free to be together without a member of the family always nearby, free to touch him and be touched in return.

Raffaella was excited by the thought of her wedding day, but she was more thrilled at the prospect of what lay beyond – her life once the cedar chest had been emptied of all its contents and she had become Marcello's wife. Ever since they were children in the schoolroom and she had willed him to choose the desk beside hers, it was all she had wanted.

As the fine linen grew warm beneath her cheek, she tried to imagine the weight of a gold ring on her finger and the new sense of belonging. It was difficult to believe that so much happiness lay in wait for her.

She lifted her head from the linen and carefully closed the lid of the chest, then eased herself back into bed. Teresa continued to sleep soundly. Raffaella listened to her sister's rhythmic breathing and felt the warmth radiating from her skinny body. One more night like this and then it would be Marcello lying there beside her.

She closed her eyes and slowly her mind quietened. At long last she slipped away into sleep.

When Raffaella finally woke, her mouth was dry, her eyes filled with sleep, and her sister's side of the bed empty. There was no sound except the crying of gulls and the lapping of water, but as she blinked and rubbed her eyes clean, she smelled coffee. She sat up in bed and ran her fingers through the tangle of her long, black hair. What time was it? she wondered. How late had they left her to sleep?

Pulling back the curtains, she saw the sun was climbing in the sky. Her father and the rest of the fishermen must have set out long ago. Now their boats would be nothing more than dark dots on the blue horizon.

The cottage Raffaella had lived in all her life was perched on a rock, overlooking the harbour and the sea beyond. Years ago it had been painted the colour of peaches, but the lash of salt in the wind had quickly peeled the paint from the walls where the sun had blistered it.

The rock was inhospitable, but a few stunted bushes clung on grimly, and at its base, well above the high-tide mark, her father had planted a white statue of Our Lady, who stared out to sea and protected the fishermen and all those who risked their lives riding the waves.

Their little house was built to fit round the curve of the rock. Every room was narrow and cramped, but the narrowest part of all was the kitchen, where the wall was carved into the rock itself. Brightly coloured plates danced across the rough grey slab, and on a high shelf, Raffaella's mother had arranged wine bottles she'd collected, her eye caught by an unusual shape or shade, and jewels of glass she'd found while trawling the beach, fragments worn smooth by the sea and the sand.

What Raffaella loved most about her mother was the way she looked for the play in life. When she had to clean and polish her house, she did it with a song or at least a hum. If she had to shake out the crumbs from a tablecloth, she amused herself by scaring away the seagulls that perched on the narrow ledge of rock below the kitchen window.

Even while she made a simple cup of coffee she was playing, heaping the fine coffee grounds in an impossibly tall pyramid, higher and higher every time, until sometimes it collapsed all over the kitchen table and she had to clean it up and start again.

Her mother's coffee shouldn't have tasted any different than coffee made by someone else's hand, but Raffaella was convinced it was better. She breathed its scent now as she climbed down the crooked steps from her room at the top of the house.

'Mamma, what time is it?' she called out. 'Why didn't you wake me earlier?'

'Ah, Raffaella, you're up at last.' She heard a laugh streak through her mother's voice. 'The smell of coffee must have woken you. I wondered if it might.'

'No, you knew it would. That's why you made it.' Raffaella stepped into the skinny kitchen and smiled at the familiar sight of her mother pouring a stream of black coffee into two small white cups and spooning in sugar.

'I knew?' Her mother looked up and smiled back in reply. 'Well, perhaps I did.'

Sliding on to the wooden bench pushed back against the hard rock wall, Raffaella reached for her cup. 'Mmm, that's strong,' she said between sips. 'I'll miss your coffee when I go. Mine never tastes so good.'

'And I'll miss you –' her mother took up her own cup '– much more than you'll miss my coffee. Why couldn't you have picked a local boy, eh? A nice boy from around here.'

Raffaella didn't smile, for she knew her mother was only half joking. All her life she had lived in the southern Italian village of Triento, nestled in the folds and ripples of the mountains where they met the sea. Triento was a divided town. Half of it, Big Triento, clung to the foothills of the mountains, and the other half, Little Triento, perched on the rocks beside the harbour where the fishing boats were moored. A steep and perilous road zigzagged from one half to the other.

When Raffaella married Marcello, she would go up in the world quite literally. She would leave the fisherman's cottage in Little Triento and head up the steep incline to her new life as the wife of a prosperous merchant's son.

'I'll miss you too, Mamma,' Raffaella replied. 'But I'll still see you, won't I? Whenever you come up the hill to market?'

Her mother laughed. It was a deep and throaty sound that Raffaella had grown used to hearing countless times each day throughout her childhood.

'Won't I?' she repeated.

'I suppose you might,' her mother replied, and then she frowned. 'Although not every day, Raffaella, I can't promise you that.'

Raffaella knew how much her mother, Anna, hated climbing the hill. She would do almost anything to avoid it: make ingredients stretch a little further, create a meal out of almost nothing.

But cleverest of all was Anna's ability to divine when one of the other wives of Little Triento was on the brink of slipping her basket over her arm and embarking on the long, slow walk up to Big Triento to shop for food. Invariably, seconds before the woman left, Anna would land on her doorstep and press a few coins on her, along with a quickly scribbled shopping list. 'Just a couple of things,' she'd say breathlessly. 'You don't mind, do you?'

Anna was tall with a low voice and a natural air of authority and few of the fishermen's wives dared say no to her. Beatrice Ferrando, Patrizia Sesto, Giuliana Biagio and the rest, all were a little afraid of her. So they would walk up the hill and carry a heavier basket back down again while Anna slipped off home and pleased herself.

Usually, she would sit with a book in her hand for an hour or so until her shopping arrived on the doorstep and it was time to start cooking dinner for her husband, Tommaso, her two daughters and her only son, Sergio.

Raffaella's mother rarely walked up the steep hill if she could help it and as a result she was softer of thigh and rounder of belly than most of the other fishermen's wives. Yet Tommaso loved her womanly curves, and she loved the stolen hours she had to herself.

But now Anna sighed a little as she sipped her coffee, almost as if she knew the steep hill was beckoning her again.

'Your brother, Sergio, often complains that the meat Beatrice Ferrando brings me is too fatty,' she mused. 'And last week Patrizia Sesto came back with rotten tomatoes. We had to throw most of them away, remember? I might as well go to the market myself more often.'

'Yes, I agree. You might as well,' Raffaella echoed, and she poured her mother another tiny cup of the strong coffee before it grew cold.

Anna tried to keep the frown from her face as she watched her daughter moving about the kitchen, putting away the coffee things. There was so much to worry about. Would Raffaella be happy with this boy she wanted so much? Would marriage be the joyful thing she expected?

Most of the mothers of Triento would be thrilled to have a daughter marry into the Russo family, but Anna didn't feel that way. She saw how Raffaella hero-worshipped the boy. And she feared that he in turn saw little beyond her beauty. When she woke in the middle of the night, her elder daughter's future was the thing she worried most about, tossing and turning until dawn.

She prayed fervently that this marriage was the right thing. But if it turned out not to be, if sadness lay in store for Raffaella, then she wanted to be there watching over her.

And if that meant putting her basket over her arm and climbing the hill to Big Triento every other day, then so be it. Anna would miss her stolen hours and hate every moment of the steep walk, but she could see no other way.

2

Wedding days in Triento were always properly celebrated. The whole village loved to come together to mark the occasion. And this was a special wedding. The eldest son of Triento's most prosperous family was marrying the town's most beautiful girl. People had been talking about it avidly ever since they were first promised to each other.

'Raffaella Moretti, she's only a fisherman's daughter, she's marrying well,' they'd mutter to each other.

'Yes, but just look at her,' sighed the women over their baskets as they gathered in the main piazza. 'Those long, black ringlets that fall to her waist, her full lips, her perfect skin . . . And she's never had eyes for anyone but Marcello Russo. They're so in love.'

'What about that body of hers, eh?' The men jabbed each other with sharp elbows as they drank and smoked together in the corner bar. 'She has the breasts of a goddess and the legs of a movie star. If I were Russo, I'd have married her as fast as I could.'

But Marcello hadn't rushed into marriage. He had held on until he'd finished serving out his apprenticeship. Two years he'd waited while he learned the family business inside out.

The Russo family made and sold the finest hand-woven linens. 'Crafted in the traditional way since 1880,' as they often told people proudly. Since he was the eldest son, Marcello had been allotted the prime job of working in the family's shop, while his four younger brothers were relegated to the workroom, where the fabrics were woven, and to the packing house, where they were carefully folded in tissue paper and sent off to customers all over Italy.

Once married, Marcello would be given the apartment above the linen shop. It wasn't much more than a couple of rooms, but for a first home it was fine. And as soon as they started having children, he planned to find them somewhere bigger to live.

Marcello wasn't nervous on the day of his wedding. As he shaved and smoothed back the dark brown hair that tended to flop into his eyes and dressed in his new suit, he felt content. He liked the way his future was looking – a beautiful wife, a good job, what more could a man want?

It was late morning and the sun had come out from behind the mountain at last and washed over the tall, skinny buildings, which were the colour of honey and sand, that lined the steep streets of Big Triento. Above the terracotta-tiled rooflines, the spires and steeples of churches soared.

Soon the bells would start ringing. One by one each of Triento's seven churches would let them peal out until the noise echoed loudly over the mountains and people began to gather in the streets to wave him on his way.

Marcello glanced in the mirror and smoothed back his unruly hair one last time. His brother Stefano would be here any moment and it would be time to go.

Just as he was reaching for his watch, he heard his brother's prompt knock on the bedroom door.

'Marcello, your days as a single man are nearly over,' called Stefano, flinging open the door as the rest of his brothers cheered and whistled in the background. 'Are you ready?'

'Yes, I'm ready,' Marcello replied, and moved to walk out of the door.

'Stop and let me straighten your tie first,' Stefano ordered, fussing with some imaginary crookedness. 'The streets are lined with well-wishers. You have to look your best for them. Agostino, Gennaro, Fabrizio, what do you think? Does he look ready?'

Agostino and Gennaro cheered and whistled again, but Marcello noticed his youngest brother, Fabrizio, had fallen silent and the expression on his face seemed half sullen.

'Fabrizio, what do you think? Do I look good enough to marry Raffaella Moretti?' he asked.

His youngest brother shrugged. 'I suppose so,' he replied, 'but it doesn't matter how much you dress yourself up. She'll always be the beautiful one.'

Stefano laughed and slapped him over the back of the head as if he'd made a joke. But Fabrizio's tone was serious, and as he followed his brothers out of the front door and down the narrow street, his face looked as sullen as ever.

The village was alive with people. Women smiled and waved at the five young Russo boys dressed in all their finery and called out, '*Buona fortuna*'. Some of the older ones dabbed at the corners of their eyes with white handkerchiefs. For the first and only time that day Marcello felt his nerves jangle.

'Come on, wave back at them, they're here to wish you well,' Stefano encouraged him over the cacophony of ringing bells.

'They're here to see Raffaella, not me.' Marcello shrugged. 'They can't wait to find out what she looks like in her wedding gown.'

All the same, as they approached the grey stone façade of the Church of Santa Trinita, Marcello lifted his hand at the crowds and they cheered and clapped in return.

Padre Simone was waiting for him at the altar in his white priest's robes, and the church pews were crammed with family, friends and any of the other villagers who had managed to find themselves a space. There were sprays of white flowers on the ends of each pew and more blossoms arranged in brass urns on either side of the altar. This was his mother Alba's work, realised Marcello. She had been up here early this morning to make sure everything was perfect.

Marcello stood at the altar, his four brothers behind him, and waited to hear the sound of the crowd cheering once again for then he'd know Raffaella had arrived at Santa Trinita in her little cart pulled by a donkey. Sure enough, minutes later, the cry went up, far louder than it had been for him.

He didn't turn round, not even when he heard the church door open and the rustle as everyone in the pews turned to see the bride. The organ began to play and Marcello knew Raffaella and her father had started their slow walk up the aisle, but he continued to stare straight ahead. Only when he sensed she was right beside him did he choose to look round.

Raffaella was as beautiful as he'd known she would be. Her white dress was full-skirted, her veil yards of embroidered tulle. She held a loosely tied bouquet of white flowers, and Marcello saw her hands were shaking.

'Don't be nervous,' he whispered, moving closer to her. 'I'm here. I'll look after you.'

Padre Simone raised an eyebrow and Marcello nodded. They were ready.

'We'd like you to marry us now, Padre,' he said calmly, taking Raffaella's hand and squeezing it tight.

The ceremony seemed to go on for ever. Throughout each long prayer Marcello held on to Raffaella's hand. He could sense her whole body trembling, and when he glanced down, he saw that behind her veil, her eyes were glistening with tears.

Only when it was time for them to exchange wedding rings did he let her hand loose. And then, as soon as he was able to, he picked it up again.

'We'll be together for the rest of our lives,' he whispered in her ear as they walked back down the aisle and stood together on the steps of the church, their families milling around them. There was Raffaella's mother, tears in her eyes, hugging them and calling out her congratulations. Her father, wiry little Tommaso Moretti, shook him by the hand, and her brother, Sergio, clapped him on the back. 'Congratulations, congratulations.' He'd never heard the word said so often by so many people.

And then his mother, Alba, was beside them, her lips pressed into a hard little smile.

'Congratulations.' She seemed to say the word to Raffaella alone.

Her veil pulled back from her beautiful face, Raffaella smiled at her new mother-in-law.

'Well?' Alba tossed her head and her tight grey curls wobbled. 'Say thank you for a lovely husband.'

Raffaella blinked and took a step backwards. 'Yes, thank you. Of course thank you,' she stammered.

Alba smiled tightly again, took her son's face in her hands and kissed him hard on both cheeks. And then she was gone, most likely to make sure the tables for the wedding feast were set up to her satisfaction.

The feast was to be held on long trestles laid out in the piazza. Almost all the village would settle there, beneath huge canvas umbrellas to shade them from the August sun, and the eating would go on all afternoon. There were ten courses in all, ending with the wedding cake, which was so big it would have to be wheeled out on a trolley.

Marcello knew his father-in-law, Tommaso Moretti, hadn't been able to foot the bill for such a lavish occasion, so his own parents had contributed generously, for they wanted things done well. A small ceremony and a simple feast might be fine for some people, but it wouldn't have looked good for the eldest son of the Russo family.

The party would go on until late into the night and it was sure to end in drunkenness and dancing. But he and Raffaella would slip away as early as they could and hide themselves away in the apartment above the linen shop. And tomorrow their new lives as a married couple would begin. Taking his seat at the head table, his beautiful wife beside him, Marcello's sense of contentment grew even stronger.

Raffaella was overwhelmed. Since her mother had helped fasten her into her dress this morning, her heart seemed to have been beating twice as fast as normal. Standing beside Marcello at the altar, she'd barely been able to keep herself from fainting. She'd hung on to his hand as if it were the only thing that could hold her up.

Somehow she'd made it through the ceremony, saying her vows in a hoarse voice and trembling as Marcello slid the gold ring on her finger. It was a little loose, she realised now, twisting it nervously as she sat beside her new husband at the wedding table. She must have lost weight since it was bought for her.

Platters of food started arriving: trays of baked rigatoni, huge wheels of bread and dishes of seafood. Raffaella couldn't have eaten it, even if she'd been hungry. Everyone wanted to talk to her, to give her their congratulations, admire her dress, tell her she looked wonderful. She felt dazed with happiness.

'Can you believe it? We're finally married,' she whispered to Marcello when there was a break in the stream of visitors to their table.

'Of course I believe it.' He brushed a kiss over her lips. 'I've planned to marry you since you were a girl. It was always going to happen.'

'I'll be a good wife to you,' she promised him.

'I know you will.' He squeezed her shoulder and then turned to his brother Gennaro, who was heaping his plate with a second helping.

'Eat, eat, you'll need your strength later,' Gennaro was laughing.

All of the Russo brothers and their father, Roberto, had plates piled high and were eating with gusto. Only his mother, Alba, was nibbling at her food, tasting a bit of this or that, then pushing the plate aside and waiting for someone to take it away. Displeasure had been carved into her face all day long, and even as she ate, she was still frowning.

Raffaella knew her mother-in-law didn't think much of her. Alba had wanted someone better for her eldest son, a girl from a merchant's family, not just the daughter of a fisherman. The thought of it made her angry, but as her own mother had pointed out, anger wouldn't get her anywhere.

'Once you're married she'll be your family. You'll just have to try to get on with her,' Anna had said more than once.

So Raffaella tried to let her anger go. Perhaps when Alba saw just how much she loved her eldest son and just how well she cared for him, she might change her mind and decide to like her. And really it wouldn't be so bad. Lots of newly married women had to live with their husband's family, but she and Marcello had their own place. She reminded herself how lucky she was. Her cedar chest was in the tiny apartment waiting to be unpacked, and so much happiness lay in wait for her. She wouldn't let one woman's sourness spoil any of it.

3

To begin with, married life was everything Raffaella had dreamed it would be. She loved waking early with Marcello beside her and making his coffee each morning before he started work. While he opened up the linen shop, she would put her basket over her arm and head to market to buy the day's food. There was time to stop and chat to neighbours in the piazza, and sometimes she might meet her mother there, still puffing from the walk up the steep hill, with Teresa carrying her basket.

Most days, once her chores around the house were done, she liked to help Marcello. It was good to be near him, and besides, she enjoyed the work they did in the dark wood-panelled shop. She would tidy the place, sweep the floor or help her husband unfold a tablecloth or bedcover for customers to admire and hopefully buy.

When no one was looking, she loved to bury her face in the neatly folded stacks of linen and breathe their unique smell.

'Like freshly baked biscotti,' she had said once to Marcello, 'with vanilla and cinnamon and something else . . . I can't quite put my finger on it.'

And he had smiled at her and continued counting up the day's takings.

At lunchtime Marcello would close the shop for a couple of hours, and if they weren't eating with his family that day, they would climb the stairs to their little apartment and she would make him lunch.

Raffaella had taken her pick of the finest fabrics to brighten their home. She had scrubbed the two rooms from top to bottom and set out terracotta pots of red geraniums on the wide windowsills and the small wrought-iron balcony. She thought the place looked perfect now.

Each day she cooked something special. Octopus stewed in an

earthenware pot with garlic, chilli and tomato; mushrooms with mashed cannellini beans and rice or his very favourite, pork with pickled peppers. She liked to sit across the table watching her husband's face as he took his first mouthful of whatever she'd created. Yet despite her best efforts, Marcello seemed to be growing thinner.

She had also noticed how he was becoming more obsessed with the business. Often she would wake early and find his side of the bed empty and cold. When she took his coffee downstairs, he'd be leaning over a ledger filled with numbers, brow furrowed and too distracted to talk. In the evenings when it grew dark, Marcello would still be there, working.

'The shop is doing well, isn't it? Why must you work such long hours?' she asked him.

After five or six seconds he looked up. 'What?' he asked. 'Did you say something?'

She repeated herself, trying to keep the plaintive note out of her voice.

'Yes, the shop is doing just as well as it ever has,' he agreed. 'But that's not enough, Raffaella. You can't stay still in business; you have to expand, and I'm trying to work out how best we should do it.'

'But I miss the time we used to spend together in our apartment. Won't you put that book away and come back upstairs with me, just for a little while?'

'I'm doing this for our future, you know.' Marcello sounded impatient. 'That's why I work so hard. We can't stay in that tiny apartment for ever. We need a decent house, some land, perhaps even a car. That's what I'm working for.'

She tried to put an arm across his shoulder, but he shrugged it away and picked up his pen. 'I'm happy in the apartment,' she told him. 'I don't care about big houses. It doesn't matter to me where I live so long as I'm with you.'

His face softened. 'You must be lonely sometimes, Raffaella. After all, you're used to having your family around you. Why don't you go down the hill more often and spend time with them? And hopefully by next year there might be someone besides me for you to look after.' He rested his hand on her stomach. 'And then you won't want so much of my company, I promise you.'

Raffaella didn't speak. She wanted a baby just as much as he did.

Every month when she began to bleed she felt disappointed. But it didn't matter how many babies she had, she would always want his company. She was completely certain of that.

She moved to a stack of already tidy linen and began to refold it slowly. Every now and then she glanced up at her husband and saw that his head was still buried in his books.

Sometimes Marcello felt as though he couldn't breathe in this place. He'd grown up in a spacious house, and since he was the eldest son, he'd had his own room. He was used to being able to close a door on everyone else and enjoy the peace of his own company. But it was so different here. In their two-roomed apartment, he never seemed able to close a door on Raffaella. She was always somewhere in his orbit. He loved his wife, but this was not how he had imagined their marriage would be.

Marcello needed silence and space and he would never find it here. That was why he'd taken to working so feverishly. If he could prove to his father that he had solid plans to increase profits and improve efficiency throughout their business, then perhaps he would agree to lend him enough money to find a bigger home. Somewhere with as many as five rooms with one of them, just a tiny one, he could set aside as his office. The idea of it had begun to dominate his thoughts.

Still, he conceded that Raffaella might be right and he had been working far too hard recently. Certainly, he was feeling more tired than he had ever been in his life and he'd noticed he was growing thinner and paler by the week.

Perhaps this evening he'd put his work aside and take some time off. He could meet his brothers in the corner bar and spend the night drinking beer, eating pizza and making too much noise. It would do him good. And the work would still be there waiting for him when he came downstairs early tomorrow morning.

4

'What are you doing to my boy, eh?' Alba's voice was shrill. 'He's wasting away in front of my eyes. Look at him, so thin and such a terrible colour. You can't be looking after him properly.'

Raffaella was helping her mother-in-law roll out dough for *rotolo*, while Marcello sat and smoked a cigarette with his father and they talked about the business. It seemed he was going to get his wish. Roberto Russo was impressed with his business plans. Right now he was considering just how much he could afford to lend his favourite son so he could buy the bigger home he seemed to want so much.

Making *rotolo* was something Raffaella found tricky. She'd been concentrating on rolling the sausage shape of pasta up into a muslin cloth and not paying full attention to her mother-in-law. But she couldn't fail to hear the anguish in Alba's voice as she complained about the way her son was being cared for.

'He's been working much too hard,' Raffaella said defensively. 'He's up half the night bent over his books. And when he does take time off, he stays out late drinking with his brothers. He needs to rest and take care of himself, I keep telling him that.'

Raffaella didn't want to admit that she was so worried she couldn't sleep at night. Surely hard work alone couldn't cause a strong young man to fade away? Even her sister had commented on how frail Marcello seemed these days. After that she'd doubled her efforts to beg him to see the doctor, but he seemed to resent her fussing over him and only grew more distant and pushed her further away.

'Enough food, plenty of rest and good care, that's all he needs.' Alba's tone was sharp and critical. 'He never looked like this when he was living here with me, no matter how hard he worked. Perhaps he should come home for a while and build up his strength again.

Yes, yes, that's it, you should both leave the apartment and move back here, and once my Marcello is strong again, then you can move into this big house of your own that you seem to want so much.'

Raffaella didn't bother to correct her. She couldn't blame Alba for being so concerned. But what her mother-in-law hadn't seen was just how hard Raffaella was trying. She was shopping for twice as much food, using every pan in the house, serving Marcello course after course. And still, behind the plates heaped with pasta, meat and vegetables, he grew thinner and paler.

While her own wedding ring was fitting snugly now, Marcello had had to stop wearing his weeks ago in case it fell off and went astray somewhere in a pile of linen.

'So that's settled, then – you'll leave the apartment and come back here with Marcello.' Alba had a plan and she was determined to follow it through.

'No . . . I don't think so.' Raffaella was in a panic. 'I'll have to ask Marcello, but I'm sure he'll want to stay near the shop.'

'The shop? One of the other boys can look after that. I'm sure Stefano is perfectly capable. My son's health is what matters here. And I think it's better if you two aren't alone up in that apartment. Perhaps it's damp or something, I don't know. But I'm sure it isn't good for him there.'

'But—'

'Just take a look at your husband, Raffaella. Does he seem like a well man to you?'

Raffaella's heart sank. How could she argue? There was something wrong with Marcello and maybe he would be better off here, surrounded by family in the house where he'd grown up, than upstairs from the linen shop and always tempted to return to work.

Fortunately, Marcello himself vetoed the plan. 'It is kind of you, Mamma, but that won't be necessary,' he told her. 'All we need is to get ourselves into a decent place of our own as quickly as possible. Stefano told me there is a farmhouse for sale halfway up the mountain. The old Allegri place, you know it. The air is good up there. There's even a little land attached, enough for Raffaella to keep chickens, maybe some goats, and to grow all our own vegetables. I'll feel better again in no time once we're there, you'll see.'

But over the next week Marcello barely had the energy to run the linen shop, never mind view the Allegri farmhouse and haggle over the price. His hipbones were jutting out now and he had complained of backache. Raffaella was convinced his skin had a yellow tinge to it. She was completely terrified.

'Please go and see the doctor. Please do it just for me,' she begged.

'If you promise to leave me alone afterwards, then maybe I will.' Marcello's tone was gruff, but she was sure he was worried too. Hard work and not enough fresh air couldn't explain the way he looked and how tired he felt.

Marcello insisted on going alone to see the doctor. The doctor examined him quickly, bundled him into a car and drove him straight to the hospital. Raffaella was taken to visit him there. Her husband seemed lost and lonely in the hospital bed, and she held his hand just as tightly as he had held on to hers on their wedding day.

He wouldn't let her stay for very long. 'Someone has to look after the shop, and it's better if it's you rather than pulling one of the boys away from work they should be doing.'

She clutched his hand, unwilling to move. Here in the hospital, Marcello looked far sicker than he ever had when he was at home and she had been able to convince herself he was just a little wan and overtired and would be well again soon.

'What do the doctors say? Have they given you medicine? How long will it take for you to get better?' She fired the questions at him and he closed his eyes and let his head sink back on to the pillow.

'Raffaella, *cara*, I love you, but I'm tired and I need to sleep. Go back home now, there's a good girl. Look after the shop and I'll see you in a week or so.'

But before the week was over, Padre Simone had come to Raffaella to break the news that her Marcello was dead. The doctor drove back to fetch his stiff, cold body, and he was laid out in the bedroom that had been his own since he was a child. Raffaella sat beside him, holding his hand in both of hers, and people came and went.

She stayed there as Alba wailed and tore at her clothes, and as Roberto held his cheek against his son's and whispered, 'My boy, my boy.' Sometimes Fabrizio came and sat beside her wordlessly for an hour or so; sometimes her mother and sister joined her. Once Padre Simone slipped in and they kneeled beside the bed and prayed together. Raffaella was sure her husband would sit up and tell them to stop fussing. Who was minding the shop? What were they doing wasting time here? But his body was rigid and empty. Marcello had gone.

It was Alba who asked her to leave. 'We need to bury our boy. And you should go home and dress in black. You're a widow now.'

Raffaella took one last look at her husband. She remembered him as a boy and thought of him on her wedding day. She remembered the first time she saw his face on the pillow next to hers, brown hair flopping into his eyes. And then she squeezed his hand one last time and left as she'd been told to.

5

For days Raffaella had felt numb rather than sad. She hadn't even been able to squeeze out a tear at the funeral as she'd watched Marcello's coffin being lowered into the ground. The wailing from those around her at the graveside had been so loud that she'd been shamed into burying her face into her handkerchief to hide the dryness of her own cheeks.

They'd gathered at the graveside, her family and his and half the village behind them. The women tore at their hair and wailed, the men shouldered the coffin and cried more quietly. Raffaella saw only one person with cheeks as dry as her own. Although she dabbed at her face theatrically with the corner of a black scarf, her sister-in-law Angelica was losing the struggle to conceal her glee. For she was married to Stefano, the second son, and once a decent length of time had elapsed, a month or two at the most, the pair of them would take over Marcello's work in the linen shop and Raffaella would move out of the apartment to make way for them.

'They're taking everything I have left,' she'd blurted out to her sister, Teresa, when the burial was over.

Teresa had squeezed her arm and hissed in her ear, 'I never liked that Angelica. She always seems to be plotting something. Look at her now – she can barely keep the smile off her face. It's not decent.'

Raffaella hadn't been able to look. Deliberately, she'd turned away.

'Never mind,' her sister had consoled her. 'When I'm married, you can come and live with me and help look after my children. You're such a wonderful cook, you can take care of us all.'

Raffaella had said nothing, for she couldn't imagine anything worse. And then the priests had come to offer words of consolation and she and Teresa had been hemmed in by their dark robes and had talked no more.

That night she went home to the empty apartment, still shocked and numb with grief, and shut herself away from the world. Each day the effort of forcing herself out of bed and washing was almost too much for her. But at night she stayed awake late, staring up at the empty black sky, and wondered why she didn't seem able to cry.

Even now, as Raffaella sorted through her clothes, pushing the finest and brightest to the back of her wardrobe and pulling the dark and the drab to the front, she felt as though all her feelings had drained out of her.

She held out a skirt the colour of rubies that Marcello had given her just six months ago. She would never wear it again. The blue dress and the yellow, the pinks, the emerald and the gold, all those colours were forbidden to her now. For Raffaella, only twenty-two and already a widow, the one decent shade was black.

Raffaella knew what was expected of her. Triento was an isolated village, bound by centuries of tradition. Here, a truly virtuous widow mourned for life, wore nothing but black and went to her grave untouched and unloved by anyone but her husband.

For the funeral Raffaella had worn a new black dress. Today she would wear it again and tomorrow too most probably. She closed the wardrobe door firmly on all her old clothes, straightened the long skirt of the black dress and buttoned up its high collar. Taking a last brief glance at her dark shape in the mirror, she put her basket over her arm and stepped into the world.

In the days since the funeral Raffaella had hardly bothered eating. Once in a while she had forced herself to swallow a little fruit or cheese or a piece of cold meat. But now her meagre supplies were finished and it was time to face Triento again.

The linen shop was closed, a bereavement notice pinned to the door and the windows dark. Raffaella let herself out on to the street, where people were beginning to gather and church bells starting to ring.

Each of Triento's seven churches was built to be bigger and more impressive than the last. This was a holy village – perhaps the holiest in all of Italy – and to give thanks to a bountiful God, its well-fed merchants, fishermen and artisans had given generously to raise churches in His name.

And still, year after year, they gave more. The coffers were filling again, thanks to a large bequest from one of the town's richest men, but no one, least of all the priests, wanted to see an eighth church built.

It was difficult to avoid a priest for long in Triento. There was always a glimpse of a dark robe somewhere as they darted about on market days or cast about for a congregation in the hour or so before a service. Today, as Raffaella walked through the streets, eyes cast down and face settled in sombre lines, she came across three priests, her favourite – Padre Pietro – among them, standing in a group with their heads together between the fountain and the town hall in the main piazza.

'My poor child,' called out Padre Pietro as he noticed her drifting past towards the market stalls. 'Come here a moment. I've been concerned about you – we all have. How are you doing?'

'I still can't believe he's gone,' she said quietly, and she saw the pain in his face and knew that he genuinely felt for her.

'You know that I'm always easily found if you need to talk,' he told her, and he might have said more had Padre Simone not interrupted.

'And in Triento God is always easily found if you want to talk to Him,' he preached at her. 'Marcello is with God, Raffaella. Come to Santa Trinita and you will be closer to them both.'

'Yes.' She tried to nod at them both at once. 'I'll come to church soon. Both churches. I will.'

The third priest, tall and handsome Padre Matteo, was looking at her speculatively. 'Oh, and I'll come to your church too, of course,' she promised him.

'My child, you're always welcome,' he replied. 'But there is something else concerning me right now – your future. What is to become of you?'

Raffaella frowned. She hadn't thought beyond the next hour, never mind about her future. All she wanted was to be left alone in the little apartment, where she could curl up in bed and imagine Marcello was still downstairs in the linen shop doing sums and making plans.

'I don't really know,' she replied. 'When Angelica and Stefano want to reopen the shop, then I suppose I'll go back down the hill and live at home with my family.'

'Tell me, my child,' the priest asked, 'is it true that you are just as good a cook as your mother?'

Raffaella flushed a little. 'Well, Mamma has shown me everything she knows.'

The priest nodded. 'That's good. Then perhaps I can help you with your future. There is a house just a little way along the coast where they'll need to hire help very soon. The place needs an airing and to be cleaned from top to bottom. And then, when the tenant arrives, it will need a good cook. So, if you like, I could recommend you.'

Raffaella wondered what Marcello would think of her taking on a job. And then she remembered her husband was gone and she was on her own. Better that she was working, earning some money for the family, than sitting uselessly at home.

'Do you think they'd consider me?' she heard herself say to Padre Matteo.

He hesitated. 'I'm not sure. But I'll make some enquiries on your behalf.'

She smiled. 'Thank you. I'd appreciate that.' And nodding good day to all three priests, she moved on to fill her basket with apples.

The priests followed Raffaella's progress through narrowed eyes. They saw the easy sway of her hips as she crossed the piazza and noticed how every man's head turned as she passed. They also saw the looks sent her way by the wives and sisters of Triento and they recognised trouble in the making.

'To be widowed so young is a tragedy,' sighed Padre Pietro.

'A tragedy for us all,' added Padre Simone.

The priests watched the baker, Alberto, fix his eyes on Raffaella's swelling breasts as she walked past him and into his shop. Lumbering up from the bench where he spent much of his day soaking in the sunshine, Alberto followed her inside, his gaze now falling appreciatively on the curve of her full buttocks.

'She can't stay here in Triento,' said Padre Matteo firmly. 'We have to be rid of her.'

'Poor child, she will lead them all into temptation,' nodded Padre Pietro, the furrows of his worried brow deeper than ever.

'Sending her away is a fine idea,' agreed Padre Simone. 'But I'm not sure about giving her the job at Villa Rosa. What if the rumours are true?'

The three men fell silent for a moment. All had heard the whispers in the days since Marcello's funeral. No one knew who had started the rumour, but Silvana, the baker's wife, had spread it about and it had grown and swelled until people in Triento could talk of very little else.

'Do you think there really was poison in the food she fed poor Marcello?' whispered Padre Matteo at last.

'Marcello's mother certainly believes it,' said Padre Simone. 'She told me so. She thinks Raffaella poisoned her son slowly and deliberately and that's why he wasted away. But poor Alba, she is mad with grief. And surely it's a crazy idea? It's only a year since I married them and it struck me then how very much in love they were.'

'Well, I can't believe it,' frowned Padre Pietro. 'Raffaella loved Marcello with all her heart, I'm sure of it.'

'But you know the old saying,' countered Padre Simone. 'Where there's smoke there's fire. Is it worth taking the risk? I think we should keep her well away from Villa Rosa.'

Padre Matteo shook his head. 'Carlotta will be there too, remember. We'll warn her to keep a close eye on Raffaella. She's a clever girl. She doesn't miss much.'

The three priests watched as Raffaella exited the baker's shop, Alberto still close on her heels. He touched her arm and then put a large hand to her waist and pulled her into the soft folds of his flesh. Pressing her close, he kissed both her cheeks and murmured what must have been stock words of condolence. And as she tried to pull away, his body held her fast, and it was only the appearance of his sharp-faced wife, Silvana, at the doorway of the shop that prompted Alberto to let her loose.

'Villa Rosa, we're agreed, then,' said Padre Simone heavily. 'Let's tell Carlotta today and get her there as fast as possible.'

6

Raffaella arranged the food she'd bought; the apples in a bowl, fresh tomatoes on the window ledge and salty pecorino cheese wrapped in waxed paper placed high on a shelf beside a paper bag filled with glossy, dark-coated chestnuts. She planned to roast the chestnuts later, once it was dark, for the peeling and eating of them as they came piping hot from the oven might fill some of the empty hours that stretched out in front of her until it was time to go to bed.

But first, there would be thin slivers of veal, dipped in egg and breadcrumbs and fried quickly in her cast-iron pan. She had bought herself meat, for her father always said that food with blood in it gave a person strength. And she was tired and weighed down with unspent tears, so strength was what she needed.

Hungry now, she cut a slice from the small flat loaf she'd bought at the bakery. As she tasted it, she remembered the baker's touching hands and his slabs of arms pulling her towards him, and the memory made Raffaella shudder. All the way through town she had known men's eyes were on her, even though she walked with her own gaze low.

When Marcello was with her, he had shielded Raffaella from the looks of other men. And before she was married, her mother always kept her close. This was the first time she had faced life as a lone woman. And she felt lonely and vulnerable.

Raffaella filled in time. She swept the floors even though she'd already swept them once that morning and no one but her had walked through the rooms to dirty them. She rearranged the apples in the bowl and turned the tomatoes on the window ledge so they would ripen evenly. She tipped the chestnuts out of the bag, slashed at their glossy coats with a sharp knife and rolled them into a single layer on a metal tray ready to be roasted. And yet still only an hour had passed.

Longing to hear a voice other than her own, Raffaella took the back stairs down to the shop below. Stefano and Angelica were there, making the place their own, rearranging the piles of linen, polishing the wood panels and the panes of glass in the door.

Angelica looked up. 'Oh, it's you.'

'I came to see if you needed any help.'

'No, no.' Angelica shook her head energetically and set her glossy black curls swinging. 'I think Stefano and I have everything under control.'

Raffaella couldn't help herself. Burying her face in the nearest pile of linen, she filled her nostrils with the familiar musty smell.

'What are you doing?' Angelica sounded alarmed. 'Don't wipe your face on the linen.'

Raffaella tilted her head up, smiling. 'Don't be silly, I'm not wiping my face, I'm smelling these sheets. Go on, try it.'

'I can't do that.'

'Why not? It's the best smell in the world. Like freshly baked biscotti, only better.'

In spite of herself, Angelica took a tentative sniff. 'Doesn't smell like any biscotti I ever baked,' she said shortly, and moved away to fold and pat the piles of fabrics she now felt that she owned.

'Are you sure there is nothing I can do?' Raffaella pressed her.

'Well,' Angelica replied slowly, 'there is one thing.'

'Yes?' Raffaella's voice was bright and hopeful.

'You could start packing up your things upstairs. Stefano and I have a lot of work to do getting things properly organised. It would be so much easier for us if we lived above the shop.'

'Weren't things properly organised before? When Marcello was looking after the shop?'

'Oh, he was a wonderful man,' Angelica said hurriedly. 'The best kind of man. But he was perhaps not the very best businessman. My Stefano has so many wonderful ideas.' She beamed at her bespectacled husband. 'I think we'll see the family's profits doubling in no time.'

Raffaella let one hand stroke the pile of sheets. 'I'll start packing soon,' she promised.

'Will you go back down the hill to live with your parents?' Angelica asked lightly.

'No, I don't think so.' Raffaella turned towards the stairs and just before she began to climb, tossed back over her shoulder, 'I've been offered a job. I'd be a fool to turn it down.'

She couldn't pack today. It was too soon to take apart the fragments of life that she and Marcello had gathered together. So instead Raffaella seized her basket and, balancing it over her arm, left the house once more. This time she didn't walk to the market square but turned left and tracked down the hill towards home.

Raffaella felt the muscles in her neck and shoulders relax a little as she laid eyes on her parents' house. A skinny cat and her kittens were skulking around the doorstep waiting for her soft-hearted sister, Teresa, to sneak out and feed them scraps. They darted away into the shadows as Raffaella climbed the stone steps and rapped on the blue wooden door with her knuckles.

'It's only me,' she called out as she opened the door. 'Hello. Is there anybody here?'

'Raffaella, at long last,' her mother's voice called back. 'I've been waiting and waiting for you to come home. Come into the kitchen, my poor child, and sit down. Let me make you some coffee.'

Anna reached for the pot and began to build a pyramid of coffee in it while Raffaella collapsed on the bench, leaned back against the rock wall and rested her basket on the marble-topped table.

'Have you brought me something from the market?' Anna asked, glancing over at the basket. Pulling it towards her, she felt about inside. Raffaella saw the confusion on her face as she pulled out a large flat object wrapped in an offcut of linen.

'What's this?' she asked, and not waiting for a reply, proceeded to unwrap it. She stopped in surprise when she saw what the package contained. 'You've been carrying this around with you?'

Raffaella nodded but Anna wasn't looking, she was still gazing at the contents of the package.

'It must make you feel a little better having it with you,' Anna said quietly. 'Like you're close to him. Like he's still there beside you.'

Raffaella felt hot tears push at her eyes, but still she couldn't seem to let them fall.

'But it's a heavy thing,' Anna continued. 'Why don't you take it out of this big glass frame at least?'

Anna was staring at the wedding portrait she held in her hands like she had never seen it before, but she must have noticed it many times in the year it had hung on the wall of her daughter's apartment. It was Raffaella's favourite shot of her husband. The photographer had made Marcello stand on three encyclopaedias so it would seem as though he were taller than her. Perhaps that was why he looked a little solemn. Or maybe a tiny part of him resented the whole day stolen from work.

But when she looked at this picture of them together, it wasn't Marcello's expression she noticed or the delicate embroidery on her beautiful white gown, but the pure, bright love shining from her face. How quickly life had changed.

'I don't want to take it out of the frame,' she told her mother. 'It might get damaged. And besides, I like feeling the weight of it in my basket. That way, I know it's there.'

Anna's mind quickly darted somewhere else as it so often did. 'Don't go back up the hill today,' she urged. 'Stay here with us. Have dinner. Stay for the night.'

Raffaella hesitated. She wasn't certain she was ready for the intimacy of family life. Her father might want to talk about Marcello, her mother would want to comfort her. She didn't think she could bear it.

Wrapping her wedding picture back up in the scrap of linen, she put it away, out of sight, in her basket. 'Oh, I don't know,' she replied tentatively. 'I bought some food for my supper. I should go home.'

'The food will keep, I'm sure. Stay here and eat with us. What I cook will be better than whatever you had planned.'

'But what are you going to cook?' Raffaella asked. 'My basket is empty. Do you have enough food in the house?'

Anna poured another cup of coffee for Raffaella and raised her own to her lips. When she'd drained it, she replied, 'The cupboards are a little bare. But it's not such a big problem because, as you say, your basket is completely empty. So you could trot back up the hill, fill it with delicious things and be back in time for me to make supper. I don't need much. Just some meat, some vegetables, a little garlic, some chilli ... oh and a big loaf of bread and perhaps a few eggs.'

'And some chestnuts. I feel like chestnuts.'

'Yes, chestnuts if you like.'

'All right, I'll go now, then.'

Anna shook her head. 'No, don't go right this minute. There's time for us to talk about whatever it is you've been doing all alone in the days since Marcello's burial. We've been worried about you. Your sister, Teresa, kept wanting to go to you even though you'd told her not to.'

'I needed to know what it felt like to be alone.'

'And what does it feel like?'

Raffaella paused. 'The strangest time is in the mornings,' she said slowly. 'At night I dream Marcello is still there. And then I wake and remember he's gone for ever. That's the most difficult time.'

Anna touched her arm lightly. 'There's no need for you to be alone any longer, my love. Come home for good. Your brother will help you move your things down the hill.'

'Not yet,' Raffaella replied. 'I'm sorry, but I'm not ready to come back home just yet.'

'All right, stay away a little while longer if that's what you really want. But will you do just one thing for me, please?'

'What's that?'

'Cry, Raffaella,' her mother said gently. 'I can see the tears there in your eyes. It's time to let them go.'

7

Raffaella felt newly washed. The storm of tears that had passed over her was finished now, although her eyes were still red and her nose all shiny. She didn't know why it had taken her so long to let herself begin to cry, but once started she hadn't been able to stop. She felt as if she were sobbing not just for Marcello, but for everything sad that had ever happened to anyone she knew. In the end, her mother had poured her a glass of the sweet red wine that she kept in the back of the cupboard beneath the sink.

'This is good stuff. But don't tell your father,' Anna had said as Raffaella took a sip.

The sweetness and strength of the wine had made her feel better. And now she was clutching her empty basket as she walked up the hill to the market.

It had been a while since Raffaella had tackled the steep incline. She'd grown soft living in Big Triento, she realised. But when she had trouble catching her breath, she could always stop and turn to look at the view that grew bigger and better with every upward step she took.

At only halfway, she could make out the curve of the coastline, the rocks tumbling into the sea and the pebbly coves jammed in between the high cliffs. There were islands out there, outcrops really, topped by ruined towers and circled by seagulls. Directly beneath her were the terracotta rooftops of Little Triento and beneath them the fishing boats, wallowing in the water beside the smart little speedboats used by the richer people from Rome and Naples who made it this far south in the summer.

Raffaella pitched onwards, leaving the road and taking a shortcut up the steps that cut through the rock behind the walled gardens of some of the bigger houses. Branches loaded with lemons and figs hung above her head, and pine trees towered above them. The shade was a relief, for the October sun still had heat in it and she was shrouded and stifling in her widow's long, black dress.

At last she was standing in the exact spot where the priests had stopped her earlier that morning. The town hall was behind her, two storeys high and one of Triento's grandest buildings. In front of her was the fountain, a circle of fish in burnished bronze spouting water, with a naked mermaid rising from the middle.

Three narrow streets branched from the main piazza. One was lined with shops and cafés, the second pointed towards the mountains, and the other down to the sea. During the week the piazza itself was lined with market stalls that were hung with strings of salami and swollen yellow gourds of waxy caciocavallo cheese or piled high with the season's produce: monstrous pumpkins, pink-and-white speckled borlotti beans, sweet red apples and the very last of summer's ripe peaches.

Raffaella retraced her steps through the market, filling her basket with green beans, thin strings of red chilli peppers and bunches of leafy broccoli. She hurried past the hanging pigs' heads and sides of ham and through the butcher's door, and bought thin slices of red meat marbled with fat. For the last stop of all she saved the place she most dreaded, Alberto's bakery. He was sitting outside it now, the flaps of his bloated body spilling over the sides of the wooden bench where he spent most of every day. Once his big hands had finished bruising the dough and his bread was baked and cooling, Alberto considered his work done. It fell to his pinch-faced little wife, Silvana, to serve his customers, wrapping the flat golden loaves in paper and taking the money, while he dozed in the sunshine or sat and stared into space.

Raffaella saw that Alberto's eyes were closed now and his chest was rising and falling, slowly and deeply. She crept past, careful not to wake him.

She found Silvana trapped behind her rows of loaves and deep in conversation with Patrizia Sesto. Their heads were close together over the counter and Silvana was whispering something urgently. Both women turned as she came in and quickly fell silent. Patrizia's pale moon of a face flushed pink, and Silvana pressed her lips tightly together.

'*Buongiorno*,' said Raffaella, but Patrizia only nodded in reply, and seizing her basket of bread, she hurried out of the shop.

Silvana managed to recover her composure. '*Buongiorno*,' she replied. 'Have you already eaten the bread I sold you earlier?'

'I need another loaf for my mother. A large one this time.'

Silvana shrugged and began to wrap the heavy, hard-crusted bread in glossy white paper.

Raffaella glanced back through the shop window. She could see Patrizia Sesto on the other side of the piazza, speaking to Beatrice Ferrando. Both women had their baskets clutched to their stomachs and they were talking quickly and staring over at the bakery. Raffaella was quite certain that she was the topic under discussion.

There was always something to gossip about in Triento, and although she wasn't very interested in the rumours, sooner or later Raffaella usually heard them anyway. She knew which husband was said to be straying, whose child had been misbehaving, who was liked and who was hated.

She had suspected there would be whispers about the way Marcello had wasted away and died, but no one dared speak them out loud to her. Instead, they must have been hissing at each other in the shops and doorways of Big Triento, gossiping over baskets filled with food or little cups of espresso, muttering behind their hands. There was a sick feeling in the pit of Raffaella's stomach as she wondered exactly what they were saying.

She took the loaf from Silvana's outstretched hands and, clutching it to her chest, left the shop without another word. Tears were pressing at her eyes and she longed to get home so she could fling herself face down on a bed and let herself cry again.

Silvana sagged a little as she watched Raffaella leave the shop. She wondered if the girl had overheard anything. Surely not, but it had been a close thing.

From the bench outside the doorway, she heard the sound of steady snoring. Her husband, Alberto, never slept quietly. For all the years of their married life, her own sleep had been frayed. He snorted as he breathed in and whistled as he let the air out again. The noise went on all night long. It was no wonder she hated him.

Some nights Silvana lay awake and fantasised about leaning over and pinching his nostrils with one hand while covering his mouth with her other. Or she dreamed of putting her pillow over his face and pressing it down firmly until the only sound she could hear was her own breathing.

He honked like the pigs on her father's farm, she thought angrily. If only she had known that about him before they were married. There had been other choices then, other paths she might have taken. She remembered a farmer's boy with hair the colour of muddy straw who had begged her to give him her heart. She had turned him down because Alberto seemed the better prospect – his family had a comfortable house as well as the shop in town, and a baker's wife would never go hungry.

She still saw the farmer's boy. But what was left of his straw-coloured hair was greying now, and he didn't work the land but sat in an office in the town hall on the other side of the piazza. He had never married and Silvana always wondered if a little bit of his heart still belonged to her. She hardly got a chance to speak to him, for she was imprisoned in the bakery all day and he was wealthy enough to pay a housekeeper to come in and do his shopping for him. She saw him, though, walking past on his way to and from his office, and she longed to abandon the loaves still left to sell and chase him through the piazza. Sometimes she thought so hard about following him that if a customer came in and spoke to her she would jump, startled to find herself still standing there behind the counter.

She only ever escaped in her mind, for Alberto was always there outside the shop, his bench a guardhouse. And even while he was sleeping, Silvana was certain that if she tried to slip past, his eyes would open.

When Marcello had died so quickly and quietly, Silvana had been shocked. And then when his mother had whispered her suspicions over the counter, she'd been intrigued. She was too weak to overpower Alberto and too tame to run away, but she hadn't surrendered completely. And now she kept thinking, if the girl had really done it – which admittedly she doubted – perhaps what had worked for Raffaella could work for her too.

The sound of a customer's voice called Silvana back to reality.

'Ah, it's so hot today. This shop is full of flies, Silvana. You ought to do something about it.'

Alba Russo was standing beside the counter wearing her custom-ary look of distaste. Shilling-mouthed and fastidious, life rarely pleased her. She was a short woman who would have been stout had she allowed herself to enjoy her food. Her iron-grey hair was disciplined into tight curls by daily use of rollers, and her feet were always thrust into shoes with four-inch heels so that she teetered over the cobbles of Triento.

'Oh, the flies, yes, they're terrible this year,' Silvana managed to reply through her daze. 'But really, what is one to do?'

'I find a rolled-up newspaper works wonders,' Alba said briskly. 'Perhaps you should try it sometime.'

'But I kill one lot and more of the things fly in.'

'Don't give up so easily, Silvana. You could at least try to keep their numbers down. It's not clean to have so many of them buzzing round the food.'

Silvana quickly changed the subject. 'Guess who you have just missed by minutes? Your daughter-in-law Raffaella was here. I haven't had a glimpse of her since the funeral and then she comes in twice in one day.'

'I'm glad I missed her,' Alba said. 'I have no desire to see the girl at all.'

'Maybe you're wrong, you know,' Silvana couldn't help saying. 'Perhaps there really was a cancer growing and spreading inside Marcello like the doctors told you.'

Alba leaned over the counter and hissed so viciously that little bits of spittle left her mouth and sprayed Silvana's face. 'A cancer?' she repeated in disgust. 'He was young, strong and healthy, then he married her and one year later he was in his grave. Cancer is a useful little word that doctors use when they're too lazy to bother finding out why someone really died.'

'But couldn't you have talked to them? Made them run more tests or something? Asked more questions?'

'I did talk to them, Silvana, of course I did. I asked a million questions. And I talked to the police too. Everyone trots out the same stupid story and excuses. Cancer, they say, riddled with it. No one believes the girl had anything to do with it. But I know what's true is true. I'm a patient woman, Silvana, and I don't forget a thing. One day, when the time is right, I will make Raffaella pay. I'll have my revenge.'

Alba's hands were curled into tight balls, and her eyes were so wide they all but popped out of her head. Silvana felt almost sorry for Raffaella.

'Yes, but what if you are wrong, though?' she dared to repeat.

Alba made a choking sound. 'I'm sorry, Silvana, I thought I needed bread,' she snapped. 'Now I realise that I don't want any after all.' And she turned on her heel and stalked out of the shop.

Raffaella's tears had turned to anger. The more she thought about what the gossips might be saying, the angrier she became. The man she loved with all her heart had died, so surely people should be kind to her. Instead, they were whispering behind her back. Taking long strides, she quickened her pace to swallow up the ground between herself and the sea, glad to be leaving Big Triento behind.

'Mamma, I'm home,' she called, as she pushed open the familiar blue door and dumped the heavy basket on the ground. Before Anna's searching eyes could look into her own and read her mood, Raffaella headed for the bathroom. 'I'm hot and sticky,' she called out. 'I'm just going to clean myself up.'

She splashed cold water on her face for a full five minutes before she felt the anger loosen its grip on her. Pink cheeks still singing from the cold, she checked her reflection in the small, square mirror above the washbasin. She looked far calmer than she felt, although her eyes were still muddied from the afternoon's tears.

'Raffaella! What are you doing in there? Come and talk to me.' Her mother's voice rang through the house.

'Just a minute, I'm coming,' she called back.

Anna had found the basket of food and was already in her kitchen. When she cooked, she prepared the food as if she were creating a painting. She laid out her carefully chopped ingredients in piles before she mixed and melded the colours and textures with a sure hand. Sometimes, when she was pleased with what she'd done, she used a tea towel to unveil the finished meal with a mock flourish.

'What are you making?' Raffaella knew better than to offer to help, for her mother had always preferred to cook alone. She swore any other hand on her knives rendered them blunt and useless, and another person's heavy touch could taint the food. Her kitchen was so cramped that two cooks could only mean constant collisions and jogging of elbows. If Raffaella wanted to learn a dish, she'd best watch and listen from the safe distance of the bench.

'I'm making simple food,' Anna told her. 'Simple but good. The beans, I'll quickly blanch, then refresh in cold water and dress with a squeeze of lemon, a drizzle of olive oil and pinch or two of sea salt. The broccoli, I'll stir round the frying pan with smashed chilli and garlic, and the meat is sliced so thinly it needs nothing more than a quick turn in hot olive oil and a gentle simmer in a sauce of tomatoes, capers and a crushed anchovy or two.'

'Anchovies? What about my father?'

'Don't worry about him – he'll only taste the salt, not the fish.'

A lifetime of pulling fish out of the sea had left Raffaella's father, Tommaso, with a loathing of their soft flesh. He hated the sea and all that swam in it, and his hatred grew stronger by the year. While he lived on a rock that rose out of the water, once he crossed the threshold of his home he was careful not to set eyes on the expanse of blue outside his windows. Every chair or bench he ever sat on pointed inwards and viewed nothing but the room, and if ever he was asked why, Tommaso would always reply, 'I stare at the sea all day. When I'm at home I prefer to stare at my family.'

If he'd had his way, the wooden shutters would be pulled closed across the windows all the time and not just when there was a storm lashing at them. But Anna couldn't live her life in darkness and she'd told him so.

'It's bad enough that you'll only eat meat. Every day meat, meat and more meat and the price of it and the slog up that hill to get it, and why we can't just eat what you catch I'll never know.'

'I see their glassy eyes and watch them die,' he always bellowed at her. 'I can't eat the ugly things after that.'

'Well, the poor farmer has to look into the eyes of the pigs that provide your pork,' she had tried pointing out. 'What do you think about that?'

'Let him eat my fish, then, if he has such a problem,' he'd bellowed again, and although he wasn't a big man, his voice came from his boots and Anna always had to step back a pace or two to escape it.

Her secret jar of salty anchovies was pushed to the very back of the cupboard and shielded by taller jars full of dried beans, bottles of preserved fruit and canisters of flour.

'Anchovies, they're hardly fish at all,' she told her daughter briskly. 'They don't deserve the name.'

'Yes, but one day he'll find out and won't he be furious?'

'I've been feeding him anchovies for over twenty years and he's never guessed yet. They're good with lamb, delicious with pasta, they bring a sauce to life, so why wouldn't I use them?' Anna replied, and suddenly there was a light in her eyes that Raffaella had never seen before. Her voice dropped to a low, confiding tone. 'Sometimes, if he's annoyed me a lot, I sneak an anchovy or two into whatever he's eating even if it doesn't really compliment the dish. And I take extra pleasure in watching him eat those meals.'

'Mamma!' Raffaella was shocked.

'Oh, you must know how infuriating husbands can be.'

Raffaella said nothing and Anna's hand flew to her mouth. 'Oh, I'm sorry, I didn't mean . . . I forgot . . . '

'That's all right. Everyone can't be tiptoeing around me all the time.'

Anna still looked mortified.

'You know what might make me feel a little better?' Raffaella tried to smile.

'Yes?'

'A drop or two of that sweet red wine that you keep in the cupboard beneath the sink.'

As she poured the wine Anna rolled her eyes. 'For God's sake don't tell your father about this or the anchovies or I'll be in trouble.'

He was only a little man, but Tommaso Moretti had the presence of a person twice his size. It was always a shock when he jumped to his feet and his head only reached as high as his wife's shoulder, for the power of his personality filled a room. And although Anna looked down on him physically, she almost always deferred to him.

When Tommaso walked through the door and sat on the kitchen bench with his back to the window, Anna would rush over with a single cigarette and put it in his mouth and light it. At mealtimes she served his food at the table and ate her own dinner over the sink, before she cleared the dishes and washed them up with the help of her daughters. If she raised her voice in argument, she was usually ready to back down if he showed no sign of moving.

He was her husband, he went to sea each day and cast his nets, and the fish he brought home helped fill their pockets with money. And Tommaso's nets always brimmed with fish. Even when other men returned with a disappointing catch, Tommaso would follow them with a full load of glassy-eyed, silver-skinned fish lining the bottom of his boat. While Anna might have her quiet rebellions, Tommaso was a good provider, and she treated him with the respect she knew he deserved.

Tonight his tough face softened as he came through the door and found his elder daughter there.

'You've come at last. We've been so worried.' He seized her and kissed her.

'No need to worry. I've been fine.'

'But now you're here,' he said happily. 'You've brought your things? You won't be going back up the hill?'

Raffaella looked at her father, his black hair stiff with salt and his wiry little body, its muscles taut from hauling at the nets, and she faltered. 'No, I . . . '

'You what?'

'I left my things up there. I'm only here to eat with you and perhaps stay tonight because I don't want to be walking back up the hill in the moonlight.'

'But why?' She felt the rise of his temper and saw him try to damp it down just like she herself always had to. 'Why don't you come home? I don't understand you.'

'I spoke to the priests,' she said quickly. 'They have other ideas for me.'

'What ideas are these?' he demanded, and her mother echoed, 'Yes, what ideas?'

'Well.' Raffaella looked from one to the other. 'There is a house along the coast where they need someone to clean and make it ready, and then they'll need a cook. And the priests thought I might be suitable.'

Anna turned to Tommaso and gasped, 'Villa Rosa!'

'It can't be.'

'What else? I told you what Giuliana Biagio has been saying. The priests have rented the place.'

'But nothing was decided.' Tommaso was furious. 'Surely they can't go ahead with this without us all agreeing.'

Raffaella had no idea what they were talking about and she tried to interrupt, but they ignored her.

'When we left that meeting, nothing was decided,' Tommaso

repeated, his rage building. 'And now this. They're going ahead without us. I'm not having it. Do you hear?'

'Don't do anything hasty,' Anna counselled. 'We don't know for sure what's going on. Perhaps we're jumping to conclusions.'

Realising her words had pushed her parents to the edge of conflict, Raffaella tried to interrupt again, more forcefully this time. 'Look, don't worry about it. I'll refuse the job if it's such a problem.'

'No!' Anna's eyes darted to meet her husband's hard stare. 'She should accept it. Shouldn't she?'

Tommaso nodded. 'Go and take the job,' he said more calmly now. 'Talk to the priests tomorrow and tell them that you want it. Your mother's right – we mustn't act too hastily. And it can only be an advantage to have you at Villa Rosa.'

Raffaella was uncertain what he meant, but she didn't like to argue. If her father thought it best that she should take this job, then that was what she was going to do.

8

Raffaella's legs were tangled with her sister's skinny limbs and they were playing their old game, tugging the sheet back and forth to try to get the lion's share.

'Oh, no, I've got none of it over me now,' Teresa complained, giving a short, strong pull. 'I'll freeze to death if you don't give me some more.'

'Nonsense,' Raffaella gasped. 'It's draped all over you. It's almost dropping to the floor. I'm the one who'll freeze.' And she pulled again, then rolled on top of the sheet and trapped it to stop Teresa from stealing it back.

They'd played this game all their lives in the bed they shared in the tiny room under the eaves at the very top of the house. Tonight, though, for Raffaella, it felt strange to have the soft body of her sister lying beside her instead of the hard male body she had become accustomed to during her year of marriage.

'You won't roll over and start trying to kiss me in the night, will you?' Teresa giggled, still tugging at the sheet in vain.

'No,' Raffaella said shortly.

'You won't start cuddling up all close to me and being soppy?' Teresa continued.

'No.' Raffaella rolled away and released an extra few centimetres of sheet. 'Here, now you won't get cold, will you?'

Teresa was silent for a moment or two and Raffaella thought she might have drifted off to sleep. But then her thin, high voice piped up again. 'Raffaella?'

'What?' She dreaded a question about Marcello's death or her marriage or, worse still, about sex, for Teresa was fifteen and relentlessly curious.

But instead her sister asked simply, 'Why do you think Papà was in such a bad mood tonight?'

Raffaella considered the question. 'I don't know,' she replied. 'It started when I mentioned the job I've been offered cleaning and cooking in a house up the coast. They got all excited about it and started yelling at each other.'

'Do they not want you to take the job?'

'Well, that's the strange thing. When they'd finished yelling, they told me that I ought to take it. But they didn't explain why.'

'Papà has been in a terrible mood for weeks now,' Teresa offered. 'Has the catch been bad?'

'No, I don't think that's it. But they shut up about it whenever I'm around. It's really annoying.'

'Does Sergio have any idea what's going on?'

'Maybe, but I hardly ever see him these days, so who would know?'

When he wasn't working beside his father on the fishing boat, their brother, Sergio, was away some place with his friends doing who knows what for hours on end. It irked Teresa that he could come and go as he pleased, a shadowy figure sometimes glimpsed late at night in a darkened kitchen with his head over a pan of leftover pasta. She was less than two years younger than Sergio and yet her every move was tracked and she rarely left the house after nightfall.

'Sergio tells me even less than they do these days,' she added mournfully. 'I've really missed you, Raffaella. It's lonely here without you. Won't you come home?'

'They say they want me to take this job.'

'But do you want to?'

Raffaella shrugged in the darkness. 'Why not? What else is there for me to do?'

'Come home. Stay here with me.' Teresa pushed the sheet back towards Raffaella. 'It's awful here without you.'

Raffaella felt half guilty and half impatient. 'I know, but soon you'll leave too. There'll be a husband somewhere for you and you'll make a home with him and then what will happen to me?'

'You'll come with me too, like I keep saying.' Teresa reached for her arm and clung to it. 'I've got a bad feeling about this job you've been offered, really I have.'

Raffaella smiled a little. 'You and your feelings.'

'No, I do,' Teresa insisted.

Raffaella let her sister press herself closer, and when Teresa pushed her head into her shoulder, she stroked her hair gently because she knew that was what she wanted. 'It'll be all right you know, *cara*. I'll be just down the coast a little way. You can come to see me whenever you want to.'

'I have a bad feeling,' Teresa repeated.

'It doesn't matter. I have no choice. I have to take this job. Surely you understand that?'

9

Carlotta was staring out of her bedroom window. It was that hour before daybreak, before the first bright streaks paint the sky, when it seems like it will never grow light. She had woken early and with a sense of excitement. This felt like the start of something that would change all their lives. For better or worse she wasn't sure, but for Carlotta, whose life in the garden was dictated by the rhythm of the seasons, any change was welcome. The seasons were beautiful but monotonous. Year after year summer followed spring and winter breathed its chill on autumn. Each season brought with it a long list of tasks, and there was little variation or scope for change. This coming season would be different, though, and whatever happened, Carlotta knew she would be part of it.

As soon as she saw the first glow of daylight, Carlotta slipped out of the house and through the high gates into the walled gardens of Villa Rosa. She turned her back on the house itself and followed the carved rock steps that led down to the sea. This was her ritual. She would stand on the rocks and look at the sea crashing beneath her. Some days it was calm enough to swim and Carlotta could have climbed down the rusting ladder bolted to the rock. But she'd seen the sea when it was a boiling mass, slapping against the rocks with a power that would dash her to pieces. She knew its strength, and even when it was calm, she lacked the nerve to so much as dip a toe in it. It was safer to stand and look down on the water as it thrashed itself into a froth of white foam.

It was only here, at the edge of the sea, that Carlotta could let her mind go free. Here, she had the luxury of thinking her own quiet thoughts for a few moments each morning. If tears streaked her cheeks, they would pass for salt spray. And if she prayed, she was sure that only God could hear her above the roar of the surf. Had there not been so much work to do, she might have stayed here for hours.

She felt for the key in her pocket as she turned to walk back up the steps, and was reassured by its hard shape beneath her fingers. She passed the terraced gardens where the neat rows of tomatoes and chilli plants were dying back, and she paused for a moment when she reached the pomegranate tree in the centre of the courtyard. The old tree had sagged further now and even the second crutch Umberto had wedged beneath its branches might not support them for much longer.

Carlotta felt a little tug of excitement as she reached the front door of Villa Rosa and pulled the key from her pocket. The house had been shut up for years and she'd never had any reason to open it. She barely remembered what it looked like inside. Now, as she pushed the door open, the stale smell of neglect reached her first. She peered into the gloom, feeling oddly guilty about stepping over the threshold.

'Hello?' she called out shyly, and immediately felt ridiculous. There was no one inside and she had every right to be there.

First, Carlotta threw open the shutters and windows on the lower floor, and then she turned to examine the rooms the light had revealed. The house was floored with white ceramic tiles that would shine once they were relieved of a thick layer of dust. There were curtains the colour of butterscotch, corded and tasselled with gold, and there were high-backed chairs that looked more grand than comfortable. Pictures of flowers hung in ornate frames, and a mirror covered the whole of one wall. Carlotta caught her reflection in it but quickly turned away from the sight of her pale face and thin shoulders.

She moved upstairs briskly, opening windows as she went. Already the sea breeze was rolling in and chasing out the musty, dank smells that had lived there so long. There were three bedrooms on the upper floor, one grand with a balcony that overlooked the courtyard, the other two more modest. Carlotta ran a finger over the chest of drawers and eyed the dust balls in the corner. There was a lot of cleaning here for someone. She had told the priests she could manage it herself, but they'd insisted she should have help.

'Carlotta? Where are you? Hoo-hoo, Carlotta?' Her father had known she planned to open up the house today, but he must have forgotten. Things not directly concerning his garden rarely stayed in Umberto's mind for long.

She leaned over the balcony and called, 'I'm up here.'

Umberto looked around in confusion. 'Where?'

'In the house,' she added, waving to attract his attention.

She saw him hesitate at the front door just as she had.

'The place doesn't look as bad as I'd thought it might,' he called to her as he climbed the stairs. 'Could be worse.'

'There's lots of work to do,' Carlotta insisted.

'Oh, not so much,' Umberto replied. 'Not enough for us to need this girl the priests want to foist on us.'

'Raffaella Moretti.'

'You know her?'

'Not really.' Carlotta rubbed her hand absent-mindedly over the dull surface of the dressing table. 'She's younger than I am, so I only just remember her from school. But I'd have to be blind not to notice her walking through town. She's a stunning girl.'

'And what else do you know about her?'

Carlotta looked uncomfortable. 'I've heard things.'

'Like what?'

Carlotta hesitated, ashamed at having listened to such poison. 'In town, what they say is she murdered her husband. He died rather suddenly, and the gossips are making a meal of it.'

Umberto raised his eyebrows. 'The gossips always do,' he said.

'Yes, but . . . ' Carlotta gazed out at the sea and the horizon, her brow creased in worry. 'What if there is some truth to it? What if the girl's not to be trusted?'

'She's Tommaso Moretti's daughter, isn't she?'

Carlotta nodded.

'Well, he's a good man. Why should his daughter be any different?'

'I don't know . . . I'm just concerned. Why would they gossip like that if there were no truth to it at all?'

Umberto's face took on the contrary expression his daughter knew so well. 'Don't judge this Raffaella girl until you've met her properly yourself. And tell the priests to let her come. Perhaps we do need her after all.'

10

From where she was sitting, Raffaella could see a pink wall and a window with its shutters thrown open. Above her head, red bougainvillea climbed over a pergola, and beneath her feet, its dropped flowers lay wilting on the terracotta tiles.

The gardener, Umberto, had been at the gate to meet her. Toothless and tanned to terracotta by the sun, despite the shade provided by the dirty cloth cap squashed on his head, he'd shifted awkwardly from foot to foot and muttered at her shyly.

'Wait here,' he had told her. 'My daughter, Carlotta, will be with you shortly.'

That had been fifteen minutes ago and there was still no sign of Carlotta. Perhaps she was keeping her waiting on purpose. Or maybe she was simply busy, cleaning already, up there in the room that lay behind the open window.

With nothing else to occupy her time, Raffaella looked around curiously. This was the most beautiful garden she had ever seen. Below the terrace where she sat, there were rows of trees, their branches hanging heavy with fruit. And ahead of her, in the centre of the courtyard, was a single pomegranate tree, its head drooping down and its limbs resting tiredly on two roughly cut wooden stakes.

Green-backed lizards ran across the low stone wall that surrounded it, disappearing into the cracks and holes with a flick of their long, black tails. Raffaella was absorbed in watching them when a soft voice interrupted her.

'*Buongiorno.*'

She looked up to find a skinny, awkward-looking girl whose face was shaded by a wide-brimmed hat.

'*Buongiorno.* I'm Raffaella,' she replied.

The girl nodded. 'I know that. I recognise you from school and I've seen you shopping in Triento from time to time. I'm Carlotta Santoro.'

Raffaella cast about in her mind for a memory of this nondescript little soul but could find none. 'Of course,' she lied politely. 'It's good to see you again.'

Carlotta nodded at the small bag of clothes at Raffaella's feet. 'Leave your things here for now,' she instructed, 'and I'll show you Villa Rosa. Later we'll pick up your bag and I'll take you down to your room.'

'I won't be sleeping here, then? In Villa Rosa?'

'No.' Carlotta looked shocked. 'That wouldn't be right at all. You'll be staying with my father and me in our house just over the way and I'm sure you'll find it comfortable enough. Now come on, we have no time to waste.'

Carlotta moved quickly and Raffaella hurried after her. She was shown a bathroom that needed scrubbing and a kitchen that needed scouring. There were dusters and a mop and bucket laid out ready for the work to begin.

'I'm doing the bedrooms and the living room,' Carlotta told her. 'The rest is up to you.'

'Will I start now, then?'

Carlotta nodded and moved to turn away.

'How long do we have before the tenant arrives?' Raffaella asked.

'I'm not certain,' Carlotta replied in a tight little voice that didn't welcome more questions.

'And who is the person who will be living here?' Raffaella persisted.

'You'll see soon enough.' Carlotta turned her back on her and called out as she walked away, 'Shout if you need anything. Otherwise I'll come and get you later on.'

Raffaella looked at the bucket and mop and sighed. The afternoon stretched ahead of her hot and full of hard work. For a moment she wished she was back in her tidy apartment above the linen shop, but that door was closed to her now. There was no escaping the layers of dirt left behind by years of neglect, and as she filled a bucket with water, she tried to decide where to start scrubbing.

Already the skin on Raffaella's hands felt rough and dry, and the scale of the job was only just becoming clear to her. With every

49

cupboard she opened, every drawer she peered into, she found more dirt. Where did the dust come from? Did it roll in under the doors and push through gaps in the windows in search of a place to pool and settle? It had misted the wine glasses so that each one would have to be rinsed and polished; it had lain down on the bowls and platters stacked on the open shelves, and sprinkled over the cobwebs that festooned the ceiling, and hidden itself in corners and high places.

There were worse things than dust when she opened the oven: baked-on grease and shrivelled fossils of food from long-forgotten meals. Whoever had cooked here last hadn't been the best house-keeper, and Raffaella resolved to take better care once she began to use the place herself.

As she scraped at the blackened fat in the oven, she wondered who would be eating the food she cooked in this big, generous kitchen. The priests had avoided answering her questions, and now Carlotta was staying close-mouthed. All this secrecy seemed ridiculous, for sooner or later the whole town would know who was living here, and anyway, what did it matter? Raffaella found herself wondering what Marcello would make of the mystery. They might have discussed it together while she prepared his dinner and he drank an *aperitivo*. And then, with a sudden shock of grief, she realised that the world was moving on without him.

She stared at the oily filth on her hands. Soon they would be red and raw. Her arms would ache from scrubbing and her legs from kneeling on the floor. Raffaella allowed herself a moment of sadness. This wasn't her life. This wasn't what was meant to happen at all.

Then she rubbed her cheek against her shoulder, dipped her scouring pad into the clean water and set to scrubbing with even more vigour than before.

The oven was shining inside and out by the time she looked up from the task and found Carlotta standing in the kitchen doorway, staring at her silently.

'Oh, how long have you been there?' Raffaella was startled. 'I didn't hear you coming.'

A trace of a smile wandered over Carlotta's face. 'Sorry, did I give you a fright? I was trying to decide whether to interrupt you or not. You looked like you were working so hard.'

'How on earth did this place get into such a state? The oven was disgusting. It doesn't look like it's been touched for ages.'

'It hasn't. Villa Rosa is a summer house, and the people who own it live up north. They used to come every August and spend the month here. But they haven't bothered with the place in years.'

'But why? It's so beautiful. If it were mine, I'd live here all the time.'

Carlotta's face looked strained. 'The Barbieri family is a rich one. They have other beautiful houses in other places so I suppose they prefer to use them in the summer.'

'Why don't they sell Villa Rosa, then?' Raffaella pressed her.

'I don't know.'

'Perhaps they think that one summer they'll want to come back here?'

'I really don't think so. They won't be back.' Carlotta sounded quite certain.

Raffaella stood up and stretched the stiffness from her body. 'Have I done a good job?' she asked, nodding towards the oven.

Carlotta smiled properly this time and her face seemed nearly pretty. 'Yes, you've done a really good job. Once I've washed all the curtains, I'll be finished with my rooms and then I can come and help you.'

'That would be good.'

Carlotta paused for a moment in the doorway. 'The tenant we're doing all this cleaning for is a man,' she offered at last. 'An American. He'll be living here for a few months at least, and the priests say he arrives in a fortnight.'

II

Anna hated making this trek up the hill. She didn't like the complaining of her calf muscles or the feeling that her lungs were fighting for air. And either the slope was getting steeper or she was becoming older and slower, for today the climb seemed to be taking an age.

As she slogged onwards, she allowed herself to think bitter things about the other fishermen's wives – Giuliana Biagio, Beatrice Ferrando, Patrizia Sesto and the rest – quite useless, each and every one of them. Oh, they'd been generous enough with the space in their baskets and brought back meat, vegetables and fruit from the market as they always did. But when it came to the other delicious titbits that Anna wanted so much, they'd held back.

'What's happening? What's the talk in town?' she'd asked them every day for the past week. And they'd shrugged or murmured and worn their blankest faces as they backed away from her.

Anna knew what that meant. Whatever was occupying the gossips around the stalls on market days in Triento must have something to do with herself or her family. She had no idea what the rumour might be, only that it was serious enough for none of the other wives to dare bring it back down the hill for her.

'I'll just have to go myself,' she'd told Tommaso the night before. 'Hear with my own ears what they're all talking about.'

He had laughed. 'Are you sure now, my love? Can't you bully it out of Patrizia or sweet-talk Giuliana into telling you? Is it really worth a walk up the hill?'

'It'll have to be because I can't get a word out of any of them. Lord knows what they're saying about us up there, but no one's brave enough to share it with me.'

'I wonder,' Tommaso had mused. 'I wonder what it is.'

'Oh, something about Raffaella, I'd imagine. What else?'

'Or something about the new tenant at Villa Rosa?'

Anna had frowned. 'Surely if it were about Villa Rosa, they'd be jumping out of their skins to tell me? But now you mention it, that gives me double the reason to go to the market myself tomorrow. If there's news to be had about Villa Rosa, I'd like to hear it.'

A knot of priests lay directly in Anna's path as she climbed the final steps into the piazza. They turned their backs when they saw her and folded their dark robes inward, and their voices fell to whispers. With no more than a sidelong glance at their tight little circle, she marched on, weaving through the market stalls towards the sweet scents of the bakery.

Alberto was slumped on his bench outside the shop as always. He half opened an eye and snapped it shut again quickly when he saw it was her. But Silvana, trapped behind the counter, couldn't avoid her so easily.

'Ah, *buongiorno*.' Anna breezed in. 'What do you have for me today, Silvana?'

'Oh, the usual.' The baker's wife shrugged. 'What brings you up to town, anyway? I haven't seen you for a while.'

'Not that long, surely? I was in here only the other day, wasn't I?'

'No, it's been longer than that,' Silvana insisted. 'I don't think I've seen you since Marcello's funeral.'

'Ah, yes, poor Marcello,' Anna said heavily. 'And poor Raffaella too.'

'So young, so sad,' Silvana murmured in agreement, but her eyes seemed to slide away from Anna's gaze and drift towards the corner of the shop in discomfort.

Anna sat down on the stool Silvana kept beside the counter for regular customers who might stay for a chat. On quiet afternoons a particularly garrulous customer could stop here for twenty minutes or more toying with the latest snippet of news, turning it over and over, just as Alberto did the dough he kneaded every morning, shaping it and reshaping it and examining it from every angle. Easily as much gossip was baked to perfection as bread in this little shop. And if there were an intriguing rumour doing the rounds or some fresh news buzzing, many of Triento's husbands found themselves being urged to eat slice after slice of hard golden bread to soak up their bean soup as their wives contrived a reason to return to the bakery for yet another loaf.

'Ah, that's better ... my poor feet ... that damn hill,' Anna grumbled as her backside thumped down on the hard wooden stool, and then she added lightly, 'So what's happening?'

'Eh?' Silvana looked startled.

'What's the gossip round town?'

Silvana shrugged.

'Come on, something must have happened. Everyone must be talking about somebody.'

Silvana shook her head. 'It's been very quiet. I can't think of anything interesting to tell you at all.'

'No gossip?'

'No.'

'None?' Anna sounded disbelieving. 'So what have you been talking about all day, then?'

Silvana shuffled loaves around on the shelves with nervous, flour-dusted hands. 'Nothing really.'

Anna shot her a disbelieving look.

'Honestly, things have been very quiet round here ... ' Silvana's voice tailed off and she focused on the shop doorway as if willing someone to walk through it. And then a sly look settled on her face as it occurred to her to turn the tables on Anna. 'Why, what have you heard?' she asked.

'It's what I haven't heard that bothers me,' Anna muttered.

'Eh? What do you mean?'

Anna shook her head. 'Never mind,' she said. 'Just give me one of those big loaves and wrap it well – I have to carry it down that damn hill.'

'Not going to Villa Rosa, then?' Silvana still looked sly.

'No, of course not.'

'And how is Raffaella getting on there? I hear she's been hired to help keep house.'

Anna nodded. 'That's right.'

'The tenant they've all been waiting for will be arriving soon, I expect?'

Anna said nothing and Silvana couldn't help but break the silence with more words.

'What's your daughter told you, then?' she asked in a low voice. 'About the tenant?'

'Nothing. My Raffaella isn't much of a one for gossip.'

'You must know something, surely?'

Anna took the wrapped loaf from Silvana's outstretched hands. 'There is one thing I know,' she said quietly. 'If this mystery tenant has anything to do with the priests and their crazy plans for the statue, then there'll be trouble.'

'The statue?'

'Yes, Silvana, the statue.'

The baker's wife stared out of the window at the mountain, her eyes empty. 'I really wouldn't know anything about the statue,' she said tonelessly.

'That's right because nothing was agreed on at that meeting, was it?' Anna said sternly. 'When Tommaso and the other men walked out, nothing had been decided. And the priests surely wouldn't have made a decision without them. Would they?'

'Who knows?' Silvana took Anna's few coins from her hand and put them away in the till. 'I expect if decisions had to be made, then the people who bothered to stay at the meeting would have made them.'

'So they are going ahead with it?' Anna's voice was steady and low. 'They're going to put that statue on the mountain with us or without us? Is that what you're saying?'

'Oh, for goodness' sake!' Silvana slammed the till drawer shut. 'Ask someone else about it. Try one of the priests, surely they'll know. But I can't help you, really I can't. I have better things to do than stand around here gossiping about statues all day.'

Striding from the shop, loaf beneath her arm, Anna held her irritation in check. She should have known better than to expect Silvana to open up. She had always been a cunning woman. Sometimes gossip spilled from her mouth faster than water gushed from the fountain in the piazza. But Silvana was wise enough to know when to hold herself in check. And if she had decided not to speak, nothing was going to coax the words from her.

As Anna stepped through the street, she glanced up at the mountain that shaded Big Triento from the sun for most of every morning. It was steep and reached a sharp point at the top like a mountain in a child's picture book. In the old days the village of Triento had clung to the very top of that peak, safe from bandits and thieves. But in more peaceful times the villagers had built new homes in the folds and foothills of the mountain and settled there. They'd abandoned the old goatherds' huts and let them fall into ruins, and all that remained was the barest trace of them – the line of a rock wall, the space where a doorway had once been, the blackened stone of a fireplace.

No one ever went up there now, for there was no reason to. But there were still a few farmhouses halfway up the mountain and an open-air chapel, where Padre Pietro sometimes said morning Mass in the summer months. One day last June he'd taken it into his head to climb the steep track up to the summit and walk through the ruins of Old Triento to the very top of the mountain to look down on the view of the glorious stretch of coastline God had blessed them with.

The idea had come to him while he stood there in the sunshine and wind, closer to the sky than the sea, musing at the loneliness of this abandoned place. They should build something up here, he realised, build to the glory of God. Not a church, though, for there were enough of those down there beneath him, spires and steeples straining upwards. He could see his own modest little church, Santo Spirito, tightly packed into the centre of Triento. It was difficult enough to find worshippers to fill its pews, even when the streets were clogged with people. A church built all the way up here in this isolated spot would be destined to lie empty. There would be no point in it at all.

Later that day he'd shared his thoughts with Alba Russo over a coffee in the little corner café near his church. She was often there in the late mornings, fussily demanding her coffee be served with a separate jug of frothed milk and peering at the pastries in the glass cabinet that lined one wall but never choosing one because, as she liked to explain, she preferred to stay trim.

Padre Pietro always listened as Alba boasted of her family's skill in the linen business or, more latterly, lamented the wasting away of her eldest son, Marcello. He listened patiently because someone had to hear her whispered suspicions and it was better him, who'd always loved Raffaella, than someone else who might believe the worst of her.

But that morning, before Alba could press him into a corner and lower her voice to an urgent whisper, Padre Pietro spoke. He told her of his climb up to Old Triento and his belief that something should be built on the wasted ground that lay there.

'But what?' he asked her. 'If not a church, then what?'

'Well, it seems obvious to me,' Alba said crisply. 'A statue, that's what you should put up there. A tall, pure white statue of Christ that will be seen for miles around, from the land and from the sea, like the one they have in Rio de Janeiro. You must have seen pictures of it.'

Padre Pietro looked dubious. 'Yes, I have. But you know, Rio is a huge city and Triento only a village. A project like that would be too much for us.'

'I don't see why. We have all that money old Signor Bertoli left the town when he died, remember. Poor man with no family, no fine young sons like mine to carry on his legacy. Wouldn't it be wonderful to build a statue in his name so that Triento will never forget him?'

'I don't know.' Padre Pietro looked dubious. 'It's too ambitious, too bold . . . and far too expensive. It's a beautiful dream, but I'm sure that anything we tried to build on that mountain would use up far more money than Signor Bertoli left us.'

'Money?' Alba rapped on the counter for more coffee. 'Well, if that's the problem, my family will certainly pledge more money. And if we do, then the other merchants will. And the fishermen will have to put in their share too. You'll have enough in no time.'

And that's how it had begun. As the plan was passed from mouth to mouth, the priests had seized on it and decided that, with God's help, and a little extra money, it could be done. But Tommaso, with the other fishermen behind him, had put up a fierce argument. He didn't see why they should empty their pockets into the collection bowls. Didn't they give enough already to the church week after week? What money they had was hard earned hauling stinking fish out of the sea in all weathers. It was easy for the merchants, warm, safe and dry in their shops, to throw money into the church coffers.

'You can't expect us to give any more,' he'd complained at the town meeting they'd held in the piazza. 'We risk our lives out there each day and we don't make as good a living as any of you. Isn't that right, boys?'

'That's right, that's right,' the other fisherman had agreed.

'Spend poor Bertoli's money on something useful, for God's sake,'

Tommaso had continued, his voice rising. 'What about a new schoolhouse to replace that damp old building our children are forced to sit in for half the day? That's a far better idea. A statue would be no more than a vanity. We don't need it – especially if it's likely to cost more than we've got. That doesn't make any sense at all. It's madness.'

The sharp elbow of his wife, Alba, had roused Roberto Russo. 'Now hold on a minute,' he'd argued. 'That statue will be for all of us, a sign of our piety for all the world to see, a glorious way to thank God for His goodness.'

'An expensive way,' Tommaso had scoffed, and the other fishermen had laughed.

But Roberto was building his momentum and he didn't let the interruption put him off his stride. 'That statue will stare down at the sea, its arms outstretched, protecting you and all fishermen for as long as it stands. If anything, you should donate more money than us, for it's you who'll benefit from the statue's greatest blessings.'

Quick to anger, Tommaso had jumped to his feet. 'Stop talking nonsense, Russo,' he'd thundered. 'There won't be any blessings. The thing will just be a lump of stone on the mountain and an expensive lump at that. It will be nothing more than a memorial of your arrogance, your self-importance and your ridiculous puffed-up pride. And we're not paying for it, I'm telling you, we're not.'

And with that, the other fishermen had risen to join him, and turning their backs on the townspeople, they'd stormed back down the hill to Little Triento, to their wives and the sanity of their kitchens, where they'd relived the meeting, and exaggerated their own part in it, long into the night.

Padre Pietro had spoken after they'd left. 'Perhaps Tommaso Moretti is right,' he'd said, his face settling into its usual sad lines. 'It was a beautiful dream, but the cost will be too high if it divides the town.'

'We're already divided, aren't we?' Alberto, the baker, had called out. 'They're down there with the fishes and we're up here closer to God. Who cares about them, anyway? We should go ahead with the statue with or without them.'

Padre Pietro had tried to object, but he'd been shouted down. Only Roberto Russo's booming tones could be heard above the babble.

'Let the statue face the land,' he had decreed. 'Let it have its back to the sea and never gaze upon a single fisherman.'

'Eh, that's right,' Alberto had agreed. 'If they're not going to pay up, then curse the lot of them, I say. Let the statue give them the cold shoulder, like Signor Russo says.'

And so the priests had quietly got on with their plans, collecting more money and seeking those with the expertise to tell them how best to raise their statue on the mountaintop. Roberto Russo had contacted his cousin in America. He worked in construction and knew the right people. Names had been mentioned, people had been recommended, and finally someone was hired. Working secretly, the priests had rented the very best house in the area, Villa Rosa, to accommodate the project manager they had found. Then they'd hired Raffaella to cook and clean for him. And down the hill in Little Triento, as whispered rumours of these plans had wafted down to them, the fishermen and their wives were left wondering exactly what was going on.

'Why do we even care?' Anna asked later that evening. 'If the money isn't coming out of our pockets, let them put a statue on every mountain in Italy.'

'It's a matter of principle,' Tommaso argued. 'We were against that statue from the start and we have just as much right to be listened to as anyone else. But no, Russo and those priests don't think we count.'

'So what are you going to do?'

Tommaso looked out of the kitchen window, glimpsed the sea and frowned. 'I don't know,' he said, turning his back on the wide expanse of blue. 'But I feel like I have to do something.'

12

For the people of Triento, there was always a church door open.
They had the chance to worship at almost any hour of the day. Seven
priests meant seven Masses to listen to, seven curtained confessionals
where sins could be spilled and washed away, seven incense-scented
echoing halls filled with pews for the faithful to sit on and wooden
rails for them to kneel on and pray.

But no prayers were being said in Triento this afternoon, and the
doors of every single one of its seven churches were pulled tightly
closed. Sinners who wanted a priest to confess to would have to walk
down the narrow alleyway that led to a dark little café tucked away
in a courtyard behind the piazza. There, an old yellow dog with an
overshot jaw was stretched out in the only patch of sunlight, and
seven dark-robed men were sitting in the shade at tables that had
been pushed together and covered in a red-and-white checked
tablecloth.

The Gypsy Tearoom had been here for as long as anyone could
remember. No one knew how it had come by its name, for it had
never served tea and nor was it run by a gypsy. Not that anyone
cared. All that mattered was that its owner, Ciro Ricci, served the
very best pizza they had ever tasted.

As they gathered round their table, the priests were distracted by
the thought of the stringy mozzarella cheese melting in their mouths,
the tang of tomato and basil on their tongues and the crunch of the
thin wood-fired crust as their teeth bit into it. Until their bellies were
filled and they were lingering over a carafe of Ciro's rough red wine
or a strong hot coffee none of them would be able to tune their minds
properly to the matter in hand.

Even so, they chatted about it in a desultory way as they fiddled

60

with the paper napkins in their laps and fidgeted with their wine glasses.

'I still think we need to have the whole town behind us before we try to do this,' remarked Padre Pietro, his kind face creased with worry.

'Once the building work starts, they'll be caught up in the excitement, I promise you,' replied handsome Padre Matteo.

'Are we certain, though?' Padre Pietro pressed him. 'Are we quite certain we want to go on with this? If we change our minds about the whole thing now, it wouldn't be too late. But if we take it much further, then we're committed.'

Padre Matteo put a reassuring hand on his shoulder. 'My brother,' he said kindly but firmly, 'we're already committed. If we back away from this now, we will lose face, we'll lose trust. Don't worry so much. And, God willing, in a year or so, we'll be sitting at this very table and raising our glasses to toast success.'

Padre Simone nodded in agreement. 'This was practically your idea,' he reminded the anxious little priest. 'When that statue is raised on the mountain, it will be a great day for you. Keep your faith.'

Padre Simone fell silent, the word dying on his lips, and he stared away into the dark pizzeria. Faith was something he hadn't felt himself for a long time. He'd had plenty to spare as a young priest. There were moments when he had burned with it. But sometime between then and now, the fire had died and the faith had seeped from him.

He'd begun to question the very existence of God, and once the doubt had taken hold in his mind, there was nothing he could do to rid himself of it. Yet still he stood at the altar, said Mass, gave Communion. Appalled at his own hypocrisy, he considered turning his back on the Church, but he lacked the courage to take the first step away from its protection. The Church was his livelihood and his life, and he could see no other path before him.

Secretly, he thought this business of the statue was a folly that was likely to ruin them all. The idea was monstrous, ridiculous. It was crazy to imagine that such a small town could accomplish so great a thing.

He was among those pushing for the plan to go ahead for one reason only. If the impossible did happen, if that statue was raised on the mountain and the faithful flocked to see it, then it would be the closest thing to a miracle he had ever witnessed. If such a feat could be achieved in a place as humble as Triento, it would prove there truly was a higher power looking after them. And he would have his faith back.

Although Padre Simone had shared none of these thoughts with the other six priests, he did ask himself in quiet moments what made each of them so keen to back the statue. Were they, like him, burdened with thirsty souls, their faith in need of refreshment?

He turned to examine the faces at the table and wondered about the men who wore them. Padre Bartholomeo had gulped the last of his wine and was turning greedy, bloodshot eyes towards the carafe. Padre Nicola was thinking only of the pizza. Padre Pietro was swinging between dreams and doubt. And Padre Fabiano was so old it was unlikely he would live to see the beginning of any work on the statue, never mind the completion.

There were two priests at the table Padre Simone was unsure about. The red-faced, middle-aged man sitting beside him, Padre Cristofono, whose poorer, smaller church was his neighbour, competed fiercely with him for a congregation. And across the table, Padre Matteo, so handsome and so pious.

If there were a dying man in Triento, you could be sure Padre Matteo would be the first to arrive at his bedside to deliver the last rites. If there were a pregnant woman, he would be somewhere nearby on the day of the birth in case of the need for a hasty baptismal. He tended to the sick and comforted the sad. And yet there was something haughty about Padre Matteo. His beautiful face was hard and impassive. He seemed unmoved as he stepped through his priestly life brushing against the joy and pain of others. Beyond his evident pride in his own godliness, it was impossible to tell what he was thinking, particularly since he had taken to the extraordinary habit of wearing sunglasses whenever he was out on the street.

If Padre Simone had known the truth, perhaps he might have felt less threatened by Padre Matteo. For the fine-looking priest had his failings. While seeming to work so tirelessly for others, in reality he thought mostly of himself. The priesthood was a job for him and a poorly paid one at that. He saw no harm in scooping up a handful of coins for himself from the collection plate. He'd saved every last coin he had rescued, and when the statue was nearly finished, he and his brother would use the money to set up a business. Just a little souvenir shop to serve the tourists who would surely travel to Triento to see the statue, selling trinkets to remind them of their trip, and all in his brother's name of course, so no one would know he was involved. Padre Matteo didn't see any harm in it. He had worked so hard for so few rewards and he believed he deserved whatever he could set aside for himself. And so it had been in his best interests to support the idea of the statue since the very beginning.

Padre Simone knew none of this. He was inclined to believe that this passion for the statue was a sign his fellow priest had a surfeit of faith, while he himself had none. The unfairness of this didn't surprise him. One of life's ironies was that it was nearly always unfair.

He pushed his glass a little way down the table and let Padre Crisotofono top it up with wine. He could smell the pizza baking and hoped it wouldn't be too long before they ate.

The Gypsy Tearoom wasn't a big place, just a single room with brightly painted ceramic tiles on the walls and an old wood-fired oven in the corner. When the weather was too bad to eat in the courtyard, everyone had to pile inside and sit elbow to elbow at the mosaic-covered tables. Sometimes the squeeze was so bad you barely had space to raise your fork to your mouth. And the noise, as each diner shouted to be heard above the other, was deafening.

An overworked Ciro would wipe beads of sweat from his dark face with an old towel he'd saved especially for the purpose, and then, pressing rounds of pizza dough with one hand, he'd sprinkle them with olives, capers, thin shavings of proscuitto or the leaves of preserved artichoke hearts with the other. He fed his creations into the fiery mouth of his oven, and when they were perfectly crisp, he pulled them out, slapped them on a plate and delivered them to the table himself while they were still piping hot.

There was magic in it, Padre Simone believed, for no matter how hot, noisy and uncomfortable the Gypsy Tearoom was and no matter how busy Ciro became, the pizza always tasted divine. Sometimes it was possible to hear him shouting at his only helper, a young boy who came in to wash the dishes, but his bad temper never infected the food. A slender young man with quick hands and a face that showed his feelings, Ciro had never yet served up a poor pizza, and he liked to boast that he didn't think he ever would.

The table of priests fell silent as the pizza arrived and only Ciro's voice could be heard. 'Who wants the proscuitto? Who wants the calzone? Who is hungry around here, eh?' he cried jovially.

The old yellow dog raised his head from the ground and thumped his tail. His overshot jaw gave him the appearance of always having his teeth bared in a snarl. Most people chased him away from their properties with a handful of stones. But Ciro let him spend his days seeking the few patches of sunlight in the shady courtyard and usually, if the old stray looked hungry, quietly left out a plate of scraps for him when there was no one else about.

Now, though, he made a show of shooing the creature away. 'No begging at my tables, you filthy old thing,' he cried, waving an arm wildly in its direction. 'Get out of my courtyard, do you hear?'

The old dog looked back at him calmly, blinked once or twice and then let his head sink sleepily back to the ground.

Padre Simone began to eat. He always chose the margherita because he believed the perfect pizza needed nothing more than moist mozzarella, the best tomatoes and a drizzle of good olive oil. The priest chewed slowly, for once the food was finished, there would be no excuse not to talk in earnest about the statue, and he was in no rush for that moment to come. Neither was anyone else, he realised, as he noticed how they savoured rather than devoured Ciro's food.

It was Padre Matteo who brought the meeting to order as Ciro finally came to clear the empty plates.

'I have some news,' he declared. 'The American project manager is on his way at last. He's expected to spend a few days in Napoli before driving down to Triento.'

'Why an American?' Padre Pietro asked. 'Couldn't we have given the work to an Italian?'

'That's what I keep telling you, my brother.' Padre Matteo succeeded in keeping the note of irritation out of his voice. 'He's an Italian really. He comes from a family of poor immigrants from Napoli who went to New York to find a better life. They worked hard for his education. I believe he's the man we must have and everything we've been told confirms this. To begin with, he's already completed successful work on some very similar projects.'

'This is going to be a very complicated business, isn't it?' Padre Pietro sounded defeated by the very thought of all that had to be achieved.

'Complicated? Well, maybe a little,' Padre Matteo continued patiently. 'We can't just erect a statue up there, that's for sure. First, we have to build a strong road all the way up to the top of the mountain. And that's why we need the finest expert help and why we went to endless amounts of trouble to find the right man for the job.'

'So let me get this straight,' put in Padre Simone, dabbing at his lips with his paper napkin. 'We have to build a strong road. We have to make a giant statue. We have to somehow get that statue up to the top of the mountain. And we don't have the support of half the town. It will take a miracle for this to happen, won't it?'

'Not a miracle, my brother, only the help of our American expert and a generous God. Have some faith. Those were your own words earlier, remember? Keep your faith.' Padre Matteo gave him what he suspected was a knowing look, although, since the priest's eyes were shielded by his beloved sunglasses, it was difficult to tell.

13

Eduardo Pagano was nervous as he got behind the wheel of the car. The roads out of Napoli were difficult ones and he wasn't accustomed to the Italian style of driving. Cars seemed to swerve all over the road, hooting their horns and creating their own lanes. He was still edgy as he drove south beyond the Amalfi coastline and down past Salerno. He'd heard tales of villages that were wild places and bandits who ambushed foreigners and held them for ransom. Not for the first time he wondered why he'd left the relative safety of New York and embarked on this adventure.

His parents had been so excited for him. They'd referred to the trip as 'going home'. But Italy didn't feel like home to him. His aunts, uncles and cousins spoke so rapidly and in such a harsh-sounding dialect he struggled to follow them. And Napoli, with its washing lines strung out across streets filled with old men selling cups of octopus soup and slices of pizza, with its noise and heat and with its pretty young girls hustled away from him quickly on the arms of their mothers, Napoli seemed decidedly foreign to Eduardo.

And now here he was driving down to a village in the mountains, to an area his Neapolitan family had told him was mortally dangerous, to meet a bunch of crazy old priests with some plan to put a statue on a mountain. He'd give it a week, he decided, and then no matter how much they offered to pay him, if he didn't like the feel of the place he'd drive straight back to Napoli.

His map on his knee, Eduardo continued to steer south, and as he drove he felt his spirits lift. The road curved past olive groves and vineyards. It hugged the rolling coastline, passing under tunnels carved out of rock and past ancient villages that clung to the tops of mountains. Once or twice he pulled to the side of the road and, putting thoughts of bandits out of his mind, drank in the beauty of the view.

As he neared Triento, the road became narrower and steeper, just as the priests had told him it would. They'd instructed him to turn off before he reached the village, tucked in the crease of the mountain, and instead follow a little lane that led down to the sea. 'You can't miss Villa Rosa,' their letter had read. 'Its gates will be open ready for your arrival, and there will be people there to welcome you.'

Sure enough, as Eduardo took a bend in the road, he glimpsed a house washed in pink behind high wooden gates that stood wide open.

'That must be it,' he muttered to himself, as he braked and eased the car through the gateway.

If there were people here to meet him, he could see no sign of them.

'Hello, there. *Buongiorno*,' he called, climbing from the car and stretching stiff legs. No one called back in reply.

There was a view of the sea from where he stood and a tiled terrace covered with bougainvillea and gardens that sloped away out of sight. It was a stunning place. He felt his spirits lift further.

'Hello,' he called again, but still no one bothered to call back. He thought he heard a sound, though, a humming and a clinking of glasses, and he decided to follow it.

He found a table beneath a canopy with six chairs drawn up beside it, and next to it was a kitchen where a beautiful young girl in a black dress was washing dusty wine glasses and polishing them dry carefully. She hadn't seen him, so Eduardo stopped to watch her. He saw that she had long, black hair that tangled in ringlets round her face, she was blessed with a soft, shapely body, and her eyes, when she lifted them to meet his, were chocolate brown.

'Oh?' she said in surprise.

'*Buongiorno*,' he said gently.

'Oh, yes, *buongiorno*. I'm sorry.' She dried her hands hurriedly on the cloth and came out to meet him. 'I'm so very sorry, but I don't think we were expecting you today.'

He shrugged. 'This was the day I was always going to come,' he said affably. 'But it really doesn't matter.'

'Someone should have been here to welcome you properly, though,' she insisted. 'Umberto or Carlotta. They'll be so upset that they missed your arrival.'

'No need to be sorry. I'm here safe and sound, that's the important thing.' He held out his hand. 'I'm Eduardo Pagano.'

'Raffaella Moretti,' she replied, putting a warm hand in his. 'I'll be your cook and help with the housekeeping in Villa Rosa. But it's Umberto and Carlotta who really look after the place. And they should be here. I don't know where they've got to.'

She stepped forward to look about the courtyard, and he followed close behind her.

'That's interesting,' he remarked.

'What is?' She turned back to look at him again and he realised that even here, surrounded by all this beauty, the girl's beauty held its own.

'That old tree held up by stakes. I've never seen anything like that before. It's very picturesque.'

'It's old.' She gave a dismissive shrug. 'If it's pomegranates you want to eat, there are better, younger trees down below to pick from.'

'Do you know, I've never tasted a pomegranate, although I've always wanted to.'

She made a face. 'Some people like them, but to me the seeds are hard and bitter. My mother knows how to make them into a syrup and then they can be good.'

'But there are stories about the pomegranate tree.' He sat on the low wall that encircled the old tree and smiled up at her. 'Do you know them?'

'What stories?' She looked guilty, as if she had work to do but couldn't quite tear herself away from him.

'Lots of them. Of all the trees in the world, the pomegranate tree must be the most interesting.'

'Why is that?' He had piqued her interest.

'I read about it once.' He patted the wall. 'Sit down here beside me and I'll tell you.'

She took a step forward and hesitated for a moment. And then they both heard other voices. A toothless old man and a thin, pale younger woman were running up the stone steps from the terraced gardens in their hurry to welcome him.

'Raffaella,' the pale one scolded. 'You haven't even offered the signore a cool drink.'

'I'm sorry. I made some lemonade earlier. I'll go and fetch it.'

And then she was gone and he was left alone with the old man and his daughter and their clumsy efforts to welcome him.

'Sit down, sit down. Where are your bags? What would you like? What can we do?' they fussed.

Raffaella came back with a tall glass of cloudy homemade lemonade on a silver tray and a dish of fat green olives.

'I won't forget about the story of the pomegranate tree,' he promised her. 'I'll tell you about it later.'

She gave him the tiniest of smiles and slipped back towards the kitchen.

Raffaella stood at the window and watched as the americano strolled around the garden, his glass of lemonade in his hand. Equally as curious, Carlotta hovered at her shoulder.

'I've never seen an American before,' she confided. 'I thought he'd look different – fat and bald with a big cigar maybe. But he doesn't look all that different from an Italian.'

'He's not how I imagined he would be either,' agreed Raffaella, still staring out of the window at the tall, handsome, well-muscled man with the striking blue eyes, lightly tanned skin and jet-black hair. 'Somehow I thought we were getting the house ready for a much older man.'

The americano glanced up through the kitchen window and met Raffaella's eyes. Turning away, she began polishing the dusty wine glasses again in silence.

She didn't see Umberto wander over to the new arrival, gesture towards the sea and then lead him down the crooked stone steps towards the rocks below. But she did look up a few minutes later and notice Carlotta still staring out of the window at the empty garden. And for a moment she seemed to have lost the guarded look that lived on her face and Raffaella thought she glimpsed the sad, lonely girl who lay beneath.

14

Raffaella stared at the pomegranate tree and wondered about the story the americano had been about to tell her in his slow and strangely flavoured Italian. If Carlotta and Umberto hadn't found them, would she have agreed to sit beside him on the low wall beneath the branches and listen to him speak?

She may have been tempted, for she had found a lot to like about him. There was the way he raised his eyebrows and smiled as though he found life endlessly amusing. The lines round his eyes crinkled and it was impossible not to smile back.

But what Raffaella had liked most was the way he talked to her. No man had offered to tell her stories about trees before. Marcello, unless he'd had a few glasses of wine, had rarely wasted words. He was a kind man, but as she'd quickly learned, he was governed by his moods. Some days he would kiss her lips and lead her by the hand to their bedroom. But she remembered other times when he had pushed her away with the flat of his hand or nudged at her with his elbow. 'Not now, Raffaella. I'm busy. Go away.'

Carlotta's voice broke in on her silence. Stress had turned up its volume and she couldn't be ignored.

'Oh, this is a complete disaster. What are we going to do?' she fretted.

The americano had stayed at Villa Rosa for long enough to let Umberto unload his bags from the car and carry them into the house, and then he had driven into Triento to meet some of the priests.

'There's so much to do before he gets back . . . his bed to be made up, food to be bought, a meal to be made . . .' Carlotta wailed. 'Oh, and I wanted it all to be perfect for him. What are we going to do, Raffaella?'

'Don't panic. I'm sure there's food enough in the cupboards for me to throw together a bowl of pasta, and putting sheets on the bed will only take a minute.'

'But this is his first meal here. It has to be special, not something you've thrown together.'

Raffaella opened the cupboards and considered their contents. 'Perhaps you're right,' she conceded. 'Why don't you see if your father can quickly drive me into town to go shopping?'

'No.' Carlotta suddenly looked prim. 'I don't think that's a good idea.'

'Why ever not?'

Carlotta couldn't tell her that the priests had said she should be kept away from Triento – and the admiring eyes of other women's husbands – as much as possible. So instead she said unconvincingly, 'Wouldn't it be quicker if I went?'

'I don't see why. I'm the one who'll be doing the cooking so it makes sense for me to do the shopping too.'

Carlotta still looked doubtful.

'Fine.' Raffaella shrugged. 'Just wait a minute while I write you a list of what I think we'll need.'

'No, no, there's no time for writing lists.' Carlotta was panicking again. 'You go. I'll run and fetch my father and have him start the car.'

The engine of Umberto's Fiat Bambina whined as they climbed the steep lanes that led to Triento, and Raffaella sat with her basket on her knee gazing out of the passenger window. She had been shut up inside Villa Rosa for the best part of two weeks and the outside world already looked strange to her eyes: bigger, fresher with richer pigments and brighter light.

'Isn't it a beautiful day?' she remarked happily to Umberto.

'Eh, do you think?' he replied, his voice oddly muffled by the false teeth he had shoved hastily into his mouth when he'd realised they had company. 'Would have been a lot more beautiful if those useless priests had given us the right date for the americano's arrival. Poor Carlotta, I really thought she was going to burst. She's been so excited by the idea of this tenant arriving and so determined to get everything right.'

'Excited? Has she? She doesn't seem it.'

He gave her a sidelong glance. 'Ah, you don't know my Carlotta.

She doesn't often show what she's feeling. But I'm her father, I can tell.'

Raffaella nodded and fell silent for a moment. Then she spoke up again. 'Signore?' she asked. 'Isn't it a blasphemy to call the priests "useless"?'

Umberto chuckled. 'When you get to my age, *cara*, you're allowed the odd blasphemy. You've earned it. And anyhow it's true that they are useless. Seven priests and every one of them a fool. Incredible!'

'What does the americano want with them?'

He glanced at her again. 'Do you really not know about the latest madness?'

She shook her head.

'You must be the only person in town. Ah, well, you'll find out soon enough, I expect.'

They were nearly in Triento and it was time for Umberto to start circling the village looking for a place to park his little Fiat. The roads were narrow and the piazza small, and when the village had become snarled up with dusty trucks and cars, the council had hired Francesca Pasquale to be the traffic officer. They'd issued her with a peaked cap and a whistle, and she wore a little white bag slung round her shoulders and spent the days pacing the streets and keeping the traffic moving. At the first sign of someone pulling over to park, she'd blow on her whistle, jab her finger in the air and screech, '*Avanti, avanti!*' Still, if you could stop quickly enough, leap out of your car and disappear up a side alley without Francesca seeing you, then it was still possible to park within Triento's walls.

'Ready?' Umberto asked Raffaella.

'Ready,' she agreed.

'OK, one, two, three, go.' He slammed on his brakes and they both jumped from the car and ran towards the corner bar. Raffaella beat Umberto to its doorway but only just.

'You're fast,' she said, panting and laughing, once they were safely inside.

'She'll be the death of me, that woman,' he grumbled. 'Running like that at my age can't be good for me.'

'Ah, well, you can sit down and have a drink now.' Raffaella looked round at the smoky little bar filled with tables of men, more or less Umberto's age, intently playing cards. 'I'll meet you here in half an hour.'

'Better make it twenty minutes. Carlotta is waiting for us,' he called to her as she disappeared out of the door.

Feeling a sudden sense of freedom, Raffaella headed towards the market. She hadn't realised how often Carlotta's eyes were on her, hadn't considered how trapped she was at Villa Rosa, but now she was alone and it felt good. She managed to ignore the sight of Angelica fussing with the linens that hung in the Russos' shop doorway, and she turned her head away so she didn't have to face the baker Alberto's brazen gaze.

She filled her basket with swordfish the hook-nosed fishmonger swore had been caught that morning. 'So fresh it still thinks it's swimming,' he promised her as he wrapped the fish in layers of paper and placed it carefully in her basket. 'And probably caught by your own father's boat too.'

It was while she was standing at a market stall, hung with strings of dried red chilli peppers and long bags of hazelnuts, that she spotted them. Padre Matteo and the americano were walking shoulder to shoulder down the street, quite a sight the pair of them with their showy good looks. She fell back into the shadows, reluctant to be seen. As they drew closer, she skirted round the edge of the market stall and disappeared up the alleyway that lay behind it.

An old yellow dog was lying halfway up the alley and he seemed to be baring his teeth at her. She stopped and eyed him dubiously.

'Don't mind him, signora,' a male voice called. 'Come on, he won't hurt you.'

Ciro Ricci was standing outside the Gypsy Tearoom smiling at her.

'Oh, hello. I was just . . . ' she began.

' . . . feeling hungry so you thought you'd come and see if I had a pizza in the oven,' he finished for her.

'Oh, no, I—'

'Well, you're in luck.' He grinned. 'I was making one for myself and I slipped in an extra in case someone hungry turned up. Sit, eat with me, be my guest.'

He pulled out a chair, and although she didn't mean to, she found herself sitting down and watching him as he laid out a knife, fork, glass and napkin in front of her.

Ciro was good-looking in a quiet way. His hair and eyes were black, his skin olive, and his cheekbones high. He was quick to smile and just as fast to anger. But what people noticed first about him was the pride he took in his work. The Gypsy Tearoom might only be a humble village pizzeria, but the plates and glasses were never chipped or smeared by someone else's lips, the ingredients were the best he could find, and the food he served never anything but delicious.

'Just a couple of minutes,' he promised, smiling at Raffaella. 'Nearly ready.'

'I shouldn't—' she began, but already he'd disappeared inside.

The smell when he returned set her mouth watering. 'A margherita with a little basil,' he said, laying it down in front of her. 'As Padre Simone always says, it's all you need.'

'I can't stay. I'm in a hurry,' Raffaella told him. 'But I'll taste a little.'

'Eat, eat,' he urged her. 'A little or a lot, whatever suits you.'

She took a bite, then another and began to eat with relish. Warm mozzarella cheese oozed into her mouth, and the sharp tang of basil and sun-soaked tomatoes nipped at her tongue.

'That's good, very good,' she told him, and he grinned again.

Ciro picked up his knife and fork, but didn't cut into his pizza. The smile had left his face and it seemed as though he had something serious on his mind. He cleared his throat rather nervously and looked down at the tabletop as he spoke.

'I'm so sorry about Marcello.'

She nodded a quiet acceptance of his condolence.

'We were only a few weeks apart in age, you know,' he continued, daring to meet her eyes now. 'When he died it shocked me. I'm still shocked.'

'You were never friends with him, were you?'

He shook his head. 'You know the Russo family; they keep to themselves. We were never close, but I always liked him.'

She nodded again and kept eating.

'He came here sometimes to eat pizza and drink beer with his brothers,' Ciro continued. 'Not for a while, though, of course. Not since he got really ill.'

Raffaella stopped eating. 'That's not so long ago,' she said softly.

Ciro stared at her for a moment, and then, in a voice as soft as hers, he said simply, 'It must be terrible for you.'

'It was terrible when he was ill,' she agreed. 'I could see him slipping away from me, growing smaller and sicker, but there was nothing I could do. When I lost him, I couldn't imagine what life would be like without him.'

'And what is it like?'

Raffaella hesitated. 'Empty, sad . . . scary,' she said at last.

'What are you scared of?'

Ciro's eyes were gentle and so was his tone. Raffaella felt a rush of trust in him. He wasn't like the other men, who stared at her so brazenly when she walked the streets of Triento alone.

'I'm scared of the future,' she confided. 'And of being on my own. I'm scared about what will happen to me.'

Ciro looked troubled. 'I wish I could help you.'

She smiled at him. 'That's kind of you. But I don't think there is anything you can do.'

'I could be your friend.' Embarrassed, he made a little motion with his hand as if brushing away a crumb. 'If you'd like me to . . . '

'My friend?' Her eyes widened.

He nodded. 'I'm almost always here at the Gypsy Tearoom. If you're feeling scared and lonely, I'm easy to find.'

Raffaella was surprised. Ciro had always been there, on the fringes of her life. But she'd hardly noticed him, never mind sought out his company. There had been no one but Marcello for her for as long as she could remember. And trying to make him love her had taken all her time and energy.

'That's kind of you,' she repeated. 'But I don't see how we can be friends. Surely you—'

He interrupted her. 'If you need someone to talk to, you know where to find me.'

His tone was so earnest she couldn't bring herself to argue. 'Thank you,' she said simply, putting down her knife and fork. 'But right now I have to go. I'm late and I'm going to be in trouble.'

It was an odd idea, she thought, as she rushed back towards the corner bar to find Umberto. How could she and Ciro be friends? And why would he think to suggest it? And yet as she felt men's eyes following her progress down the street and saw their wives scowling at her, the thought of having someone like Ciro on her side didn't seem like such a bad thing after all.

Umberto was hovering in the doorway of the bar, looking impatient.

'Come on, come on. What kept you?' he called out as he spied

Raffaella and, grabbing her arm, ran with her down the street.

They found Francesca Pasquale standing near the old Fiat, glaring at them and blowing her whistle furiously. 'No parking,' she bellowed between whistles. '*Avanti, avanti!*'

'All right, all right, you've made your point. Do you want to deafen the lot of us?' grumbled Umberto. But she was still blowing long blasts of her whistle as they drove away.

Reaching the piazza, they saw there was a hold-up. A truck had stopped right in the middle of things, and cars were trying to squeeze past on both sides, coming perilously close to demolishing the market stalls, whose vendors were yelling and throwing their arms in the air in anger and frustration.

'Watch out, you idiot! Do you want to bring the whole lot down on my head?'

'Who are you calling an idiot, *scemo?*'

'Someone move the damn truck. Where's the driver, eh? What sort of place is that to park?'

It was pandemonium.

'Where's that woman with her whistle when you need her?' complained a red-faced Umberto, who had one hand on his horn and was hooting frantically. 'This is a nightmare. We'll be stuck here for hours. Carlotta will explode.'

'No we won't. They'll sort it out. Look, here comes the truck driver now.'

'It's you who made us late in the first place,' he pointed out. 'Where were you, anyway?'

Raffaella told a half-truth. 'Buying fish,' she replied.

'How long does that take?'

The traffic was beginning to creep forward and Umberto was gradually returning to his usual colour.

'It doesn't do to rush. I had to be sure to get the best and freshest fish for the americano, didn't I?' Raffaella looked away from Umberto and out of the window as she told the lie.

Something was out of kilter, she realised, as she waited and watched, and it was nothing to do with the traffic chaos.

She saw the baker's wife, Silvana, standing beside Triento's mayor, Giorgio Lazio. Her face looked all twisted and one of her hands was resting on his arm. As the car pulled away, Raffaella turned her head and watched the pair of them until they were out of sight. The little scene had been an odd one, although she couldn't work out why.

Silvana wasn't aware of anyone watching. Her feet were planted firmly enough on the cobbled piazza, but her head was spinning.

'Helping me feed the pigs, watching the sunset together, sneaking away for a swim. Remember? Remember?' she asked. She spoke in a sort of shorthand, but the mayor seemed to understand her.

'I've never forgotten,' the mayor replied, and he smiled.

She had dreamed of this moment but never dared make it happen until this afternoon. It was all thanks to Raffaella, really. She'd seen the girl coming out of the alleyway and walking down the street with her hips swaying and her shapely young breasts pointing proudly before her. Every man in town had turned to take a good look except Alberto. He was in his usual spot on the bench outside the bakery, his chin sunk to his chest, snoring peacefully.

Just as Silvana was thinking how soundly her husband must be sleeping to miss out on a chance to leer at Raffaella, she spotted a familiar figure standing on the edge of the piazza, watching the traffic chaos.

His hair was grey, his skin pale and his face creased by time, but when Silvana looked at him, she still saw a farmer's boy with hair the colour of muddy straw and skin hued in gold. Her heart beat a little faster, and with a last glance at the sleeping Alberto, she cast off her apron and hurried out of the shop.

'Giorgio.' She stopped him with a hand on his arm.

'Yes?' He looked at her rather quizzically.

And then she had blurted out all that nonsense about the pigs and the sunsets in a bid to jog his memory.

He hadn't forgotten a thing. 'They were the best days,' he told her softly.

She checked on her husband, nervous he might be waking. 'I made a mistake,' she told Giorgio, taking her hand away from his arm reluctantly. 'All those years ago, I took the wrong path. I'm sorry.'

She made it back behind the counter without Alberto noticing a thing. The mayor was still standing outside the shop staring through the window, and she gave him a tight little smile and then shook her head.

She had thought talking to him might make her feel better, but it hadn't. She felt a hundred times worse.

He'd bungled it, Ciro thought, as he leaned against the wall of the butcher's shop and watched the commotion in the piazza. He'd made a fool of himself. She'd never take him seriously now.

Ciro had carried a picture of Raffaella around in his head for as long as he could remember. Whether he was making ten pizzas at once or yelling at that useless boy he'd hired to wash the dishes, he could stop and summon up her face in a heartbeat and it always made him feel like smiling.

She was younger than him, but even as children in the same classroom, he'd daydreamed that some day he might ask her to marry him. As they'd grown up and she'd become more beautiful, he barely dared speak to her. When she was betrothed to the eldest Russo, he was sad but resigned. It was natural that the most beautiful girl in town should marry the boy with the best prospects. There was no sense in trying to fight it.

Then Marcello had died and Ciro had been shocked that someone his age could slip so easily into the grave. He'd wondered how tenuous his own hold on life might be. And he'd vowed that one day, if ever he got the chance, he would speak up and say something significant to Raffaella.

He groaned as he remembered his words. What on earth had made him offer her his friendship like that? He must have sounded so clumsy and foolish. If only he'd been content just to chat to her for a while and suggest she return for another pizza some day. What must she think of him now? he wondered.

'Eh, Ciro, get back in your kitchen. There are hungry people around here.' Two of his regulars were standing at the entrance to the alleyway.

'No, I've had enough,' he replied. 'I'm closing up early. No more pizza today. Come back tomorrow.'

'Where have you been? What took you so long? I expected you ages ago.' Carlotta was overwrought. Two flushed patches stained her pale cheeks like splashes of crimson on a whitewashed wall. She seemed more upset than angry, and Raffaella felt guilty for the stolen moments she'd spent at the Gypsy Tearoom when she should have been hurrying back to Villa Rosa to help to make everything perfect.

'Where is he, the americano? Is he home yet?' Raffaella asked.

'Yes, yes, he came back fifteen minutes ago. He said Padre Matteo and Padre Simone are going to join him for dinner. But will you have enough food for so many?'

'Where is he now?' asked Raffaella, flicking a glance out of the window towards the pomegranate tree.

'He put on his swimming things and went below to take a dip in the sea. I hope it isn't too rough. I told him how wild it can get down there when the sea crashes against the rocks, but I'm not sure he was listening to me. And anyway, it's really too late in the year and much too cold to swim. What if he catches a chill?' Carlotta's face was strained and the two crimson spots burned brighter.

Raffaella put on her apron and tied the strings neatly behind her back. 'Stop worrying,' she said, as she pulled pots and pans from hooks and cupboards. 'He won't drown, he won't get sick, and there will be food for everyone, I promise you.'

Carlotta nodded, but still she seemed nervy as she helped unpack the shopping and prepare dinner. She almost dropped the heavy cut-glass fruit bowl, and she cut her finger on the sharp knife she was using to score chestnuts. Finally, on edge herself by now, Raffaella had to send her away.

'You go and clean yourself up. Put on a fresh blouse and skirt, and then you can serve dinner while I look after the cooking.'

'Good idea. I have a white blouse, do you think I should wear that?'

Raffaella nodded. 'Yes, if you like. Now go.'

It was a relief to be alone in the kitchen. Like her mother, Raffaella preferred to cook without help. There was a sort of poetry in it, a beauty and a rhythm as she moved about, chopping and frying, simmering and stirring. She stuffed pasta shells with melting ricotta cheese and shards of fried courgettes and covered them with a creamy tomato sauce. And then she set thinly shaved slices of the fresh swordfish on a platter and drizzled them with olive oil and the juice of blood oranges.

As she prepared the meal, she glanced out of the window every now and then, wondering when Eduardo and the priests would come and take their seats at the long table beneath the canopy and wait to be served.

At last she saw them, the two young handsome men and the shorter older one. They sat around the table and Carlotta took them a glass of *limoncello* and ice to sip as they watched the setting sun put on an extravagant performance, splashing its palette of pinks and gold across the sky.

Carlotta lit candles, for the night was a still one, and brought a jug of red wine and a basket of bread to the table. She still seemed edgy, but the men were so absorbed in their conversation they barely seemed to notice she was there.

Raffaella longed to go out herself, carry a dish or bowl to set upon the table and take the chance to speak another word or two to the americano. But something held her back. It wasn't that she was shy or nervous like Carlotta, more that the kitchen seemed a safer place for a freshly widowed woman whose feelings were bubbling and foaming inside her like boiling water in an unwatched pasta pot.

Snatches of their conversation drifted in through the open window, and although she hadn't meant to eavesdrop, Raffaella found it impossible not to listen.

'How big will it be exactly?' Eduardo was asking between mouthfuls of pasta.

Padre Simone and Padre Matteo looked at each other.

'Really big. This has to be something spectacular,' said Padre Matteo. 'Pilgrims and tourists will come from miles around to stand beneath the outstretched arms of Christ the Redeemer and have their photos taken beside him.'

'Well now.' Eduardo wiped a crusty hunk of bread round his plate to soak up the sauce. 'The statue in Rio is thirty metres tall. Surely you're not thinking of going bigger than that?'

'No, no,' agreed Padre Matteo. 'It doesn't have to be the biggest statue of Christ in the world. The second biggest will do well enough.'

'I disagree.' Padre Simone shook his head. He had little appetite tonight and had barely touched his food. 'For God, we should do our best, not second best.'

The two priests bickered between themselves as Eduardo watched them, a smile never far from his lips. At last, as Carlotta came to clear the plates, he spoke at length and the priests stopped arguing and listened.

From her post at the sink washing dishes, Raffaella continued to eavesdrop. This must be the latest madness Umberto had spoken of, she reasoned. But to her, the idea seemed a beautiful one. She longed to see Christ on the mountain with his arms outstretched, watching over them, keeping them safe. And listening to Eduardo, as he outlined the problems and came up with possible plans to resolve them, she marvelled at his cleverness.

It was a windless, warm night that owed its mood more to summer than autumn. Raffaella was lying in bed, wide awake. Thoughts and ideas churned round in her head, making sleep impossible. What should she do about Ciro Ricci and his odd but kind offer of friendship? And, more importantly, what could she cook for the *americano* tomorrow? She would pile delicious treats on his plate, and although it might be Carlotta who served him, Eduardo would know who had made the food, whose hand had stirred the sauce and added just the right amount of chilli to give it bite or pancetta to make it silky.

Then a new thought broke in – rather humdrum and unwelcome but nagging all the same. Had she left the oven still burning? She remembered pulling out the final dish from it, roasted *melanzane* stuffed with anchovies and black olives. And she could recall cleaning every last dish, wiping down the stovetop and leaving the kitchen immaculate. But she couldn't remember what she'd done about the oven. She tried to put the thought out of her mind, but the image of the blazing oven refused to leave her. Worse still, it was joined by a vision of Villa Rosa, flames shooting up through the terracotta roof, and all because she, Raffaella, had been careless.

Sighing, she rolled out of bed. One of her black dresses was hanging over the back of a chair, but she couldn't stand the thought of imprisoning her body in it again. It was only a short walk from Umberto's house, where she slept each night, to the kitchen of Villa Rosa. Up a few steps, through the gateway and she'd be there. The night was moonlit, but it was late and everyone was in bed so she was safe, she reasoned, as she slipped into the silk night robe she had been given when she married. It was palest pink, like the beginning of a blush, and it fell almost to her ankles, so it might have been a modest garment had it not been so sheer and clung to her curves the way it did.

The silk felt cool against her skin as she let herself out of the house and set off at a brisk pace. She had almost reached the pomegranate tree when she saw a pinprick of burning orange in the darkness beneath it and smelled the unmistakable muskiness of cigar smoke.

'Oh!' She stood stock still in a pool of moonlight.

'So I'm not the only one who can't waste such a beautiful night on sleeping?' Eduardo sounded amused. Raffaella could just make out the blackness of his shape, sitting on the low wall under the pomegranate tree.

Embarrassed, she tugged the robe tighter around her. 'I'm so sorry to interrupt you, signore. It was only that I thought I'd left the oven on in the kitchen. If you don't mind, I'll just check and then I'll leave you in peace.'

He didn't seem to hear her. Raffaella listened to him smoking, drawing on the cigar with a tiny sucking sound and then breathing out the scented smoke in a sigh.

Finally, he spoke. 'You see the way the moon is touching the mountaintop right now?'

She turned to look and indeed the full moon did seem to be resting its rim on the highest peak of the mountain. 'Yes, I see, signore,' she replied.

'That's where the statue will stand. Imagine how it will look on nights like this with the moon as its backdrop. It will be like the Second Coming.'

She wasn't sure what she was expected to say. 'It will be beautiful, I'm sure, signore,' she managed.

'It has to be more than that. There is already so much beauty here for it to compete with: the mountains; the sea; the trees . . . '

'I should go, signore,' she said nervously. 'I'll check the kitchen and then I'll be gone.'

'What's the hurry? Don't you want to come and sit beside me while I smoke my cigar and tell stories about the pomegranate tree?'

'I really shouldn't. At this hour . . . I shouldn't.'

'There's no one here but us. Who will know if you stay and keep me company for a while?'

The silk of her robe rippled round her legs as she moved towards the pomegranate tree and sat on the low wall about six inches away from the point of his burning cigar. She was doing the wrong thing but couldn't help herself.

'Tell me about the tree?' she asked. 'The pomegranate, what is its story?'

'They look quite delicate, don't they?' he said, his voice low and melodic. 'But don't think you can kill off a pomegranate tree easily. It hails from the East, from Egypt, Persia and Babylon. It can live through drought, survive the burning salt of the sea, cope with heat and cold. It's hardy, that's for sure.'

'Many trees are hardy,' Raffaella pointed out. 'What makes this one special?'

'Well, according to one legend, the pomegranate tree grew from blood,' he told her. 'But there are so many myths. It was said by the ancient Greeks to be the tree of love and death.'

Raffaella was entranced. 'How do you know this?' she asked.

'From books. I read a lot.'

'Are there more stories?'

'Oh, yes.' He paused to pull on his cigar. 'Do you know the myth of Persephone?'

From his tone of voice, Raffaella sensed this was something famous she ought to have heard about. 'I'm not sure . . . ' she began.

'Persephone was the daughter of Demetra, the ancient goddess of fertility,' he explained. 'She, like you, was very beautiful indeed. One day when she was with her friends collecting flowers from the fields, Pluto, the god of the underworld, fell in love with her so he abducted her. Devastated, her mother, Demetra, stopped bearing fruits so people didn't have anything to eat. The gods had to intervene and have Persephone returned. But Pluto was clever. To tie her to Hades, his underworld kingdom, he made her eat from the pomegranate fruit. From then on she spent some months in Hades, the season when nature is quiet, and then she returned, bringing fertility and new life in spring.'

'He made her eat pomegranate seeds so she wouldn't be able to leave him for good?'

'That's right.'

Raffaella stayed quiet in the hope Eduardo would fill the silence with more words.

'In Greece, even today they break a pomegranate on the ground at weddings as a symbol of fertility,' he told her.

'And so that the husband can never leave the wife?' Raffaella asked softly, thinking of Marcello.

'Perhaps, I'm not sure. But there are more stories, many more. Some people believe it was a pomegranate and not an apple that Eve plucked from the tree to tempt Adam. And there is a poem that I remember. Do you want to hear it?'

'Yes.'

'The pomegranate speaks: My leaves are like your teeth. My fruit like your breasts. I, the most beautiful of fruits, am present in all weathers, all seasons, as the lover stays forever with the beloved.'

Raffaella was aware he was sitting closer now. His cigar smoke was clinging to her hair and she could hear his breathing.

'I like that. "As the lover stays forever with the beloved,"' she repeated. 'Where does the poem come from?'

'It's a translation from ancient Egyptian. There is more, I think, but that's all I can recall.'

'I wish I knew poetry.'

He laughed and moved closer to her. 'Are you shivering a little?'

'Yes, perhaps a little,' she admitted.

She felt the sudden warmth as Eduardo's arm encircled her and he pulled her to him. She held herself rigid.

'No wonder you're cold. The silk of this robe is so fine.'

He stroked her sleeve and traced the shape of her arms. She shivered again, but this time it wasn't from the chill. She could feel the heat of his fingers through the thin fabric of her robe.

Raffaella was too stunned to move away from his touch. Instead, she sat completely still, eyes closed, allowing him to rub her shoulder with the palm of his hand. His fingers drifted gently to her cheek and he paused for a moment. There was no sound except their breathing. Then he took her chin in his hands, tilted her face and lightly covered her mouth with his.

His lips were warm and his kiss tasted of cognac and cigars. For a moment she gave herself up to it. She forgot herself completely. Then he stopped and drew back to look at her face in the moonlight, and the lazy lids of her eyes finally opened and she remembered. It was past midnight in the garden of Villa Rosa, and there were at least a hundred reasons why she shouldn't be here.

She drew a sharp breath and pulled away from him. 'No!' she said fiercely.

'I'm sorry, that was wrong of me. I'm a little drunk and very tired. But wait . . . don't go.'

It was too late. Raffaella had jumped to her feet, beyond the reach of his arms. Turning, she ran back through the gateway and down the steps towards the safety of Umberto's house. She had forgotten all about the oven that might yet be burning. But she could still sense heat on the pathways of her body that had felt the warmth of his fingers. And she could still taste his lips and smell cigar smoke in her hair.

15

The temperature had dropped overnight, and when Raffaella woke early after a restless night, she sensed the first hint of winter in the air.

Her blush-pink night robe lay crumpled on the floor where she had dropped it, and as she fastened herself safely back into her black dress, she glanced down at it guiltily. She was shocked at her behaviour of the night before. Sitting with a strange man in the darkness, allowing him to touch and kiss her; the memory of it horrified her.

But what frightened Raffaella most was the way her body had responded. She remembered how she had given herself up to the americano's kiss, felt a heat rushing through her and fought a longing to surrender further. Never in her short year of marriage had she felt that way.

She wasn't sure how she would face the americano this morning. All she could do was stay in the kitchen, out of his way and forget about his kiss and the touch of his fingers.

There was no sign of anyone at Villa Rosa and no sounds but the birdsong, the rustling of lizards in the fallen leaves and the distant crashing of the sea against the rocks below. As Raffaella busied herself making fresh bread and coffee, her eyes were drawn to the cut-glass bowl filled with pomegranates that Carlotta had left on the kitchen table. The big, leathery fruit looked like apples swollen with pride, so glossy and perfect it seemed they could hardly be real.

Raffaella plucked a pomegranate from the bowl and, taking a sharp knife, hacked it in two. The seeds spilled out like a cache of red jewels, and the juice pooled like blood on the wooden chopping board. Gingerly, she tasted the seeds. They were cool and smooth on her tongue, and crushing them with her teeth, they drenched her mouth with their sweet-tart juice. She frowned at their astringency. Perhaps Pluto had sprinkled sugar on them to sweeten them for Persephone, for she couldn't imagine why the girl was tempted to eat them otherwise.

There were trees laden with pomegranates out there in the gardens, and Raffaella wondered what Umberto did with them every year. Gave them away probably, or left them on the trees to split and rot and for the birds to peck at.

She trailed a finger through the pool of juice and licked it. Sweetened, it might not taste so bad. She remembered her mother had a recipe for making pomegranate syrup and wished she could recall it.

By the time the bread was out of the oven, Raffaella had formed a plan. She would have Umberto warm the engine of his Fiat and drive her into Triento so she would be safely out of the way before the americano woke up. If she ran down the hill, she would find her mother pottering about in her kitchen. It would be good to feel its solid rock wall against her back as they sat and drank a morning coffee together. She could forget about the way she had disgraced herself and betrayed Marcello's memory, pretend none of it had happened. And perhaps, after they had finished their coffee, her mother would pull out her old recipe book and give her some clues about what she could do to make the pomegranates palatable.

She heard the sound of someone sweeping leaves and called out, 'Umberto, is that you?'

'Yes, it's me.' He sounded fractious. 'As fast as I brush these leaves into a pile, the breeze blows them away again.'

'Forget about the leaves.' She ran out of the kitchen door and took the broom from him. 'Please, I need you to drive me into town quickly.'

'What's the rush?' he grumbled. 'I've only just woken up, you know. Give me half an hour and then maybe I'll take you to the market.'

'No, I need to go now,' Raffaella insisted. 'I'm going to go to my parents' house before I do any shopping. My mother has a recipe for pomegranate syrup that will use up some of this wasted fruit.'

The thrifty gardener in Umberto liked this idea. 'All right, then, I'll warm up the car,' he told her. 'Five minutes and then we'll be gone.'

Raffaella was impatient. She had a plan and the little Fiat couldn't carry her quickly enough towards it. Her hands gripped her wicker basket, and she tapped her foot on the floor as if that might somehow make Umberto push his own foot down harder on the accelerator and send the car speeding faster round the twists and turns of the road that led to Triento.

Now she was on her way home, Raffaella allowed herself to think about how much she missed her family. She had tried to push them away to the back of her mind in the time she'd worked at Villa Rosa. There was no sense in being homesick, no time to indulge in feeling lonely. But now she knew she would soon see her mother and she could hardly wait.

Umberto dropped her off in the piazza and they agreed on a time for him to return to pick her up. Hours of freedom stretched ahead of her. Wrapping her black woollen shawl round her shoulders, Raffaella turned into the chill of the wind that had whipped up from the sea. She took a few quick steps forward and then slowed. Looking back over her shoulder, she waited until she saw Umberto driving away. The market vendors were setting up their stalls, and the sweet smell of baking bread drifted from the bakery, but it was still early and there were few people about. She had plenty of time, and there was one small thing she wanted to do before heading for home.

She turned on her heel and walked up the narrow alleyway that led to the Gypsy Tearoom. The yellow dog was there standing sentinel, and although the door was closed, Raffaella could see a light had been lit and someone was inside moving about.

She knocked gently on the door and Ciro opened it. He seemed surprised to see her.

'Come on, come in,' he urged. 'It's cold out there.'

'I can only stay a moment,' she told him as she stepped over the threshold.

The little café was snug and scented with wood smoke and garlic. There were mirrors on the wall to make the room seem bigger than it truly was and a mosaic of brightly coloured ceramic tiles that seemed to tell a story. In the first scene, a galleon sailed past a castle on a headland, and in the next, a group of peasants danced gaily and downed flagons of wine.

Raffaella tore her eyes away from the pastoral scene and saw Ciro was already chopping ingredients and filling bowls.

'You start work early,' she remarked.

'It's good to be prepared. This place will fill up later and everyone will want pizza in a hurry. But I have plenty of time now. Would you like me to make you a coffee or some warm bread for breakfast?'

'No, I can't stop. I only came to tell you something ... ' She paused.

'Yes?' he asked encouragingly.

'It was about your offer of friendship.'

He smiled gently. 'It was a crazy idea.'

'No, not crazy at all. I need a friend right now. I'd be grateful for it.'

'Then you have my friendship,' Ciro promised, 'for just as long as you like.'

'Thank you,' she said softly. 'I'll feel better knowing you are looking out for me. I know Marcello would have appreciated it too.'

As he watched her disappear down the alleyway, Ciro was filled with happiness. This was the last thing he'd expected. He was Raffaella's friend now and he swore to himself he would do whatever he could to take care of her.

Raffaella hurried through the piazza, head bowed against the cold wind, shawl tugged round her shoulders. The walk down to Little Triento seemed longer than she remembered and it was a relief to reach the bottom of the hill and see the familiar blue door of her parents' house. She knocked and pushed it open without waiting to hear her mother call in reply.

'It's me. I'm home,' she sang out.

Book still in hand, her mother rushed to greet her. 'It's been weeks. I thought you'd never come.'

'Only two weeks, Mamma,' she laughed. 'And I've been so busy they've gone in a flash.'

'What's this?' Anna took the basket from her hands and peered inside. 'Ah, pomegranates, how lovely.'

'Do you think? Horrible, bitter things, I reckon.'

Anna shook her head. 'Give them to me, then, if you don't want them, because I know I'll find a use for them. But come here and let me kiss you. And then follow me through to the kitchen. Just two minutes ago I was thinking I should put the coffee pot on.'

Home looked strange to Raffaella's eyes and she picked out the little things that had changed the picture she was used to. A shallow dish of seashells sat on the window ledge, a string of red chilli peppers hung from the ceiling, a bowl of walnuts had been placed on the table.

Her mother had forgotten her promise of coffee and was reaching up to the high shelf to pull down the scrapbook of recipes she kept there. Of all her possessions, this was the only thing Raffaella had ever coveted. It had been on the shelf for as long as she could remember, a new recipe added to it whenever Anna came across someone who knew of a dish she'd never heard of before. The oldest recipes were family ones, handed down from mother to daughter for generations. But even more interesting were the recipes she'd collected from strangers – gypsy women and people passing through.

No matter how many recipes she had, Anna always wanted more. Sometimes she tried her hand at cooking them, but more often she only read them through, imagined how they would taste and pasted them into the leaves of her scrapbook for time to yellow and fade.

'Pomegranates, pomegranates,' she was muttering now as she flicked through its pages. 'I know there is something here.'

'I thought I remembered a recipe for a syrup,' Raffaella offered.

'Yes, yes, here it is.' Excitement caught her voice. 'Pomegranate syrup – excellent to glaze a piece of pork, to baste a goose or roasting chicken.'

Anna found a clean piece of paper and began to copy out the recipe for her daughter. 'If you make it, you must promise to bring some for me.'

'Oh, I'll make it. There are trees loaded with pomegranates at Villa Rosa. I can't imagine why anyone would plant so many. There is one that Carlotta claims is older than all of us.'

Anna paused. 'It must have been there long before Villa Rosa, then,' she mused. 'I remember when that house was built. Its owners used to come every summer. They were so glamorous, and they had boats to sail and friends who would come to the parties they threw.'

'What happened? Why did they stop coming?'

'Who knows?' Anna gave a quick evasive shrug. 'One year they didn't turn up and that was it, we never saw them again.'

'So sad to think of the house empty for all that time.'

Anna dropped her pen. 'It's not empty any more, though, is it? Tell me about the new tenant. What is he like?'

Raffaella felt a blush begin to colour her cheeks. 'The americano? Oh, I don't know. I'm in the kitchen mostly. Carlotta has seen more of him than I have. Apparently, he's here to build a statue on the mountaintop. It's going to be so beautiful, especially on moonlit nights when it will look like Christ really has come to Triento. Don't you think that will be wonderful?'

'Is that what this americano says?'

Raffaella nodded.

'So he really is going to build it, then? He believes it can be done?'

'Yes, I think so. He spends all his time with the priests talking about it.'

Anna sighed heavily. 'Your father's not going to be happy.'

'Why not? Does Papà not want a statue to be built?'

'He thinks it's a folly and I agree with him. It will use up all of poor Signor Bertoli's legacy and more. If it bleeds this town dry of money, then what will happen if we have a bad year or two? What if there are bad storms, no fish, failed crops? People won't be able to eat a statue.'

Raffaella saw the sense in what her mother was saying. 'Will Papà try to stop the americano and the priests?' she asked.

Anna looked worried. 'Don't ask me. I have no idea. Only God knows what he'll do.'

Teresa was happy to see her. 'I've missed you so much,' she told Raffaella, throwing her arms round her sister. 'How long can you stay?'

'Not long. I should leave soon, actually. I have to buy fresh meat and vegetables and then go back to work in the kitchen of Villa Rosa.'

Teresa clung to her. 'Don't go yet,' she pleaded. 'Stay and talk to me a while.'

Normally, Raffaella would be tempted to linger, but not today. Something was calling her back to Villa Rosa.

'I have to go,' she insisted. 'But why don't you walk up the hill with me? I'm sure Mamma has one or two things she'd like you to pick up from the market.'

'What a good idea.' Anna was already pushing a basket into her younger daughter's hands. 'Just some pork, fresh herbs and a bottle of good red Aglianico wine. I think I'll make his favourite meal for your papà this evening.'

With the recipe for pomegranate syrup tucked into her own basket, Raffaella walked up the hill with her sister, their backs against the biting wind, and listened to her chatter.

'Papà has been in such a strange mood, and I think Sergio knows why but he won't say, and both of them shouted at me for no reason the other day . . . ' The words came tumbling out of Teresa as though she'd been holding on to them until she could share them with her elder sister.

'So has Papà been grumpy?' Raffaella asked.

'Grumpy one minute, sad the next, and it's impossible to know what he's thinking.'

'And what about Mamma?'

'She seems worried about him and tries to calm him down,' Teresa said, breathing heavily from the effort of the climb. 'But they've been arguing too.'

'What about?'

'I'm not sure. Once, I asked them, but then Papà shut up and the next minute Mamma told me it was time to go to bed.' Teresa was indignant. 'They treat me like a child, you know. You're the only one I can talk to and you're never here any more.'

'I'll try to get back more often,' Raffaella promised, 'although I have a lot of work to do so it may be difficult sometimes. I need you to do a favour for me. Keep your ears open. Listen to Mamma and Papà arguing. If you stay quiet and don't draw attention to yourself, they'll forget you're there. And then all you have to do is remember what they've said until you see me again and we'll try to work it out together.'

Teresa looked pleased. 'I can do that,' she said.

The chilly autumn winds had blown across the piazza, swirling through the mounds of fallen leaves that carpeted its cobbles and sweeping the people of Triento off the streets and back inside their houses to shiver and light their wood-fired stoves and remark that summer was over at last.

Silvana was having a slow day. Barricaded behind her bread, she had no one to gossip with and nothing to do but think. Alberto had pulled his bench into the shop and was sitting opposite her, slowly reading his newspaper. She stared beyond him, out of the window, and imagined her life without him.

The mayor came into view, walking quickly over the cobbles, smoking a cigarette. Then Raffaella and her sister appeared on the other side of the piazza, faces pink and glowing. The three of them smiled as they passed, exchanging greetings, and walked on, braced against the wind. Silvana felt jealous of those girls and their freedom. She watched Giorgio disappear into the town hall and wished she'd been able to stop him to smile and say hello. But she was here in the prison she'd married into, and he was a thousand miles away on the other side of the bakery windows. Silvana looked at her husband, and not for the first time, she wished he were dead.

Alba Russo almost fell into the shop in her haste to avoid bumping into Raffaella. Smoothing down her wind-blown curls with a trembling hand, she sat down on the stool Silvana kept for her favourite customers and muttered, 'Madonna *mia*, whatever next?'

'What's the matter, Alba? Are you unwell?' Silvana thrust a glass of water into her hand and watched as she sipped at it tremulously.

At last she spoke. 'I'm not unwell,' she said in a low, quiet voice. 'I'm perfectly fine.'

'Are you sure? You seem a little wobbly,' Silvana remarked as Alba placed the glass carefully back down on the counter, her hand still shaking.

'Wobbly?' She took a deep breath and her voice rose. 'I seem wobbly? Well, that's hardly surprising.' She ended on a high note and Silvana realised Alba was angry rather than distressed.

'Why? What has happened?' she asked, her interest piqued. 'Who has upset you?'

'That *puttana*!' Alba leaned across the counter. 'That hussy I allowed to marry my eldest son, that's who.'

Silvana glanced over at her husband, but he hadn't bothered to lift his eyes from his newspaper. 'So tell me,' she encouraged Alba. 'What has Raffaella done now?'

Alba stared at her wordlessly, enjoying a moment of dramatic silence.

'Well?' Silvana encouraged her.

'I'm watching her, you know,' Alba replied. 'She may be hidden away from me up there in Villa Rosa, but the minute she sets foot in this town she won't make a move without me or one of my boys knowing about it.'

Silvana was transfixed. 'You're watching her? Really?' she asked.

'I knew she'd give herself away sooner or later, but even I didn't think she'd be fool enough to do it so soon.'

'What has she done?'

'Twice now she has been seen sneaking up the alleyway that leads to that Gypsy Tearoom place where all the men gather to drink beer and eat pizza all day and half the night.'

'So she wants to eat pizza. So what?' Silvana had been thrilled at the prospect of scandal and now she sounded disappointed.

'Pizza,' Alba scoffed. 'Early this morning before breakfast when there was hardly anyone about? I don't think she's going there for pizza. There must be some man involved. My son is barely cold in the ground and already she has insulted his memory.'

'But are you telling me that she's actually been seen with a man?' Silvana asked in disbelief.

'No!' Alba shouted so loud that Alberto looked up from his newspaper. 'But it's only a matter of time, I'm certain of that. She should respect my son's memory for at least two years, for God's sake. All those people who scoffed at my suspicions about her and told me I was crazy, soon they'll have to think again.'

Alba slipped down from the stool. 'I'm going to find a priest. Padre Simone, he'll know what to do.'

Alberto's eyes followed her as she left the shop. 'She didn't even buy any bread, the mad old bitch,' he remarked over the top of his newspaper. 'It's a wonder we ever make any money. There's too much gossiping and not enough spending going on in this place, if you ask me.'

Silvana stared at him for a moment with hard eyes. There was no point arguing with him. She couldn't even bear to look at him. For the second time that day she wished that he were dead and she could find a second chance for happiness.

16

Eduardo felt guilty. Last night's stolen kiss was the first thing he had thought of when he opened his eyes that morning, and although the memory brought him some pleasure, he realised he had scared the little peasant girl.

He hadn't meant to kiss her, only talk. But the beauty of the night, the outline of her body against the moonlight and his growing excitement about the statue had stirred up something in him.

She had run away before he'd had a chance to apologise properly and now she was bound to avoid him. Eduardo felt awkward. He wondered if he should try to snatch a moment or two alone with her and tell her he was sorry.

Raffaella was nowhere to be found when he went in search of her. The thin, anxious-looking one, Carlotta, was alone in the kitchen, and she rushed towards the coffee pot the moment she saw him.

'Good morning, signore. I hope you slept well. There is bread and homemade peach jam for your breakfast, and I will make a good strong coffee to wake you up.'

'Ah, yes, thank you, that would be lovely.' She was so eager to please him it was almost painful. 'But actually, I was wondering if Raffaella was anywhere around?'

'Oh.' Carlotta sounded surprised. 'You want Raffaella. But why?'

'Just to thank her for last night's dinner,' he lied casually. 'It was one of the most delicious meals I've ever had.'

Carlotta smiled. 'That's good. I'll pass on the message, if you like. Hopefully, tonight's dinner will be just as delicious. Raffaella is in Triento now shopping for it.'

'That's where I was heading myself, actually. Don't worry about making me coffee. I'll have one in the bar when I get there.'

Carlotta looked pained. 'Oh, but really, signore, it's no trouble,' she called at his back as he disappeared out of the kitchen door.

Eduardo circled through the streets of Triento four times, but there was no sign of Raffaella. On his final loop, an officious-looking woman in a peaked cap started blowing a whistle and waving at him.

'You're clogging the streets, signore. Stop driving round and round like a madman, do you hear,' she shrieked between shrill blasts of her whistle.

Reluctantly, Eduardo gave up, and taking the road that led to the mountain, he drove as far as a little settlement of houses clustered round an outdoor chapel. It was here that the narrow road became a rocky path. Abandoning his car, he set off on foot and climbed up through the ruins of Old Triento to the site where the priests planned to put their statue.

The wind was cold on his face, but he found it bracing. Reaching the summit, he stopped to let his eyes eat up the view. It was magnificent. The whole of Triento lay at his feet, with its soaring spires and steep, narrow streets. He could see the line of the coast, the bays and rocky outcrops and the vast expanse of turquoise water that washed against them.

'What a place this is,' Eduardo said out loud to himself. 'What a perfect place for a statue.'

He knew it wouldn't be an easy project. To begin with, the mountain would have to be tamed. Eduardo looked down at the steep incline and imagined how it might be done. A road would zigzag up the mountainside with strong bridges to carry it over the ravines. The rocky slope where he stood would be flattened and levelled out. And then they would bring up the huge statue section by section and assemble it right here on the top of the world.

Eduardo felt another surge of enthusiasm. The plan had caught his imagination. Gazing down at the roofs of Triento, he swore to himself that he would raise a statue on this spot no matter what it took. His name would go down in the history of this little town. Long after he had returned to Manhattan, they would talk of the American who had given them their statue.

As he climbed back down the path towards his car, Eduardo's head was filled with plans. He thought about the problems he would face and how he might go about solving them. By the time he had driven back to Villa Rosa, his dreams of the statue had pushed all thoughts of anything else out of his mind.

He pulled through the open gates to find the gardener busy sweeping up fallen leaves as the wind tried to snatch them away from him. His daughter was watering the ancient pomegranate tree in the centre of the courtyard. Through the kitchen window, Eduardo caught a glimpse of Raffaella's dark head and the memory of last night's kiss came rushing back. He wondered how on earth he would get a moment alone with her to make amends.

'*Buongiorno*, signore,' Umberto called out to him. 'Are you hungry? Raffaella is just making us some lunch.'

Eduardo nodded. 'Yes, I'm very hungry. I'd love some lunch.'

'If you go through to the dining room, my daughter will bring it to you as soon as it's ready.'

'Can't I eat in the kitchen with you?'

Umberto looked dubious. 'You really want to eat with us?'

'Yes, I'd far rather do that than sit on my own at the dining table. That's if you don't mind, of course.'

The gardener still seemed doubtful. 'Well, if you're sure that's what you'd like, then you're welcome.'

Eduardo thought he saw a deeper pink in Raffaella's cheeks as he ducked through the kitchen door. She managed to avoid his eyes and focus on the food she was preparing. There was a big pot of spaghetti boiling on the stovetop, and beside it was a wide pan slick with olive oil and sizzling with cherry tomatoes, chilli and garlic. He watched as Raffaella ladled some of the boiling pasta water in with the tomatoes, drained the spaghetti and then tossed the whole lot together in the wide pan with torn basil leaves and a little black pepper and let it cook together for a few moments.

'Just a simple pasta dish,' Umberto said apologetically as they took their seats around the kitchen table. 'And then some fresh buffalo mozzarella for afterwards.'

The food was good but the conversation stilted. Carlotta was too nervous to talk, Raffaella was determined not to speak, and Umberto was ill at ease. Between bites Eduardo filled the silence, telling them about his walk up to the site where they planned to put the statue.

'So you think it can be done, then, signore? It's not such a mad scheme after all?' asked Umberto.

'It's ambitious certainly, but it's entirely possible. Given the money, the right equipment, skilled workers, there's no reason why it can't be done.'

Raffaella was concentrating on her food, but Eduardo could tell she was listening intently.

'Everyone in town seems so excited by the project,' Eduardo continued.

Raffaella looked up from her plate and lifted her eyebrows but still said nothing.

For a moment there was silence, and then Umberto swallowed his mouthful of spaghetti and dabbed at his lips awkwardly with a paper napkin. 'Don't be so sure, signore,' he said. 'It's unlikely that everyone is behind the plan.'

'But it will bring work to Triento while it's being built and then tourists once it's completed. How can anyone complain about that?'

'It's not me you have to convince, signore.'

'Who, then?'

The three of them stared at their plates, their faces guarded, and said nothing.

'Well, what do you think?' Eduardo asked, verging on impatience now. 'Give me your opinions.'

It was Raffaella who finally spoke up. 'It's a beautiful idea,' she said carefully. 'I'm sure everyone agrees on that.'

'But?'

'You heard what was said, signore. It's unlikely that everyone is behind you.'

Exasperated, he gave up. His cousins in Napoli had told him about the people who lived in these mountains. They are close-mouthed with strangers, they'd said, slow to trust and hidebound by tradition. Be careful, they'd warned him. He wondered what he'd got himself into.

The plan for the afternoon was to pick pomegranates. Umberto had an old wooden ladder to reach the high branches, while Carlotta and Raffaella would strip the trees of the fruit they could reach from the ground.

'Can I help you?' Eduardo asked.

'No, no, signore,' Umberto said hurriedly. 'I'm sure you're busy. We can manage without you.'

'But I'd like to help,' he insisted. 'Really I would.'

And so Eduardo held the ladder while Raffaella climbed its rungs. She passed the fruit down to him and he filled the basket that lay at his feet. For a while they worked in silence, until Eduardo saw the others had moved down to a lower terrace and he seized his chance to speak.

'I'm so sorry about last night,' he whispered up to Raffaella. 'I don't usually behave like that, I promise you.'

She didn't look down at him but kept picking fruit. And then he heard her whisper in reply, 'I'm sorry too, signore.'

From where he stood, Eduardo couldn't see Raffaella's face, only the curve of her breasts and the swell of her buttocks encased in her chaste black dress. Her hand reached down with another pomegranate and her fingers touched his as she passed it to him.

'It won't happen again, I promise you,' he said quickly.

'Say no more, signore. It's best that it's forgotten.'

She began to descend the old wooden ladder carefully, rung by creaking rung, until her face was level with his, and just for a moment the urge to kiss her again was almost overwhelming. Eduardo leaned towards her and she put out a hand to stop him.

'Signore,' she said sharply. 'I am finished up there. There's no more fruit. It's time to move the ladder to another tree.'

Baskets laden with pomegranates filled the kitchen and Raffaella had to edge around them awkwardly. Her arms felt sore from reaching above her head to pick fruit, and her legs ached from climbing the ladder. She was glad they'd finished picking, for having the americano so close to her all afternoon had been a torment. She was sure she could smell the muskiness of cigars on him and the scent of something he used on his hair. And every time she passed another pomegranate to him, she touched his warm, smooth skin.

She wondered if he could tell how she was feeling. With her head up in the branches, she couldn't see his expression. But every time she climbed up or down the ladder, her face was close to his for a moment, and several times she had been certain he was going to kiss her. Carlotta and Umberto were out of sight on the terrace below, and although they could still hear the murmur of voices, it would have been so easy for their lips to touch and for her to betray Marcello's memory again.

Raffaella struggled to think about something other than the

americano as she weaved through the baskets of pomegranates, making preparations for dinner. The wind had dropped and it was a calm evening. The sound of ringing church bells drifted down from Triento to join the clang of cowbells from the mountainside behind Villa Rosa. Umberto was in the garden burning leaves, and smoke scented the air. Carlotta was still helping to carry up the last baskets of fruit from the terraces below.

'What will you do with them all?' the americano was asking her.

'Tomorrow we will make pomegranate syrup,' Carlotta replied shyly. 'It will be a lot of work. Perhaps you'll have time to help us again, signore?'

'Yes, perhaps I will,' he replied.

Raffaella glanced through the kitchen window and caught his eye. He held her gaze. So the torment of having him so close to her would begin all over again in the morning. She wondered how she would cope with it.

Silvana was cooking, jabbing her wooden spoon at the onions she was frying, clanging pots and pans around, making an angry racket. The noise she made was almost drowned out by the evening ritual of all seven of Triento's churches letting their bells ring out one after the other. Alberto seemed oblivious to it all. He was sitting in his favourite chair, his newspaper on his knee, breathing the sweet smell of frying onions.

Glancing at him, Silvana wondered if she had the courage to do it. Everything she needed was close to hand, but she was in two minds about whether to go ahead. What if he suspected? Worse still, what if he caught her? Then she thought of the days stretched out ahead of her, the rhythm of waking, working, cooking and sleeping repeated until she was too old and bent to manage it any longer. Now was her chance to change things.

She took her heaviest knife from the rack above the sink and grasped it firmly in her bony hand. With a skill born of long practice, she hacked off the head and legs from the scrawny chicken she had killed and plucked that morning, and chopped the carcass into smaller portions. Its bones were tough, but the knife was sharp and she was stronger than she looked. She was careful to catch every drop of the chicken's blood, reserving it in a jug she pushed away to one side.

Then she went to her vegetable garden. It lay on the steep terraces behind their tall, narrow house and covered every inch of the hard, stony earth. At the very top were grape vines planted by Alberto's grandfather over a hundred years ago. Their trunks were thick and gnarled, but each year they yielded a rich crop that Silvana turned into rough red wine. In the spring she grew artichokes, and in the summer tomato plants climbed up the wooden frames on the lower, more sheltered terraces. But it was to her herb patch that she went now. This was where she grew her salad leaves and other plants her mother had taught her about when she was a girl. With quick fingers, she picked a generous bunch, and then carefully, with a sly glance over her shoulder, she took a dark-green leaf or two from a small plant that grew from the cracks of a rocky ledge at the furthest corner of the patch and tucked them out of sight in the pocket of her apron.

As she came back indoors, she saw Alberto hadn't moved. His breathing had grown heavier and she was sure he would soon begin to snore again. Biting her lip, she turned her back on him and concentrated on making dinner. She fried the chicken until it was golden and then put it in a deep pan with the onions and a jar of last year's tomatoes. She flavoured the sauce with a little salt and some chopped rosemary and left it on a low heat to simmer. The salad leaves she divided into two separate earthenware bowls and then she took a deep breath, uncorked a half-drunk bottle of her rough red wine and drank a glass of it very quickly. She refilled the glass and sipped more slowly this time. The sauce would need half an hour to simmer and grow silky with chicken fat. Now she had made up her mind to do it, she could hardly bear to wait that long.

At last the meal was ready. She ladled the chicken and sauce on to two plates, a big pile on one and a modest portion on the other. All that was left to do was dress the salad. She put a squeeze of lemon and a drizzle of olive oil on the leaves in both bowls. And then, shielding Alberto's view of the food with her body just in case he woke, she took the herbs from her apron pocket, tore them up and scattered them over one of the bowls. Reaching for the jug, she drizzled the same bowl with the chicken blood she'd saved and then tossed the leaves well.

She put the bowl alongside the larger portion of food on Alberto's side of the table.

'It's ready,' she said shortly.

'Finally,' Alberto grumbled, standing up and stretching his heavy limbs. When he saw the food on his plate, he frowned. 'Is that it? Are you trying to starve me?'

He began to eat, picking up a chicken leg and biting into it, oily tomato sauce running down his chin. 'This meat is tough,' he complained, his voice muffled by the food in his mouth. 'That hen of yours was too old. It was only good for boiling.'

Then he grabbed a handful of salad leaves and stuffed them into his mouth. 'These are bitter,' he complained as he chewed. 'What's wrong with you? Have you forgotten how to cook a decent meal?'

Silvana stared at him as he swallowed down the salad. Her heart was banging so loudly and quickly she thought it must sound like last year's *festa*, when they had let off a volley of fireworks on the mountainside.

'I'm sorry,' she said, struggling to seem calm. 'It's the time of year when the plants bolt. I must have picked some of them by mistake.'

He grunted and tore a hunk of golden bread from the crusty loaf. Wiping it round his salad bowl, he soaked up the dressing. Then he bit into it, lowered his head, forked a few more leaves into his mouth and kept on chewing. He was going to eat all of it, Silvana realised with a quiet thrill, every last bite.

The plates and pot were clean by the time Alberto had finished. He had even cleared Silvana's plate of the food she hadn't touched.

'You didn't eat much,' he remarked as he reached for the last of the bread.

'I'm too tired to eat properly,' she said, watching as the food disappeared into his mouth. 'I think I'll go to bed once I've tidied up.'

Alberto settled down in his chair again, his hands resting on his belly and the last of his wine at his elbow. Silvana couldn't stop herself turning to examine his face from time to time as she washed up the dishes.

'Why do you keep looking at me like that?' he asked sourly, and her heart beat a nervous tattoo in reply.

As she crept off to bed, Alberto was shifting uncomfortably in his chair and belching loudly from time to time.

It wasn't until she woke to the sound of him retching that she thought it might have worked and she felt half sick with fear and excitement. All night he stayed, head over the sink, vomiting noisily.

When she got up at the usual early hour, well before first light, she found him in his chair looking as if all the blood had been washed out of his body.

'Alberto, are you all right?' She tried to sound concerned.

He moaned, 'No, I feel terrible.'

'Let me get you some water.'

'No, leave me alone.' He turned his face away from her.

'But you have to get up. It's four o'clock and time for you to go to work.'

'I can't.'

'But, Alberto . . . '

'My God, woman,' he said weakly. 'Isn't it enough that you poisoned me with that terrible dinner? Now won't you at least leave me alone?'

She felt herself beginning to tremble. 'It can't have been the food that made you so ill, Alberto. We ate the same thing, remember?' she managed to say.

He grunted.

'I'll go to the bakery and do your work for you, if you like.' She tried not to sound too eager. 'I've watched you enough times so I'm sure I can manage. Is that what you want me to do?'

He grunted again and waved her away with his hand.

Slipping on her coat, she shut the door softly behind her and ran down the stone steps to the dark, deserted street below. Alberto would be too ill to move for the rest of the day. She didn't know for sure if it had been the chicken blood in the dressing or the herbs she'd picked and mixed with his salad, but it didn't matter. She could hardly keep herself from smiling.

17

Customers didn't usually congregate in the Gypsy Tearoom quite this early. The day had barely broken, but the little room already smelled of sweet black coffee, wood smoke and cigarettes. The men grouped around the table spoke in hushed voices, and Ciro moved between them on light feet, bringing fresh coffee and warm bread rolls from the oven.

Raffaella's brother, Sergio, was at the head of the table with three of the other fishermen clustered around listening to him. Small and dark, like his father, Tommaso, with a fine nose and a high forehead, Sergio had always daydreamed of himself as a leader of men. At last he had a chance to prove he could be one.

'Now is the time to make a plan,' he declared, gazing round the table at the men he had gathered to help him: Francesco Biagio, loyal but perhaps not so bright; Gino Ferrando, a good man and a hard worker; and the wiliest of the bunch, Angelo Sesto.

'What we know is that the statue is going ahead with us or without us,' Sergio continued. 'I hear the americano is going back to Napoli next week. He'll start planning things from there – hiring equipment, builders, craftsmen. But there will be no building until spring, so we have plenty of time to decide what we're going to do.'

'How do you know all this?' Francesco Biagio was wearing an awed expression on his big moon face.

Sergio tapped the side of his nose. 'Don't ask,' he said gruffly. 'Just trust me.'

'But if everyone besides us is in favour of the plan, what can we do to stop them?' Francesco asked.

'That's what we're here to decide,' said Sergio. 'By the time we leave the Gypsy Tearoom, we're going to have a plan.'

Angelo Sesto was sipping coffee thoughtfully. 'What about your father, Sergio? Why isn't Tommaso here?'

'My father is the reason we're meeting up here, not down below.' Sergio nodded his head in the direction of Little Triento. 'He's more against this statue than any of us. He's been in a fury about it for weeks.'

'Then why isn't he here?' Angelo repeated.

'Because I'm frightened he'll do something rash. You know my father. We could have the best-laid plans in the world, but if he lost his temper and took matters into his own hands, he'd ruin it for all of us.'

'We've never done anything without Tommaso. I think he should be here,' Angelo insisted.

'I'm here, aren't I?' Sergio managed not to sound as impatient as he felt. 'And I have a plan if anyone is interested in hearing it.'

Francesco nodded. 'I'd like to hear it. And I'm behind you all the way, Sergio. Keep your father out of it. We don't need Tommaso to hold our hands. We can do this without him. So what's the plan?'

Sergio leaned back and looked from one to the other. 'Before I tell you, I need to know: are you all with me?'

The three men nodded, Angelo less enthusiastically than the rest.

Sergio stared at him. 'My plan . . . ' he said, pausing to add drama to his words, ' . . . my plan is sabotage.'

Angelo ran his fingers through his curly, black hair. 'Sabotage? Is that it?'

'Yes.' Sergio nodded. 'We'll sketch in the details of exactly what we'll do as we know more about what the americano is planning. But as I see it, this is the only choice we have. We can't stop them from going ahead with the statue – it's too late for that. But we can slow down the building of it. We'll tamper with the equipment; get the builders drunk; anything to hold them up. Eventually, they'll go so over budget they'll run out of money and have to abandon the project entirely. So what do you all think?'

Gino nodded his approval, and Francesco thumped his fist on the table. 'I like it.'

Sergio smiled at them. 'And you, Angelo?' he asked.

'I think it might succeed but at what cost?'

'What do you mean?'

'The whole reason your father is against the statue is that it will bleed this town of money that could be better spent another way. Your plan will make it even more expensive. It will push Triento to the edge of bankruptcy. I don't think sabotage is the answer, Sergio. We might as well let them have their statue.'

Sergio glared at him. 'What about the principle of the thing?'

'What principle?'

'We voted against the statue and they ignored us. We shouldn't let them get away with that, should we?'

'We all know it's not right, but the point is, what you're proposing is going to make things a thousand times worse.'

'You said you were with me, Angelo.'

'That was before I heard your plan.' Angelo stood up and tossed a few coins from his pocket on to the table. 'That's for the coffee. I hope you'll think this through properly. But whatever you do, I don't want to be part of it.'

Sergio stared at him as he walked out through the door. Shaking his head, he muttered, 'I thought he was a good man. I was wrong.'

Francesco thumped his fist on the table again. 'Never mind him. We're with you, aren't we, Gino? Sabotage, that's the plan.'

Sergio looked over at Ciro, who was beginning his preparations for a long day at the Gypsy Tearoom. 'What about you? Are you with us?'

Ciro looked uneasy. 'I can't take sides. The priests are customers, you are customers, and I need you all. What I can promise is that nothing I've heard today will go any further. You can trust me.'

Sergio wasn't satisfied. 'This is no time to sit on the fence. Are you with us? Or are you with them?'

Ciro's dark eyes grew blacker. 'You've already had your answer,' he said steadily. 'I don't have another one for you.'

Sergio threw his espresso cup down on the tiled floor and Ciro winced as he heard it shatter. 'You'll be sorry, Ciro Ricci. That's all I'm saying. You'll be sorry.'

Silvana hadn't been this happy in years. There was something soothing about the rhythm of kneading the dough, shaping it into mounds and feeding it into the oven. As it grew light outside, she heard the birds singing in the trees at the far side of the piazza and she worked away contentedly to the sound of their music.

It was a little late by the time she opened her door to the first customer. Her face was flushed from the heat of the oven, and the loaves weren't stacked up on the shelves yet.

'What's going on here? Where's Alberto?' Giuliana Biagio put her basket on the counter and sank down on to the stool.

'Sick,' Silvana replied briskly. 'Up all night with it, he was. I don't know what's wrong with him. We ate exactly the same thing last night and I'm fine.'

'Probably overate, didn't he? Ate himself sick, the silly fool,' Giuliana hooted. Leaning back against the counter, she looked as though she was settling in for a good long session of complaining about their husbands. 'Francesco is the same. He doesn't know when to put his fork down. I've been telling him for years if he gets any fatter, the boat will sink under him. No wonder his nets are so often empty these days. One glimpse of that sweaty, round face of his staring down at them and even the ugliest old squid probably swims off terrified.'

Silvana nodded impatiently. 'Yes, yes, but what can I get you, Giuliana? Without Alberto here, I'm run off my feet. I've got no time to chat.'

Giuliana looked mildly offended. 'I see. Well, I'll be on my way, then, if you'll just give me one of the big loaves. Sorry to have kept you.'

She bustled out of the bakery without a backward glance. Silvana wasn't sorry. Any moment now the familiar figure of the mayor would cross the piazza on his way to work at the town hall. She didn't want to miss him.

As soon as she had the bread stacked on the shelves the way Alberto preferred, the largest loaves on the left and the smaller ones to the right, Silvana turned her attention to herself. She pulled the pins out of her hair and the tight little bun she always wore tumbled into greying curls over her shoulder. She pinched her cheeks with her fingers and moistened her lips with her tongue. She was ready.

She saw Giorgio appearing at the corner of the piazza at his usual time. Darting a quick glance around to make sure no one was in sight, she poked her head out of the door of the bakery and let out a long, low whistle. He looked up at her in surprise and she beckoned him in.

'What is it, signora? You're all alone here this morning? Where's your husband?'

'Sick,' she answered shortly, shutting the door behind him. 'I don't have much time. There'll be customers here any minute. But I had to have a word with you.'

'What about? Is something wrong?'

'Yes, something is very wrong. It has been for a long time. As I told you the other day, I took the wrong path all those years ago.'

Giorgio looked a little alarmed by her words at first, and then the lines on his face settled into sadness. 'You did what you thought was right at the time. I don't blame you, Silvana.'

'I blame myself, though. All I can say is that I'm sorry.'

Giorgio studied her face. When he looked at Silvana, he didn't see a woman of forty-five, bruised by years of unhappiness. He didn't notice the wrinkles on her skin, or how her cheeks had hollowed out and her lips had grown pinched and thin. To him, she was still the sixteen-year-old girl he'd taken his first kiss from among the trees behind the pigpens on her father's farm. He'd loved to tangle his hands in her glossy black curls until he was firmly attached to her and she couldn't break away from the passion of his kisses even if she wanted to. She'd escaped him in the end, though. When she married Alberto, it had broken his heart.

He still remembered how he had been too proud to beg her to change her mind. She'd broken the news to him at the end of the summer. They'd been for a swim together down in a little cove that could only be reached by scrambling down through a hole in the rocks. It was their secret place. They were lying on the stony shelf of beach letting the sun dry their bodies when Silvana told him she had made her choice. She hated life on the farm, the smell of the pigs and the back-breaking work on the land. She didn't want to be a farmer's wife like her mother. She was going to marry a baker and work each day in a clean shop scented with the sweet smell of newly made bread.

Angry and upset, he had turned his back on her and stormed away up over the rocks. All winter long he hadn't spoken to her. And then in the spring she was married to Alberto.

In a village the size of Triento, he couldn't avoid her. Over the years he watched as she raised her two sons. He had no reason to believe she wasn't happy. Eventually, her boys grew up and moved to Napoli to find work, and she and Alberto seemed to get along together well enough.

Now, though, looking down into her face, he wondered whether he'd been wrong. For all these years perhaps things hadn't been the way he thought they were.

'It turned out all right for us in the end, though, didn't it?' he asked her lightly. 'You are married to Alberto, and I am the mayor of Triento. We both have good lives so maybe it was for the best.'

Silvana looked doubtful. 'But things might have been so different—' she began, and then broke off as she heard the shop door open. It was Raffaella, rugged up against the chill of the morning, her face curious as it peeped above her scarf.

'*Buongiorno*. Sorry, have I interrupted something?' she asked.

'No, no, the mayor just came in to buy some bread,' Silvana said and her voice sounded strangled and odd even to her own ears. She hurried behind the counter and began to wrap a loaf for him.

'It's still warm from the oven, Mayor. I hope you enjoy it,' she managed to say, and she looked into his eyes as she passed the bread over the counter.

'I'm sure I will,' he replied as he backed out of the shop.

Silvana watched him as he walked across the piazza to the town hall. Then she looked bleakly at the rows of bread in front of her and at the beautiful young girl standing across the counter waiting to be served.

'Yes? What can I get you?' she asked.

'One of the large loaves and a packet of the *tarallini piccante*.' Raffaella pointed to the packets of hard-baked dough biscuits flavoured with chilli that lined the shelves behind Silvana. 'No, better make that two packets. The americano loves them.'

Silvana felt like she barely had the strength to wrap the bread and *tarallini*. Depression had settled on her shoulders, and her limbs felt heavy and slow.

'Are you all right, Silvana?'

'Just tired. Alberto is sick today and I had to get up very early and do all the baking.'

'Oh, I'm sorry. I hope he's better soon,' Raffaella replied politely.

The words flew out of Silvana before she could stop them. 'No you don't. You don't hope any such thing. You hate my husband, I know you do.'

Shocked by her own outburst, she turned her head away from the girl.

Raffaella was too surprised to speak for a moment. When she found her voice, she said rather gently, 'I have to go. I'm making pomegranate syrup today. When it's ready, I'll bring you a bottle.'

Taking her package from the counter, she slipped out of the bakery, leaving Silvana time to think about what she'd lost when she'd made the wrong choice all those years ago, before drying her eyes and getting ready to serve the next customer.

Raffaella was intrigued. This was the second time she'd come across Silvana talking to the mayor with that expression on her face, of desperation mixed with a strange intensity. And then there was her sadness when the mayor left and what she had said about Alberto afterwards. Raffaella wondered if Silvana loved her husband. She didn't seem to. She tried to imagine how it would be to live, work and then sleep beside a man you didn't care for. She had never liked Silvana much and certainly hadn't thought to pity her before, but suddenly she saw how bleak her life must be.

Raffaella couldn't help thinking about herself and Marcello and wondering whether, had he lived, time might have soured the love she had for him. Walking past the linen shop, she gazed up at the windows of their old apartment. All the pretty geranium plants she'd arranged on the little balcony had gone and the place looked bare. She saw that the shutters were still closed, which meant Stefano and Angelica were probably still sleeping side by side in the bed where she and Marcello had once lain.

Quickening her pace, she hurried to the butcher's shop to buy meat. Slivers of fatty pancetta and a string of sausages flavoured with fennel were wrapped up in waxy paper for her.

'You're here early this morning,' the butcher remarked.

'I have a big day ahead of me. I'm making pomegranate syrup,' she told him.

She found the old Vespa where she'd left it, tucked away down the alleyway behind the bar well out of Francesca Pasquale's sight. Umberto had grown tired of driving her in and out of Triento in his Fiat. He'd discovered the Vespa in the cellar beneath Villa Rosa and cleaned it up for her to use. Riding it was exhilarating. Raffaella loved feeling the cold wind whipping her hair round her face and hearing the way the engine screamed when she pressed it to go faster.

She stowed her packages in the basket Umberto had strapped

securely to the back and took off through the town almost laughing with the pleasure of it. There was Alba Russo picking her way over the cobblestones, staring white-faced and disapproving, and there Patrizia Sesto breathing heavily after her climb up the hill, turning to look as she roared past.

The ride back to Villa Rosa blew Raffaella's sad mood away. Carlotta was in the kitchen waiting for her. Already she had diligently cleaned the glass bottles and jars ready for them to be filled with pomegranate syrup, and she was impatient to begin the next step.

'What do you want me to do?' she asked before Raffaella even had a chance to remove her shawl.

'Well, first let's put on some old clothes. My mother says the pomegranate juice will leave stains. She told me they used it as a dye in the old days. So whatever we wear is bound to be ruined.'

Carlotta nodded. She picked up one of the pomegranates and turned it over in her hand. Its skin was leathery and red with the dull glow of a hand-rubbed finish. 'It seems a shame to cut into them, they're so beautiful,' she said almost dreamily.

'That's true. But if we don't cut into them, we won't have any syrup. Let's go and change so we can get started.'

Carlotta found some shapeless paint-spattered overalls for them to wear. They couldn't help laughing at each other when they put them on.

'They're huge,' Carlotta giggled. 'You'll have to roll up your sleeves. I can't even see your hands.'

'Well, look at you.' Raffaella smiled. 'You could be eight months pregnant under there and nobody would know.'

Carlotta glanced down at the folds of billowing fabric around her belly and fell silent. When she looked up again, her smile had gone. 'Come on,' she said briskly, 'the overalls look awful, but they'll do. Let's get on with it, shall we?'

They worked as a team. Raffaella took a sharp knife and cut off the crown from each fruit, then scored down its rind. Digging her fingers into the cracks, she pulled the fruit in half, then quarters, and the juice from the burst seeds ran down her arms to her elbows.

It was Carlotta's job to separate the fleshy seeds from the useless membrane and rind. Putting them in a muslin bag, she squeezed hard to extract every drop of juice so that only the tough little seeds were left behind.

They worked together quietly for about an hour, splattering red juice over themselves and across the walls as they cut and squeezed the pomegranates. Carlotta seemed lost in her own thoughts, and her guarded expression didn't invite questions. There was something oppressive about the silence and it was almost a relief to hear the creak of the kitchen door and see the dark head of the americano ducking into the room.

'I have some free time,' he told them. 'I'd love to help. What can I do?'

Raffaella was about to refuse his offer when Carlotta surprised her by interrupting. 'You can take over from me, signore,' she said, pressing the muslin bag full of juicy red seeds on him. 'I have to go and see to something else for a while. I won't be too long.'

She rushed out before anyone could reply, and Raffaella watched curiously as she hurried not through the gates that would take her to her father's house, but down the stone steps that led towards the sea.

'That's strange,' she murmured.

'What is?' The americano was very close, right by her side.

'Oh, nothing really.' She shifted a step or two away from him. 'Just Carlotta, she's such an odd girl. I can't work her out.'

The americano was staring at her, an amused look on his face. He started to laugh.

'What's so funny?' she asked.

'With that knife in your hand and red juice running down your arms, you look like a murderess or a madwoman. And what is that outfit you're wearing?'

'These are overalls, signore,' she said, aware of how unflattering they must be. 'The red juice will stain and I don't want it to ruin my clothes.'

He was staring at her again rather intently. Uncomfortable now, she passed him the knife. 'You take a turn cutting open the fruit, signore, and I'll squeeze out the juice,' she said unsteadily.

Standing beside him at the kitchen bench, Raffaella struggled to carry on as normal. She felt unbearably self-conscious, aware of every move she made and how she must look. The americano's presence was like a prickle on her skin. As she crushed the muslin bag between her hands and the juice trickled into the bowl beneath it, she struggled to think of something to say to him. Nervously, she licked a drop of pomegranate juice from her fingers and grimaced at its bitterness. She watched as he did the same. He seemed to appreciate the tart flavour, taking another taste and licking it from his lips.

'No man has ever helped me in the kitchen before now, signore.' She managed to break the silence at last.

He smiled. 'It may seem strange, but I find that when I have a lot of tricky things to work out, it's good to keep myself occupied with something like this. It clears my head. Usually, I don't make pomegranate syrup, of course. But I do something physical: take a walk, swim, chop wood, it doesn't really matter. And I thrash out my problems in my mind.'

'And are there lots of problems with the statue?' she asked, relieved to have guided the conversation to safe ground.

'Oh, yes, countless problems. I've worked on similar projects, but nothing quite like this before.'

Raffaella filled the muslin bag with more pomegranate flesh and squeezed again. She liked listening to his voice. The way his unfamiliar accent shaped the words made everything he said seem exotic and wonderful.

'What made you come here, then, if it's going to be so difficult?' she asked, hoping to prompt more confidences.

He smiled again. 'I don't know. I suppose I must love a challenge,' he replied, catching her eye and holding her gaze until she looked away awkwardly and put her head down to work.

By the time Carlotta returned, they'd made their way through two baskets of pomegranates and they were both covered in juice.

'Signor Pagano!' Carlotta sounded shocked. 'Your clothes are ruined. Raffaella should have found you some overalls.'

'Don't worry. They're old clothes and they don't matter much.' Eduardo handed Raffaella the knife. 'But now it's your turn to take over from me. I have an appointment in Triento and I'm afraid I'm going to be late.'

Raffaella glanced at him. 'Where is your appointment, signore? With the priests in one of the churches?'

'No, no, it's not. It's in a place called the Gypsy Tearoom. I've been asked to meet some of the locals there, the Russo family. It seems they have a lot of influence in town. I expect you know them.'

Raffaella didn't reply for a moment. She was focusing on cutting the crown from a pomegranate and scoring carefully down its skin. 'You'd better get cleaned up, signore,' she said as she broke open the fruit to reveal its store of seeds. 'If you turn up at the Gypsy Tearoom looking like that, they'll wonder what you've been up to.'

She deliberately didn't look up at him as he left. Instead, she concentrated on freeing the fat, juicy seeds from the pomegranate and filling the muslin cloth for Carlotta. The pair worked together quietly again, and this time Raffaella was glad of the silence. Her mind was busy with thoughts of the americano, and her emotions were swinging from shame to a strange kind of joy she knew she shouldn't be feeling.

When every last pomegranate had been dealt with, their hands and arms were stiff and sore from so much cutting and squeezing, and they'd filled several deep stock pans with rich red liquid.

'What now?' asked Carlotta, rubbing at her shoulders wearily.

Raffaella glanced down at her mother's recipe. 'Now it's just a matter of boiling up the juice with sugar and a little lemon juice until it thickens. Then we can bottle it.'

'It had better taste good after all this hard work.' Carlotta licked some of the juice from her hands and grimaced. 'I suppose the sugar will sweeten it and then it will be nicer.'

Raffaella tasted the juice on her own fingers. Its bitter flavour reminded her of the strange, highly charged hour she'd spent working side by side with the americano and she felt a guilty flush spreading across her cheeks.

'It will be delicious,' she murmured to Carlotta absent-mindedly. 'Good to glaze a piece of pork or baste a goose or roasting chicken.'

But Carlotta wasn't listening. She was staring out of the window towards the sea. Her cheeks were pale, and the skin beneath her eyes was puffy and swollen, and looking at her properly for the first time all morning, Raffaella wondered if she'd been crying.

18

Silvana wished she'd listened more attentively when her mother had tried to teach her what she knew about herbs. She only remembered bits and pieces – herbs that were good to use in a steam inhalation to cure a chesty cough or put in a poultice to draw out an infection. But there were other things her mother had whispered to her quietly, secrets passed down to her when she herself was young. There were herbs to calm a man's passion if it became wearisome, plants to numb pain and some that were so poisonous they could fell a man in just a few hours if she only knew what they were.

She closed the shutters of the bakery with a heavy heart and prepared to return home to Alberto for lunch. She didn't think her husband would be in the mood for eating, but just in case he had recovered enough, she wrapped up one of the larger loaves and tucked it under her arm.

The herb she'd slipped into his salad was one her mother had told her to be careful not to eat, although, however hard she tried, she couldn't remember exactly why. She'd only used a leaf or two and some uncooked chicken blood and look how ill Alberto had become. As she walked the narrow streets home, nodding at neighbours along the way, Silvana wondered whether she dared feed him the rest of the plant.

Her husband was dozing in his chair when she got home. He groaned when she asked him if he wanted a plate of spaghetti. 'I couldn't even eat a piece of dry bread. I want to heave just thinking about food,' he told her.

It hardly seemed worth putting the pasta pot on to boil for one, so Silvana went out into the garden to pick some salad greens and the last of the tomatoes. Kneeling down in the brown earth, she eyed the little plant with the dark-green leaves that grew from the rocky ledge.

No one would guess anything had been picked from it. But what if she were to uproot it, hide it in her kitchen and use it liberally in Alberto's next meal? Would it be enough to finish him off?

Being a widow wouldn't be so bad, she thought. She could keep the bakery running, work hard and live quietly. And surely she would get away with it, for who would ever suspect such a virtuous woman of murdering her husband?

Standing up, she brushed the earth from her knees. Even if she picked the plant, she was certain her courage would fail her at the last. She would never dare to feed it all to Alberto.

For a moment she thought of the stories about Raffaella that she and Alba had so enjoyed spreading. Could the girl truly have poisoned her husband slowly until he grew thin and yellow and died? If so, then she must own a strong will as well as a hard heart, for, as Silvana now realised, it was far from an easy thing to kill a husband, no matter how much you hated him.

Leaving the dark-green plant untouched on its ledge, she went back inside. Alberto was snoring again, his hands still clasped over his dome of a belly. With distaste, she watched the way his pursed mouth blew in and out as he snorted through each breath he took.

Sighing, she ate her small salad with a hunk of bread and some strong caciocavallo cheese. After lunch she would take a short nap and then go back to open up the bakery. Later, Giorgio would go past on his way home from work and perhaps he'd take the chance to smile at her through the window as he walked by.

The Russo boys all knew how to eat pizza. Ciro Ricci was always pleased when they rolled up to the Gypsy Tearoom because they didn't stint on ordering. Stefano, Agostino, Fabrizio and Gennaro could easily polish off two pizzas each, washed down with a few jugs of beer. Perhaps this greed was a reaction against years of their mother Alba's small portions, or maybe the pizza simply was too good to stop at one; Ciro didn't much care. All that concerned him was that they had plenty of money in their pockets to pay the bill at the end of their meal.

They came in often enough for Ciro to know their favourites. Stefano preferred the margherita sprinkled with rocket leaves, Agostino usually chose the primavera because he liked the fresh tomatoes on it, Gennaro would eat anything smothered in anchovies and capers, and Fabrizio was addicted to seafood.

The Russo brothers had taken the table nearest the pizza oven so they could smell their food baking. The noise they made, as they all talked at once, was tremendous. Ciro might have preferred not to listen in on their conversation, but it was impossible to avoid.

'No, no, you're wrong,' Fabrizio was shouting at his elder brother. 'We'll never get any money out of them. Tommaso Moretti has told them not to pay up and they're all too scared of him to go against what he says.'

'But what if we approach them one by one?' Stefano asked. 'Angelo Sesto is a reasonable man so we could start with him. You're not telling me he doesn't have some cash tucked away somewhere.'

'Try it if you want.' Fabrizio looked sulky. 'But don't come complaining to me when he sends you packing.'

Stefano was worried. He wasn't convinced anyone had really thought things through. They'd got themselves all excited about the statue and had started making plans without really considering how much it would cost to complete the project. If they thought the legacy old man Bertoli had left the Church would cover it, then they were deluding themselves. He had tried airing the subject with Padre Simone, but the priest had only put a reassuring hand on his shoulder and said, 'We're doing God's work, Stefano, so surely if this is what He wants, then He will provide for it.'

Stefano was a businessman. He believed in planning things properly and was never happier than when his lips were forming words like 'return on investment' or 'profit and loss'. Blind faith was something he lacked. And just at this moment, he was convinced that he alone stood between Triento and financial ruin.

'I'm going to draw up a business plan,' he'd declared to his wife, Angelica. 'I'll talk to this americano about his projected costs, look at what we have so far, work out the deficit and then come up with some strategies to cover it.'

She had turned adoring eyes on him. 'What a good idea, *caro*. Where would we all be without you?'

It was easy for him to see what the first strategy should be. Stefano was determined to milk some cash from the fishermen.

'Surely Tommaso's refusal to take any part in raising the statue was spoken in anger, in the heat of the moment,' he'd said to his brothers. 'I bet we can persuade him to change his mind. It's worth a try. And if it doesn't work, we can go behind his back and talk to the others. I can't believe they're all against it.'

They'd shouted him down. 'Be realistic,' Fabrizio was saying now. 'They're a law unto themselves down there. What on earth makes you think they'll listen to a word you've got to say?'

The americano had promised to meet them here at the Gypsy Tearoom to share a pizza and talk them through his plans for the project. Stefano couldn't imagine what had happened to make him so late.

When at last he did turn up, his hands were stained red and his cheeks looked flushed.

'Are you feeling all right?' Stefano asked him once he'd been introduced and shaken each brother's hand.

'Yes, yes.' He looked down at his stained hands and laughed. 'I've been helping to make pomegranate syrup.'

Stefano nodded politely, but he couldn't help wondering what kind of man would choose to spend his morning in the kitchen.

He cleared his throat and pressed on with what he had to say. 'We wanted to talk to you about the statue, as I'm sure you've realised. What we need to know is whether you believe the project is feasible and if so what sort of budget you envisage we'll need, where you see the potential pitfalls and so forth. I had wondered if you might prepare some sort of report for us.'

Eduardo had taken an instant dislike to Stefano Russo. He'd decided he was a perfect example of the type of pompous little moneyman who never saw the big picture, never appreciated the poetry of what they were trying to achieve but only wanted to stare at columns of figures all day long.

'A report?' he said affably enough. 'Well, of course I'll be preparing a detailed one for the priests. I had thought that would be adequate. Do you not agree?'

'They are men of God, we are men of business,' pointed out Stefano, spreading his small hands out over the table. 'I think it is vital that we should have some involvement.'

Eduardo nodded. 'Get them to give you copies of my report, then. I'm sure they won't mind.'

Stefano smiled and pushed his glasses further up the bridge of his nose. 'You are a foreigner, signore, so perhaps you don't realise how things work here. The priests can be secretive at times, and they can also be impractical. They are spiritual men after all, so why should they be burdened with too many details? But there are things they haven't considered.' He lowered his voice. 'The 'Ndrangheta, for instance. Large sums of money never get spent in this part of the world without certain families taking their cut of it.'

Raffaella had heard of the 'Ndrangheta. They were the local Mafia and said to be particularly cunning and brutal. He had hoped he wouldn't come across them.

He lowered his voice too. 'Where are they?' he asked.

'They are all around you, signore. All our lives are touched by them.'

Eduardo considered his words. 'How do I know that your family is not 'Ndrangheta?'

Fabrizio interrupted before his brother could reply. 'You don't know, signore.' The threat in his voice was unmistakable. 'And that's why it would be best for you to let us see a copy of that report.'

'But I'm still working on it.' Eduardo was stubborn. 'I'm busy getting quotes and estimates of costs. I'll need an engineer's report on the site to know how best to build a road to reach it. It's going to take some time.'

Fabrizio stared at him. 'We can wait, signore. We're reasonable men.'

Eduardo stared back. 'It's the priests who are paying me, remember. I work for them.'

As he pulled pizza from the fiery mouth of the oven, Ciro listened to them bickering and sensed the growing tension in the air. In his experience, men rarely fought when there was food on the table, so balancing plates up his arms, he got on with the business of ferrying the pizza over to them.

'Now, who is it for the primavera? Ah, Agostino, how could I forget,' he said jovially. 'And the margherita for Stefano, of course. And for you, Signor Americano, my special Gypsy Tearoom pizza so you can have a little taste of everything.'

Eduardo and Fabrizio were still staring one another down. Neither made a move to pick up their fork.

'Eat, eat while it's hot,' Ciro urged them. 'I hope you like Italian food, signore.'

Above all, Eduardo hated feeling patronised. 'We do have Italian food in New York, you know,' he said icily.

'Ah, but it's not the same, though, is it.' Fabrizio sounded arrogant. 'You should be careful, signore, if your stomach is used to American food, then our Italian dishes might not agree with you.'

'I haven't had any problems so far.' Eduardo dismissed him.

'Not so far, no,' Fabrizio agreed. 'But I believe you have Raffaella Moretti cooking for you over at Villa Rosa. You may not know it, but the girl has a reputation in this town. You want to be careful eating the meals she prepares.'

The Russo brothers had fallen silent and were staring at Fabrizio wondering if he would dare to say it.

Ciro, his hands empty of pizza, stared too. He wanted to interrupt, to say something to stop the boy, but he didn't want to risk making things worse.

'Oh, really.' Eduardo sounded interested. 'What reputation?'

'Her husband died,' Fabrizio replied. 'And they say she poisoned him.'

Ciro couldn't stay silent any longer. His hand shot out and he gripped Fabrizio's shoulder. 'Stop it! You know that's not true.'

Fabrizio only smirked.

'Raffaella did no such thing, signore,' Ciro addressed the americano. 'Don't believe the words of a few old women who have nothing to do but spread rumours all day. She's a good girl, really she is.'

Fabrizio pushed his plate off the table and it broke with a clatter on the tiled floor. 'Suddenly I'm not hungry any more,' he declared.

Ciro only shook his head and didn't bother to reply.

'Tell me, Ciro, if she's such a good girl, why have I seen her sneaking up this alleyway when she thinks no one is looking? What business does she have up here, eh?' Fabrizio asked.

Staring down at the broken pieces of plate and ruined pizza, Ciro refused to speak.

'Is it you she's coming to see, or some other man? Tell me that at least.'

Eduardo looked at Fabrizio in confusion. The conversation had moved on so quickly from the statue, and the Russo family's hostility seemed to have shifted too.

'You're making something out of nothing.' Ciro's voice was calm, but his face showed he was angry.

'That's what you say. But why should I believe you? As I told you, I've seen her with my own eyes sneaking up here more than once.'

'She isn't sneaking.'

Fabrizio looked sullen. 'This is no place for a widow to come. Her husband, our eldest brother, is only just in his grave and already she is disrespecting his memory. Our family doesn't want anything more to do with her. And you ought to keep away from her as well.'

Both men had lost their tempers now and their voices were raised.

'Don't tell me what to do,' Ciro was shouting.

'Don't insult my family,' Fabrizio retaliated.

'Stop insulting Raffaella. She's done nothing wrong.'

It was Stefano who ended the fight. Deliberately, he pushed his plate of pizza off the table too and it shattered on the ground. 'Suddenly I'm not hungry either,' he said steadily. 'Ciro, I suggest you keep Raffaella away from the Gypsy Tearoom. My brother is quite right, this is no place for a woman who's only just in mourning.' Standing up, he put on his overcoat and nodded to Eduardo. 'It was good to meet you, signore. I look forward to reading your report in due course.'

As he stalked out of the Gypsy Tearoom, Fabrizio fell in close behind him.

Gennaro sighed. 'I suppose we should go too.'

'And waste all this pizza?' His brother Agostino shook his head. 'You go if you like, I'm staying here. Anyway, someone has to keep Signor Pagano company over lunch, don't they?' He dug his fork into the pizza and grinned.

Eduardo looked at the two remaining Russo brothers and then switched his gaze to Ciro, who was kneeling on the floor cleaning up the mess of smashed china and food.

'Raffaella seems to have caused trouble for you.'

Ciro gave a dismissive shake of his head. 'Don't worry, signore, she hasn't really.'

Gennaro's laugh had a hollow sound in the empty pizzeria. 'Oh, but I think she has. You'd better stay away from her, you know. Fabrizio's always been half in love with the girl himself. I don't see how it can cause anything but trouble for you if he sees her coming back here.'

Lowering his head to his plate, Gennaro began to shovel in pizza as fast as he could. He feared this would be the last meal that he'd enjoy in the Gypsy Tearoom for some time.

19

The afternoon was a cold one with the threat of rain, and there was a sea mist shrouding the top of the mountain where the statue was meant to stand. Triento was bracing itself for winter. Firewood was being cut and stacked against the sheltered side of every house, thick woollen coats were being pulled out of mothballs, and at Villa Rosa, Umberto was busy collecting heavy rocks. Once he had found enough, he would climb up on to the roof of the house and use them to weigh down the terracotta tiles before the first storms hit the coastline.

'We're in the path of the wind here,' he told Raffaella as he piled flat-bottomed stones in the corner of the courtyard. 'We don't want the americano coming back to find half the roof missing.'

Raffaella felt surprised but tried to keep it from her face. 'What do you mean, coming back? Where is he going?'

'To Napoli, of course. You didn't think he was going to spend the winter here with us, did you? No, he'll stay away until spring, and Villa Rosa will be closed up until he returns.'

'But ... but ... ' she began to stammer.

Umberto had turned away and was heading down towards the sea in search of more rocks. 'Don't just stand there,' he called back to her. 'Come and help me if you've nothing better to do.'

She followed Umberto down the stone steps, trying to make sense of what he had told her.

'He can't leave,' she said out loud. 'What about me?'

Umberto paused to open the wooden gate that lay at the bottom of the steps. He turned to look at her, frowning. 'Well, I don't know,' he said uncomfortably. 'I don't suppose we'll need you here. Carlotta and I can look after ourselves. Surely it would be best if you went home to your parents for the winter and came back to work at Villa Rosa in the spring?'

Raffaella felt stunned. Just when she thought she'd found a way she could be happy, her life was being changed again and she was powerless to stop it. She took the boulder Umberto thrust into her hands and, balancing it against her belly, turned to trudge back up the steps.

'The priests should have talked to you about this, really,' she heard him calling up to her. 'After all, it's them paying your wages.'

She walked faster to get away from him.

'You can stay here if you want to,' Umberto was calling now. 'I'm sure Carlotta would welcome the company.'

He watched Raffaella as she rounded the corner, clutching the heavy rock he'd given her, determined to make it to the top without putting it down. He felt guilty about the girl.

Somebody ought to have explained to her that the job was only seasonal. She was a hard worker and deserved to be treated better than this.

Still, he wondered if perhaps it wasn't such a bad thing she was leaving. The way she looked at the americano hadn't gone unnoticed. Umberto had witnessed the same sort of looks before. The last time he had done nothing and it had ended in disaster. He didn't want to see history repeat itself.

Clutching his own boulder against his chest, Umberto began to climb. He hardly ever thought of that time any more. He had put it out of his mind. But now and then he would catch a look on Carlotta's face as she ran down the steps towards the sea and it reminded him that she couldn't forget so easily.

He reached the top of the steps and saw the americano had returned. His car was parked in its usual spot and he was standing beside the old pomegranate tree talking to Raffaella, the boulder she had carried lying on the ground between them. Umberto took a step or two back into the shadows and watched the pair. Their voices carried on the gusts of wind towards him, and he strained to make out their words. He heard only the last thing that Raffaella called out before turning on her heel and stalking off. 'OK, goodbye, then,' she cried into Eduardo's face.

Truth to tell, Eduardo couldn't wait to get away from this place, for winter had stolen all its charm. The sun had disappeared behind

Triento's mountain and it wouldn't be seen again until spring. There was something dank and sinister about the place, something unhealthy. He noticed the sidelong looks the villagers gave him that grew to open stares when they thought he wasn't watching. At first he'd put them down to curiosity about the foreigner and the statue he was building, but now he wondered if there wasn't something hostile about those stares. Fabrizio Russo's talk of the 'Ndrangheta had rattled him, and he wondered whose blank face and curt nod might hold the threat of terror behind it.

Then there was this strange thing with the girl. Before bed he was in the habit of smoking a last cigar beneath the old pomegranate tree, and most evenings now, once Raffaella had finished in the kitchen, she came to find him there. She never let him get close enough to repeat that first night's stolen kiss. Instead, she chose to sit a safe arm's length away from him and listen while he talked about his job, the statue and his dreams of greater things.

Eduardo found himself looking forward to waiting for her beneath the pomegranate tree each evening, the smoke from his cigar mingling with the steam of his breath in the cold air. He was fascinated by the mystery of her past as much as by Raffaella's beauty. Sometimes he asked her questions, but she never seemed to want to talk about herself or the loss of her husband; she was content to listen.

Every night, unless it was wet and windy, Raffaella kept him company, and they talked until the sky was bright with stars and the moon touched the mountaintop. He had told her many things, but perhaps he hadn't mentioned he'd be returning to Napoli for the winter. He really couldn't remember. It hadn't seemed important. So he was taken aback when she came up the stone steps clutching a rock to her belly and flew at him as though she'd been fired from a cannon.

'You are going away,' she said breathlessly.

'Yes, I have to go to Napoli to complete the next stage of the project.'

She dropped the heavy rock on the ground between them. 'I didn't know. You didn't say anything.'

Eduardo noticed a movement out of the corner of his eye and saw the gardener had come up the steps and was watching them. 'I'll be back in the spring,' he said awkwardly.

Lost for words, she stared at him. Her anger had flared so

suddenly. It had burned like a fire through dry bushes, and now it was gone, there was nothing much left. She felt foolish and ashamed.

'OK, goodbye, then.' She threw the words at him and, turning on her heel, stalked away towards the kitchen of Villa Rosa.

From then on he tried to avoid her, and she played the same game, turning her back on him if she could or hunching a shoulder protectively as he passed. He stayed out of the kitchen and ate his last meals alone in the dining room. The food she cooked for him spoke the words she couldn't say. She served sliced *melanzane*, spread with a sauce of pomegranate syrup and garlic. She basted the pork she roasted in pomegranate juice and honey. Even the dressing she tossed through his salad had a hint of the fruit in it. Each bitter-sweet mouthful held a message for him.

At last Eduardo's suitcase was packed and stowed in his car and he was ready to begin the drive back across the mountains to Napoli. He wasn't sure what he was waiting for, unless it was a last chance for a moment alone with Raffaella. But the gardener and his daughter seemed everywhere that morning. As he came upon Raffaella preparing coffee in the kitchen and cleared his throat to speak to her, Carlotta's pale face came between them.

'Have you had breakfast, signore? Can I pack you something for lunch?'

Later he passed Raffaella in the courtyard, but Umberto was hanging about tinkering with something and gave him a long look that made him feel uncomfortable.

It was late morning by the time he left, and still he and Raffaella had not exchanged a word. He saw her watching through the kitchen window as he pulled out of the gates of Villa Rosa.

It was a relief for Eduardo to point his car along the steep, narrow road and put some distance between himself and the people of Triento. Spring was months away. Who knew what could happen between then and now.

Raffaella scrubbed at the dirty breakfast dishes furiously. She hadn't meant to become so caught up with the americano.

Although she knew it was wrong, she had begun to rely on the time she spent with him. She felt better when he was there, less lonely and scared. She felt like she could breathe properly.

And now she wouldn't see him again until spring. She bent her head over the breakfast plates and scrubbed harder.

'What's wrong?' Carlotta looked anxious.

'Nothing.'

'If you're worried about your job, then why don't I ask my father to speak to the priests?'

Raffaella didn't bother to reply.

'I'd like you to stay here over the winter. I'll miss you if you go,' Carlotta continued. 'It's been good having you here. Things have been better.'

Raffaella looked at her. There was something so earnest about her pale little face. She was like a child struggling to get her words out and make a serious point.

'How have things been better?' Raffaella asked gently.

'I don't know.' Carlotta reached into her mind for the best way to express it. 'I suppose it's lonely being here with my father. I like having you here too. It's been happier.'

Raffaella smiled wryly. 'You haven't seemed all that happy to me.'

Carlotta looked uncomfortable. She ran a finger over the jars of pomegranate syrup that lined the kitchen shelves. 'All that fruit doesn't boil down into much, does it?' she said at last.

Raffaella was glad to change the subject too. 'But what's there is delicious and worth all our hard work. You wait until you taste some of the dishes I'll cook with it when the americano comes back to us in the spring.'

Carlotta gave her a quick smile and a sidelong look before she slipped out of the kitchen and disappeared down the wide stone steps that led to the sea.

20

Silvana stared at Alberto. He had wrapped himself in a rug he'd taken from their bed and was sitting on his bench, leaning against the bakery wall, his eyes almost closed. She wasn't sure if he was asleep or watching her.

Since the night she'd tried to poison him, Alberto had been a different man. He still came to the bakery every day, but he took no interest in the business. He left it all to her.

For weeks Silvana had worked like a demon while he rested on his bench. As she grew strong from kneading the dough, Alberto's muscles melted into his body fat; as her face flushed from the heat of the oven, his seemed paler by the day. He didn't care how the loaves looked when they came out of the oven or how she arranged them on the shelves. Even when Patrizia Sesto gossiped with her for a full fifteen minutes and then left without buying a thing, he didn't bother to comment.

Each day Alberto complained that he felt more breathless and exhausted than ever. Once or twice Silvana noticed him rubbing at his chest as if he were in pain. But still he insisted on shuffling along to the bakery every day and propping himself up on his bench until it was time to shuffle home again.

'He doesn't seem well,' Alba Russo observed. 'Not well at all.'

'I know,' agreed Silvana. 'I suppose I should try to get him to the doctor.'

Alba gave a little hiss of disgust. 'Doctors: what use are they? Put a little chilli pepper in his food. That's what my grandmother always swore by as a pick-me-up.'

But Alberto had no appetite. He insisted she pile his plate as high as ever and then did little more than poke at the food with his fork.

Silvana found herself feeling a hint of pity for him as he pushed away the plate, looking dejected.

She didn't mind the extra work in the bakery. There was something beautiful about working the dough and feeding the oven. For the first time in years Silvana took pride in the place. Even mopping the floor or wiping down the counter and shelves brought her a certain satisfaction. She liked to stand back and look at her work, admiring the order she'd brought to the little shop.

'Will you ever stop fussing, woman?' Alberto grumbled, and she realised he had been watching her through half-shuttered eyes after all.

'I'm nearly finished. You get along home, I'll follow.'

Alberto shook his head. 'I'll wait,' he said shortly.

On the way home, he surprised her by taking her arm. It had been a long time since her husband had touched her. She felt him leaning on her as they walked.

'You know, I really ought to take you to the doctor,' she said tentatively.

He grunted in reply.

When they reached the house, he struggled up the steps. 'I'm going to bed,' he wheezed before she'd even pulled the door closed behind them. 'Don't bother cooking for me. I don't want to eat.'

It was strange putting a meal together without having Alberto in his armchair behind her, griping about something. If he had been waiting for his supper, he wouldn't have thought much of the simple soup she was preparing. It was little more than a chicken stock flavoured with celery and fatty pancetta, and bolstered with a little broken spaghetti. She ate it alone as the sound of him snoring echoed from the room above.

It was late by the time she climbed the stairs to bed. She nodded quickly at the crucifix on the wall, crossed herself and whispered the few words of prayer she'd always relied on, before sliding beneath the covers and laying her head on the pillow beside her snoring husband.

Alberto's snoring grew more explosive as the night wore on, and Silvana tossed and turned sleeplessly beside him. Prodding his arm silenced him only for a breath or two and then he began again as loud as before.

By 2 a.m. there was a hoarse, strangled note to Alberto's snoring that Silvana had never heard before. It was driving her crazy. Pulling the blankets over her head and stuffing her fingers in her ears, she began to whistle to drown out the sound.

She must have fallen asleep still whistling for she woke to silence. Alberto had stopped snoring. She couldn't even hear him breathing. Curling up beneath the covers, she savoured the last moments of rest before she had to ease herself out of bed.

Her body felt stiff and sore as she hobbled down to the kitchen to make coffee. All that hard work in the bakery was taking its toll.

'Alberto, do you want any coffee?' she called, and then louder, 'Alberto, can you hear me?'

There was no reply.

She poured a small cup of espresso and trudged up the stairs with it. 'Here, drink that and see if it wakes you up,' she said, putting it on the table beside the bed.

Alberto hadn't bothered to poke his head above the covers. He was still lying in exactly the same position he'd been in when she left, and there wasn't a sound to be heard from him.

'Alberto, are you all right?' Gingerly, Silvana touched his shoulder. He didn't move.

She pulled back the covers and gasped at what she saw. Her husband was lying cold and lifeless, his face contorted and his eyes popping.

'Madonna *mia*, he's dead, he's dead,' she wailed, and sinking down on the bed beside him, she threw her apron over her head.

Silvana sat beside her husband's corpse, rocking gently back and forth, her mind stilled by panic. She'd been there some time, maybe even hours, when dimly she registered a knocking at the door. At first she was too scared to answer it, but then the noise grew louder and she realised women's voices were calling her name.

'Silvana, are you there? Is everything all right?'

'I'm coming, I'm coming,' she replied, and stood on trembling legs to answer the door.

Patrizia Sesto and Anna Moretti were on her doorstep, their faces anxious.

'The bakery is all closed up and dark. We wondered what was wrong,' said Patrizia, pushing herself through the door.

Anna remained on the step. 'Something is the matter, isn't it, Silvana?' she asked gently as she looked into her face. 'What is it?'

Silvana stared at them both, not trusting herself to speak. 'Alberto is dead,' she finally managed to force out. 'He's gone. I don't know what to do.'

Patrizia let out a long, high-pitched scream. 'Dead? Oh my God, what happened?' The tears began to trickle down her cheeks and with one hand she covered her heart.

Anna remained on the doorstep. 'I know what to do, Silvana,' she said in a low, calm voice. 'Can I come in and help you?'

Silvana nodded. 'Please,' she said simply, and stepped back to allow Anna enough space to enter the narrow doorway.

Events seemed to unfold around Silvana after that. She stood in the hallway and watched as Anna went upstairs to close Alberto's eyes. Patrizia stayed and made clumsy attempts to comfort her, squeezing her hand and pressing a wet cheek against hers, until she heard Anna calling for a priest and a doctor and she rushed off to find them.

It was a relief to see her go. Slowly, Silvana climbed up to the bedroom and found Anna standing there, staring down at the huge mound of Alberto's inert body, with a look of pity on her face.

'I'm sorry, Silvana,' she said quietly. 'He's at peace now, though.'

'Yes, I know.'

'I think we should break the news to your sons. Why don't you tell me how to get hold of them and I'll take care of it?'

Silvana shook her head. 'You can't.'

'Why?' Anna was confused.

Silvana's eyes grew wide and she said nothing.

'The boys will have to be told, *cara*. I'm happy to take care of it for you.'

'You can't tell them,' Silvana blurted out, 'because I killed him. I murdered Alberto.'

Anna looked shocked for a moment and then she smiled. 'I'm sure you didn't.'

'No, I did.' Silvana's voice was shrill and her tone dramatic. 'I killed him. I'm a murderess and I'll be arrested and sent to prison and it's no more than I deserve.'

'How did you kill him?' Anna asked softly. 'Show me what you did.'

Silvana turned and ran down the stairs. She was breathless when she returned, clutching a plant with dark-green leaves she had pulled out of her garden. There was still soil clinging to its roots.

Anna took the plant from her. 'You fed him this?'

Silvana nodded. 'Yes, in a salad. But only a couple of leaves and only the one time.'

'I expect he had terrible stomach pains and vomiting?'

'That's right, he did.'

Anna pushed the plant back into her hands. 'You made him ill, but you didn't kill him, Silvana. It would have taken more than that. Now dig the plant into your compost heap and put those thoughts out of your mind.'

'Do you think so?' Silvana sounded hopeful.

Anna took her arm and guided her towards the wardrobe. 'Yes, I do,' she said firmly. 'We'll break the news to your sons later. First, let's have a look in here and see if you've got anything suitable to wear.'

'Yes, yes,' Silvana agreed. 'I have all the right clothes: a black dress, gloves, a sweater and a coat. I even have black earrings. I kept them all after my mother died. I'm sure I'll still fit into them.'

'I'm certain you will too,' agreed Anna, sorting through the clothes. 'You're as slender as ever, Silvana. Your mourning clothes will fit you beautifully.'

Like a child, Silvana allowed herself be clothed. Her dress was slipped over her head and Anna buttoned up her cardigan and even fastened the earrings in her ears.

'That's very good. You look perfect,' she said as she laid out Silvana's gloves, coat and hat for later. 'The doctor will be here shortly and he'll write out the death certificate. And hopefully, Patrizia will have had the sense to find Padre Pietro. We can trust him with all the funeral arrangements. So you see, there isn't all that much for you to do.'

'What about the bakery?' Silvana looked worried.

'We'll put a notice in the window to tell people you're closed due to bereavement.'

Silvana nodded slowly, and then the words flowed out of her like water from a tap. 'I hated him, Anna. I've hated him for years. I can't be sorry he's dead.'

They heard a knocking on the door. 'I know that,' Anna said quickly. 'You had every right to hate him and you have no need to be sorry. Now let me answer the door. It will be the priest and the doctor. And Silvana?'

'Yes?'

'You can talk to me about these things whenever you want to. But you mustn't be tempted to confide them to anyone else. Do you understand?'

'Thank you.' Silvana patted her black clothes with nervous hands. 'Thank you for everything.'

The doctor barely bothered to examine Alberto. He looked down at his body from some distance as he listened to Silvana describe the extraordinary noises her husband had made during the night. 'Not like any snoring I've ever heard before,' she stressed.

The doctor nodded gravely. 'Heart failure,' he declared. 'There's no doubt about it. You only have to look at the man to see that it was going to happen sooner or later. He ate himself to death.'

Silvana swallowed hard. 'You think it was something he ate?'

'I think it was everything he ate, signora. I'm afraid he's been eating himself to death for years.'

Padre Pietro was next to arrive. He put a gentle hand on Silvana's head and asked her to pray with him. Together, they kneeled beside the bed and beseeched God to receive Alberto's soul in Heaven.

There were more knocks on the door as the day wore on. Neighbours brought words of condolence and dishes of home-cooked food. They gathered round her kitchen table and discussed Alberto's unexpected death in shocked voices. Silvana felt like a stranger in her own world. She sat in silence and let the noise of women's voices rush past her.

At lunchtime the undertaker and his assistant arrived. They had a struggle to dislodge Alberto from his bed and carry him down the steep stairway. Luckily, Padre Matteo materialised to help them or they'd never have got him out of the front door.

Late in the afternoon Raffaella came. She stood in the narrow hallway with her mother, and Silvana heard them talking in low voices. Afterwards Anna came into the kitchen and told the women gathered round the table that it was best that they leave.

'Of course, of course.' Alba Russo stood up and the others followed. 'Silvana, we'll call on you tomorrow, and you must tell us if there's anything we can do to help.'

Once Anna had closed the door on them, she poured Silvana a glass of red wine and pushed it into her hand.

Silvana swallowed a mouthful. 'You're being so good to me.'

'Why wouldn't I be good to you?'

'I haven't always been your friend. Or Raffaella's.'

Anna looked thoughtful. 'Perhaps you haven't,' she agreed. 'But this is no time to worry about things like that. Drink your wine, Silvana, and then go to bed. You need some rest.'

Silvana did what she was told. She let herself be undressed and climbed between the clean sheets that had been put on her bed.

'Will you be all right on your own?' Anna asked.

'Yes, don't worry, I'll be fine.'

When Anna had left, she stretched her legs into the empty space on the side of the bed that Alberto had always occupied. He had really gone. She felt a lurch of fear in the pit of her stomach as she remembered the plant she had buried in her compost heap. And then she stretched out further until she was taking up almost all of the bed, and she felt something that she realised could only be relief. Alberto was gone and she was really free at last.

21

The first time Silvana left the house was for the funeral. It was a bleak, cold day with a wind that whipped up from the sea and bent the tops of the trees, and Padre Pietro stumbled over his words at the graveside in his rush to finish before the full force of the storm hit them.

Her sons stayed at her side, shepherding her through the service and the burial, and she only had to nod and murmur her thanks for the condolences that were offered to her. But still Silvana was glad when it was all over and she could crawl beneath the thick quilt she had pulled on to her bed and close her eyes and listen to the rain driving against the windowpane.

Her sons had decided they didn't want to take their father's place behind the counter of the bakery, and she didn't blame them. They had made their own lives in the city, and Triento seemed no more than a sleepy, backward place to them now.

'Come home with us,' they urged. 'Leave the house, forget the bakery, come and live with us for a while.'

But she had refused. Her life was here, she told them.

The day they left, they clung to her like they had when they were boys. 'We'll be back soon. We won't leave you on your own too long,' they promised.

'Don't worry about me, I'll be fine,' she said, touched by their concern. But when they'd gone, she burrowed back into her bed again, blocking out the world with her quilts and eiderdowns.

Anna Moretti came every day to check on her and bring food. Sometimes she sat with her for a while, reading a book while Silvana dozed.

'What about the bakery?' Anna asked one afternoon. 'Will you open it up again soon?'

Silvana tugged the quilt tightly around her shoulders. 'I was going to think about it today, but I haven't had the energy. I don't know, maybe next week. Perhaps the week after.'

'Perhaps you should consider getting back there sooner than that?'

Silvana grimaced. 'There's no rush, is there? I've worked all my life, surely I'm allowed a few days' rest? And anyway, I can't face the smell of the place.'

'You don't like the smell of freshly baked bread?' Anna looked surprised.

'That's right. It's so sweet and cloying when you have to put up with it day after day. And it reminds me of Alberto.'

With that, Silvana rolled over to face the wall and closed her eyes. She didn't see Anna quietly taking a key from her chain and slipping it into her own pocket before she left.

It wasn't until several days later, when Alba Russo appeared on her doorstep clutching a slab of focaccia crusted with rock salt and rosemary that Silvana found out what had happened.

'I think you had better get dressed and hurry down to your bakery,' Alba hissed.

Silvana took the bread from her, squeezed it between her fingers and sniffed at it. 'This looks good,' she declared. 'Who made it?'

'Anna Moretti and her daughter, of course. They've got that Gypsy Tearoom person helping them. They're up to all sorts.'

For the first time in days Silvana felt a prickle of interest in the outside world. 'Such as what?' she asked.

'Well, yesterday they made a bread with walnuts and chocolate in it. And today there is this rosemary focaccia and another loaf filled with sweet onions. I don't know what Alberto would have had to say about it.'

Silvana ignored the mention of her late husband's name. 'Are they selling the bread they're baking?'

'Yes, I assumed you'd given them permission. They've been there every day and the place has been full of customers.'

Silvana held the focaccia. The pungent herby scent of rosemary almost disguised the sweet yeasty smell of bread. She wondered what the other loaves were like. Taking her black coat from the hook behind the front door, she pushed past Alba and set off to find out for herself.

The scene she found in the bakery amazed her. Loaves of bread were stacked in unruly piles on the shelves and counter. Huge slippers of ciabatta had been tossed on top of flat breads stuffed with proscuitto and roasted vegetables. Crusty white loaves fought with slender panini. Sugary breads rubbed shoulders with sourdough. The sweet smell of baking was overwhelming, and even this late in the morning, Raffaella was still pulling new loaves out of the hot oven.

Silvana couldn't help herself. She started to laugh.

Raffaella looked up. Although she was already flushed from the heat of the oven, she seemed to turn an even deeper pink as she realised she was being observed.

'Where did you learn how to do all this?' Silvana gestured at the undisciplined rows of loaves.

Raffaella straightened up and put her tray of hot rolls, stuffed with nuts and reeking of cinnamon, down on the counter. 'My mother found some recipes and Ciro Ricci came up with the rest. He showed us how to work the oven and helped us out for the first day. We've sold so much bread. I have a cashbox full of money for you.'

Silvana sniffed at one of the warm rolls. 'Alberto would never bake sweetbreads,' she remarked. 'Or breads that had been stuffed with things. He was very strict about it. Only plain focaccia, crusty white loaves and ciabatta.'

'Why wouldn't he try anything else?' Raffaella asked with interest.

Silvana shrugged. 'It was tradition, I suppose. Those were the only breads his family had ever baked. Also,' she added thoughtfully, 'I think he may have been too lazy.'

'My mother thought you wouldn't mind if we tried some new recipes. She said the main thing was to get the business going again before all the customers drifted away and got their bread supplies from somewhere else.'

Silvana nodded. 'Your mother was probably right.'

Raffaella was unlacing her apron and wiping the flour from her hands. 'Now that you're well again, I expect you'll want to take over,' she said.

Silvana sat down on the stool beside the counter and eyed the bread, trying to keep the exhaustion from her face. 'I suppose I ought to,' she agreed.

'You don't have to do it all alone if you don't want to.'

'Who will help me now Alberto has gone?' Silvana said listlessly.

'Me.' Raffaella began to arrange the rolls she'd baked on the already crowded shelves. 'I can help you.'

'But don't you already have a job at Villa Rosa?'

'No, the house is closed up until the spring and there's no work for me. So I could come and do the baking with you early every morning, if you like.'

Silvana wasn't sure if it was such a good idea. 'I couldn't pay you much,' she began hesitantly.

'That doesn't matter. I'm living with my parents so I don't need much. And in the spring I'll go back to Villa Rosa. They'll want me there when the americano returns.' Raffaella knew that every time she spoke of Eduardo her cheeks grew hot. She hoped Silvana wouldn't notice. 'We can go back to making the breads Alberto preferred, if you like,' she added hurriedly. 'We'll just do plain focaccia, crusty loaves and ciabatta again.'

Silvana looked thoughtful. 'But people have been buying this bread, haven't they?'

'Yes, we've been really busy. Everyone loved the walnut and chocolate bread. We sold out so quickly.'

'Then we should keep doing it. You can show me how to make it tomorrow. We'll work together.'

Raffaella nodded and smiled. 'OK, I'd like that.'

It was strange for Silvana having another woman behind the counter. Once or twice she banged into Raffaella as they both reached for the same thing, and several times she opened her mouth to criticise something the girl had done, only to think better of it.

It turned out to be a blessing to have some help, for Silvana hardly had a peaceful moment. Every customer that came through the door wanted to stop and offer their sympathies to her. Some perched on the stool beside the counter for half an hour or more discussing their shock at Alberto's sudden and untimely death.

Patrizia Sesto hung on the longest, whispering her words urgently as though Alberto were still there, eavesdropping from his bench. 'He was cut down in his prime, Silvana,' she sighed. 'Whoever would have thought such a big, strong man would die, boom, just like that? He wasn't even ill. I can't get over it.'

Silvana was tired of listening to the same words being repeated over and over by different people. She told Patrizia what she'd said to all the others.

'It wasn't such a big shock for the doctor. He seemed to think Alberto's heart had been failing for a while but we never realised it. And he had been ill those last few weeks, remember. He barely moved from that bench, just sat there and watched me work.'

Patrizia shook her head mournfully. 'First Marcello, then Alberto ... there's been so much death in Triento. Perhaps the town is cursed. Maybe these deaths are a message from God that He doesn't want the priests to build that statue on the mountain after all. If so who will be next—'

Raffaella interrupted. 'But Marcello and Alberto had nothing to do with the statue.'

'That's not true,' argued Patrizia. 'Marcello was a Russo and his family are the ones behind the statue. They have influence with the priests. And Alberto was at the meeting when the whole idea was discussed. He spoke up in favour of it, my husband told me so.'

Raffaella opened her mouth to argue, but she saw Silvana give a quick shake of her head so she stayed quiet.

'It's a conceit for so small a town to build so big a statue,' Patrizia continued. 'That's what my Angelo says. We'll pay for our arrogance one way or another. Look at both of you, so young and already widows. Surely that's not natural? The wisest thing would be to stop now, tell the americano not to bother coming back and leave the mountaintop bare like God and nature intended it. Don't you think so, Silvana? Don't you agree?'

Silvana took one of the cinnamon rolls and broke it open, releasing the smell of burned spice and toasted nuts. 'Have you tried this new bread?' she asked. 'Perhaps I should give you a few rolls to take home and see if Angelo likes them. Here, I'll fill a bag for you. No, there's no need to pay. These are samples. Come back and buy more if you enjoy them.'

Patrizia was so astonished to receive free bread that it completely silenced her. Taking the bag of sweet rolls, she slid from the stool and out of the shop before Silvana could change her mind.

'What would Alberto have said to see you giving away bread?' Raffaella asked once Patrizia was out of sight.

Silvana cast a glance at the empty bench that lay against the far wall. 'Alberto has gone and I can do what I like,' she said firmly. 'Now come and take hold of one end of this bench and help me carry it to the back of the shop. It's not needed here any more.'

The bench was moved and the bakery seemed bigger and lighter without it. Later, once she was home and alone again, Silvana sat in Alberto's empty armchair. To her surprise, she found her eyes were wet with tears.

She wondered what she was crying about. It couldn't be sadness at losing her husband, for there was nothing about him she missed. In fact, she was sure she must be one of the happiest widows in the whole of Italy. What then? She thought of Anna Moretti taking the key to the bakery and opening it up without telling her. She and Raffaella had worked so hard and expected nothing in return. Her tears flowed faster and Silvana realised at last why she was crying. All this time the two women had been her friends and she hadn't noticed. She'd snubbed one and been cruel about the other and yet they'd given her another chance.

Silvana buried her face in her black mourning dress and began to cry noisily. If only everyone could be as forgiving as Anna and Raffaella. But she feared that she had run out of second chances. She had made her mistakes, and even though Alberto was gone now, she would still have to live with them.

22

Raffaella missed Villa Rosa more than she expected. She found herself wondering what Umberto and Carlotta were up to all alone. The winter storms would be buffeting them and the high winds tearing through the trees and bringing the garden to its hands and knees. Umberto would be grouchy and Carlotta lonely. Raffaella thought about them often.

She thought of the americano too. He was always there in the outer reaches of her mind waiting to step in and take it over.

At least the work at the bakery kept her hands occupied, even if her thoughts were still free to wander. Early each morning, well before first light, she met Silvana there and helped her bake the bread. Each day they tried something different, a bread flavoured with seeds or spices, a loaf studded with black olives. At Christmas they made panettone, light golden bread sprinkled with dried fruit and spices.

Silvana had quickly returned to her old self, chatting with the customers, lowering her voice when she didn't want Raffaella to hear what she was saying. It was amazing how quickly Alberto had been forgotten. Hardly anyone mentioned his name any more.

At times, as the gossiping dragged on, Raffaella wondered what she was doing there. Her mother had asked her to forget old grudges and help Silvana with a generous heart, and she was trying. But some days it wasn't easy.

'Just be patient,' Anna kept telling her. 'You have every right to hate her, but that's all the more reason why you should help her.'

Raffaella didn't think that made much sense. She tried to argue, but it was useless. Her mother deflected every point she made by simply agreeing with it. 'Yes, yes, I know how horrible she can be.

I've seen it with my own eyes. But ask yourself why she's turned out like that.'

'Because she was married to that awful Alberto?'

'Maybe, but don't jump to conclusions. It might be something more than that.'

Raffaella rolled her eyes.

Her mother smiled. 'When you get to my age, you'll understand things are rarely as they seem. You're missing something about Silvana, something important. Watch her more carefully. Perhaps you can help her in more ways than you think.'

'Aren't I helping her enough already?' Raffaella grumbled. 'What more do you want me to do for her?'

All the same she made a point of observing Silvana more closely. At first she didn't notice anything out of kilter. Sometimes she laughed more gaily than a widow strictly ought to. Other times she seemed distracted and it was difficult to shake her out of silence. And then, after about a week and a half of watching her carefully, Raffaella saw there was a pattern to it all.

Twice a day Silvana would glance at the clock nervously and stare out of the window, her mind not fully on whatever it was she was doing. When the mayor, Giorgio Lazio, went past, she always waved at him through the glass and he would wave back and keep walking. The mayor was a punctual man and the same thing happened every morning and afternoon without fail. Afterwards Silvana always seemed subdued.

Raffaella cast her mind back to the rare times she'd seen the pair together. There had been something odd about those little scenes, some detail in the picture that was out of place, although she had never been able to see it properly.

'The mayor seems like a nice man,' she said one morning after he had passed by.

'Hmm, he does,' Silvana agreed.

'I expect he was handsome when he was young. I wonder why he never married?'

'I have no idea.'

'But you know him quite well, don't you? I've seen you talking to him.'

Silvana shook her head. 'No, I don't know him well. I can't

imagine what makes you think that,' she said, and Raffaella thought she detected a faint pinkness in her cheeks.

'But you were talking to him in here once when I interrupted you, remember?' she insisted.

Silvana looked irritated. 'Don't be ridiculous,' she said uncomfortably. 'The mayor came in to buy a loaf of bread, that's all, and I was passing the time of day with him.'

'And there was one time that I saw you talking to him in the piazza,' Raffaella insisted. 'You had your hand on his arm.'

The pink washed out of Silvana's face and she pressed her thin lips together tightly. Turning her back on Raffaella, she began to fuss with an untidy stack of flour-dusted ciabatta. 'So quiet today,' she muttered. 'We'll never sell all this bread. It's silly both of us being here. All the hard work has been done. Why don't you go home? I'm sure your mother would be glad to see you.'

Raffaella realised she had pushed things too far and she felt guilty. She ought to apologise, stay on and keep working, but she had a better idea. This was what her mother had meant. There were other ways for her to help Silvana besides baking and selling bread.

'All right, so long as you don't mind,' she said quickly, unlacing her apron and hanging it on the hook beside the oven. 'I'll see you tomorrow, though, at the usual time?'

Silvana nodded. 'Yes, yes, tomorrow. Now have a good day and give your mother my best.'

Raffaella left the bakery, but she didn't turn down the hill towards home. With a glance over her shoulder, to make sure Silvana wasn't watching, she slipped along the alleyway that led to the Gypsy Tearoom.

Halfway there, she bent to pat the old yellow dog that was warming itself in a patch of sunlight. She was scratching it beneath its chin when she heard Ciro Ricci calling her.

'Raffaella, leave that smelly old brute alone.'

She looked up and laughed. 'You love him really. I bet you feed him scraps of food when you think no one is looking.'

Ciro smiled ruefully and the soft skin round his eyes pleated. Raffaella thought he seemed tired.

'Are you feeling all right?' She was worried. 'You don't look well to me.'

'Oh, no, I'm fine. There have been a few ups and downs in the past few weeks but nothing I can't handle.' He guided her towards a table near the warmth of the pizza oven. 'Come and sit down. Have some coffee and biscotti and tell me how it's going at the bakery.'

Raffaella sat near the fire and shed her black shawl and gloves. 'Things are going well. Thank you again for helping us that first day.'

'It was a pleasure.'

'I wondered if you could do one more thing for me?'

'Anything, Raffaella, you know that.'

When she told him what she wanted, he frowned. 'Does Silvana know you're planning to do this for her?'

'No, it has to be a secret. That's really important.'

'Are you sure she'll be pleased?'

Raffaella looked thoughtful. 'Yes, I think so. It's worth a try, anyway. And if things don't work out, then there's no harm done, is there?'

Ciro raised his eyebrows.

'Let's try it just once,' Raffaella urged. 'You want to help Silvana, don't you?'

'I don't care about Silvana. But I'll do it for you.' His gaze was so intense she wasn't sure where to look. He was staring at her like a hungry man might stare at one of his pizzas. 'You know I'd do anything for you, don't you?' he repeated softly.

She smiled nervously. 'Just this one thing,' she promised. 'And it's not really for me, it's for Silvana.'

The mayor was a man who enjoyed the regular rhythms of his life. Every morning he woke at the same time and drank two cups of strong espresso in the same café while scanning his newspaper. His secretary knew exactly when he would arrive at his office, and she left his mail in a brown Manila folder on his desk so he could read it thoroughly before starting on the business of the day. His house-keeper had his lunch on the table almost as soon as he walked through the door – always a little pasta, some meat and salad. To finish, he enjoyed an apple, peeled and sliced with a sharp serrated knife and eaten with a chunk of pecorino cheese. Three evenings a week he ate dinner with his mother, who lived halfway up the mountain in the house where he'd grown up. The other nights he spent alone, reading in front of the fire or watching the sunset from his terrace, a glass of good red wine at his elbow. He liked these habits. They were comfortable.

Now there was a new addition to Giorgio's daily routine. Each morning and afternoon as he crossed the piazza, he glanced through the window of the bakery. Silvana was always there, staring out at him. She would raise her hand to wave and he'd wave back and smile. It was a simple, silent exchange, and yet Giorgio had begun to look forward to it. He even considered changing the time he left for lunch so the bakery would still be open as he passed by.

Giorgio had worked hard to become the man he was. He came from a family of farmers who scratched out a living on poor land. For him, the thought of such back-breaking work with so little reward had never appealed. Although there were days when he felt walled in by his office and longed to feel the sun on his face, he was proud of what he had achieved. He was mayor of Triento, a thriving town, and he took his position seriously.

When Alberto died, he was among the mourners at the funeral. He offered his condolences to Silvana and her sons, and left as soon as he decently could. Once safely home, he sat at the table in his empty kitchen and stared at the wall. Giorgio was panicking. He was afraid of the emotions that Silvana had stirred up.

Distracted, struggling to concentrate at work, he tried to put Silvana out of his mind. She was a widow, grieving for her husband, and she was out of bounds. But as Giorgio signed documents with his smart silver fountain pen, as he presided over meetings and ceremonies, as he dissolved the town's niggling problems and kept it on the path of prosperity, half of his mind was on the moment he would cross the piazza on his way home from work and stare through the window of the bakery, where Silvana would be waiting for him.

In the twenty-five years she had been married to another man, Giorgio had never stopped loving Silvana.

Alone in the bakery, Silvana watched the clock slowly tick its way to late afternoon. At last it was nearly time. Casting a glance outside, she saw that the piazza was still empty. The only person in sight was Giuliana Biagio, trotting briskly across the cobbles, her basket over her arm.

'Oh, no,' Silvana murmured. 'Please don't let her be coming here.'

But Giuliana was heading straight to the bakery. Looking at the clock, Silvana realised she would be on her doorstep at the exact moment Giorgio stepped into the piazza. She prayed that for once in his life the mayor would be running late.

'Patrizia Sesto told me that you gave her free bread,' panted Giuliana as she pushed open the door. 'Lovely little rolls flavoured with cinnamon and nuts. She showed them to me.'

'Oh, yes, that's right,' Silvana said absently, trying to see over Giuliana's shoulder. 'Did she enjoy them?'

'I expect she did. How nice to be given something for nothing. I'm quite sure it's never happened to me.'

Silvana didn't reply. She was transfixed by the scene that was unfolding outside the bakery window. Giorgio was walking across the piazza and Raffaella was hurtling towards him from the opposite direction. She had left the bakery ages ago and Silvana couldn't imagine where she'd been since then. But now she was stopping the mayor in his tracks, smiling at him and engaging him in conversation.

Silvana felt angry and jealous. She would give almost anything to be in Raffaella's shoes. She wondered what they were talking about with their heads so close together like that.

'No one ever gives me free bread,' Giuliana repeated loudly. 'Even though I'm as good a customer as any of the others.'

Silvana lost her temper. She began grabbing loaves of bread. 'Take what you like,' she shouted, thrusting thick-crusted sourdough and soft poppy-seed rolls at Giuliana, stuffing them into her basket and piling them in her arms. 'Have it all if it makes you happy. Here, have some focaccia and some of these *tarallini*. Is that enough? No? Take more, then.'

Giuliana's face froze into a wide-eyed stare. Clutching her over-filled basket of bread to her chest, she edged towards the doorway.

'No, wait, you've left some. Take this one.' Silvana picked up a flat, floury loaf and hurled it at her. 'Take two of them. Have them all.'

As Giuliana slammed the door behind her, loaves of bread rained down on it.

Silvana was breathing heavily. She looked up from the mess she'd made and saw that the mayor and Raffaella had disappeared. Rushing to the door, she scanned back and forth, but there was no sign of them anywhere. Disappointed, she looked down at the bread that lay around her feet. It would all have to be thrown away. Kneeling down, she made a start on the task of cleaning up.

23

Silvana didn't know what was the matter with Raffaella. She seemed odd this morning, jumpy and excitable, and she kept smiling for no apparent reason.

'What are you so happy about?' she found herself snapping as they kneaded the dough and fed the oven. But the girl only shrugged and smiled again.

Silvana was desperate the know the details of her conversation with the mayor, but she couldn't bring herself to ask the question directly.

'What did you get up to yesterday?' she asked instead.

Raffaella murmured something unintelligible in reply.

'Was your mother pleased to have you home so early?' Silvana persisted as they pulled trays of freshly baked bread out of the hot oven.

Raffaella dabbed at her hot, red face with a cloth. She looked uncomfortable.

'I didn't go home straight away,' she admitted. 'I went to the Gypsy Tearoom to see Signor Ricci. He was so good to us that first day when we opened up the bakery and we didn't have a clue what we were doing. I wanted to say thank you and I haven't had the chance until now.'

Silvana gave her a sidelong glance. She remembered Alba's suspicion that there was something going on between the girl and Ciro Ricci.

'Did you spend a long time in the Gypsy Tearoom?' she asked.

'Yes, I suppose so. We were talking. I like Signor Ricci. He's very sympathetic.'

'You should be careful. You know how people like to gossip.'

Raffaella began lining a big basket with crusty white loaves. She put a cloth over the top and tucked it round the bread carefully.

'What are you doing?' Silvana asked.

'Signor Ricci asked if I'd take some bread over to him this morning.'

'Have you not been listening to me?' Silvana was losing patience. 'People have been talking about you and that young man. If you had any sense, you'd stay away from him and from the Gypsy Tearoom. You're a widow, Raffaella. You're still in mourning and it's not right. Surely you can see that?'

Raffaella held out the basket. 'You'd better deliver the bread, then. Perhaps people won't be so quick to start gossiping about you.'

'Since you promised him, I don't have much choice, do I?' Silvana snapped in reply. 'Give it to me. I won't be in there for long, though, Raffaella. I'll take this bread over and come straight back. I know how to behave.'

Seizing the basket and pulling the black woollen shawl round her shoulders, Silvana marched out of the bakery and up the alleyway that led to the Gypsy Tearoom. Circo Ricci might get a shock when he saw who was bringing his bread this morning, she thought gleefully. He was expecting the beautiful young widow and he was getting the old worn-out one.

But Ciro didn't seem fazed. He smiled broadly when she appeared on the doorstep. 'Ah, wonderful, you brought me some bread. Now let me make you a good strong coffee in return. I'll just be a minute. Come in and take a seat. Come on, come in.'

'No, no, I can't. I have work to do. Thank you, but no.' Silvana tried to back away, but Ciro took a grip on her shoulder and, gently but forcefully, propelled her towards a screened-off table in the corner of the room.

'You'll like it over here, I think. Come and take a seat.'

'No, I can't—' Silvana broke off as she saw who was already sitting at the table behind the screen. Giorgio had his newspaper spread out before him and he was sipping his first espresso of the day with some enjoyment.

He looked at her and smiled. 'Good morning.'

'Oh . . . good morning.' She stared at him, unsure what she should do next.

Gently, Ciro pushed her into a chair. 'You sit here. So private behind the screen, see? You're free to drink espresso, chat, whatever. No one will know you're here.'

Silvana stared at the mayor. 'We can't drink coffee here together. It's not proper.'

Giorgio looked grave. 'You're right, it isn't. But it's only coffee, Silvana, nothing more. I think I might start coming here every morning to drink my espresso, and if you arrive with Ciro's bread delivery and we sit behind this screen for ten minutes, where is the harm in that?'

Silvana felt quite desperate. 'I do want to, Giorgio. But I'm a widow, I'm in mourning, and people will talk.'

'No one need know.' He smiled at her. 'It's only coffee, Silvana. I think we should enjoy it.'

24

Winter held tight to Triento. The wind swept through its narrow streets, and rain clouds lay over the mountain.

Raffaella's days wore the same face. Early each morning there was the struggle to leave the warm bed she shared with her sister, Teresa, and the unappealing prospect of the steep, dark climb up the hill to Big Triento.

She and Silvana were glad once the ovens were stoked. As the sky got lighter, the shop grew warmer and it was filled with the sweet, friendly smell of baking bread. Raffaella often glanced out of the window if the day was a stormy one and said a prayer for her father putting out to sea in his fishing boat.

Once the last loaves were out of the oven and had been laid out on the shelves, she made up a basket of bread to be delivered to the Gypsy Tearoom. Silvana hurried to remove her apron and was ready to go the moment the basket was full. Each morning she stayed away just a few minutes longer and always returned with the smell of coffee on her breath, flushed cheeks and happy eyes.

Raffaella never commented, and Silvana never confided in her. But Ciro had let slip that sometimes he heard laughter from the table behind the screen and sometimes it grew quiet.

Nothing else had changed. The mayor still walked past the window of the bakery twice a day on his way to and from his desk in the town hall, and Silvana still stopped to wave at him.

Raffaella was in the habit of watching her and found she couldn't stop. She saw how happiness could change a person in quiet ways. Silvana moved about the bakery as if she could hear music in her mind. The frown lines that had scored her forehead seemed to soften, her curls came loose from the pins she used to anchor them, and she let them fall about her face. To another eye, she might have seemed the same person, but Raffaella could see how she was different than before.

At first she had been pleased with the success of her plot, impressed at her own cleverness. Every time she saw Silvana heading towards the Gypsy Tearoom clutching her basket of bread, she felt a little thrill. After a week or two she was surprised to find the thrill had been replaced by an unmistakable sense of melancholy. So this was all Silvana and Giorgio could have, a few snatched moments together. It seemed so paltry.

She grew more desolate as she remembered the dreams she'd had and the life she'd missed out on. The one where she grew old with Marcello, had his babies and watched them grow up to have babies of their own. Instead, here she was, a lonely, foolish girl clinging to the memory of dusk-lit conversations in the company of a stranger beneath a pomegranate tree. She wasn't so different from Silvana after all.

Raffaella was deep in her sad thoughts the day Carlotta came to the bakery. It was early in the morning and there was no one else in the shop. She ought to have felt the cold draft of air as the door opened and heard the little chinging noise it made, but she was so lost in thought it wasn't until she happened to look up and come face to face with Carlotta that she realised she wasn't alone.

'Oh!' Raffaella was startled. 'It's you! What are you doing here? Have you got news? Have you heard when the americano is coming back?'

'No, there's no news.' Carlotta's face was as bleak as her own. 'My father told me you were working here and I thought I'd come and say hello. I've been baking all the bread we've eaten this winter. It will be nice to eat a loaf made by someone else.'

'Well, we've got plenty of bread here, as you can see.' Raffaella gestured proudly towards the crammed shelves. 'My favourite is this one flavoured with dried basil and sun-dried tomatoes. It's from a recipe my mother found. Why don't I cut you a slice so you can see how good it is?'

'You like working here, don't you? I suppose that means you won't be coming back to Villa Rosa.'

Raffaella paused, bread knife in hand. 'No, no, this is just temporary, to help Silvana out,' she said quickly. 'As soon as you have some news about the americano, I'll come back to Villa Rosa. I told Padre Pietro that. He must have forgotten to pass it on.'

'What about Silvana?'

'She'll manage, I expect.' Raffaella wanted to tell Carlotta about Silvana's clandestine morning coffees with the mayor. Their meetings were now lasting thirty minutes or more, and the mayor was often heard to whistle later as he strolled past the bakery, late for work. It was such a delicious secret she was desperate to share it, but something held her back.

Instead, she cut a slice of the loaf, releasing summer's smells, a perfume of basil and tomatoes. 'Try this before Silvana gets back. She's out delivering bread at the moment, but she won't be gone much longer so eat it quickly.'

Raffaella was busy wrapping up a parcel of bread for her when Silvana returned. She wondered if Carlotta might spot the new life in the older woman's eyes, the way her steps covered more ground and she held her shoulders straighter.

'Ah, sorry, I got held up,' Silvana blustered. 'Good morning, Carlotta, what brings you here so early?'

'Just buying bread,' Carlotta said shyly.

'And how is life at Villa Rosa?' Silvana tied the strings of her apron and stepped briskly behind the counter. 'Have the storms hit you hard this year?'

'Oh, yes, they've been awful.'

'Is the house all right?' Raffaella asked worriedly.

'The house is fine, but the garden has been blown to bits. My father doesn't think the old pomegranate tree will bud in spring. He says this last winter has been too much for it.'

'No!'

'There's nothing we can do.'

'What about another crutch to hold up its branches?' Raffaella asked.

'My father says that won't save it.'

'But I love that old tree.'

'I love it too,' Carlotta said. 'We have a young one ready to plant in its place, but it won't be the same.'

Taking her package from the counter, Carlotta hugged it to her chest. She looked thinner and more angular than ever. Her fair hair was tucked under a red woollen hat, and her face seemed pinched and pale beneath it.

'Thank you for the bread,' she said. 'I'll let you know if I hear word about the americano. And don't worry. I won't let my father chop down the old pomegranate tree unless I'm certain it won't last until spring.'

Then she left and Raffaella sank deeper into her low mood. Somehow the thought of the old pomegranate tree dying slowly out there in the wind and rain seemed like a bad sign, a symbol that there was more misfortune waiting just round the corner for the people of Triento.

'Poor child.' Silvana was watching Carlotta fighting the wind as she walked across the piazza. 'I feel sorry for her.'

'Why?'

'She seems so fragile.'

Raffaella was surprised. She didn't think Silvana was the sort of woman who had sympathy to waste on other people.

'She is quite fragile,' she agreed. 'And there's a sadness about her even when she's smiling.'

'Ah, well, I'm not surprised after what she's been through.'

'What do you mean?' Raffaella asked.

'You know, don't you? You've heard what happened to Carlotta?'

Raffaella shook her head. 'No, tell me.'

'Well, it was about five years ago, the last summer the Barbieri family came to Villa Rosa. Carlotta would have been nineteen and a prettier girl than she is now. Still, you can't blame Umberto, how could he—' Silvana broke off. 'Have you really never heard any of this?'

'No.'

Silvana stared at her and an odd look settled on to her face.

'So tell me what happened,' Raffaella urged.

'I don't think I should,' Silvana said at last. 'It's Carlotta's story, and it's for her to tell you if she wants to.'

'But you know you can trust me. I can keep a secret.'

Silvana looked thoughtful. 'I've never said thank you, have I, Raffaella?' she said slowly. 'I'm grateful for everything you've done for me. For helping me in here and for the other thing—'

Raffaella interrupted her. 'There's no need to say thank you to me. I'm glad I was here and I could help.'

'I'm glad too.'

'So will you tell me?' Raffaella was desperate to know. 'What happened to Carlotta five years ago?'

'No, I don't think so. Perhaps she'll tell you herself one day, though.'

'But I promise I won't—'

This time Raffaella heard the loud ching as the door of the bakery swung open and she felt the cold rush of air as Alba Russo came in.

'I find I need bread,' Alba said haughtily. 'But ask your girl not to give me one of those huge loaves, Silvana, it will only get wasted. I'll have a small one. I only have three sons at home now, you know.'

'How are you, Signora Russo?' Raffaella asked as she began to wrap one of the small white loaves.

'Do get her to hurry, Silvana. I have a lot to get through today.'

As she pushed the loaf across the counter, Raffaella tried to catch her mother-in-law's eyes, but Alba refused to look at her.

'Put that bread on my account, will you, Silvana,' she called out instead. 'I'll be sure to settle it by the end of the week.'

Raffaella felt the anger bubble and roar inside her. She'd never cared for her mother-in-law, but she'd tried, for Marcello's sake, to get along with her. Now there was no Marcello and no need for her to be polite. Ignoring the warning look Silvana was trying to give her, Raffaella let her temper fray.

'I asked how you are, Signora Russo,' she said more insistently.

Alba threw her a glance. 'I'm fine, Raffaella,' she replied coolly. 'I would have thought that was perfectly obvious. Now if you'll give me my bread, I'll be on my way.'

Raffaella realised her hands were still gripping the loaf on the counter, her fingernails digging pocks into its soft crust. She saw Alba reaching for it and felt a sharp tug as she pulled it free.

With a toss of her head that set her tight curls shaking, Alba left the shop. Raffaella watched her bustle across the piazza, nodding to Padre Matteo and Padre Simone as she went, struggling a little on the uneven cobbles in those ridiculous heels she insisted on wearing.

'Well,' Silvana said.

'Well what?'

'I'm wondering what you did to that woman to make her hate you so much.'

'I don't know. Married her son, I suppose.'

'It must be more than that. She doesn't hate Stefano's wife,' Silvana pointed out.

'She blames me for Marcello's death, you know that.'

'But she hated you even before he got sick.'

'Did she?'

Silvana nodded. 'She's never had a good word to say about you.'

'I honestly don't know. I'm sure I never did anything to deserve it.'

'You must have done something.'

'I swear I didn't.'

Raffaella brooded about it all day. The more she thought about Alba, the angrier and more indignant she became. It was so unfair. She had done her best with the Russo family, but from the beginning she had known Alba and her husband, Roberto, didn't think she was good enough for their eldest son. They had let him marry her only because they couldn't deny their son the girl he loved.

If it hadn't been for Marcello's brothers, family life would have been unbearable. Agostino and Gennaro were sweet to her, and even Stefano, when his wife was not around, could be kind. But it was the youngest brother, Fabrizio, who was the most attentive. Often he would come and sit in the linen shop and talk to her as she waited for customers. Dark and beautiful, he looked exactly like Marcello had at his age. Raffaella liked it when he confided his hopes and fears to her. She felt like the older sister he didn't have.

Once, Fabrizio had tried to take her hand, and another time he'd followed her into the small back room where they stacked the overflow of linen, and she had suspected he wanted to kiss her. But he was young and confused, she reasoned, and she had put those incidents out of her mind almost as soon as they'd happened.

She missed Fabrizio. It had been months since he had spoken to her and she wondered why. Sometimes she caught a glimpse of him crossing the piazza, heading towards the bar on the corner. He never found time to stop at the bakery for a word or two with her. Never even glanced her way.

'You must have done something wrong,' Silvana repeated at the end of the day as she wiped down the shelves and counter, while Raffaella mopped the floor. 'Why else would that family hate you?'

Raffaella squeezed out the mop in the bucket forcefully. 'My conscience is clear,' she said. 'I haven't done anything I need to be ashamed of.' But she couldn't quite look at Silvana as she said the words. And she was glad when it was time to hang her apron on the hook beside the oven, wrap herself in her thick, black shawl and step out into the cold wind and lashing rain on the steep path home to Little Triento.

Her mother's kitchen was cosy. The shutters were closed against the sea winds, and the wood-burner had been lit. But the chill had eaten into Raffaella's bones on the way down the hill and she felt like she might never be warm again.

'I can't wait until spring. This winter is going on for ever,' she groaned.

Her father, Tommaso, and brother, Sergio, were playing cards at the kitchen table, while her mother, Anna, hung over the stove, stirring sauces and searing meat in hot fat. For Raffaella, whose nostrils were filled with the sweet scent of baking all day, the savoury smell of scalding flesh was mouth-watering.

'I'm starving, what's for dinner?' She began lifting lids and tasting a spoonful of this and that until her mother flicked her away with a tea towel.

'Go and help your sister with her homework. Go!'

Teresa had her schoolbooks spread out over the table and was doodling idly in the margins of a page. Raffaella sat close to her and looked over her shoulder.

'What are you supposed to be studying?' she asked.

Teresa looked up at her and gave a tiny shake of her head. 'Oh, nothing,' she said quickly.

'Go on, what? Tell me.'

Teresa sighed. 'We're studying great statues of the world,' she said heavily, 'like the Statue of Liberty in New York and the one of Christ the Redeemer on Corcovado Mountain in Rio de Janeiro. I'm meant to be doing a project on them.'

Tommaso and Sergio looked up from their card game.

'I didn't choose that project,' Teresa said defensively. 'The teacher said I had to do it.'

Tommaso threw his cards down on the table and slammed his fist on top of them.

'I wanted to do my project on cats, but they wouldn't let me,' Teresa said in a small voice. 'I had to do it on the statues.'

Sergio shook his head. 'It's starting,' he said.

'Don't be ridiculous.' Anna turned from her post by the cooker. 'Nothing is starting. It's only a school project, that's all.'

Tommaso reached for his daughter's schoolbook. 'Sergio is right. It's starting. They're brainwashing our children into thinking about nothing but statues all day. Soon it will be spring and the americano will be back. There'll be engineers, builders and who knows who else crawling all over the mountaintop.'

Sergio stared at him. 'What are you going to do about it?'

'What can I do? I've thought about this all winter. The truth is, I'm powerless.'

Wooden spoon poised mid-air, Anna watched her husband. She saw he was simmering like one of her sauces.

'All I can do is put out to sea, catch fish and mind my own damn business while that statue grows on the mountain,' Tommaso complained. 'Like it or not, every day when we round the harbour wall and sail out past the point, we'll see it up there – a blot on the landscape, eh, Sergio?'

'Maybe . . . maybe not, Papà.'

'What do you mean?'

'There are other people besides you in this town. Maybe one of them will do something about it.'

'Like what?'

'I'm not sure. All I know is spring may bring a few surprises for Triento.'

Raffaella felt a growing sense of excitement. Spring had always been the time of year she loved most. She looked forward to everything about it: picking the wildflowers from the roadside; shopping at the market for delicate fronds of asparagus, fat pouches of fava beans and tender baby artichokes; seeing the sun come out from its winter home behind the mountain to warm the cobbles of Triento's damp streets.

This coming spring held more promise than most. As the days grew longer and warmer, they were drawing Raffaella closer to the moment of the americano's return to Villa Rosa. She was eager to see him, but nervous too. She wondered if his winter had been as long and lonely as hers had.

'Spring is nearly here, isn't it?' she said quietly.

Her father was staring at the photographs of statues in Teresa's schoolbook. He poured himself a glass of red wine and drank it down in two or three gulps.

'Yes, it is,' he said solemnly, rubbing at his tired eyes. 'And as your brother says, it's likely to bring some surprises.'

25

Carlotta always knew spring had settled in when the pomegranate trees flowered. At first, with their red petals tightly clasped, the flowers looked like fat red chilli peppers, but then they opened into bright trumpets with jaunty yellow stamens. Carlotta never picked them, for they wouldn't last long in water, but she liked to sit under the old pomegranate tree in the centre of the courtyard and gaze up at the red flowers tangled in its branches.

This year, just as her father had predicted, the old tree stubbornly refused to bud and flower. Carlotta found some fertiliser and dressed the soil liberally, but its branches remained bare. Down on the lower terraces, the trees were a riot of blossom and colour. But it was this tree Carlotta cared about.

'Face it, the tree is dead,' Umberto said as he filled a basket with the fava beans he was picking. 'That last winter killed it off. It almost finished me off too.'

'Please give it one more chance. Maybe it's been a little slow to realise it's spring at last, but I'm sure it will come to life soon. Don't give up on it yet.'

'Carlotta, I'm getting my axe tomorrow and I'm chopping it down. The americano will be back any day and I want a strong, young sapling in its place by the time he gets here.'

'Just give it until the end of next week,' Carlotta begged. 'I promised Raffaella I wouldn't let you take it down until we were sure it was dead.'

Umberto sighed. 'But I am sure,' he insisted. 'I couldn't be any surer.'

Carlotta climbed over the low wall that surrounded the tree and wrapped her arms round its crooked old trunk. Although she tried to hold her face away from him, Umberto could see tears in her eyes.

He gave a hiss of guilt and impatience. 'All right, the end of the week,' he agreed. 'But if it's still not showing signs of life by then, it's coming down.'

Spring found Raffaella early one morning as she was pulling the last of the loaves out of the oven. The shop was stifling and she could barely breathe. She felt the sweat trickling from her scalp, dripping down her forehead and stinging her eyes.

'My God, Silvana, it's so hot in here,' she complained.

'Open up the windows and the door,' Silvana replied. 'Let some fresh air in here or we'll both faint.'

Raffaella opened the door and then helped Silvana to pull Alberto's old wooden bench from the back of the shop to the front wall outside. Together, they collapsed on it, fanning at their hot, red faces with their hands and breathing in the cool air gratefully.

'You know,' Silvana said, 'it used to drive me mad the way Alberto would come and sit out here the minute the baking was finished. But now I think I understand. If we get as hot as this now working near the oven, what will we be like in summer?'

Raffaella said nothing. By summer she would be in the kitchen of Villa Rosa with the windows open and the sea breeze blowing in to cool her as she cooked Eduardo's dinner.

'Ouf.' Silvana fanned herself with her hands again. 'I have to make the bread delivery to the Gypsy Tearoom and look at me. I'll go and splash cold water on my face. I can't be seen over there in this state.'

Raffaella stayed outside, sitting on the bench exactly where Alberto once sat, watching the world pass by. The market vendors were setting up their stalls in the piazza, arranging their goods, their cheeses, salami and vegetables, and calling their morning greetings to one another.

'Oh, Vincenzo! You think you're going to sell those onions to anyone? They are so old they are fit for nothing but compost, my friend.'

'Oh, Gino! Your cheese smells like my old man's farts. And I bet it doesn't taste much better.'

Raffaella smiled. Already people were wearing less. Their coats and scarves had been stripped away. And although the air outside was still cool, she could tilt her face to the sun and feel it touch her skin. Spring was here.

Silvana appeared with her basket of bread and walked briskly over the piazza towards the Gypsy Tearoom. 'I won't be long,' she called back over her shoulder, and Raffaella nodded at her and smiled again.

Padre Pietro hurried past, still tucked away in layers of wool, at his age feeling the cold. And then she saw Fabrizio Russo, dressed in dark clothes, snaking between the market stalls, his head down and his expression tense.

'Fabrizio,' she called loudly. 'Hey, Fabrizio. Come here a minute. Over here.'

He came, but not too close. Standing with his body angled away from her, he nodded politely. '*Buongiorno*, Raffaella. How are you?'

'I'm fine. But you know, I've missed you. I haven't seen you all winter. Where have you been?'

He shrugged. 'I've been around.'

'Why do you never come and talk to me any more?'

He looked at her and she wondered how he managed to look so angry and so sad at the same time. 'Things have changed, Raffaella, haven't they?'

'Marcello is gone. Is that what you mean?' she challenged him.

'No, it isn't. But I think you understand. You know exactly what I mean.'

'I don't, I don't.' She was angry now. 'Why don't you explain? What have I done that's so terrible and so wrong that none of the Russo family will talk to me?'

He looked away from her and stared pointedly towards the alleyway that led to the Gypsy Tearoom. 'You should have respected my brother's memory,' he said quietly. 'I don't know what's going on between you and Ciro Ricci. I don't want to know. But it was too soon, Raffaella. I understand that you're young and beautiful, but still you should have waited.'

He turned on his heel and walked away from her quickly.

'Fabrizio, wait,' she called. 'You've got it wrong. Please let me explain . . . '

But he didn't bother to glance back.

The day felt colder suddenly and Raffaella pulled her shawl around her. Just as she was about to go inside, she caught sight of a movement on the other side of the piazza. It was Silvana, black skirt flying and her basket still full of bread, running towards her.

'Guess what? Guess what?' she began calling as she raced towards her. 'Someone threw a brick through the window of the Gypsy Tearoom.'

'What?'

'It's true.' Silvana was breathless. 'I was standing there just about to give the bread to Signor Ricci when a brick came crashing through the window, shattering glass everywhere. It made a terrible noise and an even worse mess. I got the fright of my life, I tell you. My heart is still hammering away in my chest.'

'Who threw it. Did Ciro catch them?'

'No, the culprit ran away. It was a man, that's all I know. I didn't see his face. None of us did. All I can say for sure is that he was wearing dark clothing.'

Raffaella thought of Fabrizio, all dressed in black, weaving through the market stalls with his head held low. 'Is Ciro all right?' she asked.

'Poor Signor Ricci, he seemed very shocked.' Silvana sank down on the bench and lowered her voice to a whisper. 'There's more . . . I saw a note wrapped round the brick.'

'What did it say?'

'I don't know, Signor Ricci didn't show it to me, but he looked a bit pale after he'd read it. Things might be bad for him, you know. He must have offended the wrong person.'

Silvana didn't have to say any more. Raffaella, like everyone who had grown up in Triento, knew about the families who really ran the town. Their names were rarely mentioned, but the 'Ndrangheta touched all their lives. So long as they got what they wanted, there was no need to worry about them too much. For Silvana, that meant having an envelope of cash ready once a week to hand to a man who came calling at the bakery. She and Alberto had paid the protection money for years. To them, it was just another tax. But once in a while someone in town would chafe against the system and refuse to make the payment. That's when the 'Ndrangheta would show exactly why they were the most feared people in the whole of southern Italy.

'I hope Signor Ricci hasn't done anything stupid,' murmured Silvana. 'Some people are so easily upset.'

Raffaella shivered. She felt cold inside as well as out. What if she were somehow responsible for putting Ciro in danger? The Russo family were powerful and they knew the right people. She remembered the expression on Fabrizio's face as he'd stopped reluctantly to talk to her, and she wished she knew what was written on the note that someone had been angry enough to wrap round a brick and fling through the window of the Gypsy Tearoom.

The mayor was running very late. He'd stopped to help Ciro Ricci board up the broken window of the Gypsy Tearoom. Poor Ciro was shaking so much he could barely hold his hammer, so Giorgio had done it for him and now he was running behind schedule.

Frowning, he glanced at his watch as he hurried through the piazza. His whole day had been thrown by this act of vandalism. And now there was another hold-up. There was a priest in his path – Padre Pietro was lingering around the market stalls looking at him expectantly.

'Is it true?' the priest asked, and Giorgio nodded his head.

'Was it them?' The old priest's voice was always soft, but now he no more than breathed the words.

'Perhaps,' Giorgio replied grimly. 'Although he swears there's no reason for it.'

'It's been so peaceful here for so long, please God don't tell me it's going to change.'

'It's only a broken window,' Giorgio reassured him. 'No one's been hurt.'

'There was a note too, I hear. What did it say?'

Giorgio sighed. 'Yes, there was a note. It said, "You'll be sorry."'

'It's a bad sign,' Padre Pietro said anxiously. 'Next week is the *festa*. You don't think they'd cause trouble at that?'

Giorgio patted the old priest on the shoulder. 'Don't worry so much, Padre. The *festa* will be wonderful, just as it always is,' he soothed. But later, as he sat behind his shining wooden desk in the town hall, the mayor of Triento couldn't suppress a strong sense of disquiet. It had given him a shock when that brick came crashing through the window of the Gypsy Tearoom. He couldn't help wondering what else might be in store.

Carlotta found the axe herself and put it in her father's hands. For more than a week she had waited and hoped, but the old pomegranate tree still stood bare-limbed. She'd begun to dread the sight of it, stooping and useless, taking centre stage in the otherwise flourishing courtyard of Villa Rosa.

'Chop it down today. Get it over and done with,' she urged Umberto.

He took the axe from her hands. 'Well, if you're sure . . . ' he said hesitantly.

'It's dead, isn't it?'

'Yes, it's dead. And it's only a tree, *cara*. I'll plant another in its place.'

He swung his axe and Carlotta clenched her fists as it sliced into the old wood with a dull thud. Umberto pulled it out and went to swing again. Then he saw the tears flooding down his daughter's face and let the axe fall harmlessly by his side.

'Please don't cry,' he begged.

'I'm sorry, I can't help it.' Carlotta rubbed her wet cheeks. 'It's always been there, that's the trouble. I'll miss it when it's gone.'

Umberto held the axe in slack hands. He couldn't take another swing at the tree while Carlotta was watching and crying. Staring at the wound he'd already made in its gnarled old trunk, he tried to think what to say to comfort her.

'It's only a tree,' he repeated helplessly. 'But I can't bear to chop it down if it's going to make you so unhappy.'

Carlotta began to cry again. Holding her handkerchief to her cheek, she rushed past him, her pale face a blur. Umberto didn't have to turn and watch to know where she was heading. She was taking the path down to the sea and she might stay there for hours.

Swinging his axe, Umberto slashed into the tree again. It wouldn't take much effort to chop it down. Afterwards he'd have to dig out the stump and ready the soil for the sapling that would take its place. He wondered if he dared ask Carlotta to help him plant it.

Umberto had seen his daughter upset like this before. Usually, it meant days of silence as she retreated into her own thoughts. The more he tried to draw her out, the more entrenched in quietness she would become. He dreaded the loneliness of it, but he had learned from long experience that the best thing he could do was give Carlotta time to work herself free of the melancholy.

At least there was the *festa* coming up. He would try his best to encourage her to go. Perhaps the noise and the gaiety on Triento's streets would help distract her from her deep sadness.

'It's only a tree,' he muttered to himself again as he took a last swing at the trunk and watched the old pomegranate topple to the ground.

26

Spring was Raffaella's favourite part of the year, and the *festa* was the best time of all. She loved how life was lived on the streets again. After huddling indoors round their wood fires all winter, the people of Triento came out to gather in groups in the piazza, drink espresso together and swap stories. The sense of anticipation at *festa* time was better than Christmas. For weeks before it began, Raffaella could sense the excitement building.

As a child she had loved the first day of the *festa* most of all. She and the other village children always dressed all in white. The girls would weave wildflowers in their hair, and the boys had bugles to blow. They'd form a procession behind the big gold statue of Triento's patron saint, San Bonifacio, as the priests carried it from its permanent place on the altar of Santa Trinita to the humble church of Santo Spirito.

During the seven days of Triento's *festa* the statue was taken in turn to each of the village's churches. Mass was said and candles lit for the dead. There was always plenty of singing and rousing sermons, and on the final night Triento threw a party.

It was more or less the same every year. The villagers crowded the streets, where stalls sold treats like roasted pig cheeks with a squeeze of fresh lemon juice, or shards of fresh coconut and slabs of flavoured *torrone*. A brass band played in the piazza, and fairy lights were strung from the buildings and lamp posts. Usually, there was a travelling funfair, and the screams of the people enjoying the thrill of the rides echoed through the village. At midnight the sky lit up with a firework display. Raffaella loved seeing the expressions of joy on the upturned faces around her as they watched the explosions of silver and gold.

This year she had watched most of the *festa* from the doorway of the bakery. She glimpsed the statue of San Bonifacio being paraded through the streets and watched from afar as the gypsies set up their street stalls. It was never long before she was called back behind the counter to serve another customer. Raffaella felt as though there was a wonderful party going on and she hadn't been invited.

'I'm going to close the bakery early on the last day of *festa*,' Silvana announced suddenly one afternoon.

'Are you sure?' Raffaella sounded eager.

'Yes, why not? Who's here to stop us? We can do what we like.'

Raffaella couldn't help hugging herself and hopping from foot to foot like an excited child. 'I can go and look at all the stalls and see the procession when they take San Bonifacio back to Santa Trinita,' she babbled. 'And I can see the brass band and watch the fireworks.'

Silvana smiled at her. 'That's right.'

All the same, they both felt guilty clearing the shelves of bread and hanging up the closed sign on the door of the bakery on the final day of *festa*.

'Are you sure about this?' Raffaella asked. 'You've never closed at *festa* time before. You may miss out on business.'

Silvana looked out across the piazza. The mayor was overseeing the decoration of a bandstand near the fountain, and villagers were milling through the streets, buying treats for their children from the stalls and stopping to greet friends and neighbours.

'I've watched the *festa* from this shop for the whole of my married life,' she replied wistfully.

They heard the bugles blowing to signal that San Bonifacio was on the move again. 'Quickly, off you go or you'll miss seeing the procession,' Silvana urged. 'Don't worry, I'll finish up here.'

Raffaella tore off her apron and threw it towards the hook on the wall. 'OK, I'll see you later,' she called as she hurried out of the shop and headed towards the sound of bugles.

There was a crowd outside the church and Raffaella glimpsed her sister, Teresa, in the middle of it. She was wearing a lacy white dress and had an untidy wreath of yellow spring flowers perched on her head.

As Raffaella drew closer, the boys began to blow harder on their bugles and the priests appeared, all dressed in white, carrying the heavy gold statue of San Bonifacio. They'd secured it to a wide wooden platform that was balanced awkwardly between them on their shoulders. At the front, young, strong Padre Matteo barely seemed to notice the burden, while, bringing up the rear, old Padre Pietro winced beneath the crushing weight.

Raffaella heard the sound of guitars being strummed, and falling in behind the statue, the village girls began to sing. Slowly, the procession wound its way up the steady incline towards the Church of Santa Trinita.

As the crowd moved forward, Raffaella glimpsed Carlotta on its fringes. Her face looked as pale as ever and her expression gloomy.

Raffaella pushed through the crush of people to Carlotta's side. 'Are you alone? Where is your father?' she asked, kissing her quickly on both cold cheeks.

'He dropped me off and then went back to Villa Rosa. Spring is the busiest time in the garden. Really, I should be there helping him, but he insisted I come to the *festa*.' Carlotta looked about her and frowned. 'I've been before and it's the same every year. What's the point?'

Raffaella grabbed her hand. 'Don't be like that. Let's go and eat an ice cream and then take a browse around the stalls. Come on, it'll be fun.'

Carlotta seemed reluctant, but Raffaella didn't give her a chance to refuse. Tugging her towards the corner bar where they served the best ice cream, she kept up a stream of chatter.

'I'm going to have pistachio and chocolate, a scoop of each. What do you want? You seem like a strawberry kind of person. Am I right?'

'I do quite like strawberry,' Carlotta agreed. 'But sometimes it can taste a little too sweet for me. I prefer the tartness of lemon.'

'So why not have both? It's *festa* day!'

They ate their ice creams at a table outside the bar, where they could watch people pass by. Most of the faces were familiar to Raffaella, she'd known them all her life. She waved her spoon at them in greeting when they glanced her way.

Then she saw Stefano Russo approaching, his wife, Angelica, on his arm. They'd spotted her too, she was sure of it, but they marched on, determinedly staring in the opposite direction. When they were well past, Angelica turned and gawked back over her shoulder.

'Isn't that your sister-in-law?' asked Carlotta, licking her spoon. 'Why is she staring at you like that?'

'Who knows? That entire family seems to have taken against me.'

Carlotta was curious. 'Why would they do that?'

Raffaella felt a rush of anger. 'They blamed me for Marcello's death and now they've decided I'm not behaving with enough propriety. I suppose they expected me to lock myself away for ever or be crying all the time. But I don't think I should have to behave like that to mourn my husband properly.'

There was a solemn expression on Carlotta's face. 'I know,' she agreed. 'Some people like to make a lot of noise about grieving, all that screaming and wailing that goes on at funerals. But often the saddest people are the quiet ones. Some are sad for years and years and hardly anyone guesses.'

Raffaella glanced at her sharply. She wondered if Carlotta was on the brink of confiding in her. 'Talking to someone you trust can help a little when you're sad,' she said in an encouraging way. 'That's what I've found, anyway. I always talk to my mother. What about you? Who do you confide in?'

Carlotta ran her spoon round the bottom of her ice-cream dish and frowned. 'My mother died when I was very small. I hardly remember her. It was my father who brought me up.'

'And so you talk to him?'

Carlotta screwed up her face again. 'Yes,' she said uncertainly.

'But there are probably things you can't tell him, aren't there?'

Carlotta stayed silent, so Raffaella pressed her again. 'You can always confide in me. If there are things that make you sad, things you'd like to talk about, you can trust me with them.'

Carlotta seemed like she wanted to speak but her feelings had been locked away inside her for so long she didn't know how to begin. 'I've missed you this winter,' she said at last. 'It will be good to have you back at Villa Rosa when the americano comes.'

'When will that be? Do you know when he's due to arrive?' Raffaella tried not to sound too eager.

'No, we still have no news.'

'But spring is almost over. And he told me he'd be back in time for spring.'

'I know.' Carlotta shrugged. 'But he must be still in Napoli, I guess. You're in no hurry, are you? Don't you have your job at the bakery for as long as you want it?'

Raffaella clinked her spoon on the side of her empty ice-cream dish. 'Yes, but I'd rather get back to Villa Rosa. It's months and months since I've been there. I've almost forgotten what it looks like.'

'Some things have changed,' Carlotta said hesitantly.

'What?'

'The old pomegranate tree has died.' Carlotta's voice wobbled. 'My father had to chop it down.'

'Oh, no.' Raffaella remembered the hours she'd spent sitting beneath the tree in the dark listening to the americano. 'The courtyard must look so bare now it's gone,' she said quietly.

'Yes, it does. But my father is planting a new tree. That's why he's stayed home today. It'll be done by the time I get home.'

They sat together in silence while the *festa* carried on around them. Raffaella's mood had deflated. It was only an old pomegranate tree, but somehow in her mind it was linked to everything good that had happened since Marcello's death. Now it had been chopped down and the americano had disappeared, perhaps for ever. She wondered bleakly what the future held for her.

It was Carlotta who heard the high-pitched screaming sounds coming from the far end of the village.

'Listen . . . the funfair must have opened,' she remarked. 'Shall we go and see?'

Raffaella tried to pick up the pieces of her mood. 'If you like,' she said without much enthusiasm. 'But you were right, it'll be the same as it is every year.'

They weaved through the knots of people who were clogging the streets, smiling and laughing, their children clutching balloons and sweet treats and talking in high-pitched voices. Raffaella saw Francesca Pasquale, Triento's traffic officer, blowing hard on her whistle as a car tried to push its way through the crowds. She spotted Patrizia Sesto filling her basket with chocolate-covered *torrone* at a gypsy's stall. And she noticed her brother, Sergio, a tall glass of beer in his hand, joking with a group of friends.

The brass band had arrived and the mayor was shaking hands with them and making them welcome. Silvana wasn't far away. Raffaella saw her on the fringes of a group of chattering women.

They pushed onwards. The sounds of screaming grew louder, and the coloured lights of the fairground glowed. Raffaella felt her excitement flare just as it had when she was a child. She had adored being whirled and spun round on the funfair rides. But now she was a widow, still dressed in mourning, and her proper place was on the ground, standing and watching, while other people rode the rides squealing in delight.

The evening grew cold once the sun had gone down, and there wasn't much enjoyment to be had watching others have a good time. 'Let's go back and listen to the band in the piazza,' Raffaella suggested.

Taking Carlotta's hand so they wouldn't get separated in the crowd, she left the fairground and they began to retrace their steps back towards the piazza. Suddenly Raffaella heard the sound of screaming ahead of her as well as behind. 'Can you hear that? What's going on?' Raffaella asked, and quickened her pace.

As they rounded the corner, they saw that the night sky was glowing orange. 'What on earth—' Raffaella broke off as a stampede of people came rushing towards them. Quickly, she pulled Carlotta into the safety of a doorway. 'What's happening? What's happening?' she cried as the frightened faces flashed past.

'Fire, fire,' panicked voices yelled in reply.

'Where? What's on fire?'

Raffaella felt Carlotta trembling and hugged her tight. 'Stay here. Don't panic. I'm going to find out what's going on, OK?'

'Don't go, it might be dangerous . . . '

It was too late. Raffaella had slipped out of the doorway, and hugging the line of the buildings, she fought her way up through the stream of people. She could smell the fire in the air now and feel smoke tickling her throat, but she kept moving forwards.

'Run, fire, fire,' people screamed hysterically, but she ignored them.

As she reached the piazza, she saw the mayor was up on the bandstand shouting through a megaphone. 'Stay calm everyone, stay calm,' he cried ineffectually. 'The fire engine is on its way. There's no need to panic.'

Silvana was the only one obeying him. Standing beneath the bandstand, she cut a lonely figure. But there was no way Raffaella could push her way across the piazza to reach her. She would be crushed in the attempt.

The night air no longer felt so chill and Raffaella knew she must be very near the fire now. She saw Ciro Ricci rushing past her, clutching two buckets brimming with water.

'Ciro, stop,' she called after him, and he paused for a moment.

'The Gypsy Tearoom is burning,' he said grimly. 'It's burning like wildfire. If someone doesn't do something, half the town will be alight.'

'Stop.' She caught his sleeve and held him tight. 'Stay here. You're not going to put out a fire with those. Put the buckets down and come with me.'

'Let me go, Raffaella,' he pleaded and he seemed near to tears. 'I have to save the building. It's all I have.'

Raffaella felt something brush against her legs and realised it was the old yellow dog, trembling with fear, trying to creep beneath her skirts and escape the noise and the smell of fire.

'Don't be crazy. Even this old dog knows it's time to get out of here. Come with me, Ciro, please.' She tugged at his sleeve. 'Come on.'

Reluctantly, he put down his buckets and let her lead him back towards the doorway where she'd left Carlotta. She was relieved to find her still there, tears streaking her cheeks, too afraid to move.

'Let's see if we can climb the hill and get a decent view of what's going on,' Ciro said heavily.

'All right, but be careful. People are acting like lunatics.'

It was difficult to see much in the dark with the black smoke billowing up from the Gypsy Tearoom, but they heard the fire engine arrive and saw how gradually the orange glow died down and the smoke became more like steam. The three of them stood close together for warmth and didn't say much. The old yellow dog was at their feet, his nose pressed against the back of Ciro's leg.

'Dear God, I hope no one was hurt,' Ciro said at last.

'How did it happen?' Raffaella asked him gently.

'I'm not really sure. I was baking pizza and the place was filling up. There were lots of people outside waiting for tables. Suddenly someone started screaming, "Fire, fire," and it was chaos. Everyone was running, pushing and panicking. I think they all got out, but I'm not completely sure.'

Raffaella was confused. 'So it wasn't the pizza oven that caused the fire?'

'No, definitely not, I was working right next to it and everything was fine.'

Carlotta seemed dazed. She dropped down and buried her face in the yellow dog's stiff, dirty fur.

'If it wasn't the oven, what then?' Raffaella asked him. 'Perhaps someone set the fire deliberately.'

Ciro looked grim. 'You heard about the brick that was thrown through the window the other day? Perhaps the same person was responsible for this.'

'But who?' Raffaella remembered Fabrizio's strange behaviour and felt uneasy. 'And why?'

Ciro shrugged. 'I can't be sure. But there are things going on in this village that I'd have been better off not knowing about. And there are people who are angry with me.'

'Who?' Raffaella asked again, but he held a finger over his lips.

'Trust me, you don't want to know. Now I'm going back down the hill to see if there is anything I can do. You two should go home. It's been a terrible night. Get home quickly and be safe.'

27

Silvana found it difficult to think of anyone but herself as she looked at the blackened, still smoking ruins of the Gypsy Tearoom. There would be no discreet morning coffees for her and the mayor now. No more secret meetings. She could still make out the corner where Ciro had set up a table and two chairs for them behind the screen. It had all been reduced to ash.

People had been gathering since early morning to gawk at the damage the fire had wreaked and whisper under their breath about who might have started it.

Miraculously, no one had been caught in the blaze or crushed to death in the stampede of panicked people.

'God must have been looking after us,' Padre Pietro said thankfully. 'This could so easily have been a disaster.'

'Well, it is a disaster for Signor Ricci,' pointed out Silvana. 'What will he do now? How will he make a living?'

She could see Ciro talking with the mayor and Padre Matteo. He had been the first to arrive on the scene to check what could be salvaged from the blaze. There was very little left, as far as Silvana could make out. The stone pizza oven was still standing, although blackened beyond belief, there were holes in the walls instead of windows, and all the beautiful old ceramic tiles were cracked and ruined.

'He will rebuild. That's his only choice,' said Padre Pietro. 'The town will have to help him.'

'It will be a big job, though, won't it? It will take ages.' Silvana lowered her voice. 'Maybe what people are saying is true, Padre.'

'What's that?'

'The town is cursed. And it's all because of our plans for the statue. First Marcello Russo was taken, then my husband, and now Signor

Ricci's livelihood has been destroyed. We're being punished for our vanity. Either God is angry or the Devil is laughing at us.'

Padre Pietro looked as though he wasn't sure how to answer her. He was an old man and tired. There had been many days when he had cursed himself for sharing his dreams of glorying God by building on the mountain.

'The plans for the statue are too grandiose,' he conceded. 'Perhaps we should have been content with things the way they were. But it's too late to stop it now.'

'What if there's more misfortune in store?' Silvana glanced over at the mayor and thought how much she would miss talking to him every day. 'Must other people suffer?'

Padre Pietro sighed. He had no easy answers for Silvana. 'Let us pray that they won't,' he said shortly.

He was saved from the difficulties of the conversation by Anna Moretti's arrival. Her cheeks were flushed and she was still breathless from her fast walk up the hill.

'Mother of God, poor Ciro, who would do this to him?' she said as her eyes fell on what was left of the Gypsy Tearoom. 'Does anyone have any idea?'

'No,' Silvana replied, 'it's a complete mystery.'

They stood together for a while as people came and went. It seemed right to offer some words of condolence to Ciro, but nothing they could think of was adequate. They were still staring and silent when Tommaso Moretti appeared.

'What's the plan, then?' he called over to Ciro. 'What are you going to do?'

Ciro shrugged. 'What can I do? Try and find the money to rebuild it, I suppose.'

'I'm with you. When I'm not out at sea, I'll be here helping you build. And my son, Sergio, too.'

'Thank you, Tommaso, but you don't have to do that.' Ciro seemed astonished.

'I want to do it.'

The mayor spoke up. 'And me too. It's been a while since I've done any hard physical work, but I can be useful. If enough of us volunteer to help, we can rebuild the place without too much expense, I'm certain of it.'

Silvana raised her voice in excitement. 'I can't build, but I can bake. I'll feed anyone who volunteers.'

'I'll help her,' added Anna.

Ciro was nearly speechless with gratitude. 'Thank you, thank you,' was all he could say.

'To be honest with you, Ricci, I'm not doing this for you.' Tommaso strode to the front of the crowd and stood facing them. He didn't raise his voice, but he didn't need to, for everyone was already listening to him intently.

'Whoever did this thing needs to know the people of Triento aren't going to stand for it,' Tommaso announced. 'We have to show a united front. If an American can build a statue on that mountain, then we can rebuild the Gypsy Tearoom. So if you have anything to offer – materials, your time, your expertise – then come and speak to me as soon as you can.'

There was muttering among the people gathered round him. Some weren't so keen to be generous with their time. Padre Pietro realised it was up to him to turn the mood. He gathered his energy and tried to sound more confident than he felt.

'God's blessings go with anyone who gives their help to this project. You will be rewarded for your generosity. All you give, you will get back and more.'

He had captured their attention.

'There has been talk that Triento is cursed,' he continued in a stronger voice. 'That the Devil is laughing at us. But let me remind you that the Devil will find no purchase in a place where people's souls are pure and good. So let us pray together and then let us work together.'

Silvana lowered her head and clasped her hands. She prayed fervently and hoped God was listening. Her happiest moments had been spent in this blackened shell of a building. Raising her head again, she caught the mayor's eye and he gave her a long look. He was praying hard too, she was sure of it. Neither of them was ready to give up on their happiness. They'd waited such a long time for it. Now they would wait again.

28

Raffaella hung on for word that it was time for her to return to Villa Rosa, but still it didn't come. She was beyond impatient now. If her job at the bakery hadn't been so busy, then the waiting might have driven her crazy.

Things had been busy since the rebuilding work had started on the Gypsy Tearoom. Early each morning she and her mother helped Silvana bake huge wheels of flat bread filled with meat, cheese and roasted vegetables, and carried them over to the workers in baskets at lunchtime.

'It's important to keep their strength up,' Silvana declared as they packed the baskets full of food. 'The more we feed them, the faster they'll build.'

Raffaella's father was often there. He'd made a hat out of an old sheet of newspaper and wore it perched on his head at a jaunty angle. His hands grew rough and his face dusty, but he whistled as he worked. No one had ever seen him so happy.

Her brother, Sergio, was a different matter. He had refused point blank to help rebuild the Gypsy Tearoom, and there had been the loudest row that Raffaella had ever heard in their little house on the rock.

In the end, Sergio had relented, but he only showed up sporadically and never seemed to do much work. 'His clothes are certainly no more difficult to clean,' Anna remarked sharply. 'I don't know what's wrong with the boy. He can't be making any effort. Your father always comes back filthy and exhausted.'

Raffaella had never seen the Russo brothers among the workers. Eventually, Ciro told her they'd sent a message saying they were too busy running their business and couldn't spare the time, but inevitably their absence raised suspicions.

'Are they too grand to help?' Angelo Sesto asked bitterly.

'Padre Simone and Padre Matteo haven't been so proud they can't roll up their sleeves and work beside us,' Tommaso pointed out. 'No, I think something else must be going on with those Russo boys. My son-in-law, Marcello, was the only good one among them.'

Raffaella was amazed at how quickly they were making progress with the building. What had appeared in the beginning to be an impossible task now seemed achievable. Day by day Ciro was more cheerful. He worked the hardest of all. He was there from first light till dusk, and Raffaella saw how his arms were growing muscular and his shoulders seemed broader.

Each day, when she appeared with the lunch baskets, he always put down his tools and stopped to talk.

'He likes you, that boy,' her mother remarked one afternoon as they returned to the bakery.

'I know,' Raffaella said uncomfortably.

Anna fingered the black cotton of her daughter's skirt. 'You're in mourning now, I realise that, but you don't have to be for ever,' she said softly.

Raffaella took a sharp breath. 'It's much too early for me to think of other men,' she said.

Anna nodded. 'I know it is. All I'm saying is that you don't have to wear black and mourn Marcello for the rest of your life. You are young and you should be allowed to find happiness again when it's right and when you're ready.'

Silvana had been listening. 'What about me?' she chimed in. 'I'm old. Does that mean I don't deserve to be happy?'

Anna looked at her thoughtfully. She had known Silvana for a long time. They had been at school together and married within months of each other. She had watched as Silvana struggled through the years with Alberto and was glad not to be in her shoes. A fisherman's wife had a hard life. There were stormy days when Anna feared Tommaso's boat might not make it home to the harbour. But still there was never a time when she envied Silvana her baker.

'You deserve happiness too, of course you do,' she said gently.

Raffaella wanted to add her own words. But except for her quiet thank you, she and Silvana had never spoken of her secret meetings with the mayor and it would be wrong to mention them now.

'Alberto wouldn't have expected you to mourn him for ever, would he?' Raffaella asked instead.

'Oh, Alberto.' Silvana's voice was bitter. 'He never gave a thought to my happiness in the twenty-five years we were married, so why would he care what happened to me after he was dead?'

'But what if you fell in love with someone after your mourning period was well and truly over?' Raffaella said hesitantly. 'There would be no reason why you shouldn't marry again, would there?'

Anna glanced at her daughter. 'To be honest, there might be some eyebrows raised. People like to gossip. But you know, Silvana, you don't have any family left here in Triento. Your sons have moved away and you don't have the protection of a man. In some ways, it would make sense to marry once a decent period of time has elapsed. I'm sure people could be persuaded to see it that way eventually.'

'So it wouldn't be a scandal?' Silvana wondered.

'A little talk, perhaps, but not a scandal.' Anna shook the crumbs from the bottom of the lunch baskets and stacked them out of the way in a corner of the bakery. She wondered whom Silvana could have fallen in love with. She would be sure to ask her daughter later as they walked home down the hill together.

'Raffaella, Raffaella, come quick!' Carlotta was standing in the doorway, out of breath and her eyes wide with panic.

'What's wrong? What's happened?'

'The americano has come back and I wasn't ready for him. The house hasn't been prepared, and I have nothing to give him for dinner. You have to come and help me now.'

Raffaella was already untying her apron. 'OK, calm down, I'm coming. Let's hurry and buy some food and then get back to Villa Rosa as quickly as we can.'

Carlotta's eyes were wide and her pallor seemed worse than ever. 'We have to shop for extra food because the americano isn't alone,' she warned. 'He has people with him.'

Raffaella didn't waste time asking questions. Swinging a basket over her arm, she headed out to the market. She moved smartly between the stalls, buying only the freshest produce, reaching out to test it with quick, clever fingers. Her excitement at the thought of seeing the americano again was building. But it was tempered by a hint of apprehension. She remembered the awkwardness that had lain between them before he left and hoped it could be forgotten.

And she wondered who were the people he had brought home to Villa Rosa and what was their business here. Impatient to know, she finished her shopping and hurried to find out.

29

Raffaella noticed the girl first. She was sitting in the courtyard of Villa Rosa wearing a robe, her long, wet hair caught up in a turban she'd made from her towel. She was very pretty with tawny skin, high cheekbones and slanting eyes. And she was laughing.

'We must be crazy people swimming at this time of year.' Her laughter tinkled again. 'We'll catch our deaths, it's true. Mamma is right.'

'Don't say I didn't warn you.' The woman sitting beside her looked like her mirror image, only older and rounder. She was dressed in a cream woollen trouser suit, and her eyes were hidden by dark sunglasses. She shivered a little. 'July and August are the only months to swim at Villa Rosa. That's when the sea is at its warmest.'

'But it's beautiful today, I promise you.' The americano, wearing only swimming shorts, was towelling his bare chest dry. 'I may go in for another dip later. Are you sure I won't be able to tempt you to join me?'

They laughed and shook their heads, and the girl in the turban lit a cigarette. Eduardo seemed enchanted. He ignored the interruption as Umberto's rattling old car pulled up, and didn't bother to glance over as Raffaella and Carlotta scrambled out, weighed down by their baskets and clutching parcels of food.

'Oh, good – we're not going to starve.' The pretty girl in the turban took a long drag on her cigarette. 'Here comes your housekeeper, Eduardo, see.'

Eduardo looked up and smiled at Raffaella. She wished she could climb back into the car and hide. Since well before first light she'd been working, baking bread in the hot oven and serving customers. There had been no time to run a brush over her straggly hair, and she was aware her face was shiny and her clothes were sticking to her clammy skin.

The turbaned girl flicked spent ash from her cigarette on to the ground and examined her manicured fingernails. 'Perhaps you could bring us some olives and drinks?' she asked Raffaella without looking at her. She hadn't even acknowledged Carlotta and Umberto. It was like they were invisible.

Raffaella mustered her dignity. 'Signor Pagano, welcome back to Villa Rosa,' she said formally.

'It's good to be back,' Eduardo replied. 'We have visitors, as you see. Allow me to introduce you to Olivia Barbieri and her daughter, Claudia. This is Raffaella, the best cook in the whole of southern Italy.'

The older woman tilted her head at her and then looked away, disinterested. The younger one held her stare and Raffaella thought she saw a challenge in her eyes.

'Well, I'll go and get those drinks and olives.' Raffaella glanced at the americano. He smiled at her again, then waved her away with his hand.

'Yes, yes, drinks and olives, that would be marvellous, thank you, Raffaella.'

The kitchen of Villa Rosa looked the same. Everything was where she had left it, neatly stacked away. Jars of pomegranate syrup lined the shelves of the pantry. Someone had made colourful labels for them, with Raffaella's name scrawled on.

'It looks like you've been busy,' she remarked.

But Carlotta wasn't listening. She'd made no move to find the olives or a dish to serve them on. Instead, she was staring out of the window and scowling.

'Do you know them?' Raffaella asked.

'Oh, yes. Their family owns this house. They used to spend every summer here. I don't know what they're doing back here now, though.'

'You don't like them much, do you?'

'They've never given me much reason to like them.'

Raffaella was surprised. Carlotta was such a gentle person and she never had a bad word to say about anyone. She wondered what the Barbieri women had done to make her hate them.

Draining some green olives of brine, she tipped them into a bowl. 'How long has it been since you've seen them?' she asked.

'Five years.'

'So what's the rest of the family like?'

'Signor Barbieri is rich. He used to love throwing big parties here and having lots of people around. There was a son too—' Carlotta broke off.

'What was he like?' Raffaella pressed her.

'Different than the rest of them. I don't think he enjoyed all the loud parties much.'

Raffaella made a half-hearted attempt to straighten her skirt and smooth down her tangled hair. Picking up the drinks tray, she turned to Carlotta and asked, 'How long do you think they're staying for?'

Carlotta frowned. 'I wish I knew.'

The glasses clinked together on the tray as Raffaella carried it to the door. 'I expect we'll find out soon enough,' she said. 'For now I suppose I'd better deliver this to them and then make a start on the dinner they're expecting.'

Raffaella unscrewed the lid from a jar of pomegranate syrup and sniffed at its contents. Dipping the tip of her little finger into the rich, dark-red syrup, she licked it tentatively.

'Is it still OK? What does it taste like?' Carlotta looked anxious.

'It's good. Not too bitter and not too sweet.' She tried a little more. 'Like a sharper, fruitier molasses.'

'What are you going to make with it?'

'I'm not certain yet.' Raffaella had spent the dark winter evenings copying down recipes from her mother's book, but she had been in such a rush to get to Villa Rosa there hadn't been time to run home and fetch them. She would have to cook something from memory.

Whatever she made, the food would be drenched in pomegranate syrup. She wanted the flavour of it to sing in Eduardo's mouth. With every bite he tasted, he would be reminded of the nights they'd spent together talking beneath the old tree.

Raffaella wanted to steep him in pomegranate juice like the Neopolitans steep white peaches in red wine. She made chicken with a sauce of pomegranate and walnuts. She added the syrup to the salad dressing and poured it into a dish of fava beans and red onions. She put a drop or two in the prosecco they sipped on the terrace before dinner and added it to the sliced fruit and berries she would serve to them afterwards.

Eduardo was keen to eat outside with a view of the mountaintop his statue would soon dominate.

'But it's too cold,' complained Olivia. 'Let's ask the gardener to light the fire in the dining room for us. And we'll get your housekeeper to set the table and put candles on it. It will be so cosy, just the three of us.'

'Oh, no, let's stay out here,' Claudia begged. 'We can always get them to bring us rugs and shawls if we need them.'

'The heat has gone out of the day and it will only grow colder as it gets dark. We're going inside,' her mother insisted.

Raffaella was glad she wouldn't have to watch them eating. She sent Carlotta through to the dining room to serve their dinner. Dish after dish was saturated with pomegranate juice. It all looked delicious. But the plates came back with most of the food still on them, cold and congealed. It seemed like they were only picking at their meals.

'What's wrong?' she hissed at Carlotta. 'Don't they like it?'

'The signora never eats much. She's too concerned about her figure. And Claudia is too busy trying to impress the americano to have an appetite.'

'What about him? What's he doing?'

'He likes the attention, I expect. He's not eating a lot either. But don't throw the food away.' Carlotta had noticed her staring at the almost full dishes disconsolately. 'My father and I will enjoy it even if they haven't.'

'Maybe it's too rich. I must have used too much pomegranate syrup and unbalanced the flavours. Tomorrow, first thing, I'll have to go home and get my recipes.'

'The food is good,' Carlotta insisted. 'They're just too caught up in themselves to notice it.'

Grimacing, Raffaella picked up a dish, and before Carlotta could stop her, she scraped its contents into the bin.

It had been a long day and Raffaella was so tired that her limbs were heavy and her bones seemed to ache, but still she couldn't sleep. She wondered if the americano would follow his old tradition of smoking a night-time cigar beneath the pomegranate tree in the courtyard.

Neither of the Barbieri women would keep him company on such a chilly night. He'd be alone if he were there at all. This was her chance to snatch a few words with him.

Slipping out of Umberto's little house unnoticed was no problem. She had grown used to moving quietly through the darkness. The moon was half covered in cloud, and there were plenty of shadows to hide in.

It was only a short walk up the steps and through the gateway to the courtyard of Villa Rosa. Raffaella went slowly and soundlessly, straining her eyes for a glimpse of the orange pinprick of a lit cigar beside the young pomegranate tree. It was confusing, as everything looked so different now. The hunched old tree would have made a big dark shape for her eyes to find, but the sapling that had taken its place was willowy and slender. For a moment, Raffaella felt disorientated.

'Signore,' she dared to call, but only in a whisper. 'Are you there?'

There was no reply. She breathed in hard through her nose and thought she could detect the scent of a cigar making the night air all musky.

'Signore? It's me, Raffaella.'

She could make out a shape on the low wall that circled the tree, but when she grew closer, she saw it was only an old watering can Umberto had left there. There was no sign of the americano. She listened intently for noises coming from the house, but all was silent.

Perhaps they were still where Carlotta had left them, enjoying coffee, brandy and biscotti by the fireside. More likely, they were tired and had gone to bed.

Raffaella wasn't prepared to give up easily. There was a chance the americano had taken his cigar and walked down to the sea. He might be sitting on the rocks, smoking while he watched the moonlight playing over the waves.

Carefully, she felt her way down the stone steps using the boughs of the trees that lined the path to guide her. As she grew closer, she was certain she could hear something more than the sound of the waves lapping against the rocks, although she wasn't sure if it was a person or an animal snuffling about. When she rounded the last turn in the path, she saw the light of a storm lantern glimmering faintly. Her heart hammered. It could only be him.

She scrambled over the rocks towards the light, losing her footing more than once on the rough ground.

'Who is it? Who's there?' The frightened voice belonged to a woman, not a man.

'It's me, Raffaella. But who's that? Carlotta, is it you? What are you doing down here at this hour?' Disappointment made her brusque.

'I could ask the same of you.' Carlotta's voice sounded strange, husky and low.

'Hold that lantern up. Let me see your face. Are you crying? Carlotta, what's wrong? Please tell me.' Her anger turning to concern, Raffaella sat down on a smooth rock in the little pool of lamplight. 'What's happened to upset you?'

'Nothing. It doesn't matter.' Carlotta dropped her face into her hands.

'It matters to me. Surely we know each other well enough by now to trust each other with our secrets?'

'You don't trust me with yours.' Carlotta's voice was muffled and yet Raffaella still thought she heard an accusing tone.

'What do you mean?'

'I'm not stupid, you know. I've seen you talking to the americano at night, thinking the fallen branches of the old pomegranate tree were hiding you. I saw you with him many times.'

'You did?' Raffaella was shocked. 'You were spying on us.'

'I wasn't spying, just passing by. And I never told anyone what I'd seen. I kept your secret even though you hadn't trusted me with it.'

'It's not that I didn't trust you.' Raffaella cast her mind back to the times she and Eduardo had sat together until midnight. How could she not have known Carlotta was there in the shadows? 'But I shouldn't have been there. It was wrong. And I suppose that I felt ashamed. But we were only talking, Carlotta. You know that, don't you? Only talking.'

Carlotta didn't reply, and they sat together in an uneasy silence listening to the sound of the waves crashing on the rocks.

After a while the lantern began to flicker. 'You're not the only one who has done things to be ashamed of,' Carlotta said hesitantly.

'What do you mean?'

The lantern flickered again, and with a sizzle, the flame died down completely.

'Damn.' Raffaella couldn't see a thing. 'It's pitch black. Unless the clouds clear, we'll never find our way off these rocks.'

'Don't worry, I'll get us home. I've walked across the rocks in the dark enough times not to need a lantern.'

'Why do you spend so much time down here?'

Carlotta drew a deep breath. 'It's where I come to think and where I like to pray to God. And if I get sad, there's no one here to see me.'

'What makes you so sad?'

It was so dark they couldn't see each other's faces. Somehow that made it easier for Carlotta to talk.

'Remember I told you Claudia Barbieri has a brother? His name is Alessandro and he is nothing like her at all. In the old days, when they came every summer, he would always seek me out. We used to come down here secretly after dark to sit by the sea together, and he would talk for hours and hours. At first I was shy, but Alessandro didn't mind that. He said it made a nice change from all the rich girls he got introduced to in Napoli.'

She stopped talking and Raffaella held her breath and silently willed her to carry on.

'He made me feel special.' Carlotta's voice was a whisper. 'One night he told me he loved me and we kissed. The next night he said he wanted to make love to me and I let him. I didn't like it much. It was rough and I hated feeling his hot breath on my skin. But he liked it a lot and I wanted to please him, so I let him do it again and again.'

'And you got pregnant?'

'How did you know? Did somebody tell you?'

Raffaella reached out and found Carlotta's hand. 'No one told me. But that's the reason you're hardly ever happy, isn't it? What happened to your baby?'

Carlotta struggled for a moment. 'It broke my father's heart when I told him,' she managed at last. 'He sent me to the convent in the mountains, and I had my baby girl there. I called her Evangelina, and the nuns let me keep her for two weeks so I could nurse her. Then they took her away and I never saw her again.'

'What about Alessandro? He didn't offer to marry you?'

'No, his family would never have allowed it. When I came home from the convent, he had gone. That was the last time any of the Barbieri family came to Villa Rosa until now.'

'And where was your baby taken? Did you ever find out?'

'My father said the nuns would find a good family to raise her. She would never know that I was her mother and she'd be better off for it. He begged me to try to forget her, but I can't. Whenever I see a little girl her age, I stop and wonder if she's Evangelina. I think about her every single day. And that's why I come down here.'

'My God, Carlotta, I'm so sad for you.'

'She was a beautiful baby. Sometimes she cried a little, but she always stopped for me when I picked her up.'

'Have you ever tried to find her?'

'How could I? Where would I start? And my father's right. She's probably better off without me.' Carlotta sounded defeated.

Raffaella squeezed her hand. She felt sad and angry. How could Umberto have made Carlotta give up her baby? Why didn't he stand up against the Barbieri family?

'Don't blame my father. He thought he was doing the right thing.' Carlotta must have guessed her thoughts. 'The Barbieri family owns the house we live in, and the money we earn from looking after Villa Rosa is our livelihood. His only choice was to send me to the nuns. And it broke his heart as much as it did mine.'

Raffaella hugged her tight.

'I'm glad I told you. You're right, it does feel better to talk about things.'

'I wish I could do more than just listen.' Raffaella wondered how difficult it would be to find Evangelina. 'I'd like to be able to help you.'

'There's nothing anyone can do.' Carlotta shivered. 'It's late and cold. We should go back. Hold tight to my hand and come on, I'll lead the way.'

30

The morning sun washed against the pink walls of Villa Rosa. The sky was blue and the sea bluer still. Umberto had put three pots of marigolds outside the kitchen window and their golden heads bobbed as a breeze ran lightly through them. The place had never looked so perfect, but Raffaella was so unhappy she couldn't see the beauty in any of it.

She had woken late and the americano's car was gone by the time she got to Villa Rosa. Claudia Barbieri was sunning herself in the courtyard, a pile of magazines at her elbow and a cigarette in her hand. Raffaella forced herself to be polite.

'*Buongiorno*, signorina. Can I get you something for breakfast?'

'Oh, just an espresso, I think.' Claudia smiled, showing off white, even teeth. She was trying to be friendlier this morning. 'Isn't this place stunning? I can't imagine why we stayed away so long.'

'Are you sure you wouldn't like something to eat, signorina?'

Claudia wrinkled her nose. 'Food? Oh, God, no, not at this hour. Just coffee, that's all I can manage. Make it strong with lots of sugar.'

'And your mother, would she like coffee too?'

'She's still sleeping. And Eduardo's not here.' Claudia's voice was plaintive. 'He got up at some crazy hour and went to the mountain. So I'm all alone.'

Raffaella had tried to make an effort with her appearance this morning. Hastily, she had piled her hair on her head and left some wispy curls loose to soften her face. But standing next to Claudia Barbieri still made her feel frumpy and ugly.

Claudia's natural beauty was polished immaculately. She had long, slender arms and gold bracelets clasped round her wrists. Her clothes were expensive and her hair expertly cut. Her varnished fingernails were the colour of coral, and her toenails were painted to match.

'Maybe Eduardo will be back later for a swim, do you think?' She treated Raffaella to another smile. 'It's going to be hot today.'

'You should be careful not to burn in the sun, then.'

'Oh, I don't have the kind of skin that burns. I go brown as a nut.' Claudia shrugged herself free of her clothes. 'But while you're here, you could put some of this oil on my back. That will stop the sun drying me out and turning me into a prune.'

Raffaella felt awkward. She took the bottle of scented oil and began to rub it over Claudia's smooth back and shoulders. 'Mm, that feels good. You have a nice touch,' the girl told her.

'When did you meet the americano?' Raffaella had hoped not to get drawn into conversation, but curiosity got the better of her.

'Oh, it must have been about three months ago. My father heard he was in Napoli and decided he'd like to meet the man who has been living in his house, so he invited him to lunch. Eduardo is so charming, isn't he? We all loved him.' Claudia giggled. 'And I think he quite liked us.'

'We expected him to return to Villa Rosa weeks ago.'

'Yes, I know. He kept putting it off. Maybe he couldn't bear to leave us.' Claudia turned and took the bottle of oil from Raffaella's hands. 'But then Mamma came up with the idea of driving down to Villa Rosa with him. And now here we are.'

'How long are you staying?'

'Mamma said we'd probably stay for a week or so, but it's so relaxing I think I could stay for the entire summer. So nice to be away from all the parties and dinners and enjoy the simple life for a change.'

Raffaella's heart sank. 'But won't you have to go back home?'

Claudia shrugged. 'I suppose we might get bored, especially if Eduardo is up on that mountain all day.' She began rubbing oil on her legs and admiring the way they glistened in the sun. 'I'll have to see if I can find a way to keep him at Villa Rosa, won't I?'

Eduardo felt a sense of freedom as he drove alone up the road that led to the mountain. Claudia was delightful, but he would have been a very stupid man not to notice the determined way that her mother kept throwing the girl at him.

The problem was that women were so distracting. Construction was about to start on the mountain, and how could he focus on the crucial work that lay ahead if Olivia and Claudia kept lying in wait for him suggesting shared outings and meals and lazy afternoons together in the gardens of Villa Rosa?

The statue was the important thing. Eduardo had spent the winter painstakingly laying the groundwork, and he was more confident the work could be done. The engineer's reports were favourable, and the priests had signed off on the designs. Now it would take a huge push from him to drive the project to completion. He couldn't afford to let his attention wander.

When Olivia Barbieri had suggested she and her daughter should accompany him to Villa Rosa, he hadn't felt able to say no. It was their house after all. And in truth it was pleasant enough to have some company in the evenings, people to hold a lively conversation with over dinner, instead of relying on his night-time chats with the little peasant girl for entertainment.

As he rounded a bend in the road, Eduardo caught sight of the bare mountaintop. He was so accustomed to visualising the statue there it almost came as a shock to see the place empty.

Not empty for long, though, he swore to himself. The time would soon come when he would take that bend in the road and see Christ looking down on him. That was his goal, and the day he reached it would be the best of his life.

Claudia was still lying in the courtyard roasting herself like a chicken when Raffaella roared away from Villa Rosa on the old Vespa, leaving a cloud of exhaust fumes behind her. She rode past the tumbledown stone cottages where the old peasants eked out an existence on their small patches of land. Some kept chickens and a pig or two, some had a tiny walled vineyard so they could make their own wine. All of them cultivated vegetables on every spare inch of earth. There were tangles of tall fava-bean plants just starting to die back and spiky artichokes beginning to bud. Tomato plants climbed up wooden trellises with herbs planted in between. Garlic bulbs sent green shoots above ground, and rows of onions nodded their heads at each other.

The road ran between olive trees and lemon groves and clung to the edge of the coastline as it fell to the sea. It was a beautiful ride, but Raffaella was too preoccupied to enjoy it. Last night's conversation with Carlotta kept playing in her head.

If she had looked up instead of staring at the road ahead, Raffaella might have glimpsed the convent where the baby, Evangelina, had been born. It lay high in the mountains and far enough from Triento to mean the nuns seldom had visitors. Not that it was a closed order. The nuns taught in Triento's school and helped the doctor with his clinics. But once they were behind the convent's high walls, they could rely on their privacy.

As she rode her Vespa, Raffaella thought of Carlotta, lonely and scared, nursing the baby she knew she wouldn't be allowed to keep. She imagined how she must have cried as they took Evangelina from her arms that final time and she felt angry again.

She wanted to go storming up to the convent and hammer on the door until the nuns came out and told her what she needed to know. Where was Evangelina now, which family had taken her, and how could she find her?

But the nuns would be sure to send her away. Raffaella remembered them as teachers, stern and unyielding most of them, and she recalled how they had prodded her with bony fingers when she'd turned up at the doctor's clinic infected with head lice or scratching at flea bites. No, the nuns weren't going to tell her where Carlotta's baby was, but still there had to be some way of tracking her down.

Raffaella roared into Triento and went straight down the hill to her parents' house to pick up her recipe book and a few changes of clothes. Next she had shopping to do. It was only when she had filled her basket to the brim with the best of the spring vegetables from the market stalls, the most tender meat and the freshest cheese that she stopped for a moment at the bakery to say hello.

Her mother was there behind the counter, but there was no sign of Silvana.

'She's over at the Gypsy Tearoom,' Anna told her, once the shop had emptied of customers. 'She spends a lot of time there, I've noticed, but only when the mayor is among the builders.'

Raffaella laughed. 'It's good of you to help her out,' she said, refusing to take the bait.

'Well, it means I have to climb that damn hill every day,' her mother grumbled. 'But you certainly hear everything in here. Nothing happens in this town without Silvana knowing about it five minutes later.'

'Yes, she loves the gossip. Although she wouldn't tell me everything.'

'Oh, no, she can close her mouth when she wants to, that's for sure,' Anna agreed.

'For instance,' Raffaella continued carefully, 'she refused to tell me about Carlotta, even though I begged her to.'

'Refused to tell you what about Carlotta?' Her mother looked away and started brushing flour off the counter with her hands.

'I think you know, don't you?'

Anna sighed. 'You mean about the baby, I suppose?'

Raffaella nodded.

'Yes, I knew about it. The poor girl, we all felt so sorry for her. She was such an innocent little thing with no mother to guide her. That Barbieri boy took advantage of her, I expect. But his family blamed Carlotta. They accused her of seducing him. Umberto almost lost his job over it, which would have been a disaster.'

'Why didn't you tell me all this before?'

'Why didn't you tell me about Silvana and the mayor?'

Raffaella laughed again. Her mother was always too quick for her. 'OK, OK, you win. But, Mamma, what if I wanted to help Carlotta find her little girl? Where would I begin?'

'It wouldn't be easy. I can't see that you would get the nuns to tell you a thing. And she may not even be in the area any more. Sometimes they send those babies up north to rich families.'

'There has to be a way of finding her.'

Her mother looked anxious. 'Even if there is, are you sure it would be the right thing? That child has been with the family who adopted her for over four years. Imagine how you'd have felt at that age if someone had told you I wasn't your real mother and tried to take you away.'

'But what about Carlotta?'

'It's sad for her, I'm not arguing with you about that.'

'I want to do something to help her.'

'You are helping her. You're being her friend. I think that's all you can do.'

Her mother's words made sense, but as Raffaella rode her Vespa back to Villa Rosa, she grew increasingly depressed. It seemed that whatever she tried to do, a door slammed in her face. Perhaps she had been born unlucky, for other people seemed to sail through life without experiencing the slightest misfortune. Look at Claudia Barbieri. She was rich and beautiful and could have whatever she wanted. She couldn't imagine anything ever happening to her worth wrinkling her smooth brows about. Meanwhile both she and Carlotta had lost the things they loved the most. It was so unfair.

There was no sign of either of the Barbieri women when she rode through the gates of Villa Rosa, and the courtyard was empty except for Umberto, who was fussing about in the garden.

'Ah, Raffaella, *buongiorno*,' he greeted her. 'Do you like my lovely young pomegranate tree? Isn't it doing well?'

'Yes, it is.' She nodded politely.

'It didn't look this healthy when I first planted it, you know. For the first few weeks it seemed to droop and its leaves began to curl. I really thought we were going to lose it, and then, just as I was giving up hope, it must have sent its roots down deep, because it rallied. And look at it now.' Umberto took a step or two backwards to admire the tree properly. 'It's beautiful.'

'But not quite as beautiful as the old one, or at least not yet,' Raffaella remarked. 'I was sad when Carlotta told me it had died.'

'Not as sad as she was, I'm sure. She was so attached to that tree she grieved for it like it was a person. She is a sensitive girl, my Carlotta.'

Umberto looked almost comical standing there with his dirty old hat crammed on his head. He had lost his false teeth again and had taken to talking with his hand held apologetically half over his mouth.

'It's been good having you here,' he added awkwardly. 'She hasn't ever had a friend like you before. I know it's made a big difference to her . . . and to me too.'

Raffaella was desperate to ask him about the baby. There was a chance that Umberto would know where to find her. She struggled to find a way to raise the subject.

'Carlotta has had some sad times,' she began carefully.

Umberto nodded. He seemed in the mood for confidences. 'Losing her mother when she was still so young was a tragedy for Carlotta,' he said, staring out towards the blue band of sea beneath the horizon. 'My wife drowned, you know. She used to love to swim off the rocks, and one day she went down there for a swim and never came back.'

'Oh, but that's so terrible.'

'Yes, it was very terrible. My wife was a good swimmer, but the sea was very agitated that day. If she had been swept on to the rocks by a big wave and knocked unconscious, she wouldn't have stood a chance. That's what the police thought had happened. They found her body a little way along the coast.' Umberto grimaced at the memory. 'For a long time I was very angry with her for swimming when it wasn't safe. Poor Carlotta, I don't think I was much of a father for her then. She was barely three years old.'

'Does she remember her mother at all?' Raffaella was shocked.

'No, not really. She says her only memories are of sitting beneath the old pomegranate tree with her on warm days making bracelets out of flowers from the garden.'

'So that's why she loved the tree so much?'

Umberto nodded. 'I wish I could have saved it for her. But it's time had come.' He hesitated for a moment, and then, staring at the tree rather than meeting Raffaella's gaze, he added sadly, 'I'm all that Carlotta has left. What will happen to her when my time comes?'

Raffaella wondered if now was the right time for her question. 'What about Carlotta's baby?' she asked quickly. 'She has a daughter somewhere, doesn't she? Perhaps we could find her.'

With a quick glance towards the house, Umberto lowered his voice. 'It would be impossible.'

'Carlotta still thinks of Evangelina every day.'

Umberto brushed at his eyes with rough hands. 'I know she does,' he said unsteadily. 'But it's too late. That child has another family. Carlotta's not her mother any more. It's harsh, but it's the truth.'

'Is she still here in Triento?'

Umberto shook his head. 'I don't know. The nuns took her. And whenever I've asked about her, all they'd tell me was that she had many people to love her and a very big house to live in.'

'Not Triento, then – there are no big houses here.'

'She has gone, Raffaella, so don't think you can try to find her. Don't raise Carlotta's hopes. Leave things as they are. Life may not be perfect, but it could be worse.'

Picking up the old watering can he'd left beneath the tree, Umberto shuffled off towards the vegetable patch. He had pulled his hat down over his eyes and she couldn't see his face properly, but as she watched him move between the rows of young tomato plants, Raffaella was certain he was crying.

31

Carlotta sat with her eyes closed listening to the familiar sound of the sea beating against the rocks and letting the sun touch her pale face with its warm fingers. Last night was the first time in years she had talked about Evangelina, and it had given a new lustre to the memories she polished over and over in her mind. Her baby, nestling in the crook of her arm, a warm little bundle that felt like she was part of her own body still. There had been a soft fuzz of dark hair covering her head, and her eyes, when she opened them, were dark and serious.

For two weeks Carlotta had kept Evangelina in her arms, willing herself to remember every second. Only when she had to sleep herself did she lay her down, and then she pulled the crib close to her bed so she could hear the little snuffling noises her baby made and would wake up the moment she cried.

On that final morning the nuns had given her clothes to dress Evangelina. Little knitted boots for her feet, a tiny white coat and a hat to keep her head warm. She had kissed her one last time, very gently on her forehead, and then her arms had been empty.

Her body quickly forgot it had ever had a baby. Her milk dried up, the extra weight that had rounded her cheeks and belly fell away. When she looked in the mirror, she saw the old Carlotta again. But she kept Evangelina in her mind, and as the years passed, she imagined how they might be changing her.

She didn't picture her as a tiny baby any more, but as a pretty girl with soft dark hair and wise brown eyes. Perhaps a little shy, as she herself had been as a child, and maybe her skin was pale, and her body thin and awkward. But in Carlotta's mind, she was almost always laughing, and on her arms she wore bracelets made out of flowers from the garden.

Every day she prayed to God to keep Evangelina safe and well. Sometimes she dreamed of catching a glimpse of her in the street, but never, until today, had she dared to pray for the chance to hold her one more time and kiss her gently on the forehead.

Squeezing her eyes tightly shut against the bright sunlight, Carlotta imagined a small girl running towards her, arms outstretched, squealing with delight. She would scoop her up and hold her little body tight, burying her face in her hair to see if her head still smelled a little like it had when she was a baby.

It was a beautiful dream, but Carlotta could see no way of making it a reality. The nuns were the only ones who would know where her child had ended up. One or two of them had been kind to her when she had arrived, ashamed and swollen-bellied, at the convent. They had slipped extra food on her plate and whispered that she must keep herself strong. But the others had been harder. They had made her scrub the floors and sweep out the fireplaces until the morning when the birth pangs started. They had stayed at her side grim-faced throughout her labour as she cried out in terror at the pain ripping through her body. And on the day they took Evangelina from her, they'd locked her door and left her there to cry.

However much she begged and pleaded, she was certain they wouldn't tell her whose arms they'd put her baby in. Or who had pulled the woollen boots from her feet and taken the hat from her head. The nuns would still know, they never forgot a thing, but they held their secrets close. Somewhere, there was a little girl called Evangelina with dark hair and brown eyes, and Carlotta was sure she would never see her again.

The gardens of Villa Rosa grew from earth the colour of cinnamon. Turning it with his spade each planting season was what kept Umberto fit and strong. He'd worked the soil on these terraces for forty years of his life. He remembered the early days, when the ground was stony and dry and he'd had to coax the plants to put down roots in such an inhospitable spot. His wife, Mina, had worked at his side, helping him to cultivate herbs and vegetables. In the late afternoons, if she was hot and dusty, she liked to cool off by diving off the rocks into the sea. Umberto had begged her to be careful, but even when Carlotta was a baby, Mina had refused to give up her saltwater bath.

They'd argued every day of their married lives, and the day she died had been no different. Umberto remembered harsh words and broken crockery, but he had never been able to recall what the fight was about. She was a stormy one, his Mina, and beautiful too. She sat firmly in the driving seat of all their lives. When she had gone and he was left to raise their clingy, anxious child alone, he had felt like plunging into the sea himself and never coming up for air. Instead, he dragged himself through the years, toiling in the garden, putting food on the table and watching his daughter grow into a timid young woman.

It had almost been a relief when Alessandro Barbieri had focused his attention on her. There had been some colour in her cheeks at last, and Umberto heard Carlotta laugh more in those few weeks than he ever had before or since. He had suspected there might be more than just a friendship developing, but he pushed those thoughts away and let his attention wander. There had been many signs he'd chosen not to see. So when Carlotta had come to him, wild-eyed and distraught, begging him to tell her what to do, he had been shocked but not entirely surprised.

He never set eyes on the baby his daughter called Evangelina. The nuns had taken care of it all and he had been grateful. There had been long nights of tears with Carlotta, but he had been patient, and sure enough time seemed to heal her. It was a while before he realised she had merely taken her sadness elsewhere. It broke his heart every time he saw her run down the path towards the sea and return with reddened eyes and nothing to say. But guilt and regret were useless, for the baby had gone. And all Umberto could do was what he had always done – toil in the garden, turning the spice-coloured earth with his spade, planting and harvesting his way through the seasons and the years.

Taking his basket, he moved down the rows of leggy fava-bean plants, pulling off the last of the fat green pods. Perhaps Raffaella could use these in the kitchen today. She might purée them for a soup or serve them with lemon juice, garlic and slivers of pancetta. She might blanch and peel them and put them in a salad with morsels of pecorino cheese and crisp trimmings of red onion. Or maybe she would simply mash them with lots of black pepper and a little salt.

He had been glad at first to see the girl return to Villa Rosa, for Carlotta had seemed lonelier than ever over winter. But now he had misgivings. He hoped Raffaella would be too busy in the kitchen to find time to stir up trouble with her good intentions.

Breaking off a brittle stem from a fava-bean plant, he frowned. It was time to pull these out, dig the soil over and plant afresh. In a garden, the work never ends. Looking down the long rows of spent plants, he tried to convince himself he didn't feel old and tired. How many more years would he have to work this brown earth? How many harvests lay ahead for him?

Raffaella unpacked her basket and opened her book of recipes. Tonight she was determined that the plates would be clean when they were brought back to the kitchen. This dinner would be the best she had cooked. It would be irresistible.

As Raffaella hovered over the pans, she thought about Umberto and Carlotta and the layers of sadness beneath the surface of their lives. If only life were as simple as cooking. She wished there was a recipe that she could follow to tell her what to do next.

She saw Carlotta appearing at the top of the steps and watched her come towards the kitchen, touching the branches of the young pomegranate tree as she walked past it. Raffaella knew instinctively where she had been.

'Your face is pink,' she called out. 'Have you been sitting in the sun?'

Carlotta pressed her hand against her cheek to feel the heat in her skin. 'It was so beautiful down there I stayed longer than I meant to,' she said ruefully. 'I didn't notice the time going by.'

There was an awkwardness between them as they moved about the kitchen cooking and cleaning. Neither wanted to be the first to mention last night's conversation.

Raffaella broke the silence first. 'I keep thinking about your baby and how there must be some way to find her.'

'Do you really believe there might be?' Carlotta sounded hopeful.

Raffaella remembered how her mother and Umberto had both tried to discourage her from trying. 'Of course I do,' she said stubbornly. 'It's just a matter of working out how.'

'Where would we start?'

'We have to begin with the nuns. There is no other way. Surely there must be one of them we can convince to tell us something?'

Carlotta thought about it. 'Do you remember Sister Benedicta?' she asked hesitantly.

'Yes, of course I do. She used to teach at the school. I expect she still does.'

'She was always kind to me. Once, a couple of years ago, I bumped into her in the piazza. She stopped to talk and I dared to ask about Evangelina.'

'What did she say?'

'Not much. Just that she was very happy and that she had a good mother and many sisters.'

'And what about her father?'

'I asked her that too and she said something odd in reply ... '

'Yes?'

'She said, "God is her father, Carlotta," and then that was it, she hurried away.'

'God is her father,' Raffaella repeated. 'I suppose she meant her father had died but that God was looking after her.'

'I suppose so.' Carlotta looked dubious. 'But it was strange the way she said it and then rushed off as if she was sorry she had spoken.'

'Well, let's start with Sister Benedicta, then. We should go to the school and see if we can find her.'

'When?'

Raffaella pulled off her apron, turned off the gas and covered the pans on the stovetop.

'Let's go now. Come on. I'll start the Vespa and you go and find your hat. We won't be long. Your father probably won't even notice we've gone.'

Triento's schoolhouse lay on the outskirts of the village beside the Church of Santa Trinita. It was an old building surrounded by tall trees and high walls. As she pushed open the wrought-iron gate, Raffaella saw that not much had changed. There were still low benches beneath the trees and a grassy area where the boys could kick a ball around.

Like most girls in Triento, Raffaella had been taken out of school when she turned thirteen. She had been happy to leave the place behind. The sun's rays rarely reached beyond the shelter belt of trees and the building was damp and gloomy. She had memories of feeling trapped there, hemmed in by desks and blackboards and more than half afraid of the whiskery-faced old nuns who ruled the place.

Their footsteps echoed as they walked down the hallway, past the lockers and the cloakrooms, in search of Sister Benedicta. Raffaella shuddered, for the school even smelled the same, of small children and musty books and whatever they used to scrub the classrooms clean at the end of each day.

'I hated this place,' she hissed.

'Me too,' Carlotta whispered back.

They found Sister Benedicta's classroom at the far end of the schoolhouse. It was the brightest of all the rooms, thanks to the paintings and tapestries she'd hung around the walls. A small group of young children was sitting silently at their desks, and the nun was at the backboard, chalk in hand, explaining something to them.

Raffaella and Carlotta waited outside the classroom until Sister Benedicta picked up the handbell that lay on her desk and rang it three times to signal that the lesson was over. The children grabbed their books and schoolbags, and the room was filled with the sound of high, excited voices.

'Quietly, quietly, no running,' the nun called after them as her pupils rushed into the hallway.

Sister Benedicta had not changed much. The years had softened the angles of her face, and a concertina of wrinkles appeared round her eyes when she smiled at Raffaella and Carlotta. But she still had a prettiness about her, and the plainness of the dark-blue nun's habit and white veil she wore failed to disguise it completely.

'Hello, what are you two doing here? Don't tell me that after all these years you've finally decided you want to learn something.' The nun smiled at them once more. Her voice was warm, her expression encouraging and open. But still Raffaella didn't know how best to begin. She felt reduced to a small child again, awkward and powerless.

'I . . . we . . . I thought.' She stumbled over her words. Flushing, she turned to Carlotta. 'Tell Sister Benedicta why we're here.'

Carlotta seemed strangely calm. 'We've come because I've been very unhappy for a long time and I thought you might be able to help me,' she said in a clear, steady voice.

The nun's smile faded and her expression grew guarded. 'I don't understand. How could I help you?' she asked, and Raffaella was certain she had guessed what they wanted.

'I've been very unhappy,' Carlotta repeated. 'All I can think of is my daughter, Evangelina. If you could tell me anything about what happened to her, anything at all, I'd be so grateful. I just want to see her, to make sure she's all right. I know she has another mother now, but if I could see her one more time, I'd feel a little happier.'

The nun shook her head. 'You know I can't tell you anything. You gave up your baby, Carlotta. It was for the best, you must believe me. All I can say is that Evangelina is happy and healthy. There is no need for you to worry about her.'

'Do you see her?' Carlotta was eager.

Sister Benedicta fingered the cross that hung round her neck. 'I have seen her, yes, I have.'

'So she is living near here? Does she come to this school? Is she one of your pupils?'

'No, no, please stop, Carlotta. You can't ask these questions of me, for I'm not free to answer them.'

'Please tell me one thing at least. Is her family a good one?'

The nun hesitated. 'They are very devout people, good Catholics who pray hard and work hard,' she said carefully. 'There is no need for you to be unhappy, for you can trust them to care for your daughter body and soul.'

'I don't understand why I'm not allowed to see her. What if I came up to the convent and spoke to the Mother Superior? Do you think she might help me?' Carlotta's voice wobbled. 'I'm a devout person too. I pray for my daughter every day.'

Sister Benedicta's hand closed round the cross that hung against her chest and she held it tight. 'Don't go to the convent, Carlotta. You won't be welcome there,' she said quickly.

'But why if—'

'Don't go to the convent,' the nun repeated. Gathering up the books and papers from her desk, she hurried towards the classroom door just as quickly as her pupils had. Turning back to them at the last moment, she said softly, 'I'm sorry. Forgive me.'

The room was very quiet after she had gone. Carlotta sank down on a school chair and put her hands over her face. Raffaella took a piece of white chalk and began writing something on the blackboard.

'That was hopeless. We learned nothing,' said Carlotta at last in a sad, muffled voice.

'I disagree. I think we know quite a lot now.'

'What do you mean?' Carlotta looked up and saw her words on the blackboard. 'What's all that you've been writing?'

'These are the things we know about Evangelina. All the clues we have. Read the list and tell me what you think.'

Carlotta squinted at the words and began to read them out loud. 'She lives in a very big house somewhere near Triento with lots of people who love her. She has a mother and many sisters. God is her father. All of her family are devout Catholics.'

Raffaella wiped the blackboard clean. 'Where in Triento would you find a very big house full of women who pray a lot?' she asked, and she saw a look of surprise spreading across Carlotta's face.

'The convent?'

Raffaella nodded. 'I think your daughter may still be there.'

'But why? The nuns were meant to find a family to care for her.'

'I don't know. I don't understand it either.'

'Let's go there now.' Excited, Carlotta sprang to her feet. 'Let's go and find Evangelina.'

'No, wait, we can't just turn up there and ask to see her. They'll only send us away.'

'What, then?'

Raffaella frowned. 'I need some time to think. And I have a meal to finish cooking, so we should get back to Villa Rosa. Don't look so disappointed, though, Carlotta. I'm sure we're going to find her. Don't give up hope.'

Carlotta's arms were wrapped tightly round her waist, and her warm body was pressed against Raffaella. She seemed to radiate a new happiness. But as Raffaella rode the Vespa hard round the kinks and bends in the road that led back to Villa Rosa, her mind was on other things. With a growing sense of panic, she was thinking of all that she had to do to make tonight's meal perfect.

It was a relief to reach the gates of Villa Rosa. Raffaella saw that the sun was beginning to sink towards the sea, and bringing the Vespa to a screeching halt, she flew across the courtyard towards the kitchen.

Claudia and her mother were sitting at the table just outside the kitchen door. They had helped themselves to drinks and bowls of nuts and olives. Raffaella noticed that Claudia had styled her hair and painstakingly applied make up. She looked beautiful and bored.

'Eduardo isn't back yet,' she said sulkily. 'I hope he comes soon. We challenged him to a game of cards tonight, didn't we, Mamma.'

'It will be dark soon and he'll be back,' Raffaella assured her. 'Now I must finish making dinner. I'm running late.'

Olivia seemed to have no appetite. 'I'm sure we'd be happy with a little salad and some mozzarella, wouldn't we?' she said lightly.

Claudia shrugged. 'Eduardo may be hungry, though, Mamma. Men like to eat more than we do, so let her cook,' she said, and went back to flicking through the pages of her magazine.

Raffaella rolled out some pasta to serve with a sauce of swordfish, tomato and herbs. She glazed a duck with pomegranate syrup and cooked it with blood oranges and bitter onions. She made a salad of crisp shaved fennel and smoked pecorino cheese and took some tiny artichokes Umberto had picked from the garden, steamed them slowly with olive oil and scattered them with capers, garlic, parsley and black olives.

Just as Raffaella was worrying that the meal would be spoiled, she saw the headlights of Eduardo's car as he turned in through the gates.

'He's here,' she said to Carlotta. 'Now get ready. We'll let him have one *aperitivo* and then I want you to serve dinner.'

It was warmer tonight and Eduardo would brook no argument. They were eating outside in the shadow of the mountaintop where he'd been spent all day pushing his dreams of the statue a step or two nearer to realisation.

'I'm exhausted,' he declared. 'Let's relax out here, have dinner and a glass of wine and then an early night.'

'And a game of cards,' Claudia reminded him. 'You promised.'

'All right, then, just one game, but you have to be gentle with me. I've worked hard today.'

Raffaella took out rugs to keep them warm and lit lanterns to put on the table.

In the soft light, Claudia looked pretty and more girlish than ever. Raffaella noticed how she liked to touch Eduardo, grabbing his sleeve or just brushing against him as she moved past. She looked away. It was better to concentrate on the food she was about to serve than give in to the feelings she felt rising inside her.

Even Olivia ate in silence. But it was she who spoke first. 'This food is amazing.'

The others joined in. 'It's delicious,' agreed Eduardo.

'Like nothing I've ever tasted before,' marvelled Claudia.

Raffaella had heaped the food on their plates, and they finished it all and called for more. A trickle of pomegranate sauce ran down Claudia's chin and stained the tight white shirt she was wearing, but she didn't seem to care. Olivia picked up a duck leg in her hands to lick and suck at it and pull every last bit of sweet flesh from the bone. Eduardo wiped his bread round the plate, soaking up every last drop of rich sauce.

'Amazing,' he declared. 'But I couldn't eat another thing.'

Carlotta cleared the plates and Raffaella saw to her satisfaction that every one was clean. She gave them a little time to chat and finish their wine. And then she sent out more food: a tart of nuts and chocolate; biscotti studded with almonds; fruit and cheese, and tiny cups of strong espresso.

Greedily, Claudia dug her spoon into the tart and crunched on the biscotti. It was the cheese that Olivia couldn't resist, stuffing it into her mouth with slabs of Silvana's best olive bread.

By the time the moon was hanging above Eduardo's mountaintop, they had let the cutlery fall from their fingers and were leaning back in their chairs, rubbing at their full bellies.

'I've eaten too much,' Claudia groaned.

'Me too.' Olivia looked pale in the lamplight. 'I think I'm going to have to go and lie down.'

'Why don't you both go and rest?' Eduardo suggested. 'We can play our card game tomorrow night. I'm going to sit over there on the wall and smoke a cigar and then I'll turn in too.'

Claudia stifled a yawn. 'No, no, I'll keep you company while you smoke your cigar. It's unhealthy to go straight to bed after a large meal. And anyway, I haven't seen you all day long. Wouldn't it be nice to have some time to talk?'

From the kitchen, where she was hanging over a sink full of dirty dishes, Raffaella willed Claudia to change her mind. It was she who needed to talk to Eduardo. She had saved up her words all winter and she didn't think she could hold them in any longer.

'Go to bed, go to bed,' she muttered.

Raffaella scrubbed at the plates and pans. She knew without looking up that Eduardo had moved to sit on the wall beside the young pomegranate tree and Claudia had followed him. The sweet, musky smell of the cigar reached her nostrils, and she heard the sound of their voices, although she could no longer make out their words. Perhaps Eduardo was telling her the story of the pomegranate tree and how Pluto made Persephone eat from the fruit so she could never leave him for good. Raffaella didn't want to feel jealous, but she couldn't help it.

The last pan was dried and hung from its hook on the far wall. Raffaella scrubbed at non-existent stains on the stovetop. She was running out of reasons to linger any longer.

As she removed her apron and moved to turn out the lights, she heard giggling. There were now two pinpricks of orange beneath the pomegranate tree. Eduardo had lit a cigar for Claudia and she was pretending to smoke it.

Raffaella stayed in the doorway and watched as the girl dared to take a puff of the cigar and then another. She began to cough, and fanning the smoke away from her face with her hand, she held out the cigar to Eduardo.

'Oh, no, I don't like it. It's made me feel all funny.' She broke out in another coughing fit and, when she stopped, sounded embarrassed. After that, she held the cigar away from her face until the end stopped glowing orange and the ash fell from it on to the courtyard.

'I think I'm going to go to bed,' she said in a subdued, still-embarrassed voice. 'I'll see you in the morning. Perhaps you'll have time to drink a coffee with me before you go to work.'

Happy for her to go, Eduardo lit her discarded cigar, took a long drag on it and continued staring up towards the mountain, visualising his statue.

This was it, her chance. Raffaella felt nervous, but forcing her feet to take her forward, she left the safety of the kitchen.

'Perhaps the cigar was a bad idea for her on top of all that food,' she said softly.

She saw Eduardo turn to her and heard him chuckle. 'That was a wonderful meal, Raffaella, but you're right, we were too greedy and now I think the ladies are paying the price.'

She sat a hand's breadth away from him on the low wall. 'I cooked it for you to enjoy. I've been thinking all winter what I would make for you.'

He didn't reply. Perhaps he was simply lost in the rhythm of smoking his cigar. Or maybe the ease of their old intimacy had died just like the old pomegranate tree. Raffaella wasn't certain.

'How are things going with the statue?' she asked at last.

'The statue?' Suddenly he seemed animated. 'It's going pretty well, although I don't mind telling you there have been times over the last few months when I've despaired about the whole project. Getting things done in this country isn't easy. You have to know the right people.'

'I'm sure it's the same in America, isn't it?'

He gave a wry laugh. 'No, it's nothing like doing business in America. Here, it's as if there's a set of rules that everyone but you has been taught. I was just about ready to give up when I met Luciano Barbieri.'

'Is he the man who owns Villa Rosa?'

'That's right. He has family down here in the construction business. Once I told him about the problems I was having, he had a word with the right people. It was amazing the difference it made. Suddenly I was able to make some progress.'

Raffaella felt happier. He was confiding in her again. They didn't seem like strangers any more.

'So things are going smoothly now, that's good,' she said.

Eduardo frowned. 'Well, not exactly. There's been some odd stuff going on. The surveyors say some of their equipment was moved, and the engineer seemed to think someone had been playing around up there. But I don't know; it's possible they're imagining it.'

'There are people in this town who are against the statue, remember.' Raffaella sensed trouble. 'You should be careful, signore.'

'Oh, we've put money in the right pockets, don't worry about that.'

'That wasn't what I meant . . . ' she began, but he wasn't listening.

'Wait till you see it, Raffaella. It's going to be magnificent.' His voice grew louder as his enthusiasm mounted. 'Even the people who think they are against it will have to admit they were wrong. It won't be like anything else in the world. The priests keep talking about the statue in Rio. Well, this one might not be so big, but it will be more beautiful. It will be modern, stark and powerful. When we have finished, it will seem like God Himself put it on the mountaintop.'

His enthusiasm was infectious and Raffaella smiled. 'I can't wait to see it.'

'Ah, but you'll have to wait. We must build a road first, remember? We have to tame that mountain before we can build on it. So we must be patient, Raffaella, but it will be worth the wait, I promise.'

Crushing what was left of the cigar beneath his heel, he stood up. 'It's time for me to get some sleep. *Buona notte*, Raffaella.'

'*Buona notte*, signore, sleep well.'

Raffaella stayed there for a while after he had left. Unaccountably she felt happy. Eduardo had said his project would take time. That meant she had all summer to cook for him at Villa Rosa and maybe longer. Tilting her head, she stared up at the stars scattered across the night sky. Tomorrow she would make gnocchi, and she would leave a piece of pork to soak in pomegranate syrup, lemon juice and garlic, and then cook it in a slow oven, basting it in its juices. She would cook *baccalà* in water and then sprinkle the salt fish with chilli and deep-fried sweet peppers. She would pan-fry some squid and stuff it with herbs, and cook some fresh peas with finely sliced spring onions and shards of bacon. If tonight's meal had been good, tomorrow's would be a feast.

32

The first thing Raffaella noticed as she rode into Triento on her Vespa was the commotion in the piazza. Francesca Pasquale, the traffic officer, was wearing her peaked cap askew, and the whistle she kept on a cord round her neck had been ripped from her. She was pushing and shoving at someone and shouting. 'Obey the rules of our town, signore, obey the rules.'

'What's going on?' Raffaella stopped the Vespa beside Patrizia Sesto, who was watching the argument, wide-eyed and nostrils flaring.

'It's a disgrace. That stranger refused to move his car when Francesca blew her whistle at him.'

'Who is he?'

'Some northerner who's here to work on that cursed statue, I expect. And Francesca is right. If he's going to bring his car into our town, he should obey the rules . . . '

The rest of her words were drowned out. Francesca had found her whistle lying on the ground and was blowing long, furious blasts at the stranger, who was yelling back at her and waving his arms in the air.

'I told you that statue would lead to trouble, didn't I?' Patrizia said later as the stranger finally drove away, with Francesca running after him, blowing hard on her whistle, tears running down her cheeks.

Raffaella was distracted by the sight of Fabrizio Russo standing on the edge of the crowd. There was something odd about the expression on his face. He looked over and met her eyes and then he looked away.

'The statue will be beautiful,' she murmured to Patrizia. 'You'll change your mind about it when you see it.'

She followed Fabrizio's line of sight and realised what he was staring at. There was another fight going on in the piazza, a quieter yet equally angry one. Stefano Russo was standing head to head with her father, Tommaso, near the alleyway that led to the Gypsy Tearoom. His face was red and a vein jumped in his temple. Raffaella couldn't hear what they were saying, but she saw that Stefano had a finger raised and was wagging it at her father to make his point.

She looked back at Fabrizio and found he was staring at her. This time he did not look away but held her gaze.

'Beautiful? So it ought to be, the amount it's costing this town.' Patrizia was still talking about the statue. 'That's if it ever gets built. I've heard talk of sabotage.'

'Sabotage?' Raffaella broke away from Fabrizio's stare. 'What do you mean?'

'Things have been broken, things have gone missing.'

'On the mountain?'

'That's right.'

'Who's responsible?'

'I don't know, it could be a lot of people. There are those who say it might be your own father.'

Raffaella looked over towards the alleyway, but her father and Stefano Russo had gone. She glanced back to see there was no sign of Fabrizio now either.

'My father would never do anything like that,' she insisted to Patrizia.

'He's always opposed the statue. He was the first to speak out about it.'

'He spoke against it, yes, but he would never sabotage it.'

Patrizia shrugged. 'I'm just telling you what people are saying. If you don't like what you're hearing, then don't listen.'

Raffaella saw the yellow dog poking his head round the corner of the alleyway. That must mean Ciro was there, working on the Gypsy Tearoom. Hopping off her Vespa, she wheeled it carefully up the alley, the old dog at her heels.

Ciro and her father were working side by side, sawing wood and hammering. Their clothes were dusty, and the sweat dripped from their bodies.

'Papà,' Raffaella called out.

'Cara, did you bring us lunch? It's a little early.' Her father smiled at her, and Ciro turned and smiled too.

'No, I'm not working at the bakery any more, remember? I'm back at Villa Rosa cooking for the americano.'

Tommaso nodded. 'That's right, I'd forgotten for a moment. Of course you are.'

'What was Stefano Russo saying to you just now, Papà?'

'What do you mean?'

'I saw you both in the piazza. You looked like you were arguing.'

Her father shrugged. 'Oh, you know Russo. He likes to lay down the law. Must think he's important or something.'

'But what was he saying?'

Her father only laughed, picked up his hammer and went back to work.

Raffaella looked at the Gypsy Tearoom and was amazed. There was no trace of the blaze that had destroyed it. The building work was almost complete, and the place looked more or less like it had in the old days.

'Come inside and take a look,' Ciro invited her. 'We're building a bar and some benches for people to sit on, and then we'll be nearly finished. If I throw a party on opening night, will you come?'

'Of course I will. I'd love to come.' She stopped and stared around her. Inside, the place seemed very different. The old pizza oven was all that remained of the past. The mirrors and the beautiful old ceramic tiles had gone, all ruined in the fire, and now the walls were washed in plain white.

'The benches we've been making will go along the wall, and there'll be one long table for everyone to share,' Ciro explained. 'I will put out jugs of water and wine, and people will help themselves, so it will feel almost like eating at home.'

'It's going to be wonderful.'

Ciro looked rueful. 'It won't be the same as it was before.'

'Maybe it will be better than it was before,' she said, looking round at the bright, light room in wonder. 'I have to go now, but I'll definitely be here for your party. I wouldn't miss it.'

Raffaella realised it was getting late. She went directly to the bakery and found Silvana behind the counter.

'Is Mamma not here?' she asked.

'Not today she isn't. She's exhausted, the poor thing. And anyway,

I can manage on my own. You got me through the worst days, the pair of you.'

Raffaella saw that the shelves were jumbled with loaves of all shapes and sizes. The bakery looked more undisciplined than ever.

'I have a favour to ask, Silvana. Do you have any spare bread that I could take?'

'Yes, of course I do. Are you throwing a party?'

'No, I need it for something else.' Raffaella wondered for a moment whether she should confide in Silvana, but then she decided against it. 'I'm helping someone out and I need bread, as much as you can give me.'

'You're very mysterious. Are you taking lunch to our americano and his friends up on the mountain?' Silvana narrowed her eyes. 'Because if that's the case, they can afford to pay for it.'

'No, it's nothing like that. I'm doing something to help Carlotta, but I'm sorry, it's best if I don't tell you any more.'

With her parcel of bread strapped securely to the back of the Vespa, Raffaella drove out of town. Instead of taking the coast road back to Villa Rosa, she turned right on to the steep track that zigzagged up the mountains towards the convent. The engine of the Vespa screamed in complaint but still she pressed on.

The air was cooler up here and Raffaella wished she'd worn a sweater. She shivered as she parked the Vespa beside the high convent walls. Mosses and grass grew from cracks in the old stone, and the walls were so thick and sturdily built that no sound escaped from beyond them. Just a few feet away from her, a nun was hoeing the convent's vegetable garden, but Raffaella couldn't hear the sound of metal hitting the stony earth or the nun breathing heavily from the exertion. A child could be hidden within these walls and who would know. Few people came to the convent, and those who did were never allowed far inside its walls. There was a small chamber just inside the main gates for visitors, and only the priests ventured beyond it.

Raffaella took her parcel of bread and went to ring the bell that hung beside the gates. There was no response. Tired of waiting, she rang again. At last the gate swung open to reveal a tiny nun with silver-rimmed spectacles and an air of exasperation.

'Who are you and why are you disturbing our peace this morning?'

'I've brought your bread delivery from the bakery in town.'

'Our bread delivery? There must be some mistake. We bake our own bread here.' The old nun looked confused.

'But an order was placed,' Raffaella insisted. 'Perhaps you need some extra bread today. Or maybe the cook is sick.'

The nun looked even more exasperated. 'Well, no one's said a word to me, if that's the case. You had better come in and wait while I find out what's going on.'

It was cold inside the small chamber Raffaella was shown into. The room was furnished sparsely with just a bench to sit on and a plain wooden cross on the wall. But someone had left a jug of fresh wildflowers on the windowsill, and Raffaella thought she could make out the sound of chanting coming from deep within the building.

Putting her parcel of bread on the bench, Raffaella dared to leave the chamber and push open the door that led to the main part of the convent. Although the light was dim, she could see long, graceful cloisters and a tiny courtyard beyond the arches. The chanting was haunting and beautiful. It grew louder and then stopped and she heard what sounded like high, girlish laughter.

'What are you doing?' The nun was back. 'You shouldn't be here.'

'I thought I heard a child laughing,' Raffaella said.

The nun gave her a sharp look. 'Whatever you think you may have heard, there is no reason for you to be here. I checked and no one has ordered bread from the bakery in town.'

'How strange. Are you certain?'

'Yes, quite certain.' For such a tiny old person, the nun had a strong grip and she seemed determined it was time for Raffaella to leave. 'We don't need extra bread and the cook is not sick.'

'But I came all this way . . . ' Raffaella complained as the parcel was thrust back into her hands.

'We never order bread from down there. We always bake our own.' The nun gave her another sharp look. 'I'm sorry, but your journey was a waste of time.'

As she rode her Vespa back down the steep hill, Raffaella was more certain than ever the nuns were hiding something. She and Carlotta had to find a way to get inside the convent. But how could it be done? They couldn't scale the walls or break down the doors. She searched her mind for an answer.

The air grew warmer as the road levelled out, and with some relief, Raffaella pointed the Vespa back towards Villa Rosa.

33

Carlotta was in the garden helping her father to pull out the old fava-bean plants. The earth was still soft and it released the shallow roots without much struggle. She piled the spent plants into a wheelbarrow and took them to her father, who had teased a fire from some dry old branches.

'Pile them on,' Umberto urged.

'It will smoke,' she warned him.

'Yes, but my fire is roaring. They'll dry out and then they'll burn.'

There was nothing Umberto enjoyed more than a fire. He loved the smell of smoke drifting across the garden and the haziness it lent to the air. He liked standing there quietly, poking at it with a stick and thinking about nothing much at all.

'Put them on, put them on,' Umberto repeated. He saw how the flames died back when the green plants hit them, and then watched in satisfaction as they began to curl about the stalks and shrivel the leaves. Soon the plants were blackened and withered, and the fire was spitting sparks into the air.

The sun was hot on Carlotta's back, and the fire warmed her face. She took a step or two back and rested for a moment.

'Don't stand there. Get more.'

Sighing, she took up the handles of the wheelbarrow and wondered where Raffaella was. She had come home to bed late last night and then left early this morning. Carlotta had heard the roar of the Vespa and had peered out of the window in time to see her disappearing up the hill. That was hours ago and still there was no sign of her returning.

She took another barrow-load of plants to her father and watched as he piled them on the fire. Raffaella had told her to be patient, but it was far from easy. The idea that her child might have been up there all along hidden by the convent walls was taunting her. She tried to force her mind to focus on something different, but it was impossible. The same thoughts kept circling in her mind.

It was a relief to hear the whine of the Vespa's engine and see Raffaella pulling through the gates. Carlotta abandoned the wheelbarrow and ran to meet her.

'Where have you been?'

Raffaella glanced over at Umberto, but he was standing over his fire, oblivious.

'I went to the convent.'

'Without me?' Carlotta was shocked.

'Shh, wait. Come into the kitchen. I have something to tell you.'

Carlotta felt like shaking Raffaella to force the information out of her. 'What happened? What did you learn?' she asked the moment they were inside the kitchen.

'I'm sure she's there. I think I heard her.'

'How did you get in?'

'I pretended I was delivering bread. I only got inside for a moment and I didn't see much, but I heard a child's laughter.'

Carlotta sank down on to a kitchen chair. 'How can I get myself in there?'

'I don't know. I've thought about it all the way home, but I don't have any ideas.'

'I could claim I was pregnant again and see if they'll give me sanctuary,' Carlotta suggested.

Raffaella shook her head. 'I thought of that, but it won't work. If they really are hiding Evangelina, then you're the last person they'll allow in.'

'But why would they keep her? Why wouldn't they give her to a good family like they said?'

'I've thought about that too. What if there wasn't a suitable family at the time you gave birth? The nuns might have kept her until they could find one. And the years passed and then they couldn't bear to part with her.'

Carlotta thought about it. 'Perhaps you're right,' she mused. 'Evangelina was such a beautiful child. No one would want to let her go.'

'That doesn't help us, though. We still don't have a way in. And no matter how hard I think about it, I can't come up with a solution.'

'You know, I think I might have an idea.' Carlotta was excited. 'They might not let me in, but they can't stop me sitting outside.'

'What? How will that help?' Raffaella was confused.

'I'll sit outside every day for as long as it takes, summer, winter or spring. I'll sit there for years if necessary. Eventually, they'll either have to let me in or allow Evangelina to come out.' Carlotta was determined. 'I want to see my daughter.'

'When will you go there?' Raffaella had never seen this side of Carlotta before. Suddenly the thin, nervy girl seemed strong and certain. There was no point in trying to argue with her.

'I'll go right now. I'll take the Vespa, if that's all right. Don't worry, I'll be back before nightfall. But I have to do this, Raffaella, it's the only way.'

Raffaella packed a bag. She put in bread, cheese, fruit and a flask of chilled water. She made sure Carlotta had warm clothes and a rug to sit on. And then she kissed her quickly on both cheeks and gave her a hug.

'Good luck.'

Carlotta smiled. 'It won't happen today or tomorrow or next week. This is going to take time. But I'm patient and I'll wait for as long as it takes.'

'What will I say to your father if he notices you're gone? Will I tell him you've ridden into town to pick up some things I forgot?'

'No, tell him the truth. He has to know sooner or later.'

Carlotta rode the Vespa along the road that wound up towards the convent. The wind was in her hair, the sun on her face, and she was riding towards her daughter. It was exhilarating. For the first time in her life she felt brave. She felt like the sort of woman who might dare to dive head first from the rocks into the sea even on rough days.

She found a place outside the convent walls where she would be spotted easily by anyone entering or leaving the building and laid down her rug on the ground. She was glad of the warm clothes Raffaella had made her bring, for the mountain air was clear and sharp.

For the first hour or two she saw no one. The convent gates stayed closed, and the place was silent.

To pass the time, she watched the green-backed lizards warming themselves on the rocks. If she sat very still, they came tantalisingly close, but the moment she reached out to try to touch one, they scuttled away. The noise they made as they escaped through the long grass was like a whisper.

Carlotta pulled her hat over her face and listened to the birdsong. The crickets were starting their creaky summer music, and insects buzzed past through the air, adding their own sound to the chorus.

After a while Carlotta began to notice things about the place she hadn't seen before. A colony of ants was marching back and forth a foot or so away from her like a platoon of soldiers. Lichens covered the rocks like tapestries. A gusty breeze flew through and brought with it the scent of wildflowers.

She yawned and stretched her legs. Evangelina was behind those walls, she was sure of it. She should have felt angry towards the nuns, but it was impossible. If they had kept her, then they must love her, and how could she hate them for that?

Carlotta squeezed her eyes shut and said a prayer that she would soon be reunited with her daughter.

The sound of a car roaring up the hill broke in on her thoughts. It was a white Fiat Bambina with a nun in the driving seat and a priest squashed in beside her. As it parked a few feet away Carlotta recognised Sister Benedicta and Padre Pietro. They both stared over at her and Sister Benedicta's mouth fell open in surprise. She turned to Padre Pietro and said something. The old priest looked more strained and worried than ever.

'*Buona sera*,' Carlotta called out as they climbed from the car.

'*Buona sera*, Carlotta. What are you doing here?' Padre Pietro was a kind man and his voice was gentle.

'I've come to see my daughter.'

He frowned at her. 'Your daughter?'

'Yes, my Evangelina. I know she's in there. I'm sure of it.'

'What did they say to you when you rang the bell?' Sister Benedicta looked anxious too.

'I didn't bother to ring. There's no point, is there? They'll only try to send me away. I'm just going to wait here until someone decides to do the right thing.'

The priest exchanged a glance with Sister Benedicta. Neither seemed sure what to say.

'You can't stop me sitting here,' Carlotta pointed out.

'Carlotta, this is madness,' the priest pleaded with her. 'Don't you have work to do? Shouldn't you be at Villa Rosa helping your father?'

'Nothing is more important than this,' she said stubbornly.

Sister Benedicta's brow was furrowed. 'She's right. If she wants to sit here all afternoon, we can't prevent her. She'll tire of it soon enough, I'm sure.'

Carlotta watched as the convent gates swung open to let them enter. A tiny nun wearing silver spectacles peered out and then darted back inside. The gates clanged shut and all was quiet again. She settled down and waited patiently.

Only when she saw the sun dipping towards the sea and felt the temperature drop did Carlotta stand at last and stretch her stiff limbs. She had promised Raffaella she would be back before nightfall. She packed up her bag and, with one last glance at the convent, started the Vespa and rode away.

In the morning she would make Raffaella drop her off before she went shopping in Triento. If the nuns thought she would be easily deterred, they were wrong. And anyway, she liked being there outside the convent walls. It was peaceful. She realised to her surprise that this was the happiest afternoon she had spent in a long, long time.

Umberto didn't notice Carlotta was missing until dusk had almost fallen and his fire was no more than glowing embers.

'Is she down by the sea?' he asked Raffaella. 'She must have been there for hours.'

'No, she's not by the sea.' Raffaella was deep in preparations for dinner, but she paused for a moment. All afternoon she had been dreading the prospect of answering Umberto's questions.

'Is she in the house, then?' Umberto glanced over to where he could see the roof of his own home rising above the walls of Villa Rosa. 'Did she feel unwell?'

'No, not that either.' Raffaella took a deep breath and launched into her explanation. 'Carlotta's gone to the convent. She's convinced her daughter is in there and she's determined to wait outside until she's allowed to see her. I couldn't have stopped her going even if I'd wanted to.'

She had expected Umberto to be furious, but for a moment or two he said nothing. Then he took the cloth cap from his head and pressed it between his rough, gardener's hands.

'Has she really gone to the convent?' he asked at last.

There was a note in his voice that Raffaella recognised as pride. Relieved, she picked up her wooden spoon and started stirring the soup that was bubbling on the stove. 'Yes, yes, I've never seen her like that before. She was a different person.'

He nodded. 'I can imagine.'

'I hope she's not too lonely up there.' Raffaella had been worrying all day. She felt responsible. 'I hope the nuns don't keep her waiting for ever.'

The light was fading and it was a relief to hear the sound of the Vespa and know Carlotta was safely home. She looked tired and sunburned. Raffaella made her sit down at the kitchen table and gave her a generous helping of the soup she had bubbling on the stove.

'Did you see any sign of your little girl?' she asked as she watched Carlotta struggling with the food.

'No, if they have her in the convent, then she's well hidden away. But they know why I was there. And I think they'll be surprised when they see me outside the gates again tomorrow. They'll realise I'm serious then.'

'What if this doesn't work? What if it's a waste of time?' Raffaella was beginning to worry that she had raised false hopes.

'I have to try, don't I? It's no use going on like I was before, always wondering.'

'I suppose not.' Raffaella turned to Umberto, who had been sitting opposite his daughter, folding and unfolding his cloth hat nervously. 'What do you think? Should Carlotta go back to the convent again tomorrow?'

Shifting his eyes away from her gaze, he didn't reply.

'Papà?' Carlotta prompted him.

Umberto crushed his cloth cap into a ball, and his words came out in a rush. 'What do I think? I think that for too long people have been telling you what to do, *figlia*. What right do we have to interfere, and how has it made your life better, eh?'

'But, Papà ... ' Carlotta dropped her spoon into her soup bowl and seized one of her father's work-roughened hands. 'You did what you thought was best for me.'

'No, I did the easy thing.'

Carlotta stared at him. 'What do you mean?'

'If your mother had been alive, none of it would have happened.' His voice was hoarse and low. 'She'd never have allowed that Barbieri boy to take advantage of you.'

'That was my fault, Papà. You can't blame yourself.'

Umberto brushed at his dampening cheeks with his dirty old hat. 'And then I let them drive you up to that convent and take your child away. What sort of father would do that? What kind of man am I?'

Carlotta squeezed his hand so tightly that her knuckles whitened. 'No, Papà, please don't. I love you so much and I can't bear it if you're unhappy.'

Umberto shook his head sadly. 'I know what happens when you go down to the sea every day, Carlotta. I've seen you sitting on the rocks, crying to yourself. And I can't stand to watch you. I just don't know what to do.'

'I've never expected you to do anything. Please don't be sad, Papà. I hate it.'

Raffaella glanced from one to the other. She had done this. She had peeled off the scab that lay over their lives and held everything together. It was a sobering thought and for a moment she wished she had never interfered and things were still as they were when she had arrived at Villa Rosa: Carlotta's unhappiness hidden, Umberto's guilt locked away, and the pair of them quietly leading a life dictated by the seasons.

'Eat your soup, Carlotta,' she said gently. 'If you're going to sit outside the convent all day tomorrow, then you should eat properly tonight.'

They both looked up at her in surprise as if they had forgotten she was there.

'I'll take you to the convent in the morning.' Umberto lifted Carlotta's hand to his lips and dropped a kiss on it. 'I'll wait with you, if you like. I don't like to think of you up there all day on your own.'

Carlotta smiled. 'You have so much work to do in the garden. And I'll be fine alone. I was happy up there today. It was peaceful, and I really did feel as though I was close to Evangelina. I'm certain she is there.' She picked up her spoon and, to please Raffaella, tried to eat a little more of the thick tomato broth she had simmered with tender young vegetables.

Filling another bowl full of soup, Raffaella dusted it with grated Parmesan and put a jug of rough red wine and a basket of hard golden bread on the table.

'You should eat too,' she told Umberto. 'You've been standing over that fire all day, you must be hungry.'

They tried to do justice to her cooking, but neither of them had any appetite. Instead of eating, they stared at each other across the table.

'I'm proud of you, *figlia*,' Umberto said, pushing his soup bowl aside. 'You are your mother's daughter. I never realised it till now.'

Raffaella was proud of her too. But it was hard not to feel a tiny prickle of jealousy. Even Carlotta was getting on with her life. She had chosen her path.

'I'm sorry I can't finish this.' Carlotta looked anxious. 'I'm so tired. Do you mind if I go to bed?'

'Of course not.' Raffaella smiled at her. 'You've had a big day. Go and get some rest.'

Umberto escorted his daughter home. Linking arms with her, he led her past the young pomegranate tree and down towards their house beyond the high walls. Watching them go, Raffaella knew they were closer than ever and she was glad.

34

Raffaella woke early and with a new sense of purpose. Last night she'd watched Eduardo eating and laughing with Claudia Barbieri and had been gripped by a sense of hopelessness. She'd stared at the dirty dishes stacked around her in the kitchen and at the food splattered over the stovetop, and in that moment her life had seemed like a steep mountain she didn't have the strength to climb.

She had been depressed when she lay down to sleep, but this morning she felt different. There had to be things she could do to take control of her life. She knew where to start. She would take the Vespa and ride into town, and her first stop would be the Russo family's linen shop.

Carlotta was waiting for her in the kitchen of Villa Rosa. 'Will you give me a ride up to the convent?' she asked. 'Papà is still sleeping and I don't want to disturb him.'

'Are you certain you want to go back up there today?'

'Of course.' Carlotta seemed surprised to be asked the question. 'I've packed some food for my lunch and a rug in case it gets cold and I'm ready to go. So long as you or Papà come and pick me up before it gets dark, I'll be fine.'

Raffaella studied her face. The strained look round her eyes had gone, and her skin had been touched by the sun and was turning gold.

'Jump on the back and let's go, then,' she said. 'I want to get to town while it's still early.'

The morning air was fresh and the sun still had no heat in it. As the Vespa strained up the hill, Raffaella felt hopeful. If Carlotta could find the strength to take charge of her life, then so could she.

They pulled up outside the convent, and to Raffaella, its walls seemed more formidable than ever and its closed gates unfriendly. Still, Carlotta settled happily enough on the grass verge.

'I'll see you later, then.'

'OK.' Carlotta smiled.

'I hope they let you see her today.'

Carlotta was still smiling. 'I don't expect they will. But I'm a step or two closer to seeing her and that's the important thing.'

Riding the Vespa back down the hill, Raffaella thought about the linen shop and wondered how it might have changed. She hadn't so much as ducked her head in since she'd left the place. At first she had stayed away because she didn't want to see how Angelica and Stefano had changed things. And then it had been impossible to go there because she realised how much the Russo family hated her and knew she wasn't welcome.

The door to the shop lay open, but there was no sign of Angelica. The place looked different, bigger. The teetering stacks of linen that had surrounded Marcello while he worked had all been shifted and in their place were neat, tidy piles and a shining wooden table where reams of cloth and sheets could be unfolded and laid out for customers to admire.

There were other changes too: things had been rearranged; things had been cleared away. A customer's eyes might not notice it all, but Raffaella, who had got to know every corner of the shop in her year of marriage to Marcello, didn't miss a single alteration.

'What are you doing here?' Angelica had run down the stairs from the apartment above and was out of breath.

'The door was open so I assumed it was all right to come in.'

'What do you want?' There was no mistaking the hostility in Angelica's voice.

Raffaella reached out and touched the nearest pile of linen. The feel of the fine fabric beneath her fingertips was reassuring and she stroked it gently. Angelica glared at her but said nothing.

'I wanted to talk to you.' Raffaella tried to keep her tone light. 'I need to know what's going on. Why is your family so against mine?'

'I'm not against you.'

'But Stefano is, and Fabrizio and the others. I don't understand what we've done to make you all hate us.'

'You really want to know?' Angelica moved towards the pile of linen Raffaella had touched and began to smooth it out.

'Yes, yes, I do.'

'The whole town thinks you and your family are bad news. No one likes you.'

Raffaella felt sick. 'That's not true.'

'You should hear what people are saying and then you'd know it is true.'

'What are they saying? Tell me.'

'That your father has caused nothing but trouble setting the other fishermen against the statue and refusing to pay his share; that your brother, Sergio, is just as bad; and that your mother can't stop interfering in other people's business.'

Raffaella felt the anger beginning to roar inside her.

'I'm only telling you what people are saying. And you did ask.' Angelica fluffed up her curly black hair with her fingers and straightened her bright-blue skirt.

She was a pretty girl, with soft lips and almond-shaped eyes, but Raffaella noticed how marriage was filling out her figure. The seams of her blue skirt were stretching, and the flesh on her upper arms jiggled as she rearranged the linen.

'And that's not all. You should hear what they're saying about you,' Angelica said spitefully. 'Do you want me to tell you?'

Raffaella knew it would be better not to know. She should walk out of the linen shop, go straight back to Villa Rosa and stay there. But she couldn't help herself. 'Yes,' she said weakly.

'Everyone thinks that you have disrespected Marcello in the worst possible way. They're saying that you were having an affair with Ciro Ricci the whole time you were married and that you took up with him again before Marcello was cold in the ground.'

Raffaella dug her fingernails into the palms of her hands. 'No.'

'Even the priests believe it. That's why they gave you that job at Villa Rosa. They thought it might get you out of the way.'

Waves of nausea and fury were washing over Raffaella. She didn't trust herself to speak. Backing a step or two away from Angelica, she shook her head. 'No,' she repeated.

'Well, it makes sense, doesn't it?' Angelica shrugged. 'You're always being seen sneaking up the alleyway towards the Gypsy Tearoom.'

Raffaella gritted her teeth. 'Ciro is my friend. He has been kind to me, which is more than any of the Russo family were after Marcello died. Have you any idea what it was like for me? I was in shock. I could barely believe he had gone. I had to leave this shop and my home. It was such a sad and lonely time and I was grateful for Ciro's friendship. That's why I went to the Gypsy Tearoom.'

Angelica rolled her eyes. 'Why couldn't you just live quietly like a normal widow? You bring things on yourself. The way you walk through the streets in that black dress, swaying your hips and pushing out your breasts, it's no wonder you attract attention.'

Raffaella gasped. 'How dare you say that?'

'I dare to say it because it's true,' Angelica spat at her. 'You're nothing but a flirt, Raffaella. Look at poor Fabrizio. You were married to his elder brother and still stringing him along. You couldn't help yourself, could you? You needed to have him adoring you. You're one of those women who can't be happy unless men are fawning all over her, that's what everyone says. Marcello couldn't see it because he was blinded by your pretty face. But the rest of the family sees you for what you are.'

Raffaella's legs were shaking. She leaned back on the table for support. 'You've twisted things and made them ugly and untrue,' she argued. 'Fabrizio and I were only friends. I always loved Marcello. I still love him. Can't you tell people that? Can't you let them know the truth?'

Angelica tossed her black curls and laughed. 'Are you crazy? I'm not on your side, Raffaella. Surely that's obvious? Now get out. I don't want you here. You're not welcome unless you've come to buy linen. I've told you what you need to know and that's all I'm going to do for you.'

Raffaella didn't need to be told a second time. She stumbled from the shop, tears clouding her eyes and her entire body trembling. There weren't many people on the streets, but those she passed seemed to stare at her with undisguised contempt. Breaking into a run, she made for the one place where she was certain she would be treated with kindness.

As she ran towards the Gypsy Tearoom, Raffaella was filled with self-doubt. Was she the person Angelica had described? A woman who lived for the attention of men and had to have them dancing attendance on her. She had never thought of herself in that light before, but now she feared Angelica's words might be as true as they were cruel.

To her relief, she found Ciro alone. He was pottering about happily behind his newly built counter and he smiled when he saw her.

'*Ciao, bella.*' His smile faded as he saw the expression on her face. 'What's wrong? Who has been upsetting you?'

The sound of a kind voice was all it took to start Raffaella's tears flowing. She fell into Ciro's arms and, pushing her face into his chest, began to sob.

'*Cara, cara*, don't cry.' He held her tight and rocked her body gently. 'What's happened? Please tell me.'

Gradually, Raffaella's sobbing slowed and stopped. Lifting her face from Ciro's chest, she noticed that a familiar smell was filling the Gypsy Tearoom.

'You're baking pizza,' she exclaimed.

He grinned. 'The first one since the fire, and I'm glad you're here to share it with me. But before we eat, I want you to sit down and tell me what those tears were about. By the time you've finished talking the food will be ready.'

She sank down on one of the benches and wondered where to begin. 'It's nothing, really. Someone said things that upset me, but it's not important. I don't want you to worry about it.'

'But I am worried. I've never seen you cry like that before. I think you should tell me everything.'

She remembered Angelica's words and her eyes filled with fresh tears. 'Someone told me I'm a flirt.'

He laughed. 'Is that all?'

'No, the same person said the whole town thinks you and I were having an affair while Marcello was alive.'

His expression grew dark. 'Who has been saying these things?' he demanded, all the kindness seeping from his voice. 'Who has insulted us like this?'

She shook her head. 'It's best that I don't tell you. There's nothing you can do about it. And anyway, you don't need more trouble. This place is nearly finished and you have your first pizza in the oven. Things are going well for you at last. You don't want whoever set the fire to pay another visit.'

'That's my greatest fear,' he admitted.

'Do you know who it was?'

'I have my suspicions,' he said grimly, 'but I can't prove anything.

Let's not talk about this any more. It's an ugly conversation, and besides, my pizza smells like it's ready. Come and taste it. Let's see if it is as beautiful as it always was in the old Gypsy Tearoom.'

Raffaella watched as Ciro pulled the pizza from the wood-fired oven. She supposed that someone would have seen her running down the alleyway. Tongues would be wagging and word would be bound to get back to the Russo family. It would confirm all their worst suspicions about her, but Raffaella realised she didn't much care. People could say what they liked. The Gypsy Tearoom was her safe haven and she needed it more than ever.

She was still so angry and upset she was sure she wouldn't be able to swallow down any of the pizza Ciro set before her, even though the mozzarella was still bubbling from the heat of the oven and the smell of basil and tomatoes seemed to fill the whole room.

'Eat, eat,' Ciro urged. 'Quickly, tell me what you think of it.'

'It looks wonderful.'

'It's not what it looks like that matters. Taste it, Raffaella, please.'

She cut off a slice and raised it to her mouth. Just as she was about to take a bite she heard the sound of someone running down the alleyway. Silvana burst into the Gypsy Tearoom, red-cheeked and breathless.

'Madonna *mia*, you'll never guess what's happened. Tommaso Moretti has been arrested.' Her hand flew over her mouth when she spotted Raffaella. 'It's true, *cara*, your father has been taken away by the police.'

'What?' Raffaella was confused. 'Silvana, have you gone insane? How can he have been arrested?'

Silvana flopped down on the bench beside her. 'They're saying your father is responsible for sabotaging the work on the statue,' she explained, and glancing up at Ciro, she bit her lip. 'They also suspect he's the one who set fire to the Gypsy Tearoom.'

'No!' Ciro exploded. 'Tommaso is a good man. He helped me rebuild the place, for God's sake. Why would he do that if he was the person who burned it down?'

'I don't know. So suspicion wouldn't fall on him perhaps? Don't be angry with me – I'm only repeating what I've heard. Your mother has gone to the police station, Raffaella, to see if there's anything she can do. Angelo Sesto is with her.'

'I should go too.' She jumped to her feet. 'Mamma will need me.'

Raffaella began to run again, faster than the last time, her own troubles forgotten. All she could think of was her father behind bars and her mother, who loved him with all her heart, not being able to help him.

35

Time crawled slowly by at Villa Rosa. Each morning Raffaella's first thought was of her father. On sunny days she had taken to sitting in Carlotta's old spot down on the rocks and staring at the sea wishing he was out there on his fishing boat instead of locked away in a dark cell.

The police were certain they had got the right man. They had found graffiti painted on the rocks at the top of the mountain. The words 'No statue' were scrawled next to a crude drawing of a fish. And early one morning a worker had seen a short man with dark hair and a wiry fisherman's body walking away from the site. Later they found that some machinery had been tampered with and it had slowed the day's work down.

So far as Raffaella knew, they had found nothing to link her father with the burning of the Gypsy Tearoom. It was a ridiculous claim. But at times even she wondered if he might have been capable of sabotaging the work on the statue. He had been so against it from the very beginning, and who knew how far his anger might have carried him.

Umberto had been kind to her. 'The police are just as useless as the priests, if you ask me,' he had blustered. 'Don't worry, they'll have to set him free. Your father is a good man, Raffaella, just remember that.'

Carlotta, too, had been generous with comforting words, but none of them had helped Raffaella feel any better.

Perhaps the hardest thing was the way the americano was treating her. As soon as he'd realised she was Tommaso's daughter, he'd grown cold. There were no friendly smiles when she delivered a dish to the dinner table, and at night, if she walked by as he was enjoying his cigar beside the young pomegranate tree, she felt as though he was staring at her in disdain.

She wanted to talk to him, insist her father was innocent, but she was certain it would do no good. So instead she worked quietly in the kitchen, making robust meals of lamb slowly cooked in a sealed earthenware pot with potato, salami and cheese, or rolls of pork skin stuffed with garlic, parsley and chilli and then baked with a tomato sauce. She made the best meals she possibly could and followed the path down to the sea whenever she had time to indulge her own sadness.

She was sitting on the rocks staring at the crashing waves one morning when she heard her sister, Teresa, calling her.

'Raffaella, where are you? Are you down there?'

'Yes, yes, I'm here.' She saw that her sister looked hot and exhausted. 'What are you doing here? Is Mamma with you? How did you get here?'

'Ouf.' Teresa collapsed on the rocks beside her. 'One thing at a time, *sorella*. Can't you see how out of breath I am? I walked all the way up the hill and then Silvana lent me an old bread-delivery bicycle and I pedalled here. The chain came off three times on the way. Look, my legs are covered in oil.'

Teresa had grown up a lot in the past year. The child in her had disappeared and now she was a pretty young woman with long, wavy hair, a shade or two lighter than Raffaella's, and a slender figure. Her favourite colour had always been pink and as usual she was dressed from head to toe in it – pink skirt, pink blouse, even a pink ribbon in her hair. But today the colour made her skin look sallow, and the circles beneath her eyes seemed dark and tender.

'I'm so happy to see you, *cara*.' Raffaella reached over and kissed her sister on the cheek. 'I've missed you. Tell me, how is Mamma today?'

Teresa looked sad. 'The spark has gone out of her. It's awful, Raffaella. It's as though someone else is living in her body. She worries about Papà constantly, but other than taking him food each day, there's really nothing she can do to help him.'

'I feel so bad that I'm not there. Still, at least she has you and Sergio with her.'

At the sound of her brother's name, Teresa frowned and began to chew on her fingernail.

'Is Sergio not doing anything to help?' Raffaella asked.

'It's not that . . . ' Teresa stared out at the sea. 'He takes the boat out every day. His catch isn't as good as Papà's, but he's working hard.'

'That's good. I know how lazy Sergio can be when he wants. I'd thought he might slack off without Papà there to watch over him.'

'Oh, no, Sergio's not been lazy.' Teresa chewed at her fingernail again. 'Not lazy at all.'

Raffaella wondered what her sister was trying to tell her. 'There's something wrong, isn't there? Something else?' she asked anxiously.

Teresa nodded. 'Remember all those months ago when you asked me to keep watch on things at home? You told me to stay quiet and keep my ears open. Well, that's what I've been doing.'

Raffaella was surprised and touched by her sister's devotion, watching and waiting all this time even though she had forgotten ever asking her to. 'And what did you hear?' she asked eagerly.

'Oh, lots of talk about the statue; Papà and Sergio arguing about what should be done. After a while the arguments stopped. Sergio didn't seem to want to talk about it any more. And then a few weeks ago he started behaving strangely. I heard him sneaking about in the night, leaving the house and then coming back early in the morning. I asked him about it once or twice and he told me not to be a silly girl and that I was imagining things. But I know I wasn't, because one night I got up and watched him set off up the hill with Francesco Biagio and Gino Ferrando.'

'Where do you think they were going?'

'Well, the odd behaviour started at the exact same time that work began on the mountaintop,' Teresa said slowly. 'I think it's Sergio and the others who have been trying to sabotage the statue, not Papà. In fact, I'm sure of it.'

'My God.' Raffaella breathed out a long hiss. 'Could it be true? Would Sergio be so stupid?'

'Yes, I think so.'

'Have you spoken to Mamma about this?'

'No, I haven't spoken to anyone. But I couldn't keep it to myself any longer because it's been worrying me so much. I had to come and tell you.'

'I'm glad you did.'

'So what are we going to do?' Teresa stared at her, trusting that she'd find a solution.

'I'm not sure.' Raffaella couldn't imagine a worse dilemma. 'What do you think Papà would want us to do?'

'I have no idea,' Teresa said miserably. 'Sergio is an idiot, but we can't give him up to the police. But what about Papà? How can we make them believe it wasn't him? Do you suppose we ought to tell Mamma and see what she thinks?'

'No.' Raffaella was certain about that at least. 'It would kill Mamma to have to make a choice between her husband and her son. We must find a way to sort this out. I know we can do it. I just need some time to think.'

Teresa nodded. 'All right, but don't take too long, Raffaella. Remember, every day you spend thinking is another day Papà has to stay in that police cell.'

Raffaella stayed on the rocks for hours after she had gone. She forgot about everything except the dilemma she faced. Up at Villa Rosa, Eduardo waited in vain for the smell of cooking to tell him that his meal was nearly ready. And Umberto, exhausted from a day in the garden, fell into his bed early, trusting that she would pick up Carlotta from the convent as she had promised. But Raffaella stayed sitting on the rocks pondering her dilemma until long after the sun had set. Her father, or her brother? She couldn't even begin to make a decision. The moon lit a pathway over the water and the temperature dropped several degrees. The rocks were hard and inhospitable, but Raffaella didn't notice. Somewhere deep within her was an answer, and if she thought about it long and hard enough, she was certain she would find it.

Carlotta had never been worried by the dark. When the sun sank into the sea and there was still no sign of Raffaella, she wasn't concerned. She listened for the sound of the Vespa coming up the hill and wondered what her excuse would be for being so late.

It had been a slow, dreamy day. Hardly anyone had entered or left the convent aside from Sister Benedicta and a couple of the other young nuns who helped out in the school. All averted their gaze and tried to pretend Carlotta wasn't there. She didn't care. Stretched out on her rug, she had let her mind wander. She imagined the little girl who lived in the convent, what she looked like and how she passed her days. She thought of her helping to pick vegetables in the garden, learning to read from the Bible and folding her hands in prayer at night before she slept. In her mind, she constructed a whole life for the child she had never known.

Once it was dark, it grew colder and everything looked different by moonlight. Carlotta thought she saw a rat creeping towards her through the long shadows, and she heard a rustling behind her that might only have been the breeze stiffening but could have been something worse. Pulling her rug tightly around her shoulders, she wondered whether Raffaella had abandoned her and if she would have to spend the whole night here.

Carlotta was beginning to feel anxious. Staring at the high walls of the convent, she tried to occupy her mind with thoughts of what lay beyond them. She remembered there was a refectory where the nuns would be sitting down to enjoy a bowl of soup and a crust of freshly baked bread. Later they would lay down to sleep in a simple cell with a narrow bed and a cross on the wall above their heads, with nothing to trouble them but the thought of waking up in time for morning prayers. The simplicity of their lives seemed seductive to Carlotta. She wished with all her heart she was on the other side of the convent walls.

When her stomach began to growl with hunger, she knew it was well past dinnertime. More hours passed and she was sure everyone but her was asleep in bed. She longed for her own room, with its comfortable bed and flower-sprigged eiderdown. Feeling lost and lonely, she began to cry a little.

At last she could stand it no longer. Struggling to her feet, she ran on stiff legs across the road and right up to the convent gates. Hammering on them, she began to call out, 'Open the doors, please. Let me in.' Her knocking made a dull, hollow sound and she felt sure no one could hear her. Her voice fell to a whisper. 'Let me in. Please let me in.'

It seemed an age until the gates creaked open and Carlotta saw an old nun, a black shawl wrapped around her head and shoulders, frowning at her through the narrow gap.

'Why are you making such a nuisance of yourself, eh? Sitting outside our gates all day long and then knocking on our gates after dark. What's the matter with you?'

Carlotta pressed her body against the gate to prevent it being slammed shut. 'Please don't be angry with me. I only wanted to see my daughter, and then it grew dark and no one came to get me and now I'm afraid.'

'And what do you want me to do about it?'

'Please let me in.'

'You can't stay here,' the nun insisted.

'Then find Sister Benedicta,' Carlotta implored her. 'She will drive me back to Villa Rosa, I'm sure she will.'

Sensing the old nun was growing impatient, she leaned against the gate with all her weight. 'Please let me in while you go and find her. Don't make me stay out here on my own.'

The nun sighed wearily. 'Very well. Sister Benedicta is sleeping, but I will see if I can wake her. And you may come in, but you must wait in the anteroom. I don't want you trying to come any further into the convent, do you understand?'

'Yes, I won't move. I'll stay where you tell me. Oh, thank you, thank you,' she said as the gates swung further open.

The small chamber she was shown into felt safe and peaceful. The light was dim, but she sat on a smooth wooden bench beneath a cross and was sure she could smell fresh flowers. Carlotta waited for a long time, but she didn't mind. She remembered hating this place last time she'd arrived, pregnant and scared. But now it seemed different. She felt certain she was closer to her daughter here.

'Carlotta.' She started at the sound of Sister Benedicta's voice. The nun looked tired in the half-light and she felt guilty for having disturbed her sleep.

'I'm sorry ... ' she began.

'I'm sorry too,' the nun replied heavily.

'Will you take me home?'

'Yes, of course I will.'

Sister Benedicta was silent as she drove down the steep road, and Carlotta was too nervous to talk. She suspected the nun thought she was a fool for hanging about the convent gates all day long and panicking the moment it got dark.

She drove the little car surprisingly quickly and seemed to enjoy it, cornering skilfully and putting her foot down on the straight. They were nearly at Villa Rosa when she slowed the vehicle and turned to Carlotta.

'So will you be back at the convent tomorrow?'

'Yes, I'll be there.'

'How long is this going to go on for?'

'Until I'm allowed to see my daughter.'

The nun came to a smooth stop outside the gates of Villa Rosa. 'You're very stubborn,' she observed.

'Would you give up easily if you were me?'

Sister Benedicta looked thoughtful. 'No, no, I wouldn't,' she said carefully.

Carlotta stared at her. She felt sure that the nun wanted to tell her more. 'I'm very patient. I'll wait for ever if I have to,' she said in a soft voice as she opened the passenger door and climbed out of the car.

'I hope you won't have to wait for ever.' Sister Benedicta raised her hand in farewell. '*Buona notte*, Carlotta. Sleep well. I'll see you in the morning, I expect.'

The sound of the little Fiat roaring up the hill at breakneck speed cut through the silence of the night. Carlotta stood there for a moment and wondered how much longer she would have to wait to see her daughter. Sister Benedicta had never denied the child was there, behind the convent walls. Maybe she couldn't bring herself to lie. But how much longer would it be before she told her the whole truth? Carlotta was growing tired of waiting.

It was almost completely dark when Raffaella realised how chilled and uncomfortable she was feeling. A cloud had drifted over the moon, and the sea had faded into the inky blackness of the night. She panicked for a moment. How was she going to find her way safely off the rocks and back up to Villa Rosa?

Her legs were stiff and she stumbled once or twice as she picked her way slowly across the uneven ground. It was a relief to reach the steep path that climbed up through the trees and to feel her way from bough to bough towards the terraced gardens.

There was no sign of anyone when she reached the house, but it smelled like food had been cooked not long ago. Raffaella sniffed at the air. Something had been fried in a light batter, she thought, and something else had been simmered in an oily sauce of tomatoes.

Olivia Barbieri must have grown tired of waiting and prepared the food herself. She had cooked like a person who was used to someone else cleaning up after her. Tomato sauce was splattered across the worktop, and dishes were piled haphazardly over the benches.

Raffaella ate the remains of the food from the messy, discarded plates. Olivia had picked courgette flowers, stuffed them with a little ricotta and deep-fried them lightly. But even tasting them cold, it was obvious she had used too much salt in the batter and cooked them for a few seconds too long.

The salad leaves were soggy from their long soaking in lemon and olive oil. The pasta was swollen and cold. But the baby octopus she found on a dish in the oven tasted good. Realising how hungry she was, Raffaella scooped up its oily sauce with a crust of bread and savoured the sting of chilli and the fresh, grassy taste of parsley picked from Umberto's garden.

She was wiping up the last of the sauce when she smelled something more than food. The musky perfume of the americano's cigar was drifting into the kitchen. She saw he was alone in his favourite spot beneath the young pomegranate tree enjoying the night and his own company. She wondered if she dared to disturb him.

Raffaella waited in the shadows of the kitchen doorway, taking care to keep her breathing soft and slow so he wouldn't know she was there, and watched him with greedy eyes.

There was a rhythm to the way he smoked. First, he drew on his cigar, then held his breath for a heartbeat or two before blowing out the smoke in an even stream. It was a familiar sight to Raffaella, and yet watching it still felt like an intimacy.

The cigar was half spent and she could wait no longer. Moving slowly, she crossed the courtyard, as she did every night on her way home to bed. Lately, when she passed Eduardo, she had been too proud to try to meet his eye. It seemed easier to hold her face away from him and slope past pretending he wasn't there.

But not tonight, for in all those hours spent sitting on the rocks racking her brain for a way to free her father, just one thought kept returning to her – the americano could help them if he chose to. So tonight she must swallow her pride.

'Signore.' She stood before him. 'May I join you?'

Eduardo considered her for a moment and then nodded reluctantly.

She sat on the low wall just a hand's breadth away from him, and breathing the stray curls of smoke from his cigar, she waited for him to speak.

'Where were you this evening?' he asked at last. 'We were expecting you to prepare dinner as usual. What happened? Were you ill?'

'Not ill, signore, no.' She was so close to him that her skin tingled and the hairs on her arms stood to attention.

Eduardo frowned. 'Signora Barbieri had to take over in the kitchen. Her food is not as good as yours,' he complained. 'She spoiled the courgette flowers, and she cooked the pasta for too long. Still, at least we didn't go hungry, I suppose. Where were you?' he asked again.

'I didn't have the heart to cook tonight.' The moon came out from behind a long, black cloud, and she turned and tried to see his eyes. 'It's better for you to have Signora Barbieri in the kitchen just now. I can't concentrate on frying courgette flowers until they are crisp, or simmering tender *polpi* in tomatoes for you. All I can think of is my father, locked up in that police cell. He is innocent, signore, I know it for sure. Don't ask me to tell you how, only believe me, please.'

He breathed out his cigar smoke with an impatient hiss. 'You are his daughter, so of course you would say that. But the police are convinced of Tommaso Moretti's guilt and so are half the priests. They wouldn't have arrested him unless they had a decent case against him.'

'But it wasn't him. He'd never have burned down the Gypsy Tearoom, because Ciro Ricci is his friend. And someone else is to blame for sabotaging the statue. I'm completely certain of it.'

'Do you know who?'

She nodded. 'Yes, I think so, but I can't say.'

'If you want to help your father, you have no other choice.' His tone was brisk and Raffaella hesitated for a moment.

'I want to tell you, but it would cause too much trouble for me if I did. You've seen how this town works. You understand that sometimes it's safer to keep your mouth closed?' She reached out and let her fingertips brush his arm. 'Can't you trust my word?'

Eduardo ground out his cigar against the wall and frowned. 'I'm sorry, Raffaella, but you have to understand we have lost a lot of time and money on this project because of the sabotage that's been going on. Your father has committed a serious crime and he has to pay for it.'

'So you don't believe me?'

'He left his signature, remember – a drawing of a fish was found on the rocks.'

'My father isn't a stupid man. Why would he incriminate himself like that? The person who left that drawing must be someone who wants you to think a fisherman is to blame.'

Eduardo sounded weary, as if he hoped the subject could be forgotten. 'Raffaella, I don't want to argue with you about this. Surely you understand my position? The fishermen refused to pay any money towards the statue, so even if that drawing hadn't been left, suspicion would have fallen on them. It has to be one of them. If not your father, then who? Tell me that and I'll see what I can do. But otherwise I can't intervene for you and your family.'

She closed her eyes and was silent for a moment.

'Who, Raffaella? If you know something, then you should tell me.'

She shook her head. 'I have suspicions, but I don't know anything for sure.'

'Well, I can't help you.' He turned to her and touched her cheek lightly. 'I'm sorry, Raffaella, really I am.'

'I'm sorry too.' She felt her anger unlace itself and the words fell out of her mouth. 'Sorry I spent so many nights out here listening to you talk your nonsense. Sorry I wasted my time cooking and cleaning for you when I could have been at home with my family, who are good people no matter what you or anyone else in Triento says.'

She scrubbed the tears from her eyes roughly with bunched-up hands and marched back towards the kitchen, where a mess of Olivia Barbieri's dirty dishes still waited for her. More angry tears fell while she filled the sink with hot water, and as she noisily piled in plates and cutlery, she found that she was sobbing.

'Raffaella, don't . . . ' The americano was standing in the doorway. 'Please don't cry like this.'

'Go away. Leave me alone.' Her voice was raw and thick with tears.

'If I could help you, I would, but . . . '

'I said, go away.' She was shouting now. 'Just leave.'

But he didn't leave. Instead, he came up behind her, wrapped his arms about her shoulders and turned her body so her head fell on his chest. She gave herself up to the sobbing, and he rocked her gently as her tears soaked into his shirt.

It was only when the heaving sobs subsided that Raffaella became aware of the musky cigar-smoke smell of him and the hardness of his body as he leaned into her. She raised her red and swollen face from his chest so her lips were only a shallow breath away from his.

The kiss was inevitable. And as she explored the warm wetness of his mouth with her tongue and felt his fingers brushing over her body, she let everything else slip away. This time, the intensity of her desire didn't catch her by surprise. She relished the feeling of its heat seeping through her body as he kissed her harder and deeper.

It was as she spread her arms sideways for better balance that Raffaella's hand caught at the dish of discarded courgette flowers. It came crashing down and they broke apart as the sound of the old china shattering on the hard tiled floor rang through the still of the night.

'Signore, he didn't do it,' she said in a whisper.

'What?' He was confused.

'My father, he never tried to hurt your statue. I promise you that.'

'Who, then? That's all I ask. Who?'

She shook her head, the tears starting again, and he circled her waist with his arms and held her tight.

Carlotta had watched Sister Benedicta's car disappear and was about to head home to bed when she heard the sound of smashing china coming from the kitchen of Villa Rosa. Perturbed, she slipped quietly through the gates and across the shadows towards the kitchen. She noticed the smell of the americano's cigar still hanging on the night air, but there was no sign of him. The kitchen door was shut, but there was a light on inside.

She was angry rather than shocked when she saw them there folded into one other's bodies. So this was why she had been left to sit alone in the darkness up at the convent. Raffaella had been too distracted by her own pleasure to care to remember her.

Carlotta felt betrayed. She turned and, with practised silence, slipped away home before anyone could find her there. In the morning she would have to face Raffaella. She wondered what she would find to say to her.

36

Sundays in summertime were nearly always the same in Triento. It was a day to wake early and take Mass, and then, with their duty done, most people liked to cool off with a swim at the beach before heading home for a long, satisfying lunch with all their family around them.

On Sundays the fishing boats stayed moored in the harbour, their decks hosed clean and their prows nudging the rocks. There were eight of them in all, squat wooden tubs painted blue and white, with a tall cabin for the skipper to stand in and a big winch dominating the stern that was used to haul up the nets when they were heavy with fish.

But this Sunday morning there were only seven fishing boats in the harbour. The eighth had cast off from its mooring and was chugging slowly out to sea. Onboard were two men, one of them heavyset, the other more compact. From the stance of their bodies and the way they used their hands as they talked, it was clear neither of them was happy.

'How could you be such an idiot?' Sergio was furious with Francesco Biagio and angry with himself too. If only he'd been watching Francesco more carefully. He never should have trusted him to get it right. Everyone knew the man had nothing but fresh air between his ears. As he steered the boat out towards the choppy waves beyond the headland, Sergio raised his voice. 'You've ruined everything now, haven't you?'

'How many times do I have to tell you I'm sorry?' Francesco was a big man, but with his shoulders drooping and his face crumpled, he looked pitiful. 'I didn't realise how much trouble it was going to cause.'

Only the certain knowledge Francesco couldn't swim prevented

Sergio from pushing him overboard. 'You drew a picture of a fish, *stupido*. You might as well have signed our names on the damn rock,' he hissed instead.

'Well, they still don't know it was us, do they?' Francesco pointed out, and a sulky expression settled on his face as he stared out of the boat and back across the sea towards Triento.

Francesco was tired of Sergio shouting at him. He had never understood all the fuss about the statue. Quite honestly, he didn't care whether it was ever built or not. What he had enjoyed was the subterfuge of their plan. He liked to fantasise that he was a bandit as he crept around on the mountaintop after dark tampering with machinery. And he loved the feeling of having his own secret life that his wife, Giuliana, suspected nothing about. She assumed he was out with Sergio and Gino Ferrando drinking beer and wasting time. He smirked when he thought what she would say if she knew what he'd really been doing.

It had all gone so well at first. He, Sergio and Gino were like a band of brothers embarking on a risky adventure. But Sergio had insisted on being the leader of the group. He'd been unbearably bossy, insisting no one could do anything without his say-so. Gino had got sick of it first. Declaring that he was too old to spend half the night crawling about on the mountaintop, he'd refused to come out with them again. And then Sergio had been like a frustrated general with only one soldier to command and it had been no fun any more.

Drawing the fish on the rock had been an act of defiance for Francesco. It had seemed to him that they should have a symbol and take some credit for their work. But now, because of it, Tommaso had been arrested and Sergio had insisted they come out on his boat for this emergency meeting.

The Moretti boat looked no different than the others, but for some reason it had always been the luckiest. With Tommaso as its skipper, the nets were always full of fish and it was often the first to make it back to the safety of the harbour walls. But once Tommaso was locked away in prison, the boat's luck seemed to change. There was a feeling of desperation about its crew now as they trailed home with a poor catch. Sergio had become frightened, and his fear made him bossier than ever. Before too long Francesco had bitterly regretted ever getting involved with his plans.

'Sabotage was your idea,' he reminded Sergio, his arms crossed stubbornly over his great wide chest. 'I'm sorry your father is in jail, but you can't lay all the blame at my door.'

'If you'd followed my orders, everything would have been fine.'

'I don't think so,' Francesco argued. 'Angelo Sesto was right all those months ago when we had that meeting in the Gypsy Tearoom. Sabotaging the statue was a bad idea. We should have gone along with what those fools up the hill wanted. But you insisted we try to stop them and because of you Tommaso is in jail.'

'It's hardly my fault.' Sergio was indignant.

Francesco shrugged. 'It's your problem, at any rate.'

'What do you mean?'

'Your father is the one who has been locked up, and you're the one who is going to have to come up with a way of getting him out.'

It was Sergio's turn to stare out to sea. Screwing up his eyes against the bright sun, he said nothing for a moment or two. When he broke his silence, the tone of his voice had changed. 'How am I going to do that?' he asked raggedly. 'You have to help me, Francesco.'

Francesco shook his head. 'I'm sorry, Sergio, really sorry, but I can't help you any more.'

Padre Pietro was sitting at the end of one of the wooden pews in the welcome coolness of his ancient chapel. It had been a long sleepless night and he was exhausted. A few hours ago the old priest, Padre Fabiano, had finally loosened his grip on life, and he and Padre Matteo had stayed at his bedside as he slipped away.

Padre Matteo had taken care of all the necessary things, prayed for the smooth passing of the old priest's soul and performed the last rites. He had merely sat there holding one of his thin, wrinkled hands, whispering into his ear and hoping that although his eyes were closed and his breathing laboured, the old priest could hear and understand him.

He spoke all night of memories of their youth, reminding Padre Fabiano of the days when he was his mentor, helping him take the first steps along the path towards a lifetime of serving God. He thanked the old priest for believing in him and, squeezing his hand tightly, told him what a fine man he had been.

Padre Fabiano's feet twitched, and once or twice his lips seemed to form a smile. But as the day broke, he began to moan as he struggled for breath, and to the sound of Padre Matteo's practised chanting, Padre Pietro bent his head low and said his last goodbyes.

Afterwards he felt deeply saddened, and not just because he had farewelled a friend. With Padre Fabiano gone, he was the oldest of the priests. It struck him forcibly that his time on earth was growing shorter and before long it would be him lying inert on a deathbed as Padre Matteo recited the last words over him. Once the thought had come to him, Padre Pietro couldn't stop dwelling on it.

He had hurried back to Santo Spirito to say Mass, but had been unable to shake himself free of his melancholy. And now with his congregation gone, as he snatched a few moments' rest in one of his own pews, his spirit felt heavier than ever.

Hearing the creak of the old wooden doors opening, Padre Pietro assumed it was one of his congregation come to retrieve a forgotten headscarf or shawl. He was surprised to see Raffaella. With her dark hair lit by the shaft of sunlight streaming through the stained-glass window and her black dress buttoned chastely to her neck, he thought she had never looked more beautiful.

'My child, you have missed Mass,' he told her. 'You should have been here over an hour ago.'

'I know, I'm sorry.'

'I can hear your confession now, though, if that's what you want. Come and sit beside me for a moment.'

She slid on to the pew next to him and looked up at the big wooden cross on the altar. 'I didn't come here to confess, at least not exactly.'

'What, then? What can I do for you?'

'I'm not sure you can help me at all, but I had to talk to someone and I can't trust anyone but you, Padre Pietro.'

He saw that the look in her eyes was quite desperate. 'Are you in trouble?' he asked gently.

She nodded. 'Yes.'

'Tell me everything, Raffaella, and if I can help you, then you know I will.'

The relief of unburdening herself to Padre Pietro was enormous. In a hushed voice she told him about her conviction that Sergio was the one responsible for tampering with the equipment up on the mountaintop. It was good to confide in someone older and wiser than herself.

Padre Pietro listened well. Sitting quietly on the pew beside her, his expression didn't change. Raffaella never guessed that every word she spoke was like another weight loaded on to his shoulders. She never dreamed that the old priest was wishing he could reach out and touch her lips to silence her before she confided anything else he would prefer not to hear.

'What am I going to do?' she finished at last. 'I've thought about it all night long. I hardly got a moment's sleep. But I still don't know what to do.'

Padre Pietro rubbed at his eyes tiredly. 'What does your conscience tell you to do, Raffaella?'

She hesitated. 'My conscience?'

'Yes. An innocent man is in jail, and the guilty one walks free. What to you seems like the right thing to do?'

'Go to the police and tell them what I suspect? Is that what you think I should do, Padre?'

'My child, I'm not here to tell you what to do. Only you can decide that.'

'But I can't decide. That's why I came to talk to you.' Raffaella felt a sense of hopelessness sweep over her like a wave over the rocks. Perhaps this had been a waste of time after all. The old priest couldn't help her.

They both fell silent as they heard the creak of the wooden door and turned to see who was entering the church. Raffaella gasped when she realised who it was. Her brother, Sergio, his face glowing from the morning sun, was stealing between the pews towards the altar.

Sergio was startled when he saw them. 'Oh, I didn't think anyone would be here,' he mumbled. 'I missed Mass so I just came in to pray for a while. I'm sorry if I've disturbed you both. I'll come back later.'

He began to back away, but Raffaella stopped him with a word. 'No.'

She thought she saw guilt in the expression on his face and maybe something more. Fear perhaps, or panic. She felt her anger heating inside her. Raffaella loved her brother, but all her life she'd been exasperated by him and now he'd gone too far.

'It's too late to run away,' she hurled at him. 'I know what you've been up to, Sergio. And so does Padre Pietro.'

'What do you mean?' His attempt at feigning innocence was pathetic and even he seemed to know it.

Raffaella gave him a hard look. She saw that his hands were trembling, but felt no pity. 'We know about the statue and the stupid things you've been doing up there. Our father is in prison, Sergio, and it's all your fault.'

He sat down heavily on the pew in front of them and let his head fall into his hands. 'I know, I'm sorry. I thought I was doing the right thing and that Papà would be pleased with me. How could I have known it would end like this?'

Raffaella unleashed her temper. 'What sort of fool are you?' she began, but she felt Padre Pietro's gently restraining hand on her shoulder, so she bit her lip and held back the words she was almost bursting to say.

'What's done is done,' the old priest said wearily. 'Let's not waste energy on recrimination. Instead, let's think what should be done next.'

'Sergio should go and tell the police what really happened,' Raffaella said with certainty. 'He should give himself up.'

'What good would that do?' her brother volleyed back at her. 'Then we'll both be in the cells, me and Papà, and who will take the boat out to sea then? Who'll look after the family, eh? Tell me that, Raffaella.'

She thought about it and saw he was right. Just because Sergio confessed didn't mean the police would release Tommaso. They would more likely assume father and son were plotting together. And if two members of their family ended up behind bars, it wasn't going to help anyone.

'What, then?' she asked. 'What's the answer?'

'I don't know,' Sergio said hopelessly. 'That's why I came here, to pray and think hard and try to decide what's best to do.'

'I know!' The idea came to Raffaella suddenly and she was excited by it. 'Tonight you should go up the mountain and tamper with something else.'

Sergio was confused. 'How will that help?'

'Because if the sabotage continues when Papà is locked away, the police will realise someone else is responsible. And they'll have to release Papà'

'But what if I get caught?'

'Well, you haven't been caught yet, have you?' Raffaella pointed out. 'And anyway, I have the perfect alibi for you. Tonight Ciro Ricci is throwing a party to celebrate the reopening of the Gypsy Tearoom. So long as you are seen there, looking a little drunk and having a good time, no one will suspect what you've been up to on the mountain.'

Sergio looked dubious. 'I don't know, it doesn't seem like such a good plan.'

'You don't have any choice. There is no other way.'

'I can't do it.' Sergio sounded desperate. 'Not on my own, I'm sorry but I can't.'

Raffaella glanced at Padre Pietro. 'He has to, doesn't he, Padre?'

The priest hesitated. 'I don't know . . . Perhaps it's worth a try.'

'I can't do it,' Sergio repeated stubbornly.

This time Raffaella couldn't hold in her anger. 'You're pathetic. You're nothing but a coward and I'm ashamed of you.'

Sergio flinched but said nothing. Shaking out her skirt, Raffaella rose from the pew. 'You may be too frightened to do this one thing to help Papà, but I'm not,' she told him. 'Don't worry, I'll take care of it.'

She stalked out of the church, slamming the wooden door hard behind her. As she strode down the narrow lane that led to the main street, Raffaella felt energised rather than anxious. Tonight she'd slip away from Ciro's party and ride the Vespa up to the mountaintop. She wasn't sure what she would do once she got there, but she was confident she'd manage something.

37

Ciro had done all he could to put Triento in a party mood. He had decorated the alleyway with flags and fairy lights, and he'd hired a guitar player from the next village who was famous for his capacity to sing love songs all night long. The old man was gently strumming and tuning his guitar when Raffaella arrived at the Gypsy Tearoom. Just like it had in the old days, the place smelled of fresh basil and wood smoke, and behind the counter, Ciro was busy chopping food and stirring sauces, a sheen of sweat on his brow. He paused for a moment to nod and smile at her.

'*Ciao, bella*. Come in, come in. You're the first, but you're not too early.'

'I can't stay too long,' she told him and, fingering her black dress ruefully, added, 'I probably shouldn't be here at all.'

Ciro wiped down his chopping board and began to clean his knives. 'It's been almost a year since you lost Marcello, hasn't it?' he said thoughtfully.

Raffaella nodded. 'It's gone so fast.'

'How much longer will you mourn him?'

'One more year at least.'

'And then you can start to think about your future?'

'Yes, I suppose so.' Raffaella looked dubious. 'But it's still such a long way away.'

'The next year will pass by just as quickly as the last one did,' Ciro comforted her.

They were interrupted by Silvana's arrival. She bustled in, wearing her best black dress, with her hair loose about her face. '*Buona sera, buona sera*,' she greeted them, pausing to kiss Raffaella quickly on both cheeks. 'I mustn't stay long, I'm afraid. But I had to come over to wish you good luck, Signor Ricci, and perhaps to have one little glass of celebratory wine with you.'

'It would be rude not to,' Ciro agreed. 'Here, let me go and get you a glass.'

Silvana glanced quickly over at the door and Raffaella was certain she was hoping the mayor would arrive before it was time for her to leave. She seemed jittery, gulping at the glass of sweet sparkling wine Ciro gave her and drumming her fingers on his countertop.

As they talked about the bakery and the latest gossip, Raffaella sensed that she only had half of Silvana's attention. Whenever she could, she darted a glance over her shoulder, and she kept biting her lips and fluffing her hair with nervous fingers.

When a blush deepened on her cheeks and her eyes widened, Raffaella felt sure the mayor must be arriving. She turned and saw him enter, his eyes fixed on Silvana.

'*Buona sera*,' he greeted them, taking the glass of wine that Ciro offered and raising it in the air. 'What a great day this is. The Gypsy Tearoom is open again at last. *Salute.*'

'*Salute.*' Raffaella and Silvana raised their glasses in the air too and toasted Ciro's success in rebuilding his life from the ashes.

'Yes, a great day indeed,' Ciro agreed. 'And I hope I'll be seeing you in the mornings for your coffee, like I always used to, Mayor.'

Giorgio nodded and darted another glance at Silvana. 'Oh, yes, of course. I'll be here at the usual time. I'm looking forward to it.'

'And I'll start delivering bread again, if you like.' Silvana couldn't keep the smile from her face. 'I'll make sure I'm here at the usual time too. It will be just like it always was.'

Raffaella held her glass, sipped and smiled, but said very little. Her mind was focused on what she had to achieve tonight. She felt more alive than she'd ever felt and she was impatient to get started.

Gradually, more people arrived and the little place soon felt crowded. Ciro began dishing out slices of pizza and shouting to be heard above the din. Silvana and the mayor had moved to the far end of the room, pushed there by drinkers' sharp elbows, and were deep in conversation. Outside, the light was fading and it would soon be dark. It was time for Raffaella to slip away.

No one noticed her leave. She hurried to where she'd left the Vespa in a back alley on the edge of town. She felt a twinge of guilt as she roared up the road that led to the mountaintop, her black shawl wrapped round her dark hair and covering half her face. She had never broken the law before.

Things had changed so much on the mountain that Raffaella didn't know where to begin. She paused for a moment, horrified and confused by the picture before her. The ground had been churned up by heavy machinery, and where once there had been scrubby grass and wildflowers, now there was only rubble. Cement-mixers leaked dust, metal struts lay in piles, and already the huge pillars that would one day carry the road all the way to the summit were beginning to stride up the hill. What had been a peaceful abandoned place was now all ugliness and scars. Raffaella couldn't imagine how a beautiful statue could ever rise from the destruction. For the first time she understood why her father had objected so vehemently to the project and why Sergio had felt justified in trying to sabotage it.

Picking up a heavy rock, she wandered between the vehicles that had been parked haphazardly wherever the construction workers had last used them. The place was still and silent with only a whisper of a breeze through what was left of the mountain grass. Raffaella was certain she was the only one there.

It was difficult to know what to do. Should she smash the headlights of a truck, or try for something more ambitious? What had Sergio and his friends been doing to hamper the progress of the building? She wished she had thought to ask him.

She was still trying to decide when she heard footsteps chasing her, and as she jumped and turned, she felt a heavy arm fall across her shoulders.

'Got you,' a strange male voice said, and she felt him tighten his grip on her.

She struggled, but it was futile. He held her fast.

'Who is it? Pull off the scarf and let's take a look.' This voice, she recognised. It was Fabrizio Russo, breathless with excitement, pulling the shawl away from her head with clumsy fingers and shining a torch in her face.

'Raffaella!' He sounded shocked. 'What are you doing here?'

She blinked in the bright light. 'I came up to take a look at what's happening here.'

'Oh, yes, and you thought you'd come after dark and look at it by moonlight with a rock in your hand, did you?' The stranger's accent sounded northern. Raffaella tried twisting round to see his face, but he hadn't yet loosened his grip on her.

'Let me go,' she begged.

'Yes, let her go,' Fabrizio urged. 'Don't hurt her, for God's sake. She was my brother Marcello's wife.'

'I don't care who she is. She was up to no good and I'm taking her down the hill to the police. She'll be spending tonight in a cell.'

'No, wait . . . ' Fabrizio reached out and touched her cheek. 'What were you doing here? You weren't really going to damage something, were you?'

Raffaella wanted to lie to him but found she couldn't. 'Look what these strangers have done to our mountain,' she said instead, her anger fizzing. 'The place looks as though a war is being fought here. And they're bleeding the town dry for this. My father was right, the statue is a crazy idea.'

'So you're in this with him?' Fabrizio was angry too. 'The pair of you are saboteurs. And did you think that you would get away with it? Wasn't it obvious that we would post a watch up here to see if we could catch anyone else? My friend is right . . . you'll be spending the night in a cell.'

'Fabrizio, please . . . ' She realised it was pointless pleading with him. The impressionable boy who was always half in love with her had hardened into a man and he wasn't her friend any more.

She dropped the rock she'd been clutching in her hand and felt the stranger relax his hold on her. 'So you're taking me to the police?'

'That's right.' Fabrizio's face was half in shadow, but she knew his expression was stern.

'I hadn't damaged anything. I was just looking around. That's not against the law, is it?'

'You had the intention of damaging something. We both saw you. And who do you think the police will believe – us, or the girl whose father is already occupying one of their cells?'

Raffaella felt like crying, but she managed not to. Her heart was pounding and her stomach churning, but she put on a brave face. 'Well, what are you waiting for?' she spat at him. 'Why don't you and your friend take me to the police, then? I'm only glad Marcello isn't alive to see what a *scemo* you turned out to be. You were always his favourite brother. This would have broken his heart.'

'Don't bring Marcello into this.' Fabrizio's voice was fierce. 'You showed no respect to him when he was alive and even less once he was in the ground. Why did you even bother to wear black, eh? You're such a hypocrite, Raffaella.'

'You don't know anything about me, Fabrizio,' she said unsteadily.

'I know what my mother thinks of you and what she believes you did to Marcello. I tried to defend you, but now I'm wondering if I was wrong. If you're capable of coming up here to destroy things, maybe you're capable of poisoning my brother. Perhaps I should talk to the police about that too.'

Raffaella was so furious she could barely speak. 'You're an idiot, Fabrizio.'

'Yes, I am, I trusted you. I thought you were perfect and I envied my brother for having you as his wife. Now I see you for what you are and I realise both of us were idiots for not seeing it before.'

The heavyset stranger took her arm. 'That's enough. Let's get her to the police and they can decide what to do with her. You did a good job tonight, *amico*. You make a fine watchman.'

Raffaella realised she was trembling. As they led her to the car they had parked out of sight behind a truck, she felt scared. What would her father say when he was told she was occupying a cell beside his? How would her mother cope? And worse of all, what about Eduardo? He would never want to speak to her again, that was for sure. She had thought she was being so clever and she had ruined everything. This time Raffaella couldn't stop the tears from falling.

38

Triento had never been so divided. Half of the town believed Raffaella was innocent and should be released from the cells. The other half was convinced of her guilt. In Silvana's bakery and around the market stalls in the piazza, people talked of little else.

There were those in town who felt guilty themselves. Chief among them was Padre Pietro. He knew he should have stopped Raffaella. If he hadn't been so worn down by tiredness and saddened by the loss of an old friend, he might have counselled her better. He tried to make amends by convincing people of her innocence, but they didn't want to know.

Meanwhile Raffaella refused to see anyone. When Ciro Ricci turned up with a tray of pizza for her to eat, he found Silvana had already been there with a basket of bread and cheese. Neither of them even glimpsed her. She was too ashamed to see her mother or her sister and too mortified to talk to Carlotta.

So when Sergio appeared, edgy and tense, he half expected to be turned away too.

'I'm her brother,' he told the policeman on duty. 'Can I see her for five minutes?'

'She's refused all her other visitors. I don't see why you'd be any different.'

Sergio paced back and forth as he waited for the policeman to return. He didn't want to be here. It was a suffocating place. He felt like there wasn't enough air in the room to fill his lungs.

'You can go through.' The policeman sounded surprised. 'She's in the nearest cell, and your father is in the one at the end. At this rate, we'll have your whole family here.'

'I hope not,' Sergio replied nervously, and ducking through the door, he entered a short corridor of cells. The light was dim, but he saw that a chair had been drawn up next to the bars of the nearest cell. He was shocked when his eyes fell on Raffaella. She was pale, with dark shadows under her eyes, and her hair was pulled back harshly from her face. She was perched on the end of a narrow bed covered in a thin grey blanket, hugging her knees and rocking herself gently.

The policeman stayed within earshot so Sergio had to be careful of what he said.

'Raffaella, I'm so sorry.' He really meant it. 'I can't believe you're here.'

'It's my own fault. You told me it was a stupid plan.'

'What are we going to do now?'

She stared at him and chewed on her lower lip.

'Perhaps I should do what I ought to have done in the beginning?' he offered.

She shook her head. 'That won't do any good. There is only one thing I can think of that might help and even that is risky.'

'What?'

'Go up to Villa Rosa and ask Carlotta to let you see the americano. Explain everything to him. Tell him the whole story, Sergio. Don't miss anything out. If he believes you, then he might help us.'

'Why should he believe me?'

Raffaella hesitated. 'He and I were friends . . . ' she began.

'What do you mean, friends?' Sergio's voice was growing louder.

She held her fingers to her lips. 'Shush, not now. Just go and tell him the truth, Sergio.'

'And will I end up . . . ?' He looked around at the gloomy cells with their low ceilings and stale air. 'I don't think I could stand it, Raffaella.'

She shrugged. 'It's a risk,' she admitted. 'A big risk. But I don't see that you have any other choice. They're so sure we are guilty. Only the americano can help us now.'

Sergio let his head fall into his hands. He wished he could run away from this mess and start a new life somewhere else. He couldn't imagine going to the americano, cap in hand, and begging for his family's freedom. But he could picture himself here, on the other side of the bars, and the thought of it terrified him.

Sergio had never been to Villa Rosa before, and he was impressed. The house was looking particularly lovely, with the sunlight washing the pink walls, and the petals from the geraniums on the balcony drifting on the breeze down to the courtyard.

There was no sign of Carlotta, but he spotted a young woman he didn't recognise. She had a towel wrapped round her waist, and her long, dark hair was damp.

'Hello, who are you?' She smiled at him and he saw how white her teeth were against her honey-coloured skin.

'I'm Sergio Moretti,' he replied, trying not to stare at her pert little breasts with their hard nipples straining at the fabric of her swimming costume. 'I'm Raffaella's brother and I'm looking for the americano. Is he here?'

'You mean Eduardo, I suppose. He's still down there swimming. He's taken a day off work and he's decided to see if he's fit enough to swim to the island. I think he's a madman.'

'Shouldn't you be down there watching him in case he gets into trouble?'

She shrugged her shoulders and examined the way her gold bangle fell down her slim arm prettily. 'What could I do to help? I'm not going to jump in and rescue him. I'd drown myself, wouldn't I?' she said. 'And what good would that do?'

Sergio thought she had a point. He wondered if what he was about to do was madness.

'You can wait for him up here and talk to me, though, if you like.' The girl smiled again. 'Tell me about your sister in prison. Is it terrible there? Do they treat her badly?'

Sergio shifted nervously from foot to foot. 'I don't know. Maybe I should come back later,' he suggested.

The girl pouted. 'Well, suit yourself of course. But I'm bored sitting here all by myself. I'd prefer it if you stayed.'

Sergio had never seen a girl as pretty as this one. Her frame was delicate, and her skin seemed highly polished. Standing beside her, he felt like a sweating, clumsy brute.

'My name is Claudia Barbieri,' she told him. 'This is my house. Well, actually, I live in Napoli most of the time. But the city is a nightmare this time of year, isn't it? I much prefer to be near the sea.'

Sergio wished the americano would return soon. He didn't know how to talk to a girl like this. 'I'm a fisherman,' he offered, 'and I'm out at sea all day long, so to me it doesn't seem so good. I'd like to spend time in the city.'

'Well, why don't you, then?'

It seemed so simple when she said it. He wondered why he had never left Triento and tried his luck in the city. 'My family are here,' he began. 'And I have to work my father's boat and catch fish.'

'But if you don't like doing it, why bother?' Claudia sat on a wooden chair and stretched her legs out in front of her. Dropping the towel from around her waist, she wriggled into the cushions and made herself comfortable. Sergio couldn't help but stare at her tiny waist and flat belly.

'Claudia!' An older woman was crossing the courtyard.

'Yes, Mamma?'

'What are you doing talking to this man? Who is he?'

'This is the housekeeper's brother, Mamma,' Claudia said impatiently. 'I've been asking him to tell me all about what it's like in her prison cell.'

'What is he doing here? What does he want?' She sounded hostile.

'I'm sorry, signora.' Sergio was flushed. 'I'm here to talk to the americano, but he's out swimming at the moment.'

'Well, you can go over there and sit on the terrace to wait for him. Claudia, cover yourself up and come with me. Since it seems I have to do all the cooking now, the least you can do is help me.'

Claudia looked back over her shoulder as she followed her mother into the house. She smiled one last time and twitched her hand in a wave. Sergio wished he could go after her. He had never seen how rich people lived before. He wanted to look at their furniture and find out whether they had a big radiogram to play records on. And he longed to see more of the beautiful girl.

Instead, he took a seat on the hard tiled bench beneath the bougainvillea and waited uncomfortably for the americano. He was dreading this conversation. Raffaella might believe they were friends, but he couldn't see how the man could be anything but hostile towards him.

Finally, Sergio heard the slap of wet feet on the steps, and standing up, he tensed and readied himself to speak.

'*Salve*, signore,' he said as a tall, dark man with wide shoulders rounded the corner. 'Did you reach the island?'

'Yes, I did.' Eduardo couldn't help grinning. 'Do I know you? Are you one of the workers from the mountain?'

'No, signore, you've never met me before. I'm Sergio Moretti, the brother of Raffaella, and I've come here to ask for your help.'

Eduardo's grin disappeared and his tone was cold. 'I've no interest in talking to any member of your family and certainly no intention of helping you.'

'Won't you at least hear me out, signore?' Sergio hated himself for pleading like this. 'My sister said you were her friend. She believes you are the only one who can help us.'

Eduardo frowned. 'All right, I will listen to you. I owe Raffaella that at least.'

The americano wanted to sit on the low wall beside the pomegranate tree so the sun could dry the seawater on his body. Sergio felt himself sweating even more copiously as he began to talk.

It was a far from easy tale to tell. Eduardo shook his head gravely when he described the plot to sabotage the statue, and he shuddered when he heard details of how they'd gone about it. Although Sergio faltered once or twice, somehow he managed to get the whole story out.

'And that's why you have to help Raffaella,' he finished. 'She had nothing to do with this. Neither did my father.'

Eduardo rubbed his fingertips against the bristles on his chin and sat there deep in thought for a minute or two. 'Why don't you confess all this to the police?' he asked at last.

'Because they'll assume we were all in on it. I'll end up in the cells as well, and then who will take care of the family? I have a mother and another sister to look after, signore.'

'Hire a decent lawyer, then. If your father and Raffaella are innocent, as you claim, then surely that's the best solution?'

'I'm just a fisherman, signore. And lately things haven't been going well for me. Besides, the law moves slowly here and it's corrupt. There are people in this town who would make sure we were all found guilty.'

'Well, you are guilty, aren't you?'

Sergio cast his eyes to the ground and swallowed his pride. 'Yes, I am. I'm sorry, signore. I made a big mistake, I can see that now. I thought what I was doing was the best thing for Triento. We were angry that the town went ahead with plans for the statue when all of us fishermen were against it. Our opinion counted for nothing and we were insulted by that.'

'Are you expecting my sympathy?' Eduardo's voice was harsh.

'Not for me, signore, no. But for my sister, if you truly were her friend.'

Eduardo shook his head. 'I don't know.'

'You're her only chance.'

'Even if I agreed to help, what would I do?'

'My sister had an idea. She thought you could go to the priests and tell them that you've received threats saying that unless you pay more protection money, there will be more damage on the mountain . . . serious damage. They'll think it's been the work of the 'Ndrangheta all along, and if you insist that you're convinced my family is innocent, the police will have to release them. You are a powerful man in this town now, signore. People will listen to you.'

Eduardo raised his eyebrows. 'But surely the 'Ndrangheta will know this story's not true?'

Sergio spoke so quietly Eduardo had to lean closer to him to hear properly. 'The 'Ndrangheta isn't run by one person, signore, or even one family,' Sergio whispered. 'It's made up of lots of different families and they are busy with many things. Some are involved with drug-running, some prefer extortion, and the worst of all are the kidnappers. But one family doesn't necessarily know what the other is doing. And that's why this plan will work.'

'And you will get away with what you did,' Eduardo pointed out.

'Well, yes.'

'Why would I agree to that?'

Sergio remembered the pretty girl in the courtyard and her talk of Napoli. He hit on an idea. 'What if I promised to leave town? Once my father is out of prison, he can work the fishing boat again. I'll move to the city and I won't come back. It would be a second chance for me. I know I don't deserve it, but after all, what I did on the mountain only slowed the building, it didn't stop it. There will be a statue up there whether the fishermen like it or not.'

'So if I do what you want, then the sabotage will stop? The others won't continue with it?'

'Not without me.' Sergio didn't quite manage to keep the pride from his voice. 'I was the leader.'

Eduardo shook his head. 'I still don't know. You want me to lie to the priests and the police?'

'For Raffaella, signore. I don't know what happened between you and my sister, but she seems to think you cared about her a little.'

Eduardo tried to imagine Raffaella's shining beauty trapped amidst the ugliness of a police cell. 'How is she?' he asked, and some of the hardness had gone from his voice.

'She's not good. I saw her this morning and she looked terrible. We have to get her and my father out of there.'

'I'll think about it. That's the best I can promise at the moment.'

Sergio was relieved. This was more than he had expected. 'Thank you, I appreciate it.'

'But if I decide to help you – and I'm not saying that I will,' Eduardo warned, 'If I do help you, I never want to see you again or your sister. Both of you are trouble. I want to get this statue built without any more interference from either of you.'

'I understand.'

'That's all I care about – the statue. Now go before I throw you out. And don't come back.'

39

Carlotta couldn't be bothered hiding her sadness any longer. Sitting outside the gates of the convent, she let her tears fall. There seemed no end to them. Every time her sobbing eased she thought of Raffaella locked up in prison and started crying again.

Her face was flushed, her skin shiny, and the tears seemed to run from her eyes, nose and mouth. At one point she cried herself to sleep, curled up like a stray kitten on her little rug, and when she woke again, she was in shadow. She opened her eyes and squinted upwards to find Sister Benedicta standing over her.

'You can't go on like this, Carlotta,' the nun said gently. 'This is madness.'

Carlotta rubbed at her raw eyes. 'What choice do I have?' she asked in a husky voice. 'Almost everyone I love is locked away. Raffaella is in a police cell and refuses to see me. And my daughter is somewhere inside your convent out of my sight.'

'What about your father? He loves you.'

'Yes, he does, I know that. But he can't bear to see me unhappy. It's better that I cry here than back at Villa Rosa where he can find me.'

Sister Benedicta touched the cross that hung round her neck and looked thoughtful. It almost seemed as though she might be praying. She took a step or two away from Carlotta and then hesitated.

'Stand up quickly,' she ordered. 'Come with me.'

Carlotta struggled to her feet. 'Where to? Don't take me home. I don't want to go back there yet.'

'I'm not taking you home.' Sister Benedicta grabbed her elbow and propelled her towards the gates of the convent. 'Just walk quickly and be quiet. I don't want anyone to find us.'

Carlotta felt her whole body flooding with joy. 'Oh, thank you . . . thank you,' she began.

'Hush, don't thank me yet.'

Sister Benedicta bundled her through the convent gates and led her along a series of corridors. The air was cooler inside the thick stone walls, and the light was so dim that Carlotta stumbled once or twice, but the nun made her keep walking. Suddenly they were outside again, blinking in the bright sunlight. Carlotta recognised the vegetable gardens and the grove of fruit trees that grew in a sheltered sunny spot against the convent walls.

'Quickly, quickly, don't stop now.' Sister Benedicta sounded tense. She pulled Carlotta down an overgrown path that wound through the fruit trees. They rounded a corner and Carlotta saw a curious sight. In a clearing between the trees and the wall, someone had built a tiny wooden house. It had a steeply pitched roof, an open doorway and two windows with red shutters. And it was far too small for anyone but a child to fit inside.

Carlotta stopped walking and this time Sister Benedicta didn't urge her on.

A little girl was crouching inside the house chattering away softly to herself.

'Evangelina? Is that you in there?' Sister Benedicta called.

'No,' a childish voice replied playfully.

Carlotta could hardly breathe. She felt herself begin to sway and grabbed at the branches of a tree for support.

'Well, if it's not Evangelina, who else could it be, I wonder?' the nun asked in a sing-song voice. 'Is it a strange girl playing in Evangelina's house? Perhaps I'd better crawl in there and see for myself.'

The child giggled and poked her head out of a window. 'It is me, really. I was only pretending to be someone else. Don't come in or you'll get stuck like Sister Maria did.'

Carlotta drank in the sight of her daughter. She saw a smooth face, with round cheeks and dancing eyes. Her glossy black hair had been tied neatly in two long plaits, and someone had embroidered her pink pinafore dress with white daisies.

More than anything Carlotta wanted to run over, scoop up the child in her arms and bury her face in her hair. She longed to know what her daughter smelled like, to feel the softness of her skin, squeeze her chubby arms and cover her face in kisses. But as the little girl crawled out of her playhouse, Carlotta held back.

She glanced nervously at Sister Benedicta and the nun encouraged her with a smile. 'It's all right. She's not shy. You can say hello to her.'

Wordlessly, Carlotta stared at Evangelina. The child gazed back at her curiously. 'Have you come to play with me?' she asked hopefully.

Carlotta's mouth was dry and her heart pounding in her chest. 'That's right,' she managed.

Skipping two or three steps closer, plaits swinging, Evangelina smiled. 'Oh, good! What shall we play? Will you show me a new game? One that I've never played before.'

'I'll try.' Carlotta still held back. She had wanted so badly to see Evangelina, and now the child was in front of her she was paralysed. Then she noticed a tangle of wildflowers growing against the wall of the playhouse and a memory surfaced in her mind. Carefully, she picked a bunch of the flowers and, sinking down into the grass, began to thread them together the way her own mother had shown her.

'What are you doing?' Evangelina asked inquisitively.

'I'm making you a garland,' Carlotta explained.

'Can I help?'

'Yes, go and pick some more flowers – some of the yellow and the blue, and a few of the white,' Carlotta instructed. 'Make sure you pick them close to the ground so that they've got long stems.'

'And then will you show me how you make them into a garland?' Evangelina asked.

'If you want me to, I will.'

'Is it difficult?'

'Not really, but you have to be patient and gentle because the flowers are delicate.'

'I can be gentle,' Evangelina promised, and skipping over to the wildflowers, she began picking them happily.

They played together all afternoon. Carlotta didn't see Sister Benedicta slip away or notice how the sun was slipping inexorably to the west. Happily, she hung garlands of flowers round her daughter's neck and placed a circle of daisies on her head.

'So pretty,' Evangelina said admiringly. 'Now let's make some for you to wear.'

By the time Sister Benedicta returned, the patch of wildflowers had been picked bare and the two of them were sitting in the grass, side by side, with petals tumbling from their hair.

'It's time to stop playing now. You have to say goodbye,' the nun said softly.

Carlotta looked up at her and back at her daughter. 'No, I . . . '

'Yes, you must,' Sister Benedicta insisted. 'I've left you here for far too long as it is.'

Evangelina seemed unperturbed. 'Will you come and play with me again tomorrow?'

'I'd like to.' Carlotta's voice was wobbling. 'But I don't know if I can. We'll have to see.'

'Shall I kiss you goodbye now, then?' Evangelina asked. The little girl stood up and came closer. Putting her arms round Carlotta's neck, she hugged tightly and pressed soft lips against her cheek. The scent of crushed wildflowers filled the air and Carlotta squeezed her eyes shut and prayed no tears would escape.

'That's enough.' Sister Benedicta sounded nervous. 'You have to go now.'

Reluctantly, Carlotta pulled away from her daughter and brushed the petals from her hair. 'Goodbye,' she said, and it felt like her heart was breaking.

'Goodbye. I'll be right here again tomorrow if you want to come and play,' the little girl said hopefully.

Carlotta couldn't look back as Sister Benedicta led her away. The tears were already dropping down her cheeks and she didn't want the child to see them.

They hurried back through the fruit trees and past the vegetable garden. An old nun looked up from her weeding and spotted them, but Sister Benedicta held her finger to her lips and the nun did no more than raise her eyebrows.

'Will you get into trouble?' Carlotta asked.

'Not if you hurry up,' Sister Benedicta said tersely.

They had almost reached the convent gates when Carlotta noticed Sister Benedicta's back stiffen and heard her whisper, 'Oh, Madonna mia.'

In front of them, Carlotta saw the unmistakable figure of the convent's Mother Superior. She had hardly changed in the years since she'd last seen her. A small, compact woman with silver-rimmed glasses and piercing blue eyes that missed little, she commanded total respect.

'What's going on here?' she asked in a voice she had used to terrify schoolchildren for almost forty years.

'I . . . I just thought . . . well, I . . . ' Words failed Sister Benedicta. She fell silent and sent Carlotta a pleading look.

Carlotta's mind moved quickly. This might be the only chance she got to make sure she was allowed to see her daughter again. 'We've been looking for you, Mother Superior,' she said unsteadily.

'You have? Why is that?'

'Sister Benedicta was bringing me to see you.'

'And why would she want to do that?' The older nun's tone was cold and stern.

'I've been sitting outside the convent for days and days now, as you know,' Carlotta began. 'There have been lots of empty hours for me to fill with thinking and praying. And I've come to understand that I don't belong down there in Triento. This is where I want to be. I know I could be happy here.'

It was true that she wanted nothing more than to live within these walls and work hard in the vegetable gardens. It would be a peaceful life and a safe one. There were few things she would miss about her time in the outside world. And she would be close to her daughter.

The Mother Superior looked at her intently. She seemed to be having some sort of internal struggle. On the one hand, she had every reason to want to keep Carlotta away from the convent. She had broken an unspoken rule when she'd allowed the child to be brought back here. At the time she hadn't seen what else she could do – the woman who had adopted her had died; the husband couldn't care for her alone. And then weeks had passed while they searched for another family. They'd all grown attached to Evangelina, she was such a sweet girl. It had been so hard to think of sending her away again and so easy to let her stay on for another week, a month, a year or two. And now she was still here, even though she really shouldn't be, and so was Carlotta.

The nun faced a dilemma. It wasn't every day a strong young woman came and offered herself to them. There was heavy work to do in the convent, and her sisters were getting older and struggling to keep up with it. And perhaps one day this girl might even decide she was ready to commit to a life of chastity, obedience and poverty. It had been a very long time since the convent had welcomed a postulate. So she couldn't quite bring herself to turn Carlotta away.

'You want to stay here with us, work hard and live quietly?' she asked tentatively.

Carlotta nodded.

'You want to pray beside us each day and share our life serving God?'

'Yes, yes, I do.'

'And you won't miss your life down there in Triento? The comfort and the material things?'

'The only thing down there that matters to me is my father,' Carlotta replied. And Raffaella too, she added silently, for without her Evangelina would most certainly have remained undiscovered behind the convent walls.

The Mother Superior regarded her for a moment, and then suddenly she seemed to make up her mind. 'You'd better come with me,' she said crisply. 'There are things we need to talk about. Sister Benedicta, thank you . . . I'll take care of things from here.'

As Carlotta followed the Mother Superior through the convent's long corridors, she thanked God that the nuns had kept Evangelina hidden within these walls. Because of them, she had been given a second chance to love her daughter. God had kept her daughter safe for her. Even if she spent the rest of her life thanking Him for it, then it wouldn't be too long.

40

Eduardo walked between the pomegranate trees and saw how the fruit was beginning to weigh down their branches. Soon it would be time to harvest again, but with Raffaella locked away, he doubted anyone at Villa Rosa would bother making pomegranate syrup. The gardener, Umberto, was more taciturn than ever, and he hardly ever glimpsed his thin, pale daughter. Increasingly, he and the Barbieri women were left to fend for themselves.

With some regret, he recalled the meals Raffaella had prepared for him. Platefuls of chicken soused in pomegranate syrup and scattered with walnuts, salt cod creamed with lemon juice and garlic, warm potatoes with chilli and pecorino romano, and more, so much more. He remembered eating until his belly strained at the button of his trousers and then sitting beneath the pomegranate tree sipping a *digestivo*, smoking his cigar and talking on and on to the little peasant girl about his work on the statue and his hopes for the future.

Eduardo's life was all laid out for him now. Once the statue was standing proudly on the mountain, there would be another job waiting. Claudia's father, Luciano Barbieri, had plans for him, big and glorious plans. He was working on a new development transforming a neglected piece of wasteland on the outskirts of Napoli into shops, apartment blocks, restaurants and parks. It would be the most ambitious work Eduardo had ever tackled. And while he suspected his benefactor's motive was to keep him close to his daughter, it was an irresistible prospect.

Eduardo could envisage his future so clearly it was almost like a memory of something that had already happened. There would be skiing holidays in winter at the Barbieri chalet and sailing round the Amalfi Coast in summer. There would be fine houses and parties where he would move in a circle of interesting and sophisticated people. And he would never again return to this oppressive little town caught between the mountains and the sea.

Eduardo couldn't wait to leave Triento behind him. He stopped pacing and stared at the view of the sky melting into the blue of the Tyrrhenian Sea and remembered how beautiful he'd found the place when he first arrived here. Now he was too jaded to appreciate it. Once he had given the priests the statue he had promised them, he would be on his way.

He looked over towards the mountain and saw that, even from this distance, it was possible to see how the road was taking shape, winding its tail round the mountaintop, creeping a little closer to the summit as each day passed.

Eduardo started pacing again. Although there had been progress, the statue was still some way from completion. He was trapped in Triento, his future out of reach. And for now his most pressing problem was Raffaella. What should he do about the girl and her father, locked away in the police cells, accused of a crime they hadn't committed?

His dilemma was what had sent Eduardo down to the gardens of Villa Rosa. He thought he'd have the space to think here and work out the best course of action, but he had been pacing up and down for an hour or more and he was still no nearer to a resolution.

Raffaella sat quiet and still on the narrow bed in her police cell. Sometimes she and her father called out to each other, with words of comfort or regret, but most of the time she spent thinking. There was really nothing else to do.

She thought of all that had happened to her since she had left the safety of her parents' house and moved up the hill to Big Triento to begin life as a married woman. That time with Marcello had held such promise. She'd loved him since she was a girl, although she was always half in awe of him, and becoming completely his was all she ever wanted.

But now, as she retraced her year of marriage in her mind, she realised something had been badly wrong from the start. Staring at the blank walls of her cell, she pictured herself living like a wife. She'd tried so hard to do all the things she had watched her mother do for her father. She cooked for Marcello and cleaned his house. At the end of each day's work, when he sat back to rest, she lit a cigarette for him and placed a glass of iced *limoncello* in his hand.

Marcello was kind and gentle. He was a good man who loved her, but he hardly ever shared himself with her. She had expected an intimacy from marriage – to be always talking, always touching – but it never came. And the more he held himself back, the more desperately she wanted him.

Raffaella remembered how he could be funny and sweet, but he could also hide behind silence. Days would pass when there never seemed to be a good time to talk. 'Not now,' Marcello would say. 'Not now, I'm working.'

She had loved Marcello, but in moments like that her love had felt like a lonely thing.

When Marcello did allow her to come close – to snuggle into the crook of his arm or curl her body around his in bed at night – she would barely dare to breathe, never mind move, in case he changed his mind and pushed her away again. He had always left her craving more of him.

No wonder she'd looked forward to his brother Fabrizio's visits. It had been a luxury being adored by him and sitting on piles of linen in the storeroom to listen to him speak. He was immature and boastful, quick to anger and laugh, so different from her husband. She had loved Marcello, but it was Fabrizio she spent her happiest times with in her year of marriage.

Alone in her cell, Raffaella stretched out on her bed and tried to imagine what her life would be like now if Marcello had lived. Would more time together have brought her husband closer to her? If she had persisted in loving him, surely one day he might have stopped flinching when she touched him unexpectedly and let himself be kissed without a word of complaint?

Sometimes Raffaella cried, but always quietly so her father wouldn't hear. At night she woke when it was still dark, and everything seemed so much worse than it did in daylight hours. She tried not to think too much about how long they might have to stay here. The police said they were building a strong case against them and she believed it. There were people in Triento who hated her family and would be glad to see them locked away.

Raffaella was certain her only hope lay with the americano. Hugging her thin pillow to her chest and remembering the brief passion that had passed between them, she flushed with shame. And yet she found it impossible to regret allowing him to kiss her, letting him flood her body with desire the way her husband never had. She knew it was wrong and she felt bad, but she couldn't wish it had never happened.

The question was, would Eduardo remember her with enough affection to come and help her now? Would Sergio even summon up the courage to go and share her plan with him? These were the things Raffaella thought about as she sat through the long, lonely hours under lock and key. There was no shortage of time to spend turning them over and over in her mind.

The Gypsy Tearoom had been busy since it had reopened and Ciro barely had a moment to himself. If his hands weren't shaping pizza dough, they were collecting dirty plates from the tables and pouring jugs of wine. He began to wonder how he had ever managed to run the place alone. It had certainly been busy in the old days, but there was always a moment to stop and chat. Now each day seemed more frantic than the last, and when at last he fell into bed exhausted, he dreamed of feeding pizza into the mouth of his oven all night long.

But now, as the afternoon stretched into early evening, things were a little quieter and Ciro seized the chance to wipe down the tables and make sure his counter was tidy. He was surprised when the mayor came in and sat on one of the benches against the wall.

'*Buona sera*,' he greeted him. 'It's unusual to see you here at this hour.'

The mayor shrugged. 'My housekeeper is ill,' he explained, 'so this evening you'll have to cook my meal.'

'With pleasure.' Ciro smiled. 'But first let me pour you a glass of my very best Aglianico. I keep this for customers I know will appreciate it.'

The mayor sipped at the rich red wine that tasted of cherries and dark chocolate. Reading the blackboard above Ciro's head, he tried to decide what to eat. Usually, he dined on whatever his housekeeper had left for him. He wasn't used to making the choice himself.

'The pizza primavera is good,' Ciro told him. 'It's covered with fresh tomatoes and a little torn rocket. I could put some olives on it if you like and some thinly shaved pecorino. It's up to you. Tell me what you want.'

'I'm not sure.' The mayor felt out of sorts. 'Why don't you choose for me? I'm certain whatever you make will be exactly what I want.'

Ciro made the pizza he had promised, adding a pinch of crushed chilli to lift it above the ordinary. The mayor was eating appreciatively, and washing it down with a second glass of the Aglianico, when Silvana hurried into the Gypsy Tearoom, an empty basket hanging over her arm.

'*Buona sera*, signore, I saw that you were heading here,' she said quickly. 'I had to come after you. I've been thinking all day about what you said to me this morning.'

The mayor chewed his pizza and swallowed. He wiped the corners of his mouth carefully with a paper napkin. 'What was that?' he asked. 'What did I say to you?'

'*Porca la miseria!*' Silvana was exasperated. 'We were talking about Raffaella, remember?'

He nodded. 'That's right, we were. I'm sorry, Silvana, but this morning seems like a long time ago to me. I've done a whole day's work since then and dealt with all sorts of people and their problems.'

'But this is more important than any of that,' Silvana insisted. 'I've done a whole day's work as well, but I've found it difficult to think about anything else.'

Trying not to sigh, the mayor put down his knife and fork. 'Take a seat. Tell me what is bothering you.'

Silvana shook her head impatiently. 'I don't need to sit down. I just want you to understand that Raffaella couldn't have been responsible for sabotaging the statue. The girl was always working, at Villa Rosa or at my bakery. She didn't have the time to sabotage anything.'

'She was found up there on the mountain,' the mayor pointed out. 'She was caught by a security guard. Fabrizio Russo was the witness.'

'But the Russo family hate her.' Silvana sounded quite desperate. 'Surely you can see that they would say anything to discredit her.'

'Why would they hate her?' the mayor asked reasonably. 'She was married to Marcello, so she was one of them. What reason could they have to turn against her?'

Ciro had been watching quietly from his post behind the counter. Now he cleared his throat nervously. 'That might be my fault,' he offered. 'I only wanted to be Raffaella's friend but I ended up creating trouble for her. The Russo family is convinced we've been having an affair. It's not true but nothing I can say will change their minds.'

The mayor heartily wished his housekeeper hadn't caught a cold from her youngest child and that she was in his kitchen as usual, preparing something simple but delicious for him to eat in peace. He shook his head gravely. 'Even if you're right what can I do?' he asked them. 'This is a police matter now.'

'You could intercede on Rafaella's behalf,' suggested Ciro.

'You could speak for her,' Silvana added. 'The Moretti family can't afford to pay a lawyer. They need the help of someone clever like you.'

'Oh Silvana . . .' Giorgio wanted to please her but this was too much.

'Very well.' Silvana was furious. 'So you don't want to help me? Well that's up to you.' She turned on her heel, tossed her hair over her shoulders and marched out of the Gypsy Tearoom.

The mayor picked up his knife and fork, and stared disconsolately at what was left of his food. Ciro looked away and wiped down the counter again. For just about the thousandth time he wondered why the grandfather he'd inherited this little pizzeria from had chosen the name he'd given it. He wished he truly were a gypsy, for surely they all could do with some gypsy magic now.

Stoically, the mayor tried to chew through his pizza. The silence in the room was awkward and Ciro prayed more customers would arrive soon. It was a relief to hear footsteps echoing down the narrow lane and see the door pushed open.

Both Ciro and the mayor were surprised to see who entered. The americano looked pale, and there was a shadow of black stubble on his chin.

'Buona sera.' Ciro nodded at him. 'Have you come for dinner?'

'No, I've come to see the mayor. Ah, there you are. They told me I would find you here.'

Resignedly, Giorgio dropped his knife and fork again. 'What can I do for you, signore?' he asked.

'There's something I need to tell you.' Eduardo hesitated and stared for a moment at the remains of pizza on the mayor's plate.

'Yes, what is it?' Giorgio prompted him.

'There have been more threats to sabotage the statue,' he blurted before he could think twice about it. 'They've demanded more money. I suspect the Moretti family may be innocent after all. We're dealing with something bigger here.'

The mayor nodded slowly and pushed his plate away. 'I did wonder,' he said gravely. 'I wish I could say I'm surprised, but I'm not.'

'You will treat this information with discretion, won't you?' Eduardo looked nervous. 'You'll be careful who you tell?'

'Yes, of course.' The mayor's tone was soothing. 'We're used to this kind of thing here in Triento, signore. We know how to deal with it. Leave this to me. I'll make sure it is sorted out.'

41

So many things had changed in the time Raffaella had been locked away. Little things were different. Her mother had put a framed photograph of her on the window ledge so she could look at her as she prepared meals. Teresa had adopted a stray kitten that was allowed to come into the house to drink its saucer of milk. There was a strange, neglected feel about the place. Raffaella saw dust balls on the tiled floor and cobwebs in the corners of the ceiling, but her mother seemed not to notice them.

And there were bigger changes. The day after she and her father were released from the police cells, her brother, Sergio, packed his bags and caught the train to Napoli. He couldn't tell them what he would do there or when he might return. Her mother clung to him and begged him not to go, but her father seemed to accept it. He had changed too. The day he returned home, he went straight to his favourite armchair and turned it round so it faced the sea. He sat there for a long time staring out of the window at the view he had always loathed so much. Raffaella didn't think he would ever complain about it again.

Her own future was uncertain. The priests had told her she was no longer wanted at Villa Rosa, and Umberto came by to drop off her belongings. That's when she learned what had happened to Carlotta. She was surprised at first, but the more she thought about it, the more it made sense. The simplicity of convent life would suit Carlotta, for she had never cared much for pretty clothes and material things. It was easy to imagine her dividing her days between work and prayer, and Raffaella was glad for her.

'But won't you be lonely?' she asked Umberto with some concern.

His reply was gruff. 'Why should I be? I have plenty to keep me occupied. And anyway, Carlotta will still come and visit and maybe share a meal with me from time to time.'

Neither of them mentioned Evangelina, but Raffaella knew without being told that the child must be up there at the convent. And whenever she was feeling low or lonely, she thought about Carlotta reunited with her daughter and it always made her mood a little lighter.

She might not have been locked in a cell any longer, but Raffaella still felt trapped. She rarely left Little Triento, for the thought of walking up the hill and facing the stares of people shopping in the piazza was still too daunting.

Instead, she stayed by her mother's side. The time passed slowly. Some days they walked together along the beach, and her mother made her hitch up the skirt of her black dress and run into the waves to get her feet wet. It was like being a child again. She showed her how to choose flat pebbles and skim them across the surface of the water as she had done with Raffaella when she was young. And on the way back, they picked ripe, juicy figs and bit into them as they walked along, returning home with fingers and faces sticky, and pink-cheeked from the sun.

Raffaella tried to keep herself busy. She found a long broom and swept away the cobwebs and the dust balls. She shook out the bedlinen, cleared out cupboards and aired clothes. Then she pulled her mother's cookbook from the shelf and spent hours poring over it, imagining what she would make if she were still in charge of the kitchen at Villa Rosa.

Before he left for Napoli, Sergio had warned her to stay away from the americano. 'Don't be tempted to try to talk to him. He made it very clear that he doesn't want to see you.'

Raffaella knew it was for the best, but still she found it difficult not to let her thoughts drift towards him. Every time she looked up towards the mountain she was reminded of him. And at night, when she touched the parts of her body that ached sweetly, she imagined her own hands were his.

So much had changed and yet one thing remained the same. Raffaella couldn't imagine what her future might hold. Life was still as uncertain as it had been a year ago, when Marcello died and the things she expected would be hers – marriage, babies, her own home – had been taken away. As the winter winds blew autumn aside and the days grew shorter, Raffaella struggled with a mood as dark as the widow's dress she still wore.

Silvana had only half forgiven Giorgio. She was prepared to raise a hand in greeting if she spotted him walking through the piazza, but she hadn't been near the Gypsy Tearoom and so she imagined he must be drinking his two cups of espresso undisturbed each morning.

It wasn't that she was ungrateful. Raffaella was free and she knew he must have had something to do with it. But the way he'd spoken to her that evening – the weary tone in his voice, as if Silvana were just another person making demands on his time and energy – had upset her.

Silvana knew how to bear a grudge. The more she thought about Giorgio, the crosser she became. Even when she couldn't quite remember exactly what it was he'd said to offend her, she still couldn't bring herself to speak to him.

She watched out for him, though. She kept an eye on the clock and made sure to look up to see him cross the piazza at his regular times. Sometimes she nodded and treated him to a polite smile, but mostly all he got was a cursory wave of her hand.

This morning the mayor was late. Silvana wondered if perhaps he had been tempted to linger over an extra coffee in the Gypsy Tearoom. There was a chill in the air today and she wished that she too had time to wrap her hands around a cup of something warm.

She was so busy that it wasn't until she was wiping down the shelves and sweeping the floors at the end of the day that she realised she hadn't seen the mayor at all. She didn't see him the next day either or the one after that and she began to worry.

When Padre Pietro came in for a loaf of bread, she managed to trap him in a long conversation, and when her chance came, she slipped in her question.

'I haven't seen the mayor about for days. Has he gone away?' she asked casually.

'No, he's sick, I think,' the priest replied, 'too sick to work. He has been ill all week, poor man.'

'Is it serious? What's wrong with him?' Silvana was concerned.

'I don't know for sure. Padre Matteo is up at his house now seeing how he is.'

Silvana frowned. Padre Matteo could always be found hovering on the doorsteps of those who were sick or suffering. It was said that no priest had ever relished giving the last rites more than he did. Just how sick could Giorgio be?

'Perhaps I should go there too once I've finished here,' she wondered aloud. 'That housekeeper of his might not be feeding him properly. I could take him some soup and some soft white bread to dip into it.'

Padre Pietro smiled and nodded. It seemed a little odd that Silvana should want to carry food to the mayor, but he liked to encourage generosity whenever he encountered it. 'That's very good of you, Silvana. I'm sure the mayor would appreciate it.'

Silvana couldn't wait for the day to end. She closed the bakery an hour earlier than usual and hurried home, where she knew she had some good chicken stock just waiting to be simmered with celery and onions and turned into a nourishing soup.

The alleyway that led to the mayor's house was steep and narrow. There were over a hundred steps to negotiate and Silvana was tired and weighed down with food. But still she moved as quickly as she could, ignoring her aching legs and ragged breath.

Her knocking on the door brought no reply. She had expected the mayor's housekeeper to be there, but all was quiet. Tentatively, she opened the door and poked her head round it.

'Hello,' she called softly. 'Hello, Giorgio, are you there?'

'Silvana, is that you?' His voice sounded weak. Pushing the door wide open, she hurried inside.

'Yes, it's me. Are you alone? I've brought you some soup.'

'I'm in here,' he said. 'But don't come too close to me. I don't want to pass on my germs.'

'What's wrong with you? Are you very ill?' Silvana found him slumped in an armchair surrounded by everything he needed: books, handkerchiefs and a jug of homemade lemonade – all was within his reach. As she came into the room, he let out a sneeze followed by a sorrowful moan.

'Oh, you only have a cold,' she said with some relief.

'It's not only a cold,' he said tetchily. 'My throat is so sore it feels like someone has been rubbing it with sandpaper. My eyes and my nose are streaming. I feel like I'm dying. I swear I've never been this ill in my life.'

She tried not to smile. 'Why don't I heat up some of this soup for you? It will soothe your poor throat.'

'I'm not hungry.' He sounded miserable. 'And anyway, I don't think I can swallow.'

'Just try a little. It's delicious, I promise you. And it's important for you to keep your strength up.'

She stayed with him as he spooned the soup into his mouth, and beamed with pleasure when he asked for a second bowl. 'I was hungrier than I thought,' he conceded.

It was good to sit here keeping him company. Silvana looked around at the comfortable home he had created. The walls were lined with books, and the chairs were turned to face the view. The room wasn't cluttered, but what he owned was good quality.

'You've done well,' she remarked as he wiped a hunk of bread round his soup bowl. 'You've worked hard and made a success of your life.'

Giorgio had been about to put the soup-sodden crust into his mouth, but he paused and stared at her. 'Yes, I've worked hard,' he agreed. 'And I thought that I was happy enough with all that I'd achieved, but this last week or so I've realised I was wrong.'

'What do you mean?' She was confused.

'I've missed you, Silvana. Every morning I thought of some little thing I wanted to tell you, but you never came.'

She looked at him. With his red nose and watery eyes, he wasn't a pretty picture, but still she loved him. 'Yes, but what's the point?' she asked sadly. 'I don't want to be the person you snatch ten minutes with in the morning and then forget about. If I can't be more important to you than that, then I don't want to see you at all.'

'But you are important to me,' he insisted.

She sighed. 'We could go on like this for years, Giorgio. But I don't think I have the heart for it or the energy.' Standing up, she took his soup bowl from him. 'I'm sorry, but I don't want to see you any more.'

'Silvana, don't go.' He sprang out of his armchair and gripped her arm. 'Don't leave me.'

'It's for the best,' she said sadly.

'No, it isn't. I don't think you understand what it's been like for me the past few days. I've been so lonely, Silvana.' He took both her hands in his.

She shrugged helplessly. 'But what can I do . . . ?'

'You can marry me, Silvana. Once you've respected your period of mourning, you can come and be my wife.'

'What will people think? What will they say?'

'I don't care about that any more. Let them say what they like.'

'Do you really mean that?'

He kissed her and his lips tasted of lemons. 'Now you'll catch my cold,' he said softly, tangling his hands in her hair.

'But I don't care about that,' she whispered, and with a tilt of her head, she told him how much she wanted to be kissed again.

42

The streets of Triento were deserted. The bars and cafés were closed, and although it was a market day, not a single stallholder had laid out their wares in the piazza. The place felt like a ghost town.

But high above the village, right on the very peak of the mountain, was an awesome sight. Where once there had been only bare, stony ground, a colossal statue of Christ now soared towards the Heavens. Its powdered marble surface was brilliant white against the blinding blue of the sky, its arms stretched wide forming the shape of a cross, and it stood more than twenty-two metres high. To the crowds milling about its base, it seemed like a miracle.

There was a carnival atmosphere on the mountaintop. Music was playing, and people were standing in groups waiting for the official unveiling. Triento had looked forward to this day for so long and everyone intended to enjoy it. There would be speeches, prayers and a blessing. And later they would all take the new road back down to the village and wait until it grew dark so they could see for the first time how their glorious statue looked when it was illuminated against the night sky.

Eduardo didn't bother to hide his pride. It was true that many people had worked with him on this project. Engineers and construction workers had made the road, a sculptor from Firenze had designed and created the statue, and the priests had supplied the money. But still he felt that this was his moment. For without him, he was certain it would never have happened.

He gazed up at the statue with some satisfaction. His Christ had a strong, noble face, a neatly trimmed beard and a sainted expression. The sleeves of his robe fell in lifelike folds, and his hands were held out, palms up to the sky. He stood facing the mountains, with his back to the sea, turned against the fishermen who had refused to contribute towards him.

None of them were here, Eduardo realised, as he scanned the crowd. They had stayed down at the harbour, mending their nets as though this were just another day.

Although he knew it was unlikely, he had half hoped Raffaella might come. It would have been good to see her one last time and to witness the expression on her face as she marvelled at the statue.

Claudia was there, standing with her mother and the priests near the front of the crowd. She smiled at him when he caught her eye. In the past months she had gained a little weight. There was a thickness about her torso, and her face had been deserted by some of its prettiness and youth. Nevertheless he was committed to her now. He had spoken to her father and they would be married before the year's end. He smiled back briefly and turned away from her to look out over the view. This was the last he would see of Triento. He had already packed his bags, and tomorrow he would leave Villa Rosa and drive back along the tortuous road that wound between mountains and beneath tunnels, north towards his future.

Padre Pietro stared at the statue. This was his dream made real and he ought to have felt joyous, but his only emotion was relief. If he'd had the slightest idea of what it would take to build this thing, he would never have shared his vision. The statue had divided the town, innocent people had been imprisoned, and an indecent amount of money had been spent. And now here it was before him, Christ risen from the rocks, and he wasn't certain if it had been worth it. It was a modern thing, spare and minimal in its detail, not his idea of beauty at all. He thought of the statues of Rome and the grandeur of the Vatican. This didn't compare.

The other priests seemed happy, though. Padre Matteo, his sunglasses pushed on to the top of his head, was looking at the statue with a smile lighting his handsome face.

'This is wonderful, eh?' he enthused. 'It's going to make our town famous. Tourists will come here. Triento may even become a big holiday resort.'

'Your brother will do well, then,' Padre Pietro remarked. 'I hear he is opening a souvenir shop in town. That was smart of him.'

'Ah, yes.' Padre Matteo flipped his sunglasses down over his eyes, and his tone grew more formal. 'My brother is a good businessman. He will sell fine ceramics, local crafts and maybe miniatures of the statue. God willing, he'll make a good living.'

Padre Simone was standing beside them, but he didn't appear to be paying attention. He was gazing at the statue with an odd, awed expression on his face, almost as if he truly were witnessing the Second Coming.

'It is a miracle, isn't it,' Padre Pietro said to him gently.

'Oh, yes, it is a miracle indeed.' Padre Simone's words sounded heartfelt. 'If any among us needed proof there was a God, we need it no longer. Only He could have put this statue here.'

Padre Matteo laughed. 'I don't think the americano would agree with you. He would rather take all the credit for it.'

'Isn't that always the way? Man is an arrogant beast. He always thinks he knows best.' Shaking his head, Padre Simone smiled, and then he turned back to the statue and continued to stare at it, ignoring the chatter of those around him and the crowds of people that jostled him as they passed.

Silvana stood amongst the Russo family near the base of the statue. Alba was chatting to her, but she wasn't listening properly. She was watching the mayor, as he moved around the crowds, and every now and then he looked up and exchanged a glance with her. The two of them shared a secret. They couldn't tell a soul, but that didn't matter. One day not too far away they would be husband and wife. It had all been agreed between them.

Alba was still talking. She was listing all the things her family had done to contribute towards the statue. 'We gave money of course, like everyone else, although a little more than most,' she said loudly. 'And then my Stefano made sure it was all spent wisely. And Fabrizio gave his time to help guard the statue at night. It was him who caught Raffaella Moretti, you know. Of course, the girl got away with it in the end, just like she gets away with everything.'

Silvana nodded at Alba's words but kept her eyes on the mayor.

'And you know that it was all my idea in the first place,' Alba continued, her voice rich with pride. 'It was me who suggested it to Padre Pietro one day when we were taking a coffee together. Build a statue of Christ that will be seen from miles around, I told him, like the one they have in Rio de Janeiro. And now look, here it is – the most impressive statue in the whole of Italy. Don't you agree?'

Silvana nodded again. The mayor was out of sight now, behind the platform where the brass band was playing a rousing tune. She wondered what Alba would think if she knew what was going on. As delicious as it was to hug the secret to herself, she couldn't wait until everyone knew.

The mayor had reappeared. He was readying himself to make his speech.

'Impressive, don't you agree?' Alba asked again, insistently.

Silvana stared not at the statue but at the mayor. 'Yes, very impressive,' she murmured back. 'A fine figure of a man.'

43

Raffaella clutched her basket, the walk to Big Triento seeming steeper and more exhausting than ever, even with the wind at her back. As she tracked slowly upwards, the statue on the mountain came in and out of view, and every time she glimpsed it, she felt a lurching in her stomach.

She knew the americano had left town, because Patrizia Sesto had told her so. He went the day after the official unveiling and had no plans to return. But it was Patrizia's other piece of news that had driven Raffaella into her bedroom, where she tangled herself in her blankets and lost herself in her thoughts.

'The word is the americano has become engaged to the Barbieri girl,' Patrizia had confided. 'So maybe he will come back after all to spend summers at Villa Rosa.'

It was later that morning that Raffaella decided it was time to go back to Big Triento. Facing the stares of those who thought she should still be in prison wouldn't be easy. She could imagine what they had been saying about her up there. But she couldn't hide her face for ever. And besides, her mother had a long list of things she needed from the market and kept complaining she was much too worn out to make the climb today.

Viewed from the bottom of the hill, the statue seemed to be looking out over the sea. But as she climbed higher, Raffaella could see it more clearly. To her, it was a sad thing that Christ should be turned inland, facing the barren mountains and missing out on the panorama of rocks, sea and sky. And yet she had to admit that whether it was half shrouded in cloud or starkly white against a backdrop of blue, the statue was impressive. Raffaella wondered how long it would be before she could look at it without thinking of the americano.

The piazza was crowded, as she had known it would be. Raffaella walked quickly, not wanting to be caught up in conversation. Her basket grew weightier as she moved from stall to stall filling it with packages of food.

She kept her eyes cast low as she began a heavy-footed trek back across the piazza, weaving her way through the market stalls. She only looked up when she heard a familiar voice, raised in anger.

'Get out of it, you filthy little bastard,' Fabrizio Russo was yelling. 'Go on, get away.'

Raffaella flinched, thinking for a moment his angry words were meant for her. But then she noticed Fabrizio was kicking at something down on the ground. She heard the whimpering first and caught sight of the old yellow dog, its tail between its legs, trying to limp away from the toe of Fabrizio's boot.

'Leave it alone!' She was shocked to realise the shrill voice was her own.

Fabrizio froze, boot in mid-air. 'Who do you think you're talking to, *scema*?' he hissed at her.

All the fury she'd been storing up burst out of her. 'I'm not talking to you, Fabrizio,' she shouted back. 'I've got no interest in ever talking to you again. What I'm doing is telling you. Leave the dog alone. What's the poor old thing ever done to you?'

The dog was staggering towards her and Fabrizio followed it, aiming to plant another kick on its bony rump. Raffaella stopped him with a stare. 'Shame on you,' she said more quietly now. 'Have you got no kindness left in you? What happened to the boy I knew?'

She didn't bother to wait for his reply. Gripping the loose skin around the old dog's neck, she pulled him back across the piazza towards the narrow alleyway where she knew he'd find some sanctuary. Tears stung at her eyes as she encouraged him forward. 'Come on, good boy, nearly there.'

Ciro must have glimpsed her through the window of the Gypsy Tearoom because he came out to meet her.

'Raffaella, it's good to see you—' he began, and then he noticed the state the old dog was in. 'What's happened?'

'That pig Fabrizio Russo has been kicking him. I think he's badly hurt.'

'Bring him inside. We'll see if he can drink some water.'

As Ciro half carried the dog to the back of the Gypsy Tearoom, his back legs were buckling and he was panting heavily. They lay him on his side and sat down on the floor beside him.

'Do you think he's going to be all right?' Raffaella asked. She stroked the old dog gently, and as he felt the touch of her hand, his tail thumped on the floor and he tried to lift his head.

Ciro looked grim.

'He's dying, isn't he?' Raffaella didn't bother trying to brush away her tears.

'Yes, I think so.'

Raffaella kept stroking, rubbing her hands over the dog's dirty yellow coat. 'Can we do anything?'

Ciro shook his head. 'He's an old boy and he's had a hard life. His heart is giving up. But you know, he probably wouldn't have lasted much longer even if Fabrizio hadn't abused him.'

'God, I hate him,' she said angrily. 'I hate all of them, the whole Russo family.'

The dog whimpered a little and Ciro held his finger to his lips. 'Don't raise your voice or you'll upset him. Talk quietly to me and keep on stroking him.'

Raffaella looked down at the old dog hopelessly. 'But what will I talk to you about? I can't think of anything that won't make me angry right now.'

'I'll do the talking, then.' The dog's breathing was growing laboured and his sides were heaving. 'Ask me a question and I'll answer it.'

'A question? Oh, I don't know.' Raffaella searched her mind for something to ask. 'All right, why is this place called the Gypsy Tearoom? I've always wondered that.'

'A good question, but not one I can answer properly, I'm sad to say.' Ciro looked down at the dog. 'Still, I don't think we have too long now, so I'll tell you what I know. It was my grandfather who started this place and he named it. When I was a boy, I used to come and help him here. I was in a rush to learn everything. I wanted to know the recipes for his sauces and the secret of his dough. I pestered him to show me how to keep the oven up to temperature and bake a pizza so it was perfectly crisp but never burned. If I remember rightly, I tormented the poor man with questions, and most things he got round to telling me.'

Raffaella kept stroking and listening.

'There was one question I asked almost every day,' Ciro continued. 'How did the Gypsy Tearoom come by its name? My grandfather liked to tease me by never giving me the same answer twice. One day he'd tell me one tall story, the next he'd come up with another.'

'What kind of things did he say?'

'Oh, crazy stuff: that a gypsy had told him he'd put a curse on him if he didn't choose that name; that he himself was the illegitimate son of a gypsy; or that he'd always meant to serve tea, but he'd never figured out how to make it taste halfway decent.' Ciro smiled fondly. 'Crazy stuff.'

'And did he ever tell you the true story?'

'I'm sure he intended to eventually, but then one day he was knocked off his Vespa and injured very badly. He went into a coma and died without ever coming back to consciousness. Afterwards I discovered that he'd left this place to me so I took over. I didn't change the name even though I'd never found out what it meant. It stayed the Gypsy Tearoom.'

'But you must have some idea?'

'No, none at all.'

'Did your grandfather travel? Did he know a band of gypsies?'

Ciro shrugged. 'Not so far as I know.'

'There has to be an explanation,' she persisted.

'I suppose there does. But to be honest, I quite like not knowing.'

'Why?'

'Some things are meant to be a mystery,' he pointed out. 'Life isn't neat. There isn't an answer for everything. All we need to know for sure is that we're born, we live, we die, and we don't require much more than this old dog: a place to sleep; food to fill our bellies; a little comfort and, if we're lucky, a lot of love.'

The yellow dog drew a last ragged breath and then he was still. Raffaella was so absorbed in what Ciro was saying she didn't notice. 'Have you found love?' she asked him in a small voice.

'Not yet, but I hope to.' He looked at her steadily. 'But you know that, don't you?'

'I know,' she agreed hesitantly. 'I think I've always known.'

'But you loved Marcello?'

'Yes.'

'And now?'

Raffaella remembered the americano reciting a fragment of verse to her once late at night in the gardens of Villa Rosa. She repeated it now. 'Love is like a pomegranate. So smooth and simple on the outside, so red raw and bitter-sweet beneath.'

'What is that, poetry?' Ciro asked.

'No, just words I heard once,' she replied. 'I didn't realise how true they were at the time.'

At last Raffaella noticed the old dog had stopped moving and she stroked him one final time, tears falling down her face. Ciro handed her a paper serviette. When she'd dried her eyes, she stood and reached into her basket. Feeling around beneath the neatly wrapped packages of food she'd bought, she pulled out a large flat object swathed in an offcut of fine linen.

'Let me show you something,' she said.

Ciro looked puzzled as she unfolded the cloth and he saw what lay within. 'That's your wedding photograph. Why are you carrying it with you?'

'It's always with me,' she replied softly. 'Sometimes I look at the girl in this photograph and wonder who she was. See the smile on my face? I was happy. I'd found love and I was so certain everything else I wanted from life was bound to fall into place for me.'

'And it did for a while,' Ciro pointed out.

'No, not really. Love with Marcello turned out to be a far more complicated thing than I'd ever imagined.'

Ciro laid an old towel over the dog's lifeless body. 'And now you're going to give up on love? Is that what you're trying to tell me?' he asked.

Raffaella looked thoughtful. 'Not exactly, but I'm going to look for other things before I look for love.'

Ciro sighed. Moving behind the counter, he occupied his hands by kneading a batch of dough he'd left there. 'I don't understand,' he said sadly. 'You're going to have to try to explain things better to me.'

She took a deep breath and tried to order her thoughts. She was only just beginning to understand things herself, so it was nearly impossible to explain them to someone else.

'When Marcello died, I felt like I was living someone else's life,' she began. 'I'd tried so hard to make our marriage everything I wanted it to be. He was the only thing I thought of, and when he was gone, I felt lost . . . and angry too, I think.'

'Why were you angry?'

'Because I'd been cheated out of everything I'd ever wanted. And then I think I panicked. I was impatient and I looked for happiness in all the wrong places.' She thought of the americano and the comfort she'd taken in the hours she'd spent listening to him talk.

'What places?'

She shook her head. 'Never mind, it isn't important any more. I've made some mistakes, but they're in the past. From now on I'm going to try to do things properly. First, I'm going to take this wedding photo out of my basket and put it up on my wall where it belongs. And then I'm going to try to mourn Marcello properly and grieve for the good things we had. All this time I've been wearing black and trying to behave like a widow and yet I've never really managed that.'

'And then what?'

'And then I don't know. For now I'm going to stay with my family and perhaps see if Silvana could do with some help in the bakery. I can't think further ahead than that. My life is uncertain. I don't have an answer for everything, and I don't know what's in store for me any more than you know why your grandfather called this place the Gypsy Tearoom. Just like you said, some things in life are meant to be a mystery.'

She sensed his disappointment. 'So you understand? I can't promise you anything . . . ' Her voice tailed off awkwardly.

Ciro put the dough to one side and moved back round the corner. He stood very close but didn't touch her. 'To me, love isn't so complicated,' he said softly. 'It's the simplest thing of all. I love you, Raffaella. I think I always have and I'm sure I always will. So I'll wait, if that's all right with you. I'll wait and see how the mystery of your life turns out.'

Raffaella smiled. She leaned forward and kissed his face very gently. 'I have to go now. My mother is waiting for her shopping.'

He took her hands in his. 'You know where I am if you need to dink coffee or eat pizza, or you just want to talk.'

'Yes, I know I'll always find you here . . . in the Gypsy Tearoom.' She kissed him once again, lightly on his cheek, and then repeated, 'I have to go now.'

He released her hands. 'Wherever you go, whatever you do, you take my love with you,' he said quietly, and his words made her feel warm inside.

Walking back through the bustle of the piazza, Raffaella held her head high. She nodded at a group of priests, whose robes were flapping in the breeze as they lingered near the fountain for a chat; she rolled her eyes at Francesca Pasquale, who was blowing her whistle passionately at an old peasant farmer on a battered Vespa; and she waved at Silvana sitting on the bench outside the bakery, busy gossiping to the butcher's wife.

Raffaella saw, to her surprise, how not one of them bothered to raise their eyes and look away from the landscape of their day-to-day lives, up above the rooflines, right to the top of the mountain, where their new statue of Christ rose above them.

She took one last look at the imposing figure before turning to the view she loved best, the triptych of sea, rocks and the houses of Little Triento wedged almost one on top of the other on the steep cliffs that edged the harbour.

The statue at her back, Raffaella headed home.

Epilogue

The pomegranate tree stands in the centre of the courtyard. It is young and healthy with clusters of reddish-green leaves on its strong branches. An old man sits on the low wall beneath the tree, resting his tired legs. His hands are rough and calloused, his face weathered by many seasons of sun and wind.

The house behind him is shuttered and empty, and the terraced gardens falling away from it towards the sea are tangled with weeds, but the man's eyesight isn't what it was and he doesn't really notice.

Hardly anyone comes to the house any more. The old man's only visitors are his daughter, Carlotta the nun, and her child, Evangelina, who is growing into a woman now.

Most days he sits beneath the tree waiting for them, feeling the sun warm his bones and letting the memories of his past play through his mind. It has been a lonely life, much of it, but not a bad one. He knows his time is drawing to a close. Sooner or later God will weed him out and plant afresh. But as he sits there, eyes closed, his broom propped beside him, the old man prays for just a little more life.

He dozes off. And when his daughter and her child finally arrive, half an hour later than usual, he hasn't moved. He remains beneath the tree, facing the sun.

The old man is very still. His daughter goes to call his name, but then she stops herself. She realises he won't hear her. Instead, she sits beside him, covering his hand with her own. They sit there for a long time, father and daughter, the girl at their feet. The dying sun paints the sky pink, and clouds crowd the horizon, and still they choose not to move.

Acknowledgements

In Basilicata there really is a town with a giant white statue of Christ on a mountain. It's called Maratea, it's a beautiful place and you should go there if you get the chance. But Triento is not Maratea and this is not the story of how Maratea got its statue. Triento and all the characters who people it are the products of my imagination. None of it is real or even faintly biographical do you hear? I made it up!

This is only a little book but writing it has taken me quite a long time and there are people I must thank. For their guidance and patience thanks to Yvette Goulden of Orion and my agent Maggie Noach. For their generosity in letting me use their houses as though they were my own a big thank you to Antonio and Clara DeSio whose gorgeous place in southern Italy inspired me at the beginning and Grenville Main and Diana Bidwill whose wild and beautiful place in the Wairarapa saved me at the end.

By far the most nerve-wracking part of writing a book is letting it go out into the world. So thank you to my friend Jane Alexander for being the first person to read *The Gypsy Tearoom* and my first novel *Delicious* – your honesty and encouragement is always appreciated. And thanks to all my other good friends for their chardonnay and sympathy . . . you know who you are.

And finally thank you to my husband Carne Bidwill. This book is for you.